Veronica Lando is an Australian crime author who won the 2021 Banjo Prize for her then unpublished manuscript of *The Whispering*.

As a child, she grew up above her parents' Melbourne bookstore, surrounded by other people's stories. Now, as an adult, she lives in Queensland and enjoys using the uniquely wild and sometimes dangerous landscapes of the far north to shape her writing.

In 2020, she placed in the Scarlet Stiletto awards and has since had short stories published in anthologies with both Sisters in Crime Australia and the Queensland Writers' Centre.

Veronica currently lives in Townsville with her husband and three children.

*The Whispering* is her debut novel.

# THE
# WHISPERING

# THE WHISPERING

# VERONICA LANDO

**HarperCollins**Publishers

**HarperCollins***Publishers*
Australia • Brazil • Canada • France • Germany • Holland • India
Italy • Japan • Mexico • New Zealand • Poland • Spain • Sweden
Switzerland • United Kingdom • United States of America

First published in Australia in 2022
by HarperCollins*Publishers* Australia Pty Limited
Level 13, 201 Elizabeth Street, Sydney NSW 2000
ABN 36 009 913 517
harpercollins.com.au

Copyright © Veronica Lando 2022

The right of Veronica Lando to be identified as the author of this work has been asserted by her in accordance with the *Copyright Amendment (Moral Rights) Act 2000*.

This work is copyright. Apart from any use as permitted under the *Copyright Act 1968*, no part may be reproduced, copied, scanned, stored in a retrieval system, recorded, or transmitted, in any form or by any means, without the prior written permission of the publisher.

A catalogue record for this book is available from the National Library of Australia

ISBN 978 1 4607 6215 8 (paperback)
ISBN 978 1 4607 1496 6 (ebook)
ISBN 978 1 4607 4266 2 (audiobook)

Cover design by Christine Armstrong, HarperCollins Design Studio
Cover images: Landscape by Eva Elijas from Pexels; all other images by shutterstock.com
Author photograph by Francoise Baudet
Typeset in Sabon LT Std by Kirby Jones
Printed and bound in Australia by McPherson's Printing Group

*To Tito.*
*Bookmark thief, reading buddy and giver of tips.*

## PROLOGUE

The child was going to fall.
They stood too close to the edge, one back heel moving closer to the sheer drop. Rain came down hard and made the sloping ground soft. Slippery.

The child's eyes, filled with terror, glanced back over one shoulder. Over the edge. A sea of granite boulders lay below, stretching to the horizon. Giant crevasses gaped open between the rocks, grinning their toothless smiles. Dark. Still. Waiting.

A hard blink and their eyes darted forward again, the green of the rainforest towering in front.

The wind picked up and whistled through the air. The child pressed two hands against their ears, trying to block the sound. The old rhyme danced through the air, whispered by the wind, and fought to wedge its way between fingers held tightly together.

> *The whispering wild will take your child,*
> *If you dare to look away.*
> *When she hears the call, she will meet her fall,*
> *Never again to play.*
> *Winds from the boulders will snatch and hold her,*
> *Where forever she will lay.*

Tears and rain blended together and, with one last glance at the impenetrable wall of green in front, the child dropped backwards over the edge, the sea of granite rushing up from beneath.

# CHAPTER ONE

The air conditioner strained, and the wipers darted across the windscreen. Callum went to turn them up a notch but they were already on max. The screech of rubber blades against the glass barely pierced through the downpour of rain pounding on the roof.

A thin sheen of sweat coated his palms. He leaned a little further over the peeling steering wheel and squinted through the rain-streaked windscreen. A wall of green loomed in the distance.

What the hell was he doing coming back?

Green, more green. Not much else visible through the downpour. He lifted his foot off the accelerator and his eyes lingered in the rear-view mirror, taking in the long stretch of highway behind.

*Could just turn around.*

He forced his attention forward, and something in his gut stirred as he turned off the highway and onto a dirt track. The front left tyre of his rental car caught a pothole and his leg gave a sharp stab.

The search had been underway for less than twenty-four hours, yet a line of cars had already formed on the shoulder of Kingfisher Way. The road forged a path between a thick barrier of trees. They towered across the way to form a canopy overhead, blocking the grey clouds from sight. Blocking the outside world. He tried to take a slow breath, soften his shoulders, but the surrounding rainforest pressed back against him.

The end of the road opened up into a large car park blocked off by a strip of chequered police tape fluttering in the wind. A group of local news vans were parked, noses to tape, like a pack of wild dogs sniffing for a good story.

Callum scanned the area before double-parking behind a beat-up Hilux. He killed the engine, and the cabin immediately began to heat up, the air from outside seeping in through every crack, inching towards him. He hesitated a beat before the ache in his leg forced him to shoulder the door open.

A wave of humidity slammed into him as the wind whipped his shirt collar up and rain flew in sideways. His glasses fogged up, and sweat beads began forming on his forehead. The earthy scent of the tropics, heavy in the air, was a welcome relief after the wet-dog rental car stench.

He used the door to help lever himself out of the car and into the deluge of rain. The tiny hatchback hadn't been built for a man his size but it was all that had been available at such late notice. Supporting his weight through his right leg, he flexed and straightened his left knee a few times before gingerly placing his foot on the ground. Two flights from Hobart to Cairns, followed by the almost two-hour drive north-west, hadn't done his leg any favours. He looked down and his shoulders dropped: he'd placed his left foot in a murky puddle. His shoe was probably soaked through.

A yellow flit across the sky snatched his attention. His eyes snapped up with a jolt of recognition as the bird was swallowed by the towering trees in front, wings beating too fast to be certain. Gone.

*Amblyornis newtonianus*: golden bowerbird.

*Maybe.*

He made his way towards the police tape and the lone officer who had pulled the short straw and was in charge of manning it.

The officer eyed his tan chinos and buttoned-up shirt. 'Press?'

*Shit, should've dressed the part.*

'No.' The lie came easily. 'Old family friend.'

The officer, barely old enough to be out of school, took in Callum's size and gave a curt nod before lifting the tape.

The area beyond was heaving, as if everyone in Far North Queensland had shown up. At least half-a-dozen marquees had been erected to offer shelter to the searchers. Three police cars and one ambulance were parked at the far end and a coffee stand stood beneath the nearest shelter. People milled underneath, drinking from styrofoam cups and exchanging hushed words.

He made a beeline for the caffeine, and what he hoped would be an update on the search. He'd been following the snippets on the news. But a thirty-year-old man missing in the rainforest in the far north wasn't considered the stuff of headlines.

He'd first read the news just over ten hours ago. The name Granite Creek had jumped off his iPad and slapped him hard in the face.

The name Lachlan Wyatt had hit him even harder.

A punch in the guts.

He stepped under the marquee and the cloying humidity intensified. His glasses fogged again, and he took them off to wipe on his shirt. It was soaked through.

*Damn the tropics.*

He jammed them back on his nose and got in line for a coffee behind a couple of gruff-looking men, mud splattered up their legs and hair plastered to their foreheads.

'Bad business all that stuff back then.' The older of the two men heaped a spoonful of sugar into his cup, his voice sombre. 'She was doomed from the start, poor little dot.' He sounded familiar. A vague memory of banana picking for him one summer as a teenager. Callum should know his name.

'Yeah, but Lachie's not a kid. He knows the lay of the land. He'll show up soon enough.'

'Not gonna show up if he heard the whispering.'

The two men half smirked at each other before their faces fell back to neutral, eye contact broken. They moved off and Callum trained his eyes on their backs, the vivid green of the trees beyond.

'Cal?'

He turned back to the coffee stand. The woman behind the table grinned at him.

'Callum Haffenden? I thought that was you.'

He took in the woman's tousled auburn hair and rosy cheeks, and racked his brain, registering her hazel eyes and the way her left cheek dimpled when she smiled.

A faint memory of kissing her in the cemetery in grade ten, during a game of spin the bottle. She'd tasted of vodka and mango lip gloss. The woman in front of him was a far cry from the teenager he remembered with heavy eyeliner and black nail polish. She wore a navy tank top that revealed sculpted arms, and a pair of high-waisted shorts that hugged her hips and were worn a little shorter than most women in their mid-forties would normally dare. In fairness, she looked about fifteen years younger than Callum knew she was.

'Steph? Steph Pemlington?'

'Thought you didn't recognise me.'

'I almost didn't. You look great.' The words flew out of his mouth before he could stop them. He swept his hair off his face in time to see her blush. 'It's been, what, thirty years?'

'Something like that. I haven't seen you since your ...' Her eyes flickered to his leg.

He waited.

She cleared her throat, met his eye. 'What on earth brings you back here? You couldn't have known Lachie.'

'Just wanted to see if I could help out.'

'Long way to come. Aren't you based in Brisbane?'

'Hobart.'

She smiled. 'Even further.'

A shrug. He returned her smile.

Her mouth formed a firm line, dimple gone. 'We're all in a bit of shock actually. It's not common for a local to go missing. Unless …' Her eyes glassed over, and Callum fought to ignore the tingle down his leg. A gust of wind blew a stack of styrofoam cups over and she blinked, hard.

'Did you know him well?' he asked.

'Lachie?' She seemed surprised by the question, her eyes clear. 'Not really. He was a fair bit younger than me. But everyone in Granite knows everyone, I guess.' She moved around the table and righted the cups, filled one with hot water from the urn and smiled. Their fingers brushed as she handed him the cup, the heat through the styrofoam uncomfortable in his already sweaty palm. She reached up and took his glasses off, the top of her head barely level with his chin. She wiped the lenses on a paper napkin, placed them back.

'There.' That smile again. 'Much better.'

A line of people had formed behind him and an older volunteer nudged past to reach the urn, knocking Callum off-balance. A sharp stab of pain flooded just below his left knee as he found his footing. Steph gripped his upper arm.

'Thanks.' He gave a small smile. 'So, any news on the search?'

'Just a lot of wet and hungry volunteers. But you should ask your mate.' She gave his arm a squeeze and nodded towards the next marquee.

Callum squinted through the rain until the stocky frame and sloped shoulders of one of the men huddled there came into focus.

'You've got to be kidding me.' A lightness spread through him. 'Thanks for the coffee, Steph.'

Pitching himself forward to shield his cup from the rain, he made it inside the edge of the largest marquee. A man in a blue police uniform was talking to a group of SES volunteers, a large map spread open on a trestle table between them, its corners weighed down by bottles of water and first-aid kits. Eddy Quade swept his hand over one edge of the map before looking up and indicating the dense rainforest in front. The volunteers scattered, a few patting Eddy on the back as they passed.

Callum waited a breath before calling out.

Eddy turned and his exhausted face moved from confusion to recognition, from surprise to delight. He closed the distance between them with half-a-dozen strides and embraced Callum. After a moment, he pulled away but didn't let go. He held on to Callum's shoulders, taking him in at arm's length. 'Cal? Jesus, what on earth are you doing here?'

'I was about to ask you the same question.'

Eddy's dark hair now had a spattering of grey at the sideburns and there was a vertical line running between his eyebrows that hadn't been there the last time they'd caught up. But the way his eyes crinkled when the corners of his mouth lifted hadn't changed in over three decades.

Eddy let him go. 'Dealing with this bloody nightmare.'

'Since when were you back in Granite?'

'Since Sunday.'

*Four days.*

'And I've walked into a right shitstorm.' Eddy's shoulders slumped. Droplets of rain glinted on the three white arrows on his epaulettes—the same Callum's dad used to sport.

'Some local bloke's wandered off into the rainforest and is yet to wander out again. Didn't show up for work yesterday morning. Alert went out later in the arvo. Bloody Brett Wyatt's son if you can believe it.' He met Callum's eye. 'Half my luck. Wife and kid are in a right state.'

'Anything so far?'

'Not much. His car's over there.' Eddy indicated a white ute, blocked off by police tape, at one end of the car park. 'Found his gear up at the camp site. No other leads.' He glared, eyebrows drawn, in the direction of the rainforest and stepped further under the marquee. Callum followed. 'We won't be able to keep this up much longer though. Conditions are set to worsen. There's talk of a bloody cyclone forming off the coast.'

Callum nodded. Not great news. Shit news, actually. He bit his bottom lip. 'Have you checked the north-west boulders?'

'We've got a chopper scouring the area, but it's not likely they're going to find anything. Lachie's a local and, from what I gather, not an idiot.' Eddy looked at him sideways. 'Sorry.'

A jolt deep down. He nodded once and Eddy continued.

'Look, the locals know not to go out there nowadays. Especially in this weather. Besides, the camp site is this side of the creek. He would've had to cross it to get to the boulders. That thing's running like a washing machine at the moment. So far we've kept the search south of the water.' He blew out a long breath, eyes dropping to the map on the table.

It showed the forestry to the north of the town. The serpentine creek that gave rise to the town's name weaved through the green mass, running at an almost forty-five-degree angle, from near the bottom left to towards the top right. South-west to north-east. The sprawling greenery that spread out south of the creek was wedge-shaped, widening the further east it moved.

The distance to be covered was enormous. Callum ran his fingers across the map.

'About a hundred and twenty square kilometres,' Eddy said. 'That's what we're dealing with.'

'Jesus.'

Callum's eyes were drawn to the grey contour of lines at the top left-hand corner of the map: the boulders.

Eddy's shoulders slumped further. 'Please don't tell me you're here in an official capacity?'

'Definitely not. Just a concerned citizen.'

Eddy raised an eyebrow, didn't push it. 'How's Milly?'

'Fine.' The word soured in his mouth. 'Actually, she's not talking to me at the moment. Normal teenager stuff.' A twinge as he recalled the argument he'd had with his daughter that morning. He pulled out his phone, suddenly heavy in his pocket.

Nothing. No messages. No reception.

A young constable, blue uniform drenched through, jogged over. He stood back a few metres and shifted his weight from one foot to the next, waiting for Eddy to look his way. 'Sarge, they're just about to dismantle the camp site before the wind does it for us.'

Eddy's brow eased. 'I'd better go supervise. Hopefully, we get some sort of lead soon. Last thing I need is Brett bloody Wyatt breathing down my neck.' He started striding off then stopped, turned. 'Pop round to mine later. I'm going to check in on Dad about eight-ish if I can get away. He'd skin me alive if he knew you were in town and I didn't invite you round.' He jogged off without waiting for a response.

Callum stepped up to the edge of the marquee. Overhead, a helicopter disappeared into a cloud of mist, the *thump, thump* of its rotors drowned out by the heavy rain falling on the canvas above. He shifted his weight from side to side, matching the trees swaying in the wind. His shirt was plastered to his chest and back, and the air began to close in, pressing against him. His skin prickled. The rainforest was alive. Watching him. Waiting.

*Stay put. Don't go in.*

But there was a tug within. A pull. His feet loosened in the sodden mud. One step out from the protection of the marquee. Then a second.

His mind screamed at him to turn back, but his feet carried him forward.

The rainforest was calling.

# CHAPTER TWO

What the hell was he doing back in the rainforest? This wasn't part of the plan.

Ahead, a figure in a pair of fluoro yellow pants, mud splattered up the legs, cut through the vibrant greens and muted browns. Callum could just make out the orange jumpsuits of several SES volunteers beyond. He was trailing one of the search party groups, struggling to keep pace. The camp site wasn't far from the main car park, less than a kilometre. A ten-minute walk for most, probably fifteen to twenty for him.

*Don't lose sight of the others.*

He gritted his teeth and ploughed on.

The rainforest was eerily quiet, the pounding of the rain diminished by the canopy above. His ears had taken a moment to adjust, and the sounds of the forest had crept in slowly, weaving their way into his head, smothering the protests within.

A shrill call split the air, sharp.

*Tanysiptera sylvia*: buff-breasted paradise kingfisher.

His eyes darted upwards but the canopy above was free of the blue wings and yellow underbelly. Nothing.

He pushed on.

The searchers had strung overhead spotlights in the trees and light splashed across the track. He approached the end of the first spotlight's reach. The light faded and the darkness crept up to meet his toes, drawing him forward. A pause. The next light cast shadows on the ground only a few metres ahead. The surface between a dark mystery. He squinted through his glasses. Still fogged.

*No contacts. No short sleeves. A+ for poor packing efforts.*

Thirty years out of the tropics and he'd forgotten that chinos and business shirts weren't appropriate attire.

He felt out into the darkness with his right foot. The person in the fluoro yellow pants was getting further away. A panicked breath, then a step. Another. A moment later and he stood in the glow of the next spotlight. He let out a long exhale, tore his eyes from the ground. The person had stopped only a few metres ahead. A woman. She slapped the back of her neck. Midges.

He lengthened his stride to catch her and his left foot slid out on the wet and mossy undergrowth. He added shit choice of shoes to his list of poor packing choices.

The woman set off again.

Callum pressed on and the voices of the volunteers ahead pushed through the rain drumming on the canopy above.

'... no salties this far up the range at least. Plenty of freshies though. And ya need to keep an eye out for those cassowaries.' A large man with a wild ginger beard and ruddy full cheeks had his head half turned back over one shoulder to speak to the woman. He was like an oversized garden gnome. The bright orange of his SES uniform made him look extra cheery. 'They can run fifty kilometres an hour through the scrub and they'll gut ya like a barramundi.'

The woman turned to her left, scanned the trees.

'And watch out for that Gympie-Gympie.' He jabbed a fat finger at a shrub that stood about a metre tall at the edge of the path. Its small pink and purple fruits shone against green heart-shaped leaves.

'Pretty,' she said.

'Pretty bloody painful is what it is. Covered in stinging nettles. Touch the bugger and you'll be in agony for weeks. Most dangerous plant in the world.'

She gave it a wide berth.

'Though, that's not the worst thing you have to worry about out here.'

She snorted. 'Worse than killer plants and prehistoric birds that'll gut me?'

'I didn't say it'd kill ya. Plenty of people have lived to tell the tale of run-ins with cassowaries and toxic plants.'

'So, what are we talking about? Some tropical Ivan Milat or bodies in a barrel kinda thing?'

A shrug. 'Some weird shit goes on up in this rainforest, that's all I'm sayin'.'

'Like?'

Another shrug. 'People disappearin'. Kids …' The man's voice was muffled, lost in the heavy air. '… rainforest callin'… lurin'…'

Another snort. 'Luring.' She shook her head.

'I'm not the one making this shit up.' The man stopped and held back the slim trunk of a sapling that grew across the path. He was about to let it fling back when he noticed Callum. Callum gave a nod of thanks as he followed the woman through. The man stepped in behind.

'It's folklore.' The man raised his voice to reach the woman, Callum now inserted in the middle of their conversation.

'Sounds like a load of rubbish,' she said.

The man paused. 'Say as you will, but that doesn't explain all the missing folk.'

'It's the rainforest. Missing folk is part of the deal for anyone stupid enough to go bush bashing.' She didn't bother to turn her head back, her dark ponytail swishing in front of Callum. Her words carried easily. 'Kids included.'

The trio pressed on, a few grunts coming from behind

Callum. At least he wasn't the only one struggling with the uneven, sodden terrain.

The woman slowed her pace. He forced himself to pick his up.

'So, what's involved with this *luring* then?' she asked.

Callum's lips tingled with the response. He waited for the other man to answer, but he was a few paces back, plucking a wait-a-while vine from his beard. They pulled up under the glow of a spotlight.

'It's called the whispering.' The words slipped out of Callum's mouth.

'The whispering?'

'Yeah. It … *whispers* to you.' He raised his head to look at her properly. She was young. Late teens, twenty at best.

She smirked. 'Whispers?'

He shrugged. 'Apparently.'

She ran her eyes down his once white shirt and dirty chinos. She stopped at his lace-up business shoes, cocked an eyebrow but said nothing.

Freed, the bearded man caught up, his cheeks glowing from the effort. 'Several Indigenous clans were killed out here during white settlement. Men, women, kids. Whole families. Bodies dumped at the boulders.'

Tension around Callum's jaw set in. Granite Creek's history was no secret. The whole country had the same sordid past, written in blood. Hard to swallow yet easily swept under the rug. His mind shifted gears as the man's voice pushed through his thoughts.

'The whispering's supposed to be the kids who lost their lives, singin' for playmates. Luring 'em off the boulders.'

Callum rubbed his slick palms on his chinos, the drenched fabric useless for drying anything.

He swallowed the lump in his throat and found his voice. 'It's just the wind. A geological phenomenon, really. When the wind picks up enough, usually pre-cyclonic, it whips through the gaps in the boulders on the northern side of the creek. It makes a whistling sound that reverberates through the valley and flies over the rainforest. Everyone here's heard it. It's nothing.' The words felt like sandpaper in his mouth.

'So why can't we hear it now?' she asked. 'It's pretty damn windy.'

'The rain drowns it out.' Along with everything else. 'It's just something local kids talk about to freak each other out, or parents tell their kids to stop them traipsing off into the rainforest and getting lost.' Or killed.

Callum worked his way over a fallen trunk blocking the path, putting his left foot in a sodden patch of earth on the other side. It made a loud squelch as he pulled it free, a slight tug below his knee followed. He carried on, a fluttering of unease starting in his gut. He pushed it down.

'Well, a thirty-year-old grown man isn't exactly the target victim then,' the woman said over one shoulder. She skirted a dark puddle in the centre of the path. A beat later a breath of wind carried her mumbled words. 'Most likely the dickhead just got himself lost.'

Callum's eyes flitted to the side of the path. Thick foliage rose up either side of the narrow track and his dad's warning from his childhood echoed in his ear.

*Never step off the trail.*

The man behind made a non-committal noise. 'I ain't a local, but Lachie sure as hell was. Would've known this place like the back of his hand.'

The woman scoffed, lowered her voice and Callum struggled to catch her words. 'Clearly not well enough, or we wouldn't all be traipsing through this slush. Too cocky for his own good.'

'And from what I hear, locals ain't stupid when it comes to this place.' The man snorted behind him, spat. 'There's at least one tourist every dry season. They're usually found soon enough. A little shaken up with bruised egos and a newfound respect for the bush. Every now and then though it's a local. Swallowed up by the boulders most likely. The gaps between some of those bastards are big enough to stow a campervan.'

'But grown firefighters who grew up in the area?' the woman said.

'Yeah, the locals that've gone missing are usually a bit younger.' The man paused, grunted. A branch snapped, the sound splitting the air. 'Kids. You know, wander off from the family camp site, that sort of stuff.'

A flit of green eyes, gold rimmed, dashed across Callum's mind. Gone. His thoughts shifted to his own daughter. He shook her from his mind. She was miles away. Safe.

'Ah, the whispering.' The woman nodded, the suggestion of a smirk lacing her words.

The trio broke through a final barrier of foliage and emerged in a clearing. The canopy of trees gave way to the sky where grey clouds hung low and the rain pelted down. The area was a muddy mess. Trampled footprints scattered everywhere, divots and puddles rife.

Some faded yellow lettering on weather-beaten, rotted timber read 'Granite Creek Campground'.

Callum took in the words, then tore his eyes away.

Orange cones marked intervals around the edge. Figures in high-vis gear ducked in and out of view, pushed their way through the thick foliage. Entry points into the forest.

A blue one-man tent was barely erect on the far side.

Limp. Wet. Abandoned.

Just beyond sat another track. The entry was defined by a clear gap in the trees that allowed searchers to move more freely. Callum knew where it led, had spent most of the hotter months of his childhood hanging in the cool waters of the creek that lay beyond. By the time the dry season rolled around, however, the temperature dropped and the water was icy enough to rival even a Tassie creek. Barely anyone ventured out then, the path grew over, and the forest swallowed the faint track back up. A spattering of smaller granite rocks, not quite boulders, spanned the distance from the camp site to the creek, leading the way like a trail of breadcrumbs.

It was the same on the other side of the creek, leading the way to the boulders.

He shook his head and closed his eyes.

Something in the air shifted, pressed against him.

His eyes flew open. The rain had stopped, the sudden silence in his ears a scream. He strained to hear, listening for the usual thrum of the rainforest: the hum of the cicadas, the bustle of leaves, the descending whistle of the brush cuckoo.

Nothing.

He tore his eyes from the far side of the camp site, looked around. The hive of activity had come to a standstill, all eyes on the fortress of trees on the opposite side of the clearing. Watching. Waiting.

A pause, then a rush of birds swept from the canopy and out through the clearing. The beating of wings echoed inside the small space.

They vanished, the silence thick as the air pressed back in.

Then it came. It whispered a soft melody at first, before a whistling sound pitched up and out of the canopy of trees, reverberated off the boulders that lay beyond and echoed around.

A wave of darkness swept over Callum, and he fought to keep his feet firmly grounded and his body upright.

# CHAPTER THREE

Callum limped back through the slopping mud of Kingfisher Way, his car up ahead in the distance, the rainforest on all sides. Green filled his peripheral vision, always hovering on the edge.

The rain had started up again, though not as heavily as before, and the high-pitched whistle of the kingfishers in the towering fig trees above now pierced the air.

He picked up his pace.

His shoes squelched on the sodden track, his left foot struggling for purchase with each step. If he'd been able to run, he probably would have, but the ground had formed an obstacle of slush puddles and hidden divots waiting to trip him up.

His heart rate slowed a beat for every step he put between himself and the looming trees behind him. His breathing was back to normal, but he still couldn't rid himself of the sense that the boulders were calling.

Why the hell had he come back to Granite Creek?

His eyes snagged on a clump of blue and white, stark against the tawny mud. He stopped, hesitated. Then took a step forward. Another.

The small mass lay on the ground at the base of a car tyre. A soft round stomach, white, and a long blue tail held upwards. A pale blue head and a set of vacant eyes trained on the forest beyond.

A wrench in his chest.

*Malurus amabilis*: lovely fairy-wren.

Still. Perfect. Lifeless.

A sudden urge to scoop the tiny bird up and take it far away.

He leaned his hands on the car in front of him. The world blurred, swam. A hard blink and a dash of blue streaked across his hands. He thought of the lifeless bird at his feet. Not the bird this time. Chequered blue tape fluttered in the wind, whipped against his fingers, and tangled in the roof racks. He snatched his hands away, stumbled backwards.

Lachie's ute.

Police tape plastered to its fenders on one side, the wind causing it to flap wildly on the other. His rental car was only fifty metres away, calling.

He stepped closer to the ute again. The sky overhead had dimmed, more night than day now.

He wiped the driver-side window, peered inside. Dark. The interior took a few moments to come into focus. It was a pigsty. High-vis clothes strewn across the back seat, bits of camping gear, and the passenger footwell littered with takeaway wrappers and empty beer cans.

'Haffenden.'

He froze. The gruff voice raked into his consciousness. He should've kept walking, driven away. Never bloody come back.

'I said Haffenden.'

He pulled back from the ute and turned. Despite being over six foot tall, he still had to look up to meet the cool blue gaze of the man approaching him. 'Brett.'

Brett Wyatt cut an impressive figure. While his buzz cut was now grey instead of dirty blond, and his waistband a little tighter, thirty years on, Brett still managed to retain the kind of presence that made you want to run for cover or piss your pants.

Callum's mind jumped to Pip, Brett's wife. Lachie's mum. He squared his shoulders and shifted his weight onto his right leg, planting his foot firmly in the mud.

Brett's face twitched. Several scratches—short and long—covered his cheeks, the skin red and smarting. He was coated in mud from the waist down. 'You have no right to be here.'

'I have every right to be here.'

'Hoping to get a good story, are ya?'

'I'm not here for work.'

'Why then? Because of her? Pip?' He spat her name.

Something stirred within. 'Yes, because of Pi—'

'Don't you dare say her name.'

Callum's leg throbbed. He needed to rest. Try a different tack. 'Look. I just wanted to see if there was anything I could do.' He spread his hands open. 'To help.'

Brett's gaze flashed to Callum's leg and the anger wavered from his face. Something else washed over his features. It was gone before Callum was sure he'd even seen anything. He could only register the heavy set of Brett's eyebrows, the thinness of his lips. His fury.

'You stay away.' Brett took a step forward and Callum's mind raced back thirty years. His heart rate quickened, breath shortened.

'This is my family. My son,' Brett said. 'And she doesn't need you anymore.'

A stab of anger punched through Callum. He tried to push it down. 'I—'

'You nothing. Keep your journo nose out of it and bugger off back to the city.' Another twitch of his face. Eyebrows hooded, shoulders rounded and head down against the rain that had now picked back up, Brett stalked away.

Callum stood, leg screaming, until his breath had settled and his heart had slowed enough so that the only sound in his ears was the thrum of the rain on the car roof and the echo of Brett spitting Pip's name.

\*

By the time Callum pulled up at the town's sole motel, the rain had eased off enough that he'd switched the wipers to low speed. The once-white stucco of the squat building, with its red bold letters welcoming travellers to the Rainforest Inn, gave it a clinical feel. The giant plastic green tree frog and overflowing swimming pool on the front lawn did not.

A handful of people dashed across the uncovered driveway as if there was a torrential downpour.

Out-of-towners: locals never ran.

It'd taken Callum several minutes to gather himself after his run-in with Brett. He'd focused on his breathing and tried to push all memories of granite boulders and pure, numbing fear from his mind. By the time he'd limped to his car, a weight had burrowed inside him, and he battled with a raw urge to leave Granite Creek and never return.

He'd checked his phone. Still nothing.

The motel was a U-shaped building. Room doors dotted around its internal perimeter, all opening in towards the car park at its centre. He pulled into the last remaining car space between two hatchbacks, both equally as unequipped as his for the rugged terrain and rain-slick roads of the far north. All of the cars in the lot screamed *tourists*.

Not tourists though. Volunteers. Feet on the ground and hope for Lachie Wyatt.

Taking his time to retrieve his luggage from the boot, he scooped up a pair of elbow crutches and rested them across his overnight bag, which he slung over one shoulder. He lumbered towards the main reception, past closed door after closed door.

A handwritten sign on the reception's glass door read 'No Vacancies'. He pushed the door open, his eyes flashing to the Cane Cutters' Tavern—the town's only watering hole—directly across the road. At least there was food within limping distance.

The rain tingled on his skin as the welcome coolness of the reception hit him. The scent of cheap air freshener and turpentine mixed with the deep earthy scent of the outside filled the air, and the middle-aged couple talking to the man at reception sardined themselves against the counter to allow for Callum's bulk.

His leg ached.

*Nearly there.*

He scanned the poky room for a seat, came up empty. A shift of his weight and the end of his crutches jabbed into the woman. She winced. He gave a small smile of apology.

*Just suck it up and stand.*

An old perspex shelf clung to a peach wall displaying an array of tourist brochures, faded and dog-eared. Scuba dive the Great Barrier Reef. Croc cruise along the Daintree River. Nothing actually for Granite Creek.

A small yellow bird stood out from one of the brochures. Long tail, short beak.

*Amblyornis newtonianus:* golden bowerbird.

*Definitely.*

He tore his eyes away.

Behind the reception desk, an impressive sketched map of the town hung framed on the wall. The main road cut the township almost perfectly into north and south halves. Sugar cane fields dotted the perimeter of the town, and beyond the outskirts, to the south, lay the ranges that sported the one road that led in and out. It twisted and wound, until it met the edge of the page. Eventually, it would bend east and lead to the Daintree Rainforest, Cape Tribulation and, at last, the sea.

The northern part of the map spawned the sprawling and unforgiving local rainforest. In the north-west corner nestled a cluster of small grey lines of dips and curves. They looked harmless.

Callum's skin prickled and he wiped his palms on his trousers.

The boulders.

He focused his attention on the conversation between the couple and the man at the reception desk.

'... such a tragedy. After everything that family's already been through.' The woman's head shook as she continued to rub her arm where Callum's crutches had hit her. 'Daryl here worked with Lachie and his dad, what's his name?'

'Brett.' The guy behind the reception didn't look up, his voice barely a grunt. A large vase of gaudy plastic flowers sat dusty on the countertop.

'Yes, Brett,' she continued. 'After that last cyclone came through. Took the week off work and drove up to lend some muscle, didn't you, love?'

The man nodded. 'Bloody mess, the town was.'

'He was good to work with, that Lachie, wasn't he, love?' She looked to her husband. 'A good bloke, you said.'

He nodded along. 'A good bloke.'

'Have come up a few times over the years, haven't you, love?' she continued. 'You know, when there's been people that have wandered off. Worst one was that little—'

'All done.' The guy behind the counter fished a key out of a cardboard shoebox and slapped it down, cutting the woman off. A garish frog keyring, bug eyes bulging, stared at them all.

The couple took their key and left, a wall of humidity pressing through the door as they opened it. Callum stepped forward.

The man behind the counter—*Mike, here to help!*—ran his hands through his limp brown hair. It hung below his jawline on either side of his face, parted down the middle like curtains opened just enough to give a sneak peak of the show behind. He gnawed his bottom lip. He had an overbite that made him look not unlike a ferret.

'Reservation?' His lips barely moved.

Callum nodded. 'Haffenden.'

Mike busied himself at the computer—a PC with a boxy grey monitor. Not much in Granite Creek had changed then.

'You're lucky.' Mike's eyes didn't leave the monitor. 'Got our last room.' He tapped deliberately at the keyboard using just his two index fingers. The nails were bitten down to the quick.

'Usually booked out?'

Mike shook his head, hair swaying as if in a breeze. 'Not for over a decade.'

Callum's gut knotted.

'Says here you're from down south?'

'Yeah, came up to see if I could help. You know, good bloke like Lachie and all.'

A grunt. More tapping at the keyboard.

'Did you know him well?' Callum asked.

A brief flicker of eye contact. 'Nah.'

Steph's words rang in his head. 'Still,' Callum continued, 'a town this size, you've got to sort of know him.'

A shrug, followed by a non-committal noise somewhere between a grunt and a throat clearing.

'Reckon he stands a chance out there?' Callum nodded his head towards the deluge of rain outside and the rainforest that lay beyond.

Mike's fingers froze over the keyboard, his eyes narrowing to squint at the screen. 'Sure.' After a pause, he started tapping away again, offered nothing else.

The lights flickered, came back. Through the glass door, a woman in high heels, wearing a lanyard that swayed dangerously in the wind, rushed past. She battled with an umbrella turned inside out.

Mike looked out and Callum saw his eyes run the length of the woman's body before he shook his head. 'Bloody press,' he said. 'Good for business. Bad for everything else.'

Callum nodded, shifted gears. 'And what about his dad? Brett, isn't it? Do you know him at all?'

Mike's eyes pulled away from the door, gave a flash of something before he returned to his focused typing. He let his shoulders rise up to his ears—both pierced and adorned with silver studs—before letting them fall. He looked several years older than he probably was. Thirty? 'You know about the Wyatt family?'

Callum's turn to shrug. 'I grew up here.'

'Then you'd know not to ask too many questions.' Mike reached into his cardboard shoebox again, selected a key. His eyes turned back to his computer monitor. After a beat, his eyebrows lifted enough to cause a spattering of shallow crevices to span across his forehead.

'Haffenden, eh?' He slid a key across the counter.

The name carried some weight to it. A cautionary tale to the kids of Granite Creek; parents whispering warnings instead of bedtime stories.

Callum pocketed the key—attached to his very own plastic frog, a large number eight painted on its back—opened the reception door and stepped back into the rain. Mike's eyes burned into his leg and followed him all the way to his room.

\*

Callum changed out of his saturated, muddy clothes but didn't bother to shower. He unpacked his small travel bag, careful to keep things he might need overnight within arm's reach.

His feet squelched with every step he took in the only pair of shoes he'd bothered to pack. Ignoring his soaked right sock, and the toes that had begun to rub, he placed his worn shoehorn on the middle shelf of the cupboard, brushed his fingers across the raised letters of Milly's name adorned along its length in pink glitter pen by the shaky hand of a six-year-old. The *y* distinctly written backwards. A warmth on his fingertips lingered.

His mind drifted to Hobart.

'Are you sure you want to go back there?' his dad had asked him when he'd dropped Milly off.

'I have to.'

His father had nodded once and waved goodbye, his lips a firm line.

Milly, ear buds in and eyes avoiding his, had marched past without a backwards glance. He'd caught a few bars of her voice, humming, as her backpack disappeared into his parents' house.

He continued to unpack, hanging three spare shirts in the wardrobe until all that was left in his bag was a small metal box, gunmetal grey and cool to the touch. It was about the size of a kid's lunch box, its front locked with a sturdy padlock. He squeezed the hard metal until his fingertips lost their colour and his knuckles ached. A pair of eyes, crinkled at the edges, swam into view. A top lip, turned up just slightly in a smile. He pushed the image away and placed the lockbox in the cupboard, wedging it between the folds of a blanket he wouldn't need.

He threw one last glance at the closed cupboard before pulling his motel room door shut behind him. The wind pressed back against the timber, fighting every inch of the movement.

## CHAPTER FOUR

A waft of beer and greasy food hit Callum as he pushed his way through the front door of the Cane Cutters' Tavern. The pub was heaving. Small circular tables with rickety chairs, and about half-a-dozen booths lining the walls, all overflowing with bodies. Most of them sweaty, muddy and still in high-vis gear.

The chatter was loud enough to drown out the wind buffeting against the windows. Callum jostled his way between the volunteer searchers, emergency workers and the odd journo, the soles of his shoes sticking to the grimy floor with each step.

Snippets of conversations ebbed and flowed as he passed.

'... call it off, cyclone's worsening.'

'Another bloody local ...'

'Not a kid at least.'

He nudged his way between a stocky man in a mud-splattered orange SES jumpsuit and the woman he and Mike had seen struggling in the gale outside the motel. She looked vaguely familiar. The lanyard around her neck, along with her make-up and lack of mud, confirmed she was a journalist with a major news organisation. She twisted her glass of red wine and gave him a slight smile. He must've looked as out of place as her in the sea of orange and fluoro yellow.

Callum gave her a curt nod and scanned the room. He caught the eye of a dark-haired girl, hair pulled back in a tight ponytail.

The one from the track.

She raised her beer to him in recognition. She looked like she should still be in school. Jesus, he must be getting old.

He gave her a nod, turned back to the bar and placed his hands on the counter, only to pull them back. A thin layer of grime now coated his palms.

He ordered a beer and two takeaway pizzas.

'Here for work?' the journalist next to him asked.

A brief pause before Callum turned to her and shook his head once. 'No.'

A lanky man pressed between them, dumping his empty pint glass on the counter. It was filled with sauce-covered serviettes scrunched into tight balls and adorned with a white blob of chewed-up gum. Mud ran the length of his fluorescent shirt, the fabric sporting a large tear along the sleeve.

The journalist eyed Callum's chinos and button-up shirt, cocked her head to the side. 'Well, you don't look like one of the volunteer searchers.'

'I like to shower.'

She took a sip of wine. 'At least it's not another kid. All that hoo-ha with that missing toddler thirteen years ago. Christ, what a mess.'

He couldn't bring himself to speak.

She didn't seem fazed by his silence and took a large mouthful of wine, before she continued on. She was clearly used to talking at people. 'And then that girl before her. She was only what? Fourteen? Fifteen? And almost no search. About twenty years ago.'

'Thirty.' Callum's voice came out jagged, the inside of his mouth raw. A flicker of granite grey skittered across his mind. He shifted his weight off his left leg and took another sip.

Her eyes scanned the pub. 'Apparently the town cop had some family emergency and the new boy in blue did the bare minimum. The whole search was called off in less than forty-eight hours.' She snorted into her wine. 'What a right cock-up that was. Still …' She smiled. 'Made for a great story.'

Something in Callum's chest tightened and he took another drink, the glass almost slipping from his hands. He wiped his palms on his trousers.

Jesus, how bloody far away were his pizzas?

Raised voices from the opposite end of the bar cut through the rumble of the pub. Callum and the journalist both turned to look. A man tried to stand up from a bar stool, staggered and was eased back down by another man with an impressive walrus moustache.

'… still not bloody looking into it, are they?' The man stood again, brushed off the other man's attempts to steady him, and leaned heavily on the counter.

A hushed murmur from the man with the moustache, the shape of the words blocked by the dark bristles above his top lip.

'They should be looking into the bloody school,' the man called, quieting the entire pub. 'Chasing down that Thacker prick. The same creep that took my Josh, that's what's got to Lachie at last.'

He raised one hand off the counter and knocked his pint of beer over. The pub watched on in silence as the amber liquid glided across the countertop.

With a firm hand from his friend, and a lack of eye contact from nearby patrons, the man was escorted out of the pub. His gusto had spilled out along with his beer.

'Sounds juicy.' The journalist raised her eyebrows.

'Haffenden!' The barman held two pizza boxes aloft, scanning the room.

*Thank Christ.*

Callum scooped up his pizzas, readjusted his weight and, with a half nod to the woman, pressed his way back through the crowd before she could open her mouth again.

\*

An empty pizza box, two beers and a glass of water sat on the old timber coffee table on the Quades' back deck. The scent of rain hung heavy in the air. Thick, dense, and pressing itself around Callum. A pleasant warmth coursed through his body, more to do with the good company than the mediocre food.

Forty minutes earlier, Callum had raised a hand to knock on the timber front door and wondered when—if ever—he'd knocked on the Quades' door. It was familiar. Unlike the roof. The telltale peeling bottle-green metal had been replaced by a more modern, slick grey Colorbond roof.

Most likely a result of the last cyclone.

Aside from a neat row of cardboard moving boxes lining the hallway, everything inside seemed as it had been three decades earlier. An odd sense of coming home had stirred something unexpected in his chest.

Eddy's dad, Bill, had given Callum a lopsided smile. He'd leaned heavily to his right as he'd pushed himself up out of an old armchair that Callum recalled from his childhood. Barely reaching Callum's chest, Bill held on to each of Callum's shoulders—the same way his son had only hours earlier—and gave them a squeeze. The scent of tobacco drifted between them.

Time had not been kind to Eddy's dad. Rounded shoulders and a posture that swayed a little to one side, as if the wind had been blowing Bill Quade steadily to his right his entire life. Weather-beaten skin, several shades darker than his son's—a legacy of a lifetime spent under the harsh Queensland sun—

and laughter lines around his mouth that sank inward like great ravines, carving their way through his flesh.

'Haven't changed a bit, have you?' Bill's words slurred as he spoke, each clinging on to the next as if it were a life raft, desperate to escape his mouth, to be spoken. To be heard.

The stroke had hit him hard, and a sudden flush of guilt washed over Callum. He should've visited when he'd heard the news.

Now, Bill leaned back heavily in a rattan outdoor chair that looked dangerously close to toppling backwards. His eyes were closed, his face peaceful, and he seemed unfazed by the rain that pushed in beneath the deck awning, wetting his bare feet. Yet Callum still couldn't be sure he was asleep.

'So, why are you really back in Granite?' Eddy threw a half-eaten pizza crust into the open box.

Callum met his eye, then looked back out to the darkness beyond the deck. The thrum of rain ricocheted around inside his head.

Eddy's stare didn't lessen. 'Pip.' It wasn't a question.

A nod. Enough said.

'And Milly's good?'

Callum's chest tightened at the sound of her name. 'Yeah. Just pissed off because I didn't let her come up here with me.' He forced a nod. Images of his daughter filled his mind, fresh faced and beautiful. Scowling and sullen. 'She got her nose pierced without telling me last month.'

Eddy laughed.

A beat later, the corner of Bill's mouth turned up.

'She's a good kid though.' A warmth surged through him. 'Just, you know, it's tricky with a fifteen-year-old girl.' With no mother. After a pause, he added, 'I don't remember us being such little shits.'

A snort from Bill this time and another laugh from Eddy, rich and warm. Thirty years had done little to change it. 'Are you kidding me? We were total shits.'

'Us?'

A slight noise of agreeance from Bill's still figure.

Eddy reached for his water and Callum saw a flash of a black, yellow and red tattoo visible on the underside of his arm—a tribute to his Indigenous heritage. 'Nicking your dad's beer and this guy's fags.' Bill's right eye opened a fraction, closed again. 'Sneaking around the boulders and doing anything we could to piss off Brett Wyatt.'

'As I recall it, we generally tried to avoid Brett as much as possible.'

Eddy shrugged, scooped up his glass of water, had a scull. 'Don't you remember? The prank calls. The toads. The dog shit.'

He stared at Eddy and a vague memory of jamming cane toads into Brett's school bag scrambled to the surface. He'd forgotten most of that stuff.

'Yeah, but Brett had it coming,' he said.

Eddy nodded, returned his glass to the table. 'All I'm saying is, maybe getting her nose pierced isn't all that bad.'

Callum sipped his beer, already warm, and a gentle snore started from Bill. 'So, how is it being back?'

'Weird. Didn't think I'd end up back here.' Eddy leaned back into the cane chair, his blue sergeant's shirt hanging over the back. He eyed his snoozing dad, lowered his voice. 'But Dad needs a hand. He's been slowing down since his stroke, and, with Mum gone, there's no one else to help out.' Like Callum, Eddy had been an only child. 'Then the sergeant's position came up and it all seemed to just fall into place.'

'And have you fallen into place?'

The rain drummed on the roof. Tension lines formed across Eddy's forehead.

'Hardly. I haven't exactly been welcomed back into the fold with open arms. Since your dad left, there's been nothing but mediocre law enforcement in this town.' A pause, more tension lines. 'Can't be too harsh on them though. Not one of them's been a local. Not even spitting distance of the north, really. Few wanted the posting. Most just shunted up here. The handful that did volunteer for the gig were deluded enough to think that they were moving up for some relaxing reef and rainforest experience.'

Callum snorted. 'Didn't realise they were moving up to a town of fifteen hundred, most of them ageing farmers?'

'Exactly. Did their time, kept things relatively in order, and then swanned back to the city once they were fed up with breaking up Sunday arvo brawls at Cutters.' He turned to Callum. 'No one's really given a shit, know what I mean?'

Callum nodded.

'Can't really blame anyone here for not having much faith in the policing system though,' Eddy continued. 'All that stuff thirty years ago with Amelia. Hell, all that stuff thirteen years ago. That kid wasn't even two.' He shook his head. 'What a nightmare. Worse than what we're dealing with at the moment.'

Callum's mind jumped to the search that took place over a decade ago. From what he'd gathered, the whole town had rallied together—the whole country for that matter. News footage every night for almost a fortnight. The first few days, the search had been particularly rampant. After about a week, the cameras had begun to drop away and the searchers retreated, as people realised that they were no longer searching for a little girl but a body. The rest of the country soon lost interest.

Until, of course, they found the body.

Small, frail and dragged from a gap between two of the boulders. The image had been splashed across the country's media outlets. No one had been spared from seeing the lifeless figure.

Callum wiped his hands on his trousers, pushed the thoughts of thirteen years ago from his mind and dragged his attention back to the present.

'So how are things going with the search?'

Eddy blew out a slow breath. 'No more news so far. Not much to go off really.'

'Odd for a local to wander off.'

Eddy shrugged. 'He probably got up for a piss in the night and wandered a little too far into the scrub. You remember what it's like out there. Two or three steps off the track and you can't see it behind you. Five or six steps and you're almost certain to have lost it. Ten or twelve steps and you're officially screwed.' He leaned forward, resting his elbows on his knees, and ran his hands through his hair. 'We've got the best there is out there. SES guys from all over this end of the state have trekked up for it. He's got as good a chance as he could hope for. Still …'

Eddy's brow knitted together.

*Not much of a chance, then.*

'Not like a local to go camping in this weather,' Callum said.

'Apparently it wasn't unheard of for Lachie. His wife said he did it now and then. To clear his head.'

'How was she when she found out?'

'As expected. Shocked. Didn't say much. Their son, Jack, was there when I spoke to her. He's only nine or ten, by the looks of it. He looked dreadful. Thankfully, it's school holidays now.'

Something snagged in the back of Callum's mind.

'Was there some business up at the school that Lachie was caught up in?' Callum glanced at Bill. No movement, no reaction. Still snoring.

'What sort of business?' Eddy asked.

'Not sure. Just something a bloke at the pub mentioned.' Rambled. 'Something about a guy called Thacker, maybe?'

'Don't know. But I haven't even been back a week. And it's been over a decade since Lachie was in school.'

'Have you heard much about Lachie?'

A shrug. 'Snippets. Seems well-liked enough. He's a firey, coaches his kid's footy team, does some volunteer work for a local conservation group. Friends of the Forest, or something like that. A good bloke is what they all say.' Eddy leaned back in his chair, closed his eyes. 'Still, who knows what will come to the surface.'

Callum took another sip of his beer.

Bill's chin was now resting on his chest and the three of them sat quietly for a few minutes. The rain ebbed slightly and the clicking of a gecko could be heard in the rafters overhead.

Eddy sat up suddenly, and Callum's body jerked upright in response.

'Found something yesterday while I was unpacking.' Eyes alert and lips hitched, Eddy got up and strode back inside the house. Callum could hear him rummaging through boxes.

'Drove ... mother mad ... said.' Bill's voice, husky from a two-pack-a-day habit and slurred by his stroke, was almost swallowed by the sound of the rain.

Callum leaned in towards the older man, who still had his eyes closed. 'What was that?'

'... melia.'

A lurch in Callum's chest. 'Amelia?'

A nod. Bill cleared his throat, a hacking sound that caused his chest to heave and spasm. Callum passed him his beer. A sip, a small swallow, and a nod of appreciation as Callum returned the bottle to the table.

'All those kids ... missing.' Bill's voice was clearer now. Steady almost. 'But the little one.'

Callum nodded. Everyone who grew up in Granite Creek knew the history of kids going missing, usually in the rainforest. Back when Bill was a kid, there were quite a few—several found out at the boulders, fallen from the edge; some drowned in the creek. Young kids. The kind that couldn't swim yet or find their way back to the track once they'd stepped off it. Usually families out camping or going for a picnic at the creek. Callum's generation had grown up with these stories. Cautionary tales. People seemed to heed the warnings and not much happened for decades, except the odd tourist.

But then the Amelias. The first fifteen years old; the second, not quite two. Both missing, seventeen years apart. Only one ever found.

'Amelia,' Bill repeated. 'The little one ... after she went missing ... when they found the body ... they said.' He took a deep breath, paused. 'It's what drove her mother mad.'

A twist in Callum's gut.

*Not even two years old.*

An image of his daughter flooded his mind. He thought back to her second birthday. She was unhappy the whole day—tears and tantrums. His parents were the only ones who'd come to celebrate. None of them had even touched the cake his mum had bothered to make.

An ache in his chest at the memory, an urge to hold his daughter now. He didn't know what he'd do if he ever lost her. He couldn't think about it. Wouldn't. He shook her image from his head.

Eddy returned, a grin on his face and a stack of books nestled in one arm. He handed Callum a fresh beer, pulled up a seat and plopped the books on the table, the image on the cover of the top book immediately recognisable.

Bold letters in green: 'Granite Creek District School Yearbook 1988'. Callum flipped through the small stack and selected one from the middle of the pile: 1992. Their final year of school.

The book was thin, the school never particularly big. It'd been fortunate that there'd even been a high school in a town so small. This far north it wasn't uncommon for kids to have to trek an hour and a half each way to attend a school at the next closest town. It was either that or boarding school.

He flicked through the pages, familiar images flashing by. Classrooms, sports grounds, school camps.

He paused on a page. Faded green pictures with smiling faces shining out. A senior year school excursion. In the local rainforest, nowhere fancy. It was meant to be an opportunity to blow off steam after they'd finished their mid-year exams.

Callum looked at the photos. All the faces were familiar, some more so than others. One stood out. Eyes crinkled at the edges, top lip slightly curled upwards as she smiled at the camera. Pip. A tightening in his chest.

Her smile, her eyes, all etched into his memory. He tore his eyes away, searched for another image. Two boys, gangly and bare chested, about to jump in the creek. Callum couldn't help but smile. He and Eddy had that awkward way of holding themselves that all teenage boys have. Not quite confident in their changing bodies, yet trying their hardest to look like grown men at the same time.

Callum's eyes focused on his seventeen-year-old self. He'd had no idea what lay ahead. A tingle below his left knee and he flipped the page.

Brett Wyatt stared from the next page and the image sent an odd sensation through him. Somehow, Brett seemed to look much younger than Callum had ever recalled. Still a towering giant with hooded eyebrows, Brett's face was softened by youth, his cheeks rounded, his eyes open wide as if he'd been caught by surprise.

Callum snapped the book shut. He placed it on the pile and leaned back in his chair. He'd seen enough of Brett's face for one day.

He turned to Eddy. 'Brett giving you much grief?'

'Surprisingly not,' Eddy said. 'I felt a little sick when I learned it was his son out there. Thought I was going to have him on my back the whole time. But he's mostly done what he's been told. Helping out with the search.'

Helpful didn't sound like the Brett whom Callum recalled. But who knows how he'd changed in thirty years.

Very little, if today's run-in held any bearing.

'So, what's the vibe like on the ground?' he asked.

A pause. 'Morale's dwindling. The weather is really affecting everyone. This cyclone's like a ticking time bomb. Still, Lachie's a local, and a smart guy from what I understand. It's been just over twenty-four hours, so he's got a good chance surviving out there. And there's nothing like a good old dose of town guilt to keep everyone searching.'

No one in Granite Creek had forgotten the pathetic search for fifteen-year-old Amelia Dyer three decades earlier. Four hours back in town and Callum had already figured that out himself.

He'd caught snippets about it from his parents. They'd left Granite Creek by that stage, but were still looped into the town's gossip.

*Ran away. Skipped town. Moved to the city to track down her dad.*

That was the best of it, spoken aloud, reasons to call off the search.

*Caught up in a drug ring. Working the streets to pay for her habit.*

The worst was muttered in hushed voices over beers at Cutters or on the footy field sideline, and had woven its way into the ears of Callum's family some sixteen hundred kilometres away.

The Haffenden family had been well respected in Granite Creek. Respected and kept at arm's length. His mum had been the only GP, his dad the only cop. No one wanted to be mates with the person who checked their haemorrhoids or gave them speeding tickets.

But Eddy's parents had been a reliable source of information, and decades later Cal's dad still phoned Eddy's regularly. That's how they learned about the aftermath. The almost non-existent search. The pregnancy. The marriage. The guilt.

A tingle below his left knee. He rubbed his palms down his trousers again.

Eddy's voice jolted him back. 'I think it's in the back of everyone's mind that, you know, we might find *her*.'

## CHAPTER FIVE

The ground beneath Callum's feet was soft and he sank a little with each step he took into the rainforest. Behind, the dim glow of his high-beam headlights struggled to penetrate the thick foliage, faint shadows splashing in front. Shitty car, shitty headlights.

After leaving Eddy's, the image of Pip had stuck in his mind, and before he'd registered what he was doing, his car had been jostling back along Kingfisher Way. He'd pulled over on the shoulder and hadn't put much thought into his actions as he'd walked to the start of a smaller, lesser-known walking track.

Pip. Her head in his lap, her long hair spilling over his thighs and across the boulders. Light against the dark granite grey.

The faint glow of the search headquarters was just visible at the end of the road. The car park was a good base with entry to the main track that led to the camp site.

Help wasn't far.

He took a steady breath and stepped beneath the canopy.

This track, along with the main one that he'd walked only that afternoon with the search party, led to the camp site. This path wasn't sign-posted though, its entrance almost completely shrouded, and the shoulder of the road was narrow, offering little in the way of parking. Walking distance from town, it was the same track he knew well from his teens.

He'd been certain some others had known of it back then. But how many people knew of it now?

The overgrown path suggested few.

As he ducked into the rainforest the outside world disappeared, the thick canopy of trees overhead drowning it out.

No sky. No light. No sound.

He strained his ears, let the rainforest burrow in. The rain, thunderous on his car roof, was now a mere patter, landing softly on the upper layers of the tallest trees, some thirty metres above. Wind that had whipped at him only moments earlier had now died. Instead, the damp muggy air was still, rigid.

His ears pricked, caught a soft whistling. He paused, straining to hear. His heart was banging loud enough to fill his head. The whistle drew nearer, and a slick sheen of sweat coated his body. A piercing shriek split the air, then the rush of wings and the rustle of a tree.

*Tyto multipunctata*: lesser sooty owl.

His heart rate slowed. The darkness crept around him.

What the hell was he doing in the rainforest at night? Idiot. It was one thing to go traipsing around with a search party along a lit track, but another to trek out alone in the pitch black.

No one knew he was here. There was no phone reception. No light.

*Time to head back.*

He went to turn but his feet had sunk down into the sodden mud. Decaying leaves and scrub masked the track, and the long leaves of ferns and branches crisscrossed over the path, concealing the way forward.

And back.

His mind returned to the last time he'd walked this path. The greenery thinner, the track clearer. It hadn't been this dense, the shrubbery hadn't pressed in this close.

*Never step off the trail.*

His car headlights shone only a few metres behind him. The road was right there. Still ...

The sooty owl whistled softly above him once more. A haze of memories took shape in his mind: his last day in Granite Creek, walking along this very track, the boulders ...

The images never quite sharpened, always blurred at the edges. Three decades of not remembering that day. He reached for the memory, but it was whipped away as if by the wind.

Retrograde amnesia, the doctors had told him. Not uncommon after an accident.

He lifted his arms, checking the space in front was clear, then swept them out to his sides. Soft elongated leaves and a moss-covered trunk brushed his fingertips. He snapped his arms back but his left sleeve snagged, the rainforest trying to keep him near.

A thrash of his arm, wildly pulling, the sound of fabric tearing and the sharp, familiar drag of a thorny vine tore at his skin. He snatched both arms to his chest.

Beneath his hands, the thumping of his heart reverberated and filled his ears. The muggy air stuck to the insides of his airways. He tried for a deep breath, failed.

Seconds passed. Hours.

A siren pierced the air. The faint flash of red and blue flickering somewhere behind. His head cleared.

Help wasn't far.

At last, his lungs filled. The siren faded and the sounds of the rainforest returned. He focused on the soft patter of rain on the canopy above, on the steady rise and fall of his chest beneath his hands.

He turned with some difficulty, his legs stubborn, as if they hadn't moved for days. Prising his shoes from an inch of mud, he willed himself to walk.

He was surprised when he reached his car within only a few paces. Not buried in the bowels of the rainforest after all, just mere metres from the cusp of the road.

He took a breath, easy at last.

*Jesus, get a grip.*

He steadied himself on the car roof, sucked in hot, heavy air. The flash of blue and red lights at the end of Kingfisher Way. His left shirtsleeve was torn, and a long, shallow scratch had formed beneath, the red of the blood already washed away in the rain.

He turned, looked back at the wall of trees lit up by the headlights. A splash of colour caught his eye. Another flicker of blue and red, this time against the sea of greens and browns.

Just inside the mouth of the track, beyond a large kauri pine, a long, thin vine hung down. Sharp barbs jutted out and, snagged among them, hung a vibrant thin strip of fabric.

It took a moment to extract it, and he received several sharp pricks from the vine for his efforts. Coloured thread, woven intricately, the strip was only about ten centimetres long with an additional length of loose thread at each end. He shifted the piece between his hands and a soft tinkle broke through the rain.

*Ting. Ting.*

Knotted within its threads were three small silver bells.

\*

Callum's eyes tracked Eddy as he strode from his police SUV. Face set and shoulders rounded against the rain, Eddy ducked beneath the police tape and was swallowed by a sea of volunteers moving in the opposite direction.

Only a few minutes earlier, Callum had stood with the lure of the rainforest less than a metre away and the pressure of the small bells in his clasped hand. Another set of red and blue flashing lights had pierced the darkness, and an ambulance had sped past his car towards the end of Kingfisher Way.

He clambered out of his rental car now and hurried along to keep Eddy in his line of sight. He pushed his way through a group of volunteers headed back towards the line of parked cars—high-vis vests glowing, heads bowed, faces sombre.

*Shit.*

Ignoring the dull ache below his knee, he picked up his pace.

'What's happened?' He placed his hand on the back of Eddy's shoulder as he reached him.

Eddy spun and a split second passed between them. Face blank and mouth thin, Eddy didn't have to say it: Lachie Wyatt was dead.

'Where?' Callum asked.

A pause.

Eddy looked Callum square in the eyes. 'The north-west boulders.'

## CHAPTER SIX

*Thirty years earlier*

I stashed my bike at the base of a thick kauri pine tree and ducked onto the track, stopping a few steps in to let my eyes adjust to the darkness. The back of my neck already felt burnt from the short ride to Kingfisher Way, and my skin prickled with the sudden drop in temperature. I yanked my t-shirt, drenched and plastered to my body with sweat, over my head and jammed it into the pocket of my shorts.

My glasses slid down my nose and I pushed them back up as I waited for the forest to come into focus. After a few moments, the outline of the trees took form, the faint track between the scrub just visible. I picked my way forward.

The day was dragging, one of nine long empty days in the middle of school holidays. A few days snorkelling in Cairns with Mum at the start and then a birding trip with Dad in the Daintree at the end marked out the two weeks. Mum's requests for now were simple: entertain yourself, don't trash the house, don't consume the entire contents of the fridge.

On my first day, I'd gone in to shadow Dad around the station. After about a hundred hours of making him cups of tea and watching him type at his computer, he was finally called out. Mr Moretti had gone missing.

Thirty seconds into our search, we'd found the old geezer walking down the main street in his pyjamas and we'd taken him back home. Mrs Moretti had whipped his arse with a tea towel and ushered us inside for some biscotti and strong coffee that Dad wouldn't let me drink. As we'd gone to leave, she'd held Dad's face firmly between two hands and kissed him right on the lips. Then she'd done the same to me. Not even her bag of takeaway biscotti had made up for her wet lips and hairy chin tickling mine. I decided not to go back to work with Dad after that.

It wasn't the kind of policing I was going to do anyway. None of this small-town cop business. Sitting on your arse, chatting to the locals. Specialist Response Group or Riot Squad. Something more exciting. That's where I was heading next year.

I ploughed on. The path was deserted. Eddy and most of the other kids from school had been shipped off down south to family for two weeks. Only a few of us from school lingered.

*Bored. Bored. Bored.*

I dodged the sharp barbs of a wait-a-while vine and took in the sounds of the rainforest. Bird sounds.

A shrill squeak: azure kingfisher.

A loud whip-crack: eastern whipbird.

Three quick ascending trills, repeated twice: noisy pitta.

They were talking to me.

The trickle of the creek crept up and I jogged the last few metres to the top of the steep bank. Time to get drenched with something other than sweat.

A quick skid down the bank, then I stripped off my shorts and glasses and dived under the still water.

*Ice.*

Freezing ice. The water clawed at my skin like the talons of a grey goshawk, sharp and angry, and the air in my chest caught.

Granite was far enough north to keep you in a constant state of sweat all year round, but far enough up the range that, in the dry season, the waters ran like the cold blood of a salty.

I broke the surface and sucked in a warm mouthful of air that made my chest ache. My legs churned under the water, and after a few minutes some feeling began to come back.

Upstream, a belt of granite boulders—grey on green—traversed the creek, connecting the two sides of the banks: the town side and the boulders side.

The safe side and the, well, who-the-hell-knows side.

The dangerous side?

People had fallen. Though Dad said they were mostly stupid tourists who didn't know what they were doing.

But there were those kids all those years ago. Eddy's dad talked about it a bit. Eddy said he was spinning shit, just trying to keep us off the boulders, out of trouble.

The kids at school said it was something else though.

Either way, everyone said not to go out there. So, of course, we'd all been.

Eddy and I snuck out there years ago, when we were nine or ten, still in primary school. It's pretty cool. The end of the rainforest, a cliff edge, and a drop to a floor of giant granite boulders that scatter all the way to the horizon. Like a gang of giants had been playing marbles, grown bored and left them behind.

The ground to the edge sloped downwards and the wind had picked up just as a whistle pitched across the boulders and the air had pressed against us. Eddy's Volleys had slipped, and he'd tripped over the roots of a huge strangler fig tree that clung to the cliff edge. He'd landed on his stomach with one foot hanging over the ledge and had spent the next two weeks telling everyone at school that he was nearly taken by the whispering.

*Idiot.*
We'd never gone back.
I lay back in the creek and let my toes break the surface and the water rush into my ears.
Silence. Just the jagged sound of my breath and the pounding of my heart.
A green roof overhead, pierced briefly by a yellow blur, flitting across the canopy. A male golden bowerbird. I didn't need my glasses: its size and shade of yellow gave it away. It landed on a nearby branch, head turning my way.
I wasn't alone.
I stood up, the splash of the water loud in the calm. My eyes moved over the bank and caught on a figure sitting on the boulders' bridge, watching me.
Her soft blonde hair was swept into a messy ponytail that slipped out from underneath a pale blue cap. Her legs poked out the bottom of worn denim shorts and dangled over the edge of the boulder, bare feet swishing softly in the water below.
Only metres away. She smiled and my mouth was suddenly dry.
Pip.
'Hey,' she said.
'Hey.'
*Think of something else to say.*
Blank.
'What are you doing out here?' Her eyes darted to the bank. The boulders' side.
My feet slipped on the mossy creek bed and I took a moment to find my footing. 'I could ask you the same question.'
She laughed. It was soft and crisp, like the call of the northern fantail. Her face fell flat, her laugh cut short.
*Say something, dickhead.*

'Umm, nice day, isn't it?'

*Shit. Not that.*

She smiled again, stood and looked around. Her eyes landed on my clothes, thrown at the water's edge. A laugh.

'Nice day for a walk.' She looked around again. 'Wanna come?'

I scrambled out of the creek, slipped once. Shit, why hadn't I kept my shorts on? Wet white jocks was not what I wanted Pip Dyer to see me in. She didn't bother to look away as I jammed my glasses back on and wrestled into my shorts. Wet fabric on wet skin.

*Great.*

She picked up a satchel that had been on the boulder beside her, threw it over one shoulder and slipped her feet back into her sneakers. No socks.

She stepped off her boulder and landed in front of me on the sloping bank. Close. Less than a metre away. I could have counted the freckles spattered across her nose, neat as pinpricks, like the spots on the breast of a star finch.

Her eyes caught mine. Gold flecked around the green irises. Little halos. I'd never noticed before. A loose eyelash sat just below her left eye, and I fought the urge to sweep it away.

Or pocket it.

I looked back to her nose. Safer territory.

She turned and her ponytail whipped against my chest. My hand flew up. What was I going to do? Tell her not to leave? Kiss her?

*Don't be a dickhead.*

After a few steps, she turned, one foot back on the boulders that spanned the creek, her satchel swinging against her thigh. 'Are you coming?' she asked.

My mouth filled with cotton wool, and I had to push the word out. 'Where?'

A smile. 'The boulders.'

# CHAPTER SEVEN

Dead. He'd arrived too late.

Callum sat in his underwear on the edge of the motel bed, mattress sagging beneath his weight. Wet clothes hung over the back of a lone rattan chair that sat at the small desk. They wouldn't dry. Nothing would dry in this place. His hair was wet, his skin was wet, and although he'd only been in Granite Creek just over six hours, it was as if he'd been drenched to the bone for weeks.

Still, he'd been too late. Lachie was dead.

Eddy had sent him back to the motel. 'There's nothing you can do to help, mate,' he'd said, jaw set. 'It's probably going to take the team a few hours to extract him. You may as well get some rest.'

Eddy's eyebrows had pulled together, his face rigid. Of all the times that the two friends had caught up over the decades, Callum could only recall a handful of occasions when Eddy didn't have a grin plastered on his face.

The first time he'd seen his friend so stony faced, they'd been seventeen. Callum had watched from the hospital bed as Eddy hovered awkwardly in the doorway, his eyes flitting towards his mate. It took a grin from Callum, as he used the triangle dangling overhead to heave himself up the bed, to entice Eddy into the room. Eddy's shoulders sagged and the corner of his mouth lifted a fraction. Within minutes the two friends were carrying on loud enough that the cranky old bastard in the bed next to Callum's had told them to shut the hell up. The two boys had grinned at each other, Eddy sitting comfortably on the end of the bed in the vacant space where Callum's left leg used to be.

The light in the motel room was dim, lit only by the bedside lamp. The scent of rain and wet earth drifted in between the window panes and under the door and blended seamlessly with the smell of damp sheets and musty carpet.

Callum rubbed his swollen left knee, and looked at the skin just below, where his leg came to an abrupt end. The skin over his stump was red, angry and sore to the touch. Still, he'd seen it in worse states. A night's rest was all it needed. His prosthetic leg rested, alongside his crutches, within arm's reach against the bedside table, a soggy shoe still attached to its end. Its partner was by the wardrobe, laces fully removed and innersole lying next to it. He doubted it would be dry by morning. He doubted even he'd be dry by morning.

His eyes ran up the outside of the wardrobe door and lingered at the top. It was firmly closed. He stared at the timber as if he could make out the folded polyester blanket beyond, the lockbox hidden within. He fought the urge to get up, limp across the room on his crutches, and check. If he had two functioning legs, he would have.

He stared at the cupboard door until his vision clouded.

*Jesus, get it together.*

He snatched his glasses off and pressed his thumb and forefinger into his closed eyes. They were hot, heavy. When at last he opened them, a splash of colour on the bedside table caught his attention through the blur.

He returned his glasses and reached for the small red and blue braided strip with its three bells. He turned it in his hands.

*Ting. Ting.*

The chime was crisp and clear even over the downpour outside. He'd known, from the moment he'd untangled it from the vine, what it was: a homemade friendship bracelet. Kids wore them even in his day. Only a few years ago, Milly also wore some. He shifted it in his hands again.

*Ting. Ting.*

The bells were something different though, a new addition.

He placed the small strip around his left wrist. It didn't fit. He'd known it wouldn't. Too small; a child's bracelet.

A sense of unease ran over him and he returned the bracelet to his bedside table.

Snatches of the day paraded through his head. The dead fairy-wren at Lachie's car. The scratches along Brett's arms. The closeness of the rainforest, the tightening of his chest, the catching of his breath.

The whisper of the wind.

He'd thought he had his panic attacks under control, had learned to rein them in. Subdue them. It'd been years since his last one. He cast a last glance at the bracelet and picked up his phone. Two bars of reception—a third flickering—lingered in the corner now that he was back in the centre of town. A frustratingly message-free screen stared back. It was 11.17 pm. Late. But not too late for a fifteen-year-old during school holidays. He didn't like his chances of getting a response but fired off a text anyway.

*Sorry I ditched you this morning. Hope you have a great time with Nan and Pop. Talk soon. Love you.*

A brief pause and then he hit send. He held the phone for a beat longer than necessary, waiting for the telltale three dots that would show Milly was responding. Biting back his disappointment, he placed the phone next to the bracelet.

She'd been pissed off—not that he'd come to Granite Creek, but that he'd refused to bring her with him. She often asked about where he'd grown up. He'd told her about the stifling heat and the endless green. About the crisp water and the sooty boulders. She always asked why they never visited and he never knew what to tell her.

It was the same when she asked about her mother.

Outside, a sudden burst of wind rattled the window.

All he knew now was that with every additional kilometre between Milly and Granite Creek, the safer he could keep her.

# CHAPTER EIGHT

The taste of bad espresso lingered on Callum's tongue as he left the bakery and wandered along the main street, limping slightly. A night of tossing and turning had done little to settle the swelling that had formed in his stump from a day of being cramped in a too small aeroplane followed by a too small car. A strong stomach and much swearing had allowed him to jam it into the fibreglass socket of his prosthesis forty-five minutes earlier.

The main street wasn't especially long, the town not especially big. The squat, single-storey shops were the same as those that decorated any small town: grocer, hardware, post office. The usual. At least half looked as if they sported new roofs.

Large solid awnings jutted out from their fronts to reach the edge of the footpath. Protection from the scorching sun during the dry season and from the torrential downpour the other half of the year. Unfortunately, they did bugger all to protect you from rain that flew in sideways.

A few people ducked and weaved from one shelter to the next. He didn't bother to rush: his leg never fared well on wet surfaces, and he'd resigned himself to being wet for the duration of his stay in Granite Creek.

Hopefully not too much longer.

He paused at a driveway that led to a rear car park behind the shops. A dash of a memory: rear-ending Ivan Schapiro's ute hard enough that the L-plate from the windscreen of his dad's SUV had flown off into his lap. His dad had sworn under his breath, replaced the plate and gone to console a seething Mr Schapiro.

Callum shook the memory from his head, crossed the driveway and stopped outside the next shopfront. By the looks of it, the Outdoor Store stocked everything from birding binoculars to Nordic walking poles. He was surprised such a business could survive in a town the size of Granite Creek, but Eddy had mentioned tourist numbers were picking up in the drier months. The outside of the shop looked tired, the paint near the bottom was stained and swollen from flood damage, popping out like mustard-coloured bubble wrap. The sign, however, looked fresh and welcoming, and Callum could see a curvy blonde woman stocking a shelf near the window. She caught his eye and flashed him a smile. He gave her a nod and moved on, his body protesting as fatigue settled into his bones.

He'd tossed and turned on the saggy motel mattress for what had felt like most of the night. Flashes of green eyes with gold flecks had come in fits and bursts, and he'd eventually woken in a puddle of sweat, the sound of the air conditioner straining. He'd rolled to check his phone: 3.24 am and still message-free.

He continued down the street and, a few moments later, with the help of the handrail, lugged himself up the three familiar steps of the local cop shop. A cool breeze welcomed him as he pushed the glass door open and entered. A voice rang out across the small reception area and a surprising lightness washed through him.

Steph sat behind the desk, phone wedged between her shoulder and her ear, her hands flying across a keyboard. She looked up, smiled. Her left cheek dimpled.

He waited for her to hang up, his eyes roaming the familiar space. Not much had changed in thirty years. A lick of paint and some fresh carpet appeared to be as far as the state budget would stretch. The door behind Steph, with its opaque window and chipped timber, was the same as when his dad had been stationed there, and the plastic light fittings were cracked and faded. A bunch of native heliconias, sitting in a glass vase to the side of the desk, brightened up the room and, he suspected, had more to do with Steph than Eddy.

'Well, hello there.' Steph clicked the phone down.

'Hi. You work here.'

She laughed. 'Missed your calling as a detective. You looking for Eddy?'

'He around?'

'Not just now. Had to go out to the morgue in Cairns. Did you hear they found Lachie's body?'

'Yeah.' He swallowed, pushed an image of Milly from his mind. 'Any word on when the funeral will be?'

'Probably next week sometime. They usually take a day or two to release the body.' Her eyes glinted. 'Thinking of sticking around for it?'

He should. 'Probably not.'

'Well, if you do stay on a bit longer, it'd be nice to catch up. Properly. Grab a bite to eat.'

The door behind him opened and Eddy was carried in on a wave of hot air. A cardboard box was wedged under his arm, and he looked up and nodded to Callum. Not surprised to see him then.

'Any messages?' he asked Steph.

'Just Sammie Morgan wants to contest his speeding fine from Monday.'

'He can contest away. I've got him on camera clocking thirty-five over the limit.' Eddy propped up a hinged portion of the desk. He cocked his head towards Callum who followed him through.

'Coffee?' Steph called.

'God, yes,' Eddy said. 'Thanks.'

'Think about that catch up,' Steph said to Callum as he walked past.

He smiled. 'I will.'

\*

'Long night?' Callum looked at Eddy. Exhaustion lines were etched across his friend's face.

'It's still going.'

'You haven't been home yet?'

Eddy shook his head, pressing the heels of his hands firmly against his closed eyes. 'Took them nearly four hours to extract his body.'

'Four hours?'

Eddy's forehead glistened despite the coolness of his office. 'Weather conditions were awful. And he was pretty messed up. Half his body had fallen into a gap between two of the boulders. One leg got stuck.' He met Callum's eyes. 'They had to break it to get his body out.'

A fire began to smoulder below Callum's left knee.

Just a break.

It didn't matter anyway. Lachie was dead.

'It was just dumb luck that they found him, really,' Eddy continued. 'Dumb luck he hadn't fallen all the way down into the bloody crevasse, and dumb luck that the chopper was coming back the way it did.' He shook his head. 'They'd already flown over that part of the boulders a dozen times or more. The pilot just happened to come back at a different angle or something. Caught a glimpse of Lachie's fluoro pants poking out the edge of the crevasse. They choppered him to the hospital in Cairns. I've been down there most of the night.'

Eddy plopped himself down in a worn office chair behind the desk. The cardboard box he'd carried into the station sat on top. A second cardboard box next to it. Callum could see several framed certificates and photos, along with a sad-looking potted peace lily, all waiting to find their new homes. A small Aboriginal flag seemed to be the only thing that had been unpacked. It stood on the desk, its mast bent slightly as if it'd been caught out in the gale.

'Bloody Brett's been on the phone all morning. Surprised I didn't have him breathing down my neck at the morgue,' Eddy said. 'Wants to know what the hell killed his son.'

Callum blew out a slow breath and sat down. He could hear Steph bustling about in the kitchenette one room over. The clank of a mug and the clatter of cutlery, followed by a muffled 'Shit'.

'What did you tell him?' he asked Eddy.

'Nothing yet. It's too early to say. The guys that extracted him said it was a fall, no doubt about that.'

'You didn't go to the site yourself?'

'Went as far as I could.'

Callum nodded. The boulders were notoriously dangerous. You'd have to be either extremely experienced or extremely foolish to risk scaling down them. Eddy was neither.

'It didn't look good from what I could see from the cliff ledge.'

The cogs in Callum's head chugged around slowly, as if pushing through mud.

Eddy's eyes narrowed, surveyed Callum. 'Look, don't go reading too much into it, mate. Plenty of people have had accidents off the north-west boulders. It doesn't mean anything.'

'So you're calling it an accident?'

'At this stage.' Eddy paused. 'I don't know if I'm ready to say the word *suicide* to Brett just yet.' He sighed and moved the box with his belongings off the desk and placed it on the floor alongside a large plastic tub, filled with sopping-wet orange and blue fabric. 'God, what a shitstorm.'

He began unpacking the contents of the box in silence. Each of Lachie's items was handled with care and turned over several times before he placed it down on the desk.

A pair of mud-covered boots. Socks, still wet. A t-shirt and a pair of fluoro yellow pants: fireman's pants. Folded neatly.

A multipurpose tool and a wedding ring.

Callum's eyes focused on the shirt. Navy. Almost granite grey when wet. No wonder they didn't spot him first—or twelfth—time around.

A clatter as Steph reversed into the room, pushing the door open with her back, two cups of coffee in her hands. Callum jumped up to help her and was rewarded with a sharp jab from his leg and a broad smile from Steph. She placed the mugs down on the desk and her eyes roamed over Lachie's belongings.

'Is that his stuff?'

'Just what was actually on him.' Eddy cleared his throat. 'Or around him.'

Callum watched as her brows knitted together, her full lips pulled tight. She reached across and slid the cardboard box towards herself and peered inside. Empty, Callum knew. She scanned the items on the desk again.

'Where's his torch?'

Both men's gazes turned back to the desk.

She was right. No torch.

'Maybe he didn't need one,' Callum said. 'It doesn't get dark till almost seven this time of year.' He knew the concept was rubbish before the words even came out. It got darker earlier in the rainforest, the fading sunlight unable to penetrate the dense canopy overhead. Anyone camping would need a torch. Still, he looked at Eddy. 'What time did he leave to go camping?'

Eddy flipped through the pages of a manila folder sitting on the desk. 'Tess said he left around six-ish.'

'And how long to drive out to the site, hike to where his gear was found, and set up?'

Eddy shrugged. 'Forty-five minutes. An hour tops.'

'Was there a torch in his gear at the camp site?' Callum asked.

Eddy's gaze turned towards the plastic tub on the ground beside his desk. A puddle of water had formed on the floor beneath a swathe of vibrant blue fabric that puffed up over the edge.

'Just his tent and sleeping bag,' Eddy said. 'No torch.'

'That's all? Tent and sleeping bag?' Steph asked. 'No food? Water?'

Eddy shook his head. 'Tess said he often didn't take food with him if he just went for the night. Went late, back early. Has been doing it his whole life apparently. Brett used to take him camping a lot as a kid.'

'Still, no water,' Steph said.

Faint frown lines spattered Eddy's forehead. He turned over a few more pages in the folder, before placing it opened on the desk. 'Here's the inventory of everything he had at the camp site. No food. No water.' He ran his finger down the list. 'No torch.'

Steph snorted. 'Maybe he was more of an idiot than we thought.' Her auburn hair swept her cheeks as she turned on her heel and walked back out to the main reception area, two sets of eyes on her back.

Eddy's frown deepened as he picked up Lachie's t-shirt from his desk and placed it in the box. Callum bundled up the yellow pants and placed them alongside the rest of Lachie's things. His fingertips burned, sent a trail of fire all the way to his eyes, suddenly heavy. There was something to be said for touching a dead man's belongings.

He blinked once, dragged himself back.

Eddy's voice grew in his ears. 'Just because we haven't found a torch, doesn't mean he didn't have one on him. You've seen the size of the gaps between those boulders. It could easily have dropped into one as he fell. Same goes for a water bottle.'

'How thorough a search was done at the site?'

'Very thorough. Several guys kitted up and canyoned down the closest crevasses. They spent hours scouring the area. They like to bring everything they can back to the families.'

A pause. 'So, the north-west boulders, hey?'

'Yeah.' Eddy stopped packing and looked up. 'Look, there's no story to be uncovered here, so don't you go getting any ideas.' He pointed a muddy boot at Callum, before placing it in the box alongside its partner. 'Not in this weather.' He paused. 'And not in your condition.'

Surprise shot through Callum: over the three decades since his accident, Eddy had rarely mentioned his leg. And never as a limiting factor.

'Look.' Eddy eyed him. 'From what I've heard, most locals don't even go out there nowadays. Not even when the weather's good. The track that we used as kids is mostly overgrown and a lot of the younger locals probably don't even know about it. Since you left, it's generally been considered too risky.'

'I'm like some kind of cautionary tale?'

Eddy shrugged. 'Something like that.'

They fell silent, the air between them heavy. Through the thin walls, Steph could be heard on a phone call, her tone reassuring, soothing.

'So, what now?' Callum spoke at last.

'Nothing. Lachie's death isn't considered suspicious. He fell, like others before him.' Eddy placed a hand on the cardboard box. 'I'll give this stuff back to Tess and let his family do their grieving.' A pause. 'And you'll be able to catch the next flight home.'

Home. The word rolled in Callum's head and images of Milly flashed before him.

The groan of the air conditioner battled against the sound of the window rattling in its frame. A beat later, Steph popped her head in, alerted Eddy to a call-out and he was up out of his chair.

'A missing cat?' Callum tried not to smirk.

Eddy shrugged and picked up his keys, heading towards the door. 'Beats dealing with missing kids.'

He paused, one hand on the door, turned back. 'Seriously, mate, don't go getting a bee in your bonnet. It's been great seeing you, but you really should head back home, Milly needs you.' His mouth hung open a fraction longer than necessary, as if he were going to add something. After a beat, he snapped it shut, gave one of his trademark grins that, this time, didn't quite meet his eyes, and walked out the door, leaving Callum alone in his office.

*Milly needs you.*

Callum blinked once, then scanned the room, his eyes falling on the closed manila folder on the edge of Eddy's desk. A glance over his shoulder at the closed door, and he leaned forward, sliding it closer and flipping the cover open.

He flicked past a few official-looking documents. Lachie's details. Date of birth. Next of kin.

He focused on the form until his eyes ached and the letters on the page began to blur.

He blinked and flipped it over.

An image stared up at him.

A photo. A photo of Lachie.

Dead.

The image was printed on A4 paper in pixelated, grainy colour. The quality was crap. But the content was clear: Lachie Wyatt, legs wedged down a gap between two boulders, his fluoro yellow pants just visible and stark against grey granite.

His face was turned to the side, his neck at an odd angle. Like a tree trunk growing crookedly in the rainforest, a desperate bid to reach sunlight. To reach life.

He flipped the photo over. Another followed. He flipped again. And again.

Image after image of Lachie's broken body shone from the pages.

His mouth pooled with the acidic taste of bile. He snapped the folder shut, and the groan of the air conditioner ratcheted up a notch, drowning out the downpour outside and the scream inside his head.

# CHAPTER NINE

The air was pungent. Wafts of sweaty bodies and beer swirled around Callum. Relieved to finally be off his leg, he shifted a little, his wet trousers protesting against the faux leather covering of his bench seat. A sticky layer of grime coated the wooden tabletop in front of him, a patch of dry tomato sauce—almost dark brown—smeared in one corner.

The Cane Cutters' Tavern was heaving. It was Friday lunchtime and he suspected many of the locals had decided to call it quits—the discovery of a dead local the excuse they needed to start their weekend early. The news of Lachie's death had spread through Granite Creek like a dark mould, coating the town in a thick shadow, and they'd flocked like thirsty kingfishers to Granite Creek's only watering hole; their bodies huddled together, beady eyes bouncing around, their feathers rustling at unexpected sounds.

Judging by the number of people crammed into the dank room, he suspected many of the out-of-towners were staying on for a drink and debrief also. No cops though. The few that had been sent up to help Eddy with the search must've headed back to Cairns already.

He caught the eye of Mike from the motel seated at the bar alongside the bearded SES guy from the track yesterday. He gave them both a nod and the SES man raised his glass. A quick scan of the room told him the journalist from the night before wasn't there. Thank Christ.

Despite the number of bums on sticky seats, the atmosphere in the pub was subdued. Hushed voices and mumbled words over clinking glasses. The rain, drumming on the old tin roof, was a constant background rhythm.

'Wow, haven't seen a line like that for the loos since I used to hit the clubs in the city in my twenties.' Steph slid into the booth opposite him.

Back at the station, Callum's stomach had given an audible protest as if on cue to remind him to eat. As a rule, he generally skipped breakfast. He was a tall guy and maintaining a healthy weight was crucial for him to be able to fit his stump into his prosthesis, as well as minimising the amount of weight it had to support. More weight equalled more pain. At home, he was diligent with his exercise routine: three times a week swimming and twice a week doing light upper-body weights to maintain his arm strength for when he needed to use his crutches.

A few days of pub meals and beer, along with the constant heat and humidity, were going to wreak havoc with his already angry stump.

Still, he hadn't been able to say no when Steph had insisted on shouting him to a beer and lunch.

Now, he avoided resting his hands on the tabletop, and tried to put the squirming sensation in his stomach down to hunger.

'So how long do you think you'll stay?' Steph leaned over the table, her elbow dangerously close to the tomato sauce dollop.

'Not sure. I should probably get back sooner rather than later.'

'Someone special waiting for you at home?' Her hazel eyes twinkled, her mouth turned up at the edges.

'Yes, actually.'

If she was disappointed, she didn't show it. She took a sip from her glass of house white, which had been poured to the brim in true country town style, and smiled. 'Well, she's very lucky.'

'Someone needs to tell her that.' Callum took a sip of his beer. 'It's my daughter.'

'Oh.' She placed the glass down and a little wine sloshed over the edge. 'I didn't know you had any kids.'

'Just the one. She's fifteen, going on thirty.' He tried not to think about his argument with Milly the day before, or the fact that she still hadn't returned his text. His phone sat heavy in his pocket.

Steph's laugh was full and floated across the table, unnatural in the muted pub. A few heads turned their way. Callum couldn't help but smile.

'And you?' he asked. 'Kids?'

'Just the one. Noah. He was ten in September.'

'And the father?' The question slipped out before he could stop it.

She shrugged. Her eyes roamed the crowd, moving from face to face, before she turned back to him. 'He's not around.'

'Oh, I'm sorry.'

'Don't be. He was more trouble than he was worth.' Her smile returned. 'What about your daughter's mum?'

'Same.' He paused. 'Not the more trouble bit, just not around anymore.' He took a sip of his beer, let the lie slide down the back of his throat and form a familiar lump in his chest. 'It's just Milly and me.'

She looked at him sideways. 'It's tough, isn't it? The whole single parent thing?'

'Yeah. Especially when she was little.'

Callum recalled holding a screaming, red-faced Milly, unsure as to what to do to calm her. Those early months had been awful. The constant crying, the sleepless nights. He tried to block out the memory of how utterly hopeless he'd felt and how he'd been so certain that he was going to fail as a father.

'Still, a teenage girl without a mum. That's tough.' She spun the stem of her wineglass in her fingers. 'For both of you,' she added.

'Same for you with Noah, I guess.'

'Yeah. He'd love to have a dad.' She lifted her glass and tilted it towards him. Her mouth lifted as she cocked her head to one side. 'Move back to Granite and we could team up.' A slight pause, then her laugh filled the air again as she gauged his expression.

Their meals arrived and Steph ordered a second glass of wine. The past few minutes rolled around in Callum's head and made his stomach knot. Cardboard textured chicken probably wasn't going to help either.

'So, Noah's ten?' he said. 'He mates with Jack then? Lachie's son.'

She nodded.

*Yes, he's ten? Yes, they're friends?*

'No. Not really,' she said once she'd finished her mouthful. 'But they're in the same grade and the school's small.'

He took another forkful.

While she tucked into her steak and chips, Steph told him about how she'd moved back to Granite Creek eleven years ago when her mum was diagnosed with breast cancer. Once she'd realised she was pregnant, it'd just seemed like the logical thing to stay in town where she'd have her parents' support.

'Unlike you,' she said.

'Me? Mum and Dad help out a lot. Always have. They moved down to Tassie not long after Milly arrived.' Almost immediately. 'Didn't want to be too far from what I'm sure they knew was going to be their only grandchild.' A warmth spread through his chest as he thought of his parents. Their move, their support. He couldn't have done it without them. 'And I think they knew I'd need all the help I could get.'

She gave a laugh. 'Well, look at you, single parent and career man then.'

He looked at her, his face blank.

'Big shot journalist,' she said.

He snorted, followed by a few strong coughs as a piece of salad lodged in his throat. 'Hardly.'

She raised an eyebrow.

'Not anymore at least.' He took a sip of his drink, washed down the lettuce. 'Writing about local council issues and feature articles for the local rag. No one reads that rubbish.'

'But earlier.'

He nodded. Earlier had been different.

'Why'd you leave your job in Brisbane?' she asked. 'You'd made quite a name for yourself. Even us folk up north caught wind of it.'

A shrug. 'Needed a sea change.' The lie rolled off his tongue before he had time to contemplate it.

'Hobart?'

'I like the cold.'

She raised an eyebrow.

A pause while he took a slow drink. 'I moved for Milly's mum.'

She nodded. Like everyone, she just accepted the answer. It was plausible. 'So why are you back now? You didn't know Lachie.'

'No, but, you know, he's a local and—'

'After everything that happened thirty years ago you wanted to ease your moral conscience?'

A knit of his eyebrows. The concrete feeling was back but he couldn't pinpoint why.

'I guess you'd left by then though.' Her eyes shifted to the table as if able to burn a hole through the sticky timber to his missing leg. She put her fork down, steak forgotten. 'No one looked for Amelia. They did a brief stroll through the forest, but nothing like this.' She shook her head. 'Her bike was found at the start of the track. It was obvious she was in the forest. She was fifteen and they didn't bother to look for her.'

He nodded. Everyone knew the search had been called off in less than forty-eight hours. A waste of manpower and resources, isn't that what they all said?

*She ran away. Skipped town. Drug ring. Working the streets.*

'Even before that, everyone turned a blind eye to the Dyer girls,' Steph continued. 'God, they had it rough. Remember their mum, Rita? What a right piece of work she was. Had a different man traipsing through that house more often than she showered. I mean, I know that no one really ever knows what goes on behind closed doors, but I think it's safe to say that nothing nice was happening to Pip and Amelia at home.' She looked out at the crowd again. 'This town is forever trying to make up for how they failed those girls.'

His eyes followed hers. The pub was chockers. The volunteers' shirts were like a sea of orange and yellow sunbirds, bright against the muted browns of the pub. His mind returned to the search for the toddler thirteen years ago. It had been more extensive, if the news had been anything to go off.

He took a long drink from his glass while his eyes roamed the pub. His gaze landed on a hulking figure hunched over a beer in the corner of the room: Brett.

Callum tore his eyes away, jaw set. Just what he needed.

Steph noticed, and her eyes shifted to where Callum's had just been. 'Poor guy.' She took a sip. 'Pip was lucky in some ways, I guess.'

Callum couldn't bring himself to speak, or even nod.

He watched as the barman placed a large pint in front of Brett, the amber liquid sloshing onto the table. The barman indicated a group of firemen at the bar, and Brett, barely lifting his head, raised his glass to them.

Most of the other patrons seemed to be giving Brett a wide berth.

'So, what was Lachie like?' Callum asked.

'Oh, you know.' Steph shrugged, moving a chip around her plate with her fork. 'Everyone liked him. Did a lot in the community.' She stabbed at the chip and held it aloft, smiled. 'That kind of guy.'

As if on cue, the fireys at the bar clanked their glasses.

'To Lachie,' one of the younger men called out and the other men echoed his call. The pub fell silent.

Callum, along with the other patrons, raised his glass. Steph's remained firmly planted on the table.

'See,' she said, swallowing her mouthful. 'The whole fire department's here to send him off. Better hope there's no emergencies while they're wetting their palates.' She raised her glass to the men and took a swift drink.

He waited before speaking again. 'Do you know Tess very well?'

'Hmm?' Steph turned from the group of firemen, her eyes glazed.

'Tess. Do you know her?'

'Lachie's wife?' Steph's gaze came back into focus. 'Not well. But in this town you're bound to run into everyone at some stage.'

Callum raised his eyebrows and let the silence sit, deepen.

'She keeps to herself mostly,' Steph said.

'No friends or family?'

She spun the stem of her wineglass, her fingertips white, her eyes focused on the straw-yellow liquid within. 'She's gorgeous. Clever too, from what I've heard. Left some promising career in the big smoke to be with Lachie up here. She probably could've had any bloke she wanted back in the city. Must've fallen for his country boy charm.' She drained her glass. It had been over half full. 'Probably not the idyllic little town she had in mind though. She's never made much of an effort with us locals. We don't hang out.'

'Oh?'

She laughed. 'I'm a fair bit older than she is, and a country bumpkin in her eyes, no doubt. Guess I'm just not her cup of tea.' She fiddled with an earring, slid her empty glass to the edge of the table.

*Or she isn't yours.*

After a pause, he asked, 'Do you know how things were between her and Lachie?'

'Good, I assume.' She hesitated, gave one shake of her head. 'But, like I said, I don't really know her well.'

He eyed her empty glass. 'One more?'

'No, I shouldn't. I don't normally drink. This lot will probably send me over the edge.' She laughed and glanced at her watch. 'Besides, I should be getting back soon.'

Callum cocked his head to the side and raised one eyebrow. 'Can't persuade you for old times' sake?'

Her eyes flittered to the edge of the pub. 'Oh, go on then.' Her dimple returned.

A few minutes later, Callum placed two brimming glasses on the table and tried to wedge himself back into the booth. He glanced at the far side of the pub, Brett's unmistakable figure still hunched over his table, beer glass empty. Two other figures, nursing their own drinks, sat opposite him. One young bloke, the other older, wrinkled and weather-beaten. The three heads leaned in towards each other, conversing. Conspiring. Brett's head snapped up, looked Callum's way. The two other men's eyes followed, seeking him out through the sea of bodies. One of them smirked and raised his glass to Callum.

Callum's mouth filled with sawdust.

'You okay?' Steph's voice cut through.

'Yeah, fine.'

A moment later and Brett sat alone, his two companions having moved on to the far end of the bar. Shoulders rounded, head drooped, Brett looked like a man defeated. Callum tore his eyes away and an idea scratched at the back of his head. He took a large drink of his beer, washing the sawdust down.

'Did you ever hear of anything that happened up at the school?'

She looked at the table, contemplating her wine.

'Was there some sort of trouble at some stage?' he pressed. 'Something with a teacher? A Thacker maybe? A kid called Josh?'

She gazed forward and he could almost see the pieces clicking together behind her eyes.

'Yeah, maybe,' she said after a moment. 'A long time ago though, before I came back. It was hushed up pretty good from what I understand. But you know how it is here. Lots of things get hushed up.' She gave him a wry smile. 'That is, until they get out.'

He looked at her expectantly and she leaned a little across the table.

'Look, I don't know a lot,' she said. 'But something happened to one of the teachers, maybe your Thacker. I'm not sure exactly. But the guy got into a confrontation with Brett and came out worse for wear. Had the living daylights beaten out of him from what I understand.' Her voice lowered. 'Thing is, he didn't press charges and it was never officially reported. Left town soon after. Moved south, I think. Adelaide or Melbourne, depending on who you ask.'

Callum nodded. He could understand wanting more distance from Brett.

'And Josh?'

She shrugged, looked at her watch. 'Shit.' She stood suddenly. 'It's after one. I need to get back.' She slipped out of the booth and slid her handbag strap over one shoulder, sweeping her hair out of the way as she did. Even in the dim pub, the auburn strands seemed to catch a little light. 'Don't tell Eddy I was late back from lunch.' She gave Callum a wink and turned, edging her way through the crowd with ease. He watched her until she was swallowed from view.

He stretched his left leg out under the table and shifted uncomfortably on the seat, his phone digging into his thigh. He reached in to pull it out of his pocket. Maybe Milly had texted him back. A thin, rough rope met his fingers, followed by a firm round object. His mind drew a blank and he pulled it out.

*Ting. Ting.*

The bracelet. He'd forgotten he'd stuffed it in his pocket that morning. The silver bells shone bright in his open palm, the red and blue thread still damp.

'Oi, Haffenden.'

A creep along his skin. He tore his eyes away from the bracelet and moved his gaze to the table that had housed Brett on the far side of the pub. Vacant. Except for more than half-a-dozen empty glasses.

A shadow fell across his own table.

Shit.

'Brett.' Callum turned to meet the man's glare, lifted his chin. Brett's eyes were red, the skin below puffy and raw. He looked as if he hadn't slept in a month.

He swayed. Like he'd been drinking for a month also.

'Haven't fucked off back to the city yet?'

'Not yet.'

'Perhaps I didn't make myself clear yesterday.' Brett leaned in. 'You're not welcome back here.'

'You've made yourself abundantly clear. But apart from you, I've felt pretty welcomed so far.'

'Don't be smart.'

'It just comes naturally to some of us.' The words slipped out.

*Shit. Don't bait him.*

Brett hunkered down and rested his hands on the table, his fingers brushing Callum's, his face inches away. His breath was hot, pungent. 'Don't think I'll go easy on you just because you're a cripple.'

A burst of anger. Callum pushed it down. Brett's son had just died. Maybe let him have this one.

Brett straightened. 'Keep your journo nose out of my family's business, if you know what's good for you,' he spat. 'Go and sniff out a story elsewhere.'

'I'm not here for a story,' Callum heard himself say, but the words sounded as if they came from someone else.

'No, I know. You're here for Pip.' Brett laughed, dry and short. 'Well, she's forgotten all about you, Haffenden. Time to move on.' He stood, laughed again and stalked away. The crowd parted for him.

# CHAPTER TEN

The air conditioner rattled, the wipers at last still. Callum sat in the stationary car, the view through the rain-streaked windscreen a blur of green and white. The house in front was not as he remembered. An extension out to the side made what was once a tiny worker's cottage into a sprawling family home, the entire thing elevated on a set of stilts. Flood-proof.

Behind the white timber house, the green of the rainforest loomed, the trees dark and uninviting under grey clouds that hung low enough to touch the tallest branches. Several trees towered over the property. Encroaching on the residence, preparing to swallow it whole.

His run-in with Brett at the pub grated at the edge of his thoughts. Why the hell had he come back to Granite Creek?

His daughter's face blazed into view. A wave of nausea. He could taste the bile at the back of his throat as Milly's smile, usually warm and bright, faded in his mind.

Heading back to the motel and then home, that's what he was doing. Just one brief stop first.

He climbed out of the car and, gravel crunching underfoot, ducked through the rain. A kid's red bike rested against one of the stilts underneath the house. He used the handrail to guide his way up the wooden steps of the veranda, the rain on the roof overhead duller than he'd expected. The drumming of his heart against his rib cage was louder.

A neatly swept front porch, with hanging baskets of ferns swaying wildly in the wind, welcomed him to the Wyatt house. A timber rack by the front door housed several pairs of shoes, neatly lined up side by side. Callum stood, dripping on the mat, eyes focused on three sets of hiking boots, like a family in descending order—large, medium, small. His eyes settled on the largest pair, knowing they wouldn't be worn again. He blinked several times as something pulled in his chest.

A woman's voice, pitched high, pierced through the wooden door and Callum, suddenly remembering why he'd come, raised his hand and knocked.

Muffled by the door and the rain, the voice grew steadily louder. Callum felt footsteps approach and the door was flung open to reveal a woman in a loose cotton dress. She was thin to the point of being almost gaunt, with the exception of her stomach, which was swollen to—what Callum could only guess was—full-term pregnancy. Her body didn't look as if it should be able to sustain another life.

The smile left her face and her brow wrinkled. She looked at least five years older than Callum had expected. Perhaps a day's grief could do that to some people.

She took him in with one quick sweep and didn't bother to conceal her actions as she pushed the door closed a few inches, fingertips gripping the timber and one foot firmly placed on the floor behind it.

'Yes?' Her voice was clipped and held a hint of an accusation.

So much for small-town pleasantries.

'Hi.' He kept his voice light.

Her eyes flicked over his khaki chinos and white shirt with the sleeves rolled up. 'Press?'

'No.' He tried to mask the guilt from his voice. 'I was just driving past and wanted to stop by …' He faltered under her stare. 'And offer my condolences.'

She remained silent and the sound of the rain didn't do much to drown out the awkwardness that was building.

'I'm sorry. Tess, is it?'

'Who are you?' Definitely defensive.

His mind reached for the first answer, grasped it. 'I'm with Eddy Quade.'

'Quade? The new cop.' It wasn't a question. She exhaled slowly, her grip on the door loosening enough that her knuckles, at least, were no longer white. Her lips lifted a fraction with what Callum was certain was immense effort. The smile didn't make it beyond her mouth.

'Mum?' A small voice trailed down the hall behind her.

Tess turned, pushing the door slightly closed again. 'Just a few minutes, Jack.' She turned back to Callum, not bothering to open the door fully again. 'Thanks for stopping by. We appreciate your condolences.' This time, the smile lasted no longer than a second, and she began to close the door.

Callum reacted fast. He placed one hand on the door, preventing her from shutting it. He registered the alarm on her face, followed by a flash of fear, before he quickly removed his hand and held both up to her, palms forward.

'Sorry,' he said. 'It's just that I'm leaving town today and had a few follow-up questions I needed to ask.'

She stood rigid, her fingers gripped back into the timber of the door.

'Mum?' The voice was closer this time, reaching Callum's ears before it was snatched away by the wind.

She looked over her shoulder again, then back. She hesitated a beat as the wind picked up, before pulling the door open a fraction further. 'Come in.'

He wiped his feet. The mud clung to his shoes as though they were a life raft. Removing them wasn't an option. A wet sock and no shoe on a prosthetic foot was asking for trouble. He wiped them again.

Inside, he felt as if he were walking through a *House and Garden* magazine. She led him through a narrow corridor with rooms shooting off from the left and right until they entered a large open-plan kitchen and living area. Every surface was immaculate. Very little was out even to suggest that a family lived there, let alone a ten-year-old kid. A few clean mugs in the drying rack, a family calendar tacked to the wall—several dates filled with neat, legible writing—and a kid's book on a side table that had been folded open, its spine creased, to mark its page.

'You've got a beautiful home,' he said, aware that he'd left a trail of water behind him on the polished timber floors.

'Thanks. I was studying interior design before I met Lachie.' It was the response of someone used to receiving compliments about her house.

She hovered awkwardly, uncomfortable with his presence. The dark shadows under her eyes and her sallow skin seemed to contrast with the crisp white louvres and slick marble benchtop. Tess, somehow, managed to look out of place in her own home.

After a pause, she said, 'Take a seat.' Her hand lifted in a half-hearted gesture towards the sitting room before dropping back down to her side.

He took in the low-set plush couch and opted for a firmer looking chair with sturdy armrests. The last thing he needed was to have to ask her for some leverage to get up. By the looks of her, she'd probably give birth on the lounge room floor. He sat, grimacing as he sank further into the seat than he'd anticipated, his knee bending painfully. He stretched his leg out.

'I'm sorry about Lachie. That must have been a big shock.'

'Of course it was a shock.' A snap to her tone; her eyebrows drawing in. She remained standing, one hand resting on her lower back, the other on her stomach.

'Mum?' A young boy poked his head around the door. His short sandy hair and blue eyes, rimmed red, startled Callum.

'Hi, Jack.' Callum leaned forward in his chair and offered a small wave. 'I'm Callum. Went to school with your grandparents.' Something gnawed at his insides. The thread of an idea. He pushed it away, buried it.

'You didn't say that.' Tess's tone was accusatory.

'Didn't I?'

'No. You said that you worked with that new cop. Quade.'

He nodded, forced himself to meet her eye. 'I also went to school with Brett and Pip. Knew them quite well.' He turned to Jack. 'Especially your grandma.'

Tess placed her hand on Jack's shoulder. 'Well, Brett's not here if that's who you're looking for.' Her face blank. 'Probably at the pub. And we didn't really ever meet Pip. Not properly.'

He nodded.

Green eyes with flecks of gold, crinkled at the edges, rushed through his mind. He pushed them aside and met Tess's granite gaze, her eyes the same colour as the boulders.

The kid stepped into the room away from his mother's grip. Tess's hand lingered awkwardly for a moment before she rested it on her stomach.

'I'm sorry to hear about your dad.'

Blue eyes cast to the floor, Jack scuffed one foot along the plush rug.

A melodious ring engulfed them all. Tess looked over her shoulder, her eyes narrowed as if daring the phone to continue. A hesitation, one last glance at Jack, and she turned and left the room without a word.

Callum and Jack listened in silence to her muffled voice before they turned to face each other, the air suddenly lighter.

'I used to live around here, you know,' Callum said.

No response.

'Not for a long time though.'

Silence.

'Had an accident,' Callum continued. 'My parents moved us to the city afterwards. Better doctors down there.' He hitched his left trouser leg to reveal his prosthesis. A cheap shot, but he wanted to get the kid talking and suspected he mightn't have much time until Tess returned.

'Wow, cool.' Jack stepped forward and crouched down to the ground, level with Callum's leg.

'Yeah, pretty cool.'

It was anything but.

A few inches of the titanium pylon shaft were visible. A fibreglass socket housing Callum's stump at one end, and a carbon fibre foot covered in a muddy shoe at the other.

'How'd it happen?' Jack reached out, caution forgotten.

'I had a fall.' He hesitated, lowered his voice. 'Near where your dad was found actually.'

The boy froze, hand mid-reach. Somewhere in the house a door slammed shut.

'Sorry,' Callum said. 'I know it must all be a bit of a shock to you.'

Jack's hand fell to his side and his eyes moved towards the edge of the room. Callum's followed. A large sideboard sat beneath the window, sparse, except for a single framed photo. Jack with his parents. Lachie in the centre, arms around his wife and son, holding them close. A roundness to Jack's cheeks, and a gap where a front tooth had once been, put him somewhere around six or seven.

A sudden memory of a seven-year-old Milly. Her pure delight as she'd found the dollar coin under her pillow after the tooth fairy's visit.

Jack's voice cut through the memory. 'Did you hear it?'

'I'm sorry?'

'Did you hear it? Is that why you went out there?' The boy chewed his bottom lip, didn't meet Callum's eye. His voice was a mere wisp of sound and Callum had to strain his ears to catch it.

'Hear what?' An unnecessary question. Callum knew the answer.

'Sorry about that.' Tess stood in the doorway, one hand on the frame to steady herself. She looked as if she could crumple at any moment. The last twenty-four hours had clearly taken their toll. Her eyes darted from Callum to her son crouched on the floor and back again. 'I'm sorry, but what did you say your name was?'

He hesitated. 'I didn't. It's Callum.'

'Callum?'

'Haffenden. Callum Haffenden.'

A long pause, then her stern features set. She let go of the door frame and stepped into the room with more purpose and confidence than Callum had, only a moment earlier, believed feasible.

'Haffenden?' Her gaze settled on his leg, his exposed prosthesis. He could see the cogs turning behind her eyes: the name, the leg. Her expression flashed, her voice firmer.

'You're that reporter,' she said. 'Brett's warned me about you. Come up from the city for a good story, have you?' Her voice rose, some colour coming to her cheeks at last.

Bending his knee with some difficulty, he hoisted himself out of the chair.

Jack, stunned, almost copped a knee to the face.

'I'll show myself out, shall I?' Callum headed down the corridor.

'Damn straight you can show yourself out. You should be disgusted with yourself. Lachie's only just died and you're preying on his son.' She waved her arm towards Jack. 'Get out.' She stormed down the hall behind him.

Callum turned to look back at Tess, to apologise, but his vision snagged on something on the wall. Next to the opened door to a washroom—drop sheet on the floor, walls half painted pale blue—were a pair of eyes, flecks of gold glinting. On the edge of a sea of Wyatt family photos on the wall, the picture threw him: Pip.

'Get out.' Tess's voice was distant, foggy.

Pip smiled at him. He remembered the feel of her curled upper lip pressed against his. He squeezed his eyes shut. He wanted to push her out of his head, and yet hold on to the memory at the same time.

'I said, *leave*.' Tess's tone was sharp.

'I'm sorry,' he said. 'I didn't mean to upset you. I didn't come for a story.'

The guttural roar of a diesel engine and the hard slam of a car door cut through the rain. Tess froze, her mouth open, her voice lost on its way out. The colour that had filled her cheeks only moments earlier had drained, and she placed one hand on her stomach, the other reaching behind for Jack. The boy stood rigid. His eyes wide, lips ajar.

A beat passed, then Tess's features smoothed back over, replaced by her granite stare and tight lips.

'You need to leave,' she said.

He opened his mouth to speak, but closed it again. Instead, he nodded once and pulled the door open.

The wind slammed against him and he made his way down the rain-soaked veranda stairs, knuckles tight on the rail, placing both feet on a single step before tackling the next.

'What the fuck you doing here?' Brett stood on unsteady legs at the bottom, the outline of a stark white ute blurry behind him. His voice would've been lost in the wind if he hadn't yelled.

'I'm just leaving.'

'That didn't answer my question.'

'I just …'

*Just what? Came to see Pip's grandson? Came to see where her dead son used to live? Came to see the place where you used to beat the shit out of her?*

'I told you to stop sniffing around.' Brett swayed. The wind had picked up while Callum had been inside, and if he hadn't known Brett—and his heaving bulk—better, he'd have thought that the larger man was about to be swept away. More likely he was just ten beers down. 'You think just cos you're some hot shot journo in the big smoke, you can stick your nose in everyone's business.'

Callum had reached the bottom step as Brett stepped forward, their faces once again closer than Callum would've preferred. At least they were at eye level. Brett's breath was heavy, and the scent of beer lingered in the air between them.

Fingers aching from his grip on the rail, Callum shifted his weight to his right leg in the hope of holding steady if Brett socked him one.

'Fuck off back to the city and leave my family alone,' Brett spat. His next words were whisked away by the wind, and Callum squinted through his streaked glasses to see Brett's lips forming the silent threat. Unmissable. Unignorable.

Milly's fresh face burst into view. A wave of anger washed over Callum, as he saw Brett's words take shape.

*Or I'll come after yours.*

# CHAPTER ELEVEN

Callum pulled up on the edge of the car park at the end of Kingfisher Way. With the engine idling, the air conditioner sputtered and groaned. He banged the dash and it stopped working altogether.

Apparently, a last-minute booking meant not only were no sizable cars available, but that the only one free was a total piece of shit. The cabin began to heat up, air thickening, fogging his glasses. He wound the window down and rain flew in sideways, slapping him in the face.

A last clench of the steering wheel and a glance at the rainforest in front, and he threw the door open and heaved himself out.

Better soaked than cooked.

Earlier, as he'd jammed the keys in the ignition, keen to pull away from the Wyatt property, a glance in the rear-view mirror had shown a hulking Brett dragging Jack across the veranda and into the house. Tess, just behind, had pulled the front door shut, blocking them all from view. Before he'd realised where he was driving, the rental hatchback had begun to trudge its way along the dirt track of Kingfisher Way.

Now, the rain weighed down his clothes and the dense air pressed against his skin, tightening its grip. He struggled to put the foggy images swimming through his head into some sort of logical order.

Brett's furious face. Lachie's broken body. Tess and Jack's fear.

One image, however, was clear: a pair of crinkled eyes and an upturned smile. But it wasn't Pip's face that was lodged in his mind. It was Lachie's. The photo had been hanging next to the one that had initially caught Callum's eye. The one of Pip. Lachie stood alongside his parents; Brett was a head taller than his wife and son. It was old. Well over a decade. Callum could tell because Pip's eyes were clear, her stomach swollen.

Bile rose up in his throat and his eyes roamed the car park. The space was deserted, a tail of chequered police tape tied to the trunk of a sturdy whitewood flapped in the wind. The rain had washed away most of the evidence that a man had ever been missing; local citizens ever concerned.

His eyes focused on the far corner where Lachie's ute had been parked, draped in the same chequered tape. He fished around in his memory, trying to drag up what it had looked like. He couldn't remember the make or model—he'd barely paid attention to the details of his rental car, aside from it being too cramped and smelling like a wet dog.

What had he seen? The panels had been clean, the car a crisp white; any mud washed away by hours in the rain. The tyres, low in the earth, had sunk into the pliable ground as puddles of water pooled around the black rubber. The inside had been chaos. It hadn't look as if it belonged to the same man who'd lived in the display-quality home he'd just visited.

He tried to fully recall the interior of the car. Empty takeaway wrappers had been strewn across the back seat, alongside worn clothes, some basic toiletries, a few loose tools, some fishing gear and a head torch.

Something caught the edge of his mind.

The head torch.

His mind ticked over. The sun would've been below the tree line when Lachie had set out to his camp site, no light would've penetrated the rainforest. Walking through the rainforest in the near dark—weighed down by a pack and tent—how could anyone leave their torch behind? One step under the dark canopy and you'd go back to retrieve it.

Callum tried to imagine it. The sound of Lachie's boots muffled on the sodden ground as he'd trudged in the dark, the canopy overhead masking any glow from the sky above. Callum felt a flicker in his chest and he tried to steady his breath.

*It's Lachie in the rainforest. Calm down.*

A little pull at the side of his mind again. Something about the image wasn't right. He took a deep breath and let the footage play out, watching a dead man walk to his death. One step after another. One boot after another. Another wisp of an idea.

Something about what he'd seen at the station floated into view, fuzzy at first, then sharper. Callum closed his eyes and the sound of the rain intensified until it was all he could hear. He pictured Lachie's items, lined up on Eddy's desk: boots, clothes and wedding ring.

The boots.

What was wrong with them? He recalled the three pairs of boots lined up neatly outside Tess's house. Hiking boots.

His mind jumped to Tess, standing at her front door. The flash of terror across her face, the protective hand over her stomach, the other reaching behind for her son. What had happened to scare her? Callum knew the answer well before he'd wanted to admit it to himself. Brett. Brett had arrived.

He felt sick.

A new image—one Callum had spent years trying to push down—clawed its way from the trenches of his memory and paraded itself in front of him. Pip. No smile. No crinkles of laughter dancing around her eyes. Her pale skin had made the bruises look much worse than he had hoped they'd felt.

He squeezed his eyes shut. Trying to lock the memory back away, where it belonged. That's not how she'd want him to remember her. He should have done more. He'd known what Brett was capable of. She'd deserved better.

Her son had deserved better.

A nearby sound. He whipped his head around, his eyes shooting towards the edge of the rainforest where the tawny mud met vivid green, and a foraging bush turkey ventured a little closer.

The rain came down in torrents, the animal unperturbed. Beady eyes stared back and the two surveyed each other.

Callum weighed up his options.

'What do you reckon?' His voice rang in his ears. 'See this thing out, or time to bail?'

The bush turkey cocked its head to the side. A brief hesitation, then with an indignant cluck, it turned and disappeared under the canopy without a backwards glance.

Callum blew out a long breath. 'Just as I'd thought.'

# CHAPTER TWELVE

*Thirty years earlier*

The sun splintered through the thick canopy, and a fleck of light caught Pip's hair for a second. Yellow. Like the breast of a golden whistler.

I pressed my lips together and continued to pick my way through the thick undergrowth a few metres behind her. Neither of us had said much for the last ten minutes.

'You're late,' she'd said as I'd dumped my bike next to hers against the old kauri pine at the start of the track. She glanced at her watch, her face set.

'Sorry. Dad needed a hand in the yard and—'

'I can't stay out long today, I've gotta get back to Amelia and ...'

I waited. Nothing.

She bounced up and down on the balls of her feet, her eyes darting back down the road. 'I just need to get home later on, that's all.'

The corner of her mouth lifted, and then she turned and strode along the track.

'Is everything oka—'

'Fine.' She didn't look back.

A few minutes of watching her milky legs stride out in front, a dark bruise shining out from the back of her right thigh, about the size of my palm. An urge to place my hand over it, measure it for size. Check it didn't hurt.

'So does your dad know you're out here?' Her voice cut through my thoughts.

I snorted, stopped myself in time from automatically returning the question. Pip didn't know who her dad was, nor did her sister. Two different dads for two different sisters.

Pip with her long legs and short shorts, Amelia with her dyed black hair and too much make-up. They were totally different. Amelia was weird. Pip was, well, hot. My stomach fluttered like the wings of the yellow-billed kingfisher.

Different, but the Dyer girls always stuck together.

'Tsk, tsk.' The corner of her mouth lifted as she turned her head to look back at me. 'Sergeant Haffenden won't be impressed.'

'Well, Sergeant Haffenden doesn't need to know.'

'Remember when he came out to school in grade seven before we went on school camp?'

A fire burned under my cheeks. 'I'm mentally scarred from it. I was kinda hoping no one else remembered.'

'Never step off the trail,' she put on a deep voice, nothing like Dad's, then laughed. 'He seems all right though. Kinda cool.'

'Dad?'

She shrugged, her shoulders rising beneath the skinny straps of her singlet. One blue strap was twisted, entwined with the purple lace strap of her bra. 'Yeah, I mean, he seems like an okay dad.'

'He'd skin me alive if he knew we were out here.'

She laughed. 'See, a good dad.'

We'd passed through the camp site, crossed the creek, and now followed the breadcrumb trail of granite rocks that marked the way to the north-west boulders. Nestled in the thick undergrowth, the scattering of rocks ebbed and flowed, like a dry creek bed between green ferns and mossy tree roots.

It was our fourth time out to the boulders together. We'd sit with our legs dangling over the cliff edge, each time our thighs getting closer to touching.

Ahead, Pip swiped at vines and fern leaves that extended out like long fingers across the path, trying to touch her.

All around us the sound of birds brought the rainforest to life.

A high-pitched whistle split the air: crimson rosella.

I hoped.

The whistle echoed in my head, whispering, and I scanned the treetops, hoping for a splash of red. Nothing. A prickle ran across my skin, wiggling its way beneath my sweat-drenched t-shirt.

My body slammed against something. Pip. I managed to grab her before I bowled her over.

'Shit, sorry.'

She dug her fingers into my forearm while she found her footing.

'Why'd you stop?' My hands lingered, holding her, and my eyes followed hers.

A bright yellow mass, small and frail atop a bed of rotten and muddy undergrowth in the middle of our path. A dull yellow head—almost olive—and a short, curved beak. Two wiry legs stuck out skyward, like a pair of spindly twigs, from the bright yellow underpants and belly.

A golden bowerbird.

'Is it ...' Pip's voice barely a breath. 'Dead?'

My hands dropped, letting her go. I stepped around her and bent down.

Two glassy eyes stared blankly up. Black and rimmed with golden circles. Not unfamiliar.

I nodded.

'What do you think happened to it?' she asked.

'Dunno.'

I reached forward, my fingers itching to touch the soft yellow. I'd never been this close.

Smooth, but my skin gripped to it, like contact on a school book. I pulled my fingers back and a single golden feather pulled away. I held it between two fingers. Warm.

My eyes roamed the ground, and it didn't take me long to find what I was looking for. Wedged between a fallen moss-covered log and a large trunk, a group of twigs and sticks bowed together to form a curved roof over a small twiggy floor. I peered inside.

'What are you doing?' she asked.

'Looking for eggs. It's mating season.'

'Excuse me?'

I pulled my head back from the empty nest, felt my face heat up. 'Oh, um, for birds. For this bird.' I pointed to the perfect yellow lump. 'Golden bowerbirds.'

'Okay.' She sounded out the word slowly, hesitantly. 'And how the heck do you know that, you birdie weirdo?' Her mouth hitched a little.

'Oh, um, my dad. He's into it. We do it sometimes together.'

'What, hunt around the forest floor for birds' nests?'

'No.' My voice rose, on the defence. 'Just come out and, you know, watch them. Take photos. That kinda stuff.'

Her eyes widened. 'Okay, so I did not know that about your dad.' She laughed. 'Or you.'

'I know it sounds weird, but he's into it and no one else out here is, so I do it with him. Keep him company. Don't look at me like that.'

'I'm not looking at you like anything.' She laughed again. 'Sounds like you have all the makings of a birdie stalker.'

'Shut it, will you.'

She was close. Closer than before.

Closer than ever.

Her freckles spanned her nose, connecting one cheek to the other. Like a little bridge. I wanted to trace its path.

The feather in my hand burned my fingertips and, before I realised what I was doing, I reached up and tucked it behind her ear. The bright yellow of the feather now dull.

The air between us thickened. Like a wall.

*Come on, you pussy, just do it.*

I swallowed, my mouth dry, my tongue too big.

*What if I'm no bloody good?*

My feet were rooted, my chest twisting.

A shift in the air, a golden flicker of her eyes, and Pip pressed through the wall, her lips against mine.

## CHAPTER THIRTEEN

A lone ambulance was visible through the streaked windscreen of Callum's rental car, its fluorescent yellow stripe cutting through the fading afternoon light. It sat, unassuming, in the Quades' driveway. Callum climbed out with a hot, greasy bundle tucked under one arm and a gutful of concern.

As he made his way up the short driveway, the rain swept in sideways, wetting the entire right side of his body. He swapped his package to the other arm and continued.

The front door opened and a figure in a bottle green uniform emerged, a large first-aid bag slung over one shoulder. Callum climbed the three steps up the front veranda as Eddy appeared in the doorway. The paramedic placed one hand on Eddy's shoulder, mouthed a few words and walked past Callum with a nod.

Forty minutes later, Eddy and Callum sat opposite each other, sheets of greasy butcher's paper on the dining table between them. A handful of cold chips and a few calamari rings all that remained of their dinner. Callum could just make out the sound of Bill's snores over the wind buffeting the window.

'Dad pressed the emergency alert button on his necklace,' Eddy said. 'I think he's losing the plot. Honestly, I thought it was just the stroke, but maybe there's more to it.'

Callum had known Eddy's dad since he was a kid. The

memory of him with his broad chest and arms like the trunks of a pine tree from a lifetime of labour on the land was hard to replace with this new, frailer, image of Bill Quade.

'We were out of teabags, that's why he pressed it.' Eddy's face was deadpan. 'Teabags. He wanted a cup of tea, and we were out. Apparently an emergency.' He shook his head again, blew out a long breath. 'Yesterday Steph found him wandering down the main street without his shoes on. I don't know how he's carried on this long on his own.'

Callum nodded slowly. 'Mate, I'm sor—'

Eddy waved him off. 'Well, that's why I'm here now.' He took a scull from his water. 'So, why are you still here then?'

Within the last three hours, Callum had cancelled his return flight, extended his hire car rental and booked into the motel for another three nights—surprisingly easy to do given it'd been a nightmare to get a room to begin with. He'd also phoned his parents, and when they'd told him Milly had gone to the movies with friends, he'd tried her mobile. For what little good it did.

That little thread of something that had been nagging him had continued, and he hadn't been able to shake the image of Tess and Jack terrified at the sound of Brett's return.

He'd taken a long shower, the cold tap running warm. He'd stood, palms flat against the tiles, head bowed, his weight fully supported by his right leg, his prosthesis propped in the other room next to the bed. A morbid slide show of images had played through his head. Lachie's ute, torch on the seat. Tess's house, shoe rack out front, calendar on the wall. And Lachie. Framed and smiling from the photo on Tess's hallway wall. Eyes crinkled at the edges and a top lip slightly curved upwards.

Lachie at the boulders, broken.

The shower water had run over him, as constant as the rain outside. He'd thought back to the deserted car park at the search site. An idea had scratched at the corner of his brain, like the foraging bush turkey scratching at the sodden undergrowth. He'd closed his eyes, digging deeper into the boggy mud of his thoughts.

Mud. Footprints. Boots.

Then his eyes had opened. Wet tiles at the bottom of the shower had swum into view. One lone bare foot, white against the grimy floor.

A few moments later, he'd been back sitting on the bed—towel around his waist and his crutches propped next to him. He'd called Eddy.

Now, at the Quades' dining table, Eddy chewed slowly on a cold chip and eyed Callum. 'Are you sure about this?'

Callum wiped his hands on a clean napkin, folded it up and placed it on top of the butcher's paper. 'No. But something just feels ... off.'

'The family were pretty accepting of it being ruled an accident,' Eddy said.

'You mean Brett?'

Eddy paused. 'Yeah.' He ran his hands through his hair, a shower of rain sprinkled onto his lap. 'Tess was there too, but she was pretty vacant. Didn't really react to anything I said.'

'And the kid?'

'Jack wasn't there. Well, he was when I arrived at the house, but Tess sent him to his room.' More rain fell onto Eddy's trousers. 'Kid's been through enough as it is without having to hear us discuss whether his father accidentally fell to his death or jumped.'

Callum shook his head. 'It wasn't suicide.'

'Why? Because you're convinced Brett killed his own son?'

'No.' Callum's answer came too fast, he paused a moment before continuing. 'Maybe. But that's not why.'

Eddy raised his eyebrows.

'When I was at their house—'

'You were at their house?'

Callum gave a slight shrug, pushed down his guilt at the memory and continued. 'There was a calendar in the kitchen. It was busy. Dentist appointment, birthday party, boys' trip to Cairns, footy match.'

'So? They've got a kid, of course they're busy.'

'It was all for Lachie. For the coming weeks.'

Eddy eyed the last few calamari rings and Callum gave him a nod.

'I'm telling you,' Callum said. 'People planning to kill themselves don't make plans for the future. They just don't.'

Eddy chewed slowly.

'I did a feature, a few years back, on family members of people who'd committed suicide.'

'Sounds grim.'

'It was. They all said that they were shocked at the time of the death, but that in hindsight they should have known because the person who'd suicided didn't commit to anything. No plans. Nothing. Not even a barbecue with the neighbours.' Callum felt a slight buzzing inside. The same kind he used to get when he was in the crux of a good story and knew he was barking up the right tree. He hadn't felt it in over a decade, didn't get the same kind of kick from reporting on local council waste issues or regional food and wine festivals. 'They certainly weren't booking in dentist check-ups and boys' weekends away.'

'Okay, say it wasn't suicide …' Eddy wiped his mouth with a serviette, scrunched it up and dumped it on the table. 'An accident then.'

'I thought that too.'

'But?'

'The boots.'

Eddy's brow furrowed, the line between his eyebrows deepening.

'Think back to the boots he was wearing,' Callum said, 'the ones at the station. They weren't hiking boots. They were his work boots. The fireys at the pub today had the same ones on. They looked sturdy, but surely he wouldn't hike in his work boots?'

Eddy hesitated this time, and Callum felt the buzz inside intensify a little.

'I don't know,' Eddy said after a moment.

'I saw his hiking boots at the front door of his house. They were flash. Why wouldn't he wear them camping? He went home first, right?'

'Yeah. But they could've been someone else's you saw. Brett's?'

Callum shook his head. 'Too small.'

'So, what are you saying?'

'His camping trip was unplanned. Think about it. No food or water. No torch. He didn't jump. And from what I've heard he was a smart guy who knew the lay of the land.' Callum narrowed his gaze. 'What the hell would he be doing out at the boulders in the middle of the night with a cyclone en route? What the hell was he doing even camping in this weather?'

Eddy leaned forward, rested his elbows on the table, and pressed the heels of his hands into his closed eyes. The wind outside picked up and the closed window vibrated in its frame.

Callum watched his friend closely. A small pulse was flicking in Eddy's neck, the overlaying skin due a shave. He blew out a long breath, then sat himself back up. He nodded, slow at first, as the pieces fell into place.

'Jesus Christ.' Eddy's lips barely moved. 'He was pushed.'

## CHAPTER FOURTEEN

Callum woke with his breath caught in his chest and heart pounding against his ribs. A blanket of grey clouded his view and there was a stabbing pain in the left calf he knew he no longer had.

He lay still, frozen in position, the sheets beneath him damp.

Wide eyes filled with terror. The sea of granite below. And a voice.

*Please, no ... please, don't ...*

He closed his eyes, tried to hold on to the words. What were they saying? Don't what?

It'd been years—decades—since he'd heard that voice. Each night following his accident, he'd wake with its echo in his ears. For weeks, months. He'd never known who it was. What he shouldn't do.

But he'd always wondered ...

He pushed the thought away, squeezed his eyes and rubbed his palms on the sheets, trying to wipe away the lingering sensation of a vice tightening around his hands.

The wind whipped through his window and across his face. His eyes flew open. The curtains billowed inward, lashes of rain splattering onto the carpet.

He swung his legs over the edge of the bed and snatched his glasses from the bedside table. He flicked the switch of the bedside lamp. Nothing.

*Shit.*

He grabbed for his phone, the screen illuminating the small space around him. It was 3.24 am. He managed to focus his eyes on the open window in front.

*What the hell?*

He definitely had not opened it.

He spun his torso to look behind. The vacant doorway of the bathroom stared back, like a gaping black hole as dark as the space between two boulders. Big enough to swallow a man whole. He gripped the edge of the mattress. His chest tightened.

*Get it together.*

He could tell by the stillness beyond that the bathroom window was closed, the room empty. Still, his heart pounded fast enough that his chest rippled, and he couldn't shake the feeling that he wasn't alone.

He scanned the rest of the room, the outline of the furniture coming into focus. The small desk. The rattan chair. The wardrobe, its door firmly closed. Some of the tension left his shoulders, and he swallowed back his relief. His eyes flicked back to the open window and the car park beyond. Nothing moved outside.

Exhaling deeply, his eyes fell to his prosthetic leg, sprawled on the floor alongside his crutches a few metres away.

Leaning heavily to his right side, he heaved himself up and, using the wall for support, he bypassed his leg and crutches and hopped his way towards the open window. His foot squelched through the already soggy carpet, and the rain lashed his bare chest. He fumbled with the curtains before leaning two hands heavily on the windowsill and peering out.

Nothing. No one. The parking lot was full of cars, empty of people. The dim glow of a television, flickering in the darkness, shone from the window of the room next door.

Across the road, the boxy outline of the Cane Cutters' Tavern was silhouetted against the dark looming rainforest. Trees pulsated in the wind, bowing down to a silent call.

He blinked and the trees came back into focus. Closer now.

He shook his head. *Don't be stupid.*

He stood up and his head smashed into the wooden window frame. A blinding white filled his vision. Hands fumbling, he grasped the slick wood and slammed the window down. The sound echoed around his room.

Deep breaths.

His vision cleared and he tried the light switch next to the door. Nothing. Outside, an illuminated 'No Vacancies' sign cut through the darkness. A large figure, visible in the dim glow, emerged from the reception office and turned towards Callum's room. A brief panic before he recognised the ginger of the SES volunteer's beard, which briefly caught the light glowing from the reception.

Callum snapped the curtains shut and a few moments later the door of the room next to his slammed.

Ignoring the pounding ache that was growing in his head, he settled himself back into bed, propped up by two flimsy pillows that deflated under his weight.

He'd only managed a few hours of sleep so far. Flashes of granite grey, downpours of rain and a jarring pain in his left leg had pushed through his dreams all night.

Not unfamiliar.

In the months that had followed his accident Callum hadn't slept a night through. He'd dreaded the nights as much as he'd dreaded a future with only half a leg.

Disabled. Stared at. Pitied.

Each night he'd wake in a pool of sweat, the same dampness on his skin he must have felt that night he'd spent stuck out at the north-west boulders. The rain had come down in sheets, so he'd been told. He never knew if he was screaming from the dreams or from the ripping pain below his left knee. Eventually, his mum and dad had sent him to see a psychologist.

These days the nightmares came in spatters rather than full-length feature films. Still, it'd been a long time since they'd been this vivid.

Bloody Granite Creek.

He rubbed his palms against the sheets again, eyed the painkillers on the bedside table and downed two. He picked up his phone and scrolled through his text messages with Milly, checking—pointlessly—if she'd replied. He opened the notes app on his phone instead.

As he typed each word, his mind cast back to his conversation with Eddy.

'It's always worth looking at what he got up to that last day,' Eddy had said. 'Chat to his colleagues, see if Tess can give us any more information.'

'Tess? She's about as chatty as a brick wall.'

'Even so, we should try. Phone records could also help.'

'And bank records,' Callum said. 'It might help clarify that it wasn't suicide. You know, if he'd made some big purchases recently.'

Eddy nodded.

'And how about the school?' Callum asked. 'All that stuff that happened up there with that teacher all those years ago. Was Lachie involved? Brett sure as hell was.'

'It's a bit of a long shot, don't you think?'

Callum shrugged, bent and stretched his left knee. There was nothing like twenty-five years as a journalist to drum into someone the need to fact check.

After a beat, Eddy nodded. 'Right you are.'

'And the crime scene should be reviewed.'

'Easy on the word *crime*, mate,' Eddy said. 'And you won't be reviewing anything.' He nodded to Callum's leg.

'I can still get around all right.'

Eddy raised an eyebrow. They both knew he was lying.

'That cyclone off the coast is picking up,' Eddy said, 'and if it hits, the last thing I need is another bloke lost in the rainforest. So, try to keep your arse out of there if you can.'

Callum pursed his lips, inhaled deeply.

'We can check out the photos,' Eddy said.

A poor man's consolation prize.

'The recovery team took plenty and the choppers may even have some footage that we can review.'

A flicker of guilt as Callum recalled the file on Eddy's desk. The images of Lachie, body mangled, neck twisted.

Now, with his pillows flattened beneath him and a steady pounding growing at the back of his head, Callum looked at the list he'd typed on his phone, glowing in the darkness of the motel room.

*Retrace Lachie's movements.*

*Phone records.*

*Bank records.*

*Teacher/school.*

*Review boulder photos.*

He looked at the end, where the cursor blinked on the blank line. He chewed his bottom lip and then, with shaking hands, typed:

*Visit north-west boulders.*

# CHAPTER FIFTEEN

Callum sat in the small office, an archive box at his feet, an empty mug at his elbow. A small pile of high school yearbooks was stacked on the table and another lay open in front of him, glossy pages reflecting the fluorescent light that hummed overhead. Outside, the rain pounded a constant beat against the closed glass louvres. Inside, the air conditioner rattled with the effort to ward off the encroaching heat. Losing its battle, by the feel of it.

The school sat only three blocks back from the main road. He'd stepped out of his motel room an hour earlier, taken one look at his cramped car and another at the grey clouds above that hadn't yet opened, and decided to walk.

The power in his motel room had still not returned so, ignoring the clumped sachet of instant coffee and the tree frog at the bottom of the kettle, he'd opted for a shot of diesel-flavoured coffee from the bakery. The back of his throat burned, but at least he'd be able to ward off the effects of a shitty night's sleep.

He'd been surprised to learn that the same administration lady that had been working the front office when he was at Granite Creek District School was still there thirty years later. He'd been even more surprised when she'd remembered who he was.

'I never forget a student,' Mrs Fenton had said when they'd met out the front of the low-fenced property. Three decades had done nothing to stifle her enthusiasm for garish lipsticks, nor her ability to apply it to her cigarette-stained teeth.

'We all heard about that work you did a few years back.'

Nearly fifteen years ago. Time must stand still in Granite Creek.

'Made quite the name for yourself, catching all those crooks. We were all so proud.'

Eighteen months of endless research and bending the rules with too many close calls with the law, and with a four-thousand-word feature article Callum had blown the lid off one of the country's leading drug syndicates, whose tentacles ran through the federal police and stretched all the way to Parliament House.

He'd become an overnight sensation, and unfortunately had made a few enemies—and evidently fans—in the process. The move from Brisbane to sleepy Hobart had been a no-brainer, especially once Milly had come along.

'Doing a piece on the school now, are you?' She didn't wait for a response, and he didn't bother to correct her, she'd agreed to come in on a Saturday after all. 'It's about time we attracted some attention. Might send some much-needed funds our way.'

They walked along a narrow tree-lined path through the deserted school. Thirty years ago, the primary and high schools had shared the same grounds; the low fence running to their left and the wooden play equipment on the other side suggested that was still the case today. The wind sent debris and leaves snaking around their ankles and whipped low-hanging branches against their faces. Grass and weeds escaped from the garden beds and spilled over onto the path. Apparently, the school budget didn't stretch to a gardener over the summer holidays and the endless rain meant that the school grounds were more wilderness than garden.

As they entered the foyer of the squat brown brick administration building, a dank, musty smell swarmed over them, pushing to escape out the open door. It'd been five weeks since school had wrapped up for the year; long enough for all the surfaces to glisten with a slight sheen of condensation and the fusty scent of mildew to begin its domination.

He scanned the room. Little porcelain animals sat blu-tacked to the front desk, lined up like soldiers. The bug eyes of a lesser sooty owl glared at him, its white speckles all wrong. Nothing had changed, not even the rigid maroon chairs had been updated in thirty years. A memory rushed at him, as unexpected as it was unpleasant. He'd sat, split lipped, in that very chair. Brett Wyatt opposite, knuckles smarting.

He reached up and traced one finger along his bottom lip, where a fine groove was still palpable. His jaw ached at the memory. He'd needed three stitches.

Now, he'd been sitting in the tiny office for at least half an hour.

He picked up the next yearbook—2004—and, stifling a yawn, began to flip through its pages.

Glossy images of kids in green and yellow uniforms smiled up at him. Playing footy, performing on stage, holding aged instruments. Frozen in time.

He stopped and turned back a page. There. The crinkled eyes and upturned smile that was etched in his memory. A twelve-year-old Lachie smiled back. Lachie playing footy. He turned a few pages. Lachie holding a model of the solar system. Another page, another image. Lachie at school camp.

Two other faces smiled back alongside Lachie. Callum bent his head lower, reading the kids' names captioned below the photo.

*You've got to be kidding.*

'Here's another cuppa for you.' Mrs Fenton strode into the room and Callum's head snapped up.

'Thanks.'

She turned to leave.

'Mrs Fenton.' He couldn't bring himself to call her Valerie. 'Can I ask you a question? About Lachie?'

She walked back towards the desk, shaking her head. 'What a tragedy.'

'Do you recall him from his school days?'

'Like I said, I never forget a student.'

'In this photo here ...' Callum pointed to the image of the three boys at camp. 'Were these his friends?'

She bent down slightly, the fug of cigarettes cutting through the stagnant air. 'Oh, yes. Thick as thieves, that lot. Not unlike yourself and Edward Quade.'

Callum nodded, impressed with her memory for students long graduated.

'And his kid, Jack, what's he like?'

'Quiet. Suppose he'll be quieter now ...' Her eyes glistened. 'Keeps to himself a lot.'

'Any friends?'

She shrugged. 'He's a good boy. Friendly enough, just ... doesn't mingle with the other kids as much as some of the others, I guess.'

*Probably because he's got a dominating shit for a grandfather.*

'He does spend a fair bit of time with that Noah Pemlington though. A bit like brothers, those two.' Her eyes glinted again, not tears this time. 'Noah was having a few issues with bullying. Jack stuck up for him. Yes, they're quite chummy.'

He nodded, unsure what to say. Hadn't Steph told him that Noah and Jack weren't good mates? The branches of an old fig tree smacked against the window, breaking the silence.

'A real tragedy, everything that's happened to that family,' she continued. 'All that business thirty years ago. Though, she was a real piece of trouble, that Amelia Dyer. Not her fault, I suppose. No father, useless mother, and that sister of hers wasn't much better. Still, wouldn't wish what happened to poor Pip on anyone. She's better off now though, really. Blessing in disguise.'

A jolt of anger swept over him. He pushed it down, plastered a smile on his face. 'And how about teachers? Do you ever forget them?'

She scoffed, a little spittle landing on her chin. 'In a school the size of Granite Creek? Not likely.'

'What did you make of the teacher that got caught up in all that saga with Brett? Thacker.'

'Simon Thacker.' She ran her tongue across her lipstick-stained teeth. 'That was a terrible business. Lucky he survived really.'

'What do you mean?'

She stiffened a little. 'Those boys.' She pointed a nicotine-stained finger at the open yearbook. 'They pushed him off the boulders. Nearly killed him. He broke his arm, I think.'

Callum rubbed his left knee. Lucky bugger.

'Still, there were no charges ever pressed. He said he slipped. Probably didn't want to ruin the future of three of his students. Always thinking of the kids, that Simon.'

She straightened the stack of yearbooks on the desk. 'There was a bit of he-said-they-said going on. All a big misunderstanding. Poor fellow had to leave town, the threats he was getting.'

'Threats?'

Her gaze shifted to the outer office and back again. 'Well, you of all people should know what Brett Wyatt is like.'

\*

Callum increased his stride along the overgrown school path, ignoring the rain and the protest from his left leg. He'd left the school office with a few yearbooks tucked under one arm and a promise to return them before he left town.

His knee had stiffened from lack of movement, and the dull ache soon turned into a sharp stab with each step. He pulled up at a peeling wooden bench, wet despite its overhanging shelter.

A groan escaped his lips when he sat down and he started to massage his left knee. He could feel the heat radiating off the stump even through his trousers.

A spattering of words on the exposed brick wall next to his seat jumped out. Scratchy print tucked next to a stainless-steel trough lined with bubblers.

He read the first line, tore his eyes away.

*Bloody school kids.*

He pushed the words out of his head and recalled the image of Lachie and his mates. He flipped the yearbook open to the page he'd bookmarked, and the three boys grinned up at him.

He jammed his hand into his pocket, searching for his phone.

*Ting. Ting.*

A moment's confusion, and he pulled out the bracelet. His fist closed around the damp strip of fabric and its three hard bells.

A dart of recollection. In the cramped office he'd been searching for older yearbooks, of students past. The books had been stacked in the archive box and the image on the cover of the top book had jumped out. A moment to realise what had caught his attention. A group of six or seven kids were pictured on the front, all smiles and broad-brimmed hats. The green of the background and poor lighting suggested that they were in the bowels of the rainforest. They stood shoulder to shoulder, holding a long snake skin between them. It must've been at least three metres in length. It wasn't the snake skin that had caught his eye, however. Tied around each kid's wrist was a woven coloured bracelet, silver bells reflecting in the camera's flash.

The book was dated last year.

He jammed the bracelet back into his pocket and pulled out his phone instead.

Blank screen. Still.

He suppressed the jab of irritation he felt towards Milly and typed a name into his search engine, checking the spelling in the yearbook. A quick search, then an even quicker phone call.

He hung up and looked at the photo of the boys once more.

He called Eddy.

A few minutes into the conversation and the silence stretched on. Callum pressed the phone against his ear, not wanting to miss Eddy's response.

'Are you sure?' Eddy said.

'I've got the photo right here in front of me, mate.'

Another pause. Then something that sounded like a long exhale, although Callum couldn't be sure it wasn't the wind.

'Okay. I'll meet you there in twenty minutes.'

With one last glance at the photo, Callum snapped the yearbook closed and heaved himself up. He ducked his head and stepped out into the worsening rain. The words of the whispering, graffitied in leering black print on the brick wall, burned into his back as he went.

# CHAPTER SIXTEEN

'So, these were Lachie's movements on his last day?' Callum held the small notebook, flipped open to reveal Eddy's messy scrawl.

'Yep. I did some asking around this morning. Tess wasn't home, but I spoke to a few blokes out at the fire station and the pub. Looks like after he knocked off his shift at four in the afternoon, he went straight for a drink. Was there for about an hour or so. Must've gone straight home and done a quick pack. Tess told us he'd headed out around six.'

'And this name?' Callum pointed to a few letters, barely legible.

'They had a drink together.'

'He told me they weren't mates.'

'Well, they're clearly mates. Then and now.'

Eddy tapped his finger on a photo in the yearbook that lay sprawled open between them. Three boys stood grinning, the green of their school uniforms blending into the background of trees, ferns and scrub. One boy, with his crinkled eyes and smile so like his mother's, was Lachie. His arms were slung around the other two, one unfamiliar. Josh Swindley, the name beneath the photo read. Callum had looked him up. Josh had died twelve years ago, no details on how. A short phone call to his dad and he'd learned that Josh had committed suicide. Jumped from the boulders. Callum's leg tingled at the thought.

He turned his eyes to the second boy with Lachie. A kid with the distinct bone structure and overbite resembling a ferret smiled back.

*

Callum and Eddy stepped into the motel reception, the cool air a relief after the stickiness outside.

'Good news,' Mike called out. 'Sparky was busy. Few outages already from these bloody winds. Managed to get the maintenance guy to come and have a look though. Power should be back on in your room. Not sure what happened there.'

'Great, thanks.' Callum placed the yearbook open on the reception counter.

Mike looked down at the book, took in the photo of the three friends. The seconds ticked by. He shifted behind the counter, limp hair flopping forward, concealing half his face.

'You said you weren't mates.' Callum kept his tone light.

'We're not.'

Eddy pointed to the photo and Mike recoiled from the gesture.

'Not anymore,' Mike added.

'Have a falling out?'

'It wasn't like that.'

'You were seen at the pub with him four nights ago.' Eddy's voice was stern, no-nonsense.

Mike lifted his head, appeared to take in Eddy's blue police uniform. Even so, he chose not to meet either man's gaze, focusing on a spot on the reception door between them.

A shrug. 'Don't know if you've noticed, but it's the only pub in town. We bumped into each other.'

'What did you and Lachie talk about when you bumped into each other on the last day that he was seen alive?' Eddy asked.

Mike flinched. 'Just catching up.'

'Did he happen to mention he was going camping that night?'

A grunt.

'Excuse me?'

'No.'

'So, what exactly did you catch up about?'

Mike rested one hand on the photo, his fingertips—skin raw—brushing the faces of the three boys. 'We had a lot of history.'

'Josh?'

A shrug. 'Yeah. It was his anniversary.' He traced the face of the third boy. 'Twelve years.' He looked up. 'That's why we had a drink. Lachie and me. For Josh. Old times' sake.'

'Thought you just bumped into each other?'

Another shrug. 'Small town.'

'And did you talk about Thacker? For old times' sake?'

Mike's head snapped up. 'No.'

'Didn't talk about what happened all those years ago?'

'We never talk about it.'

'Can you talk about it with us? Tell us what happened?'

'Nothing happened.'

'A local teacher fell off the boulders and just afterwards you and your mates were seen sauntering back from the same spot.' Eddy thrust one finger down on the photo. Mike jerked his own hand back.

'We didn't do anything.'

'Did you push him?'

'It wasn't like that.'

'Why would you push a teacher?' It was a loaded question. 'From what I heard, Thacker did nothing but shower you with attention.'

Mike's eyes darted from the photo to the door and back again.

'He was quite hurt from his fall. I could look more into that. See if charges should have been pressed.'

Mike gnawed at his fingernails, shifting his weight from side to side.

Eddy opened his mouth to speak, but Callum cut him off, taking a step forward, until his torso was flush against the counter.

'Look,' he said. 'We know it was an accident. Thacker slipped and fell, end of story.'

Eddy tensed beside him.

Callum pushed on. 'You were just kids. We're just trying to find out what happened to Lachie. Then and now.' He met Mike's gaze. 'Can you help us figure out what happened to your mate? Did Thacker hurt him?' He dropped his voice. 'Did Brett hurt him?'

Mike's shoulders sagged and he took his fingers away from his mouth. He nodded, cleared his throat. 'Thacker. He hurt Lachie. He hurt all of us.'

'Hurt how?'

'He was ...' Mike's voice dropped. 'He did stuff.'

'What kind of stuff?' Callum asked.

Mike's face hardened. 'You know the kinda stuff I'm talkin' about. The kinda shit those sorta monsters get off on.' He bit his nails again, as if to stop himself from speaking.

'Can you tell us what happened?' Callum barely caught his own voice.

A pause. 'It was only small stuff to begin with.' Mike's fingers were still at his mouth, his words muffled. 'And then it got worse.'

'How much worse?'

Mike shifted again, didn't speak for a moment. He took his hands from his mouth, the nailbeds rimmed red with blood. 'At school camp, he caught us with a bottle of vodka. He took us into his tent and made us drink the whole bottle in front of him. Then he said that he'd be happy to keep our secret, not tell our folks, if we promised to keep his secret.'

'What happened?' Callum asked.

Mike shook his head. 'You know exactly what happened. He was a sick prick that got off on young boys.' Mike's eyes met Callum's at last. 'We were only twelve, for fuck's sake.' Eighteen years of anger and distrust burned behind his eyes. And something else. Shame?

'And you didn't tell anyone?' Eddy's voice, riddled with surprise.

'There was no one to tell. I lived with my nan and pop, they didn't need that kind of hassle. And Josh lost his mum when he was a kid. He was the eldest, was expected to help out, not give his dad more grief. Nearly killed his dad though, losing Josh like that. Never been the same since, that bloke. He still ain't over it.'

An image, vivid and sickening, burst into Callum's mind: Milly's body crumpled on the boulders.

He'd never be the same if he lost her.

'And Lachie? Did he tell his parents?' he asked.

Mike snorted. 'Brett? I heard you went to school with him. You should know what he's like.'

'What about his mum? Pip?'

'I don't know.' Mike gnawed at his fingers again.

'So, Brett—'

'Cal, come on.' Eddy shifted next to him. 'Brett again?'

'Lachie never complained,' Mike said. 'But we could all tell Brett was a jerk.'

'What makes you say that?' Eddy asked.

'As we got older, Lachie would sometimes come to school with bruises and scratch marks on him. He'd shrug it off, say he fell, or the scratches were from roaming round the forest. But we all knew it was Brett.' Mike shook his head at the memory. 'And I saw Pip covered in bruises more than once.'

A wave of nausea swept over Callum. Why hadn't he come back for her?

'Josh died at the same spot as Lachie,' Eddy said. 'What do you make of that?'

'Coincidence.'

'Brett?' Callum fought to keep his voice neutral.

Eddy cleared his throat but didn't speak.

Mike snorted before he caught himself and his face fell blank. 'Nah. Josh jumped.'

'How can you be sure?' Callum asked.

'Just am.' Mike met his eyes. 'He was messed up. We all were.' His eyes dropped back to the photo of the three friends. 'Had a gambling problem. It gave him a bit of a rush, I reckon. When he won, that is. Felt like he had some power or somethin'. It got outta hand though. He got caught up in some sorta trouble.'

'What sort of trouble?' Eddy asked.

'I heard he got caught nicking some stuff from his boss. Sold it for cash. Knocked himself off not long after that.'

'Who was he working for?' Callum's skin began to prickle.

Mike's face was set. 'Brett.'

The three men paused, the wind pummelling the glass front door.

Mike uncurled his fists on the desk, his eyes trained on the image of the three friends in the yearbook. Two now dead. 'I wouldn't be surprised if Brett threw that girl off the bloody boulders thirteen years ago.'

A pause.

'Which girl?' Eddy asked.

'The toddler.'

Callum's ears whistled with the wind and rang with the name before Mike even spoke it.

'His daughter,' Mike said. 'Amelia Wyatt.'

\*

'What do you make of his story?' Callum sank down into the chair at the small desk in his motel room, relieved to be off his leg.

'Which part?' Eddy stood by the window, rain dripping from his uniform on the already sodden carpet.

'All of it.'

'Dunno. He seemed reluctant to tell us much at the start. Spilled his guts eventually though.'

'He's probably kept it bottled up for the last eighteen years. It was bound to spill over. Think they were really meeting for Josh's anniversary?'

Eddy shrugged. 'Seems plausible. Easy enough to find out if Josh actually did die on the eighteenth. Might corroborate the story a bit at least.'

Callum nodded, stretched out his leg. 'I should chase up this Thacker.'

'Seems like a dead end,' Eddy said after a moment.

'Probably. But you never know how long some people hold grudges for.'

'Sounds like he had it coming to him if you ask me.'

'Agreed. But still, I should check it out. He shouldn't be too hard to track down.'

Eddy held his gaze. 'Mate, you shouldn't be doing anything. I appreciate your help and all, but this isn't your domain.'

A jerk in his gut. 'Well, you should be following up Thacker then. And Brett. We should chat to him.'

'I don't know if *we* should be doing anything. You're just going to get yourself in trouble sticking your nose in Brett's business. I doubt thirty years has done much to soften his feelings towards you.'

'That's even more reason to bump him up the list of suspects.'

'Look.' Eddy shook his head. 'I'm not saying it's not him. But your judgement's a little clouded when it comes to Brett Wyatt.'

'He was a jerk to you too, you know.'

'I know.' Eddy frowned. 'But we're not high school kids anymore.'

'You heard what Mike said about how Brett treated Lachie.'

'Town gossip.'

'And Pip? Black eyes aren't gossip.'

'Still, I think it's best that you let me handle Brett. Last thing I need is to have to throw my best mate in the slammer for assault.'

Callum went to speak, snapped his mouth closed.

The musty fug of the motel room was giving him a headache. He slid his glasses off and pressed his index finger and thumb into his eyes. Mike's words banged against the inside of his skull, desperate to escape.

*I wouldn't be surprised if he threw that girl off the bloody boulders thirteen years ago.*

Amelia Wyatt.

Brett and Pip's daughter.

He'd been surprised when he'd learned that Pip had called her daughter Amelia, the same as her younger sister. Maybe it'd helped give her some closure. All those years of not knowing what had happened to her. Maybe it made the wound less raw.

He thought back to the search for the missing toddler thirteen years ago; the body pulled from the boulders. It had been splashed across the nation's headlines.

His stump throbbed as he recalled the footage of the lifeless remains being hoisted out from a massive gap between two boulders.

He blinked, bringing the room into focus. The closed wardrobe door stared back.

'And the boulders?' He turned to Eddy. 'I think we should check them out.'

'You're kidding, aren't you?'

A rogue palm frond slammed into the closed window. Both men turned to look outside.

'Stop thinking about bloody Pip,' Eddy said. 'She's gone.' The silence hung thick and stagnant. 'Think about your family. Your folks aren't getting any younger. And Milly. Last thing she needs is her dad keeling over on some wild goose chase through the rainforest.'

Callum sucked in a long breath, nodded. Eddy, satisfied enough, walked to the door and opened it. He threw a last glance at Callum, then pulled the door shut behind him.

Callum's leg throbbed. He tilted his head to the ceiling and closed his eyes, snapped them open at the sound of the door opening. Eddy poked his head back into the room, face grim.

'You better come see this,' he said.

Using the desk for leverage, Callum heaved himself up and followed his friend outside.

He traced Eddy's gaze and squinted through his already fogged glasses. The outline of his rental car began to take shape at the end of the car park. He took a few steps towards it. His leg jerked under his weight. An earthy fug filled his nostrils and a stab of irritation hit him as the car came into full view.

*Shit.*

All four tyres had been slashed.

# CHAPTER SEVENTEEN

*Thirty years earlier*

My lips stung from all the snogging. We'd been at the boulders for almost an hour and had barely come up for air. That morning Mum had finally removed the three stitches Brett had given me in my bottom lip, and I'd slipped a note to Pip in English to meet me after school. When she'd arrived, my stomach had flittered as if the tiny wings of hatchlings were beating inside. The bright yellow feather was stitched to the side of her hat.

The afternoon sun sat low and cast long, misshapen shadows across the boulders. Granite grey was interspersed with large patches of black, the boulders' abysses concealed in the darkness. The light caught the pale hair on Pip's thighs pressed against mine as our legs dangled over the edge of the cliff. The huge strangler fig tree clinging to the edge of the boulders marked the end of the rainforest and the beginning of who the hell knows what.

*Just boulders, dickhead.*

The tree's roots reached down over the cliff towards the rocky floor below, like the claws of a massive eagle gripping for perch. I scanned the sky. Nothing.

Pip reached one hand out and paused, her fingertips

millimetres from my swollen lip. She closed the distance and traced the vertical line where the stitches had pulled the skin tight. A tingle ran across my raw lip. Across my whole body.

'You haven't even told me why he did it.' Her hand dropped to my thigh. Another tingle.

A flash of Brett's fist flying towards my face. 'He's just a prick.'

She nudged me. 'Come on, even Brett needs a reason to sock someone.'

I sucked my bottom lip, thought about how much to tell her. I shrugged. 'Just guy stuff.'

She rolled her eyes. 'Righto, guy stuff.'

Ten days ago, I'd spotted Brett sticking something through Pip's locker door. A scrap of paper, one corner just sticking out. What the hell was he doing leaving notes for Pip? My Pip. I yanked it free, tried to have a read. He caught me. His fist moved too fast for me to even register it coming before he sucker-punched me across my jaw.

'Well, he's a jerk for punching you,' she said.

I tried to shrug it off. 'It's nothing.'

She laughed. The sound reverberated around the boulders and even the kingfishers overhead stopped to listen. 'I bet your mum thinks it's a bit more than nothing. Heard she had to patch up Brett's fist as well. You must have a jaw of steel.'

My lip ached at the mention of it, but something inside me tingled with pleasure at Pip's words. *Jaw of steel.* More like Brett had a bloody fist of steel. Didn't know Mum had to patch him up though. She never said anything.

But Pip knew. And Brett had been leaving notes for her.

A stab of something bitter and ugly within.

Pip's voice cut through it. 'Anyway, you don't need to pretend around me. I know what Brett can be like.'

'I'm fine. Seriously, it doesn't even hurt anymore.'

A smile tugged at the edge of her lips. The smell of coconut and fresh rain swarmed me as she leaned in. A golden halo shone around her, and all I could see was her face. She pressed her lips against mine, hard, and grazed my bottom lip between her teeth as she pulled away.

'Ouch!'

She smirked, raised an eyebrow at me.

'Okay, point taken. It does still hurt.' I sucked my bottom lip. The metallic taste of blood blended with Pip's coconut lip balm. 'A bit.'

She laughed again, wiped the blood from my lip with her thumb. 'Sorry.' A pause, she sucked on her thumb. 'So what did your dad have to say about it?'

'Dad? Not much, why?'

'Dunno. Just thought a copper would have something to say about his kid getting socked.'

'Told me I should've kept my nose out of other people's business.'

She laughed again. 'Sounds about right.' A pause. 'See, your dad's cool.'

I snorted. 'Cool? The guy's barely got any mates.'

'So cool he doesn't even need mates.' She laughed.

I thought about how Dad had come to pick me up from the school office. He'd had a long chat to Mr Ulrich, who'd pulled Brett off me.

'He was happy it got reported at the school,' I said. 'Doesn't wanna see other kids copping it, I guess, but he didn't want to take it any further. Reckons Brett's got enough going on as it is.'

Enough being a grade A prick is about all Brett's got going on.

But Pip nodded.

'What, you agree?' I asked. 'Brett's a jerk.'

She shrugged, didn't speak.

Jesus, did she fancy him?

I didn't want to know the answer, but the question slipped out of me all the same. 'Have you got a bit of a soft spot for him?'

'No.' Her answer came quick. She swung her feet, heels banging against the granite wall, and trained her eyes out over the field of boulders. 'But, you know, he just doesn't have it as easy as some of the other kids at school.'

'Some of the other kids?'

She turned to me, smiled. 'Yes. Other kids.' She gave my shoulder a soft nudge. 'Like you.'

'Me?'

'Don't act all surprised. Son of a cop and a doctor.' She smiled again. 'Basically hit the parent jackpot.'

A heat rose up my cheeks as I realised that I'd never stopped to consider it. Mum and Dad were all right. More than all right actually. I'd never thought about anyone else's home life. Pip's. Even bloody Brett's.

We sat in silence.

After a few moments, she pulled her satchel over from where it lay. She unclipped the two buckles at the front and flipped it open, taking out a large notebook and pencil case. Pictures sketched in grey pencil skipped by on each page.

A frog. The rainforest. A girl.

Amelia.

Not a notebook then. A sketchpad.

'You draw?'

She shrugged, turned her body so that she was facing me, her back pressed against the trunk of the fig tree. She rested her sketchpad against her bent knees so I could no longer see the drawings.

They were pretty good. The one of her sister's face had a softness to it that I didn't recognise. Wide eyes and mouth slightly open, she looked younger.

Pip unzipped her pencil case, started sketching, her eyes focused downwards. She didn't look up.

The scratching of her pencil filled the space for maybe five minutes. Maybe an hour. Time didn't really move in the rainforest. I leaned back, resting on my elbows, and closed my eyes. My lips still stung a little.

A shriek above, like a downscale whistle: a lesser sooty owl. I let the sound wash over me.

Pip's pencil scratching stopped. I opened my eyes, scanned the sky. Empty. The sun sat low, but it was still a bit too light for a lesser sooty owl.

I sat up, cracked my knuckles and craned my neck, leaning over her sketchpad. She pulled it close to her chest.

'It's not ready yet.' She smiled.

'What are you drawing?'

'I'll show you when it's done. Later.'

She slipped the sketchpad back into her satchel, along with her pencils.

The air was crisp, and within moments the temperature had dropped a few degrees. She sidled back up alongside me and I slung my arm around her shoulders. Her hair tickled the inside of my elbow.

The smarting in my lip had settled but something that she'd said earlier began to nag at me.

'What did you mean when you said, "I know what Brett can be like"?'

She shrugged beneath my arm. 'I dunno.'

'Yeah, you do. Come on, you almost just re-split my lip.'

She smiled, before her face fell flat, blank. 'It was nothing.'

I raised both eyebrows at her. 'Come on, tell me. I lie better than you.'

She laughed, but the sound barely left our ledge and the birds overhead carried on. 'It was nothing. Stupid really.' She banged one of her heels against the granite.

'What was stupid?'

I felt her shrug again. 'It was a few months ago. Over the holidays. He was with his dad out at our place. My aunt was visiting and had organised getting a few things around the house fixed, you know, that Mum didn't worry about.' She shifted at the mention of her mum. Everyone knew that Pip's mum spent more nights pissed at Cutters than she did at home with her daughters.

'Brett was helping his dad out,' she continued. 'He's supposed to be finishing up school early, going full-time with his dad.'

I couldn't speak, my mouth dry.

Brett was in Pip's house.

The sour stab returned. I felt sick.

'I didn't know my aunt had teed 'em up to come and she'd gone out to the shops with Amelia. Mum was asleep.' She paused a moment, her eyes stared out over the growing darkness of the boulders. 'It was nothing, really. But when Brett and his dad arrived, they'd been arguing.' She paused. 'Or actually, it was just his dad yelling. Telling him off, I think. Anyway, his dad stayed outside, fixing something on the veranda and Brett just let himself in. The door's always unlocked. I think he was just looking for the kitchen cos he had a toolkit with him and the sink has been leaking for months. He walked past my room, and I had the door open. I'd just come back from the creek and was still in my togs. I turned and he was just there, in the doorway, staring at me.'

A burst of something in my chest. Concern? Anger? Jealousy?

'Sounds like a creep,' I said.

She nodded. 'Yeah, I guess it was kinda creepy. Kinda sad too.'

'Sad?'

A shrug as she banged her heel absently against the granite ledge. 'Anyway, I asked what the hell he was doing in my room, and he just kept staring a bit longer. Then he kinda just snapped out of it. He got all awkward and mumbled something about coming to fix the tap.' She shrugged again.

I felt a ripple of anger bubble within.

'Brett was in your room?'

I'd never even been in her house.

'I didn't invite him in.' Pissed.

'Shit, sorry. Yeah. What a creep.' I looked at her sideways. 'A sad creep.'

Another shrug. 'He didn't actually do anything. It was just weird, the way he was staring. Like he'd never seen a girl in her togs before. He's not so bad, I guess.'

The wave of anger built, became a tsunami.

'You should've told me.'

'Why? Nothing happened.'

'No, I don't mean because of that, I just mean, you know.' I looked at the boulders, almost completely dark. The lesser sooty owl called again, shrieked. We should have left by now. 'I could've done something. Said something to him. Told him to piss off and leave you alone.'

She turned to me, the corner of her mouth lifted, and her eyes crinkled at the edges, the last of the light catching the golden flecks.

'What? I could take Brett Wyatt.'

She laughed again, reached and touched my lip. 'I don't want someone who can take Brett Wyatt.'

A lightness swam over me. I'd only just registered the relief when it was replaced by a heat creeping up my body: shame.

We watched the last of the orange sun sink below the granite in silence. The shadows and darkness extended like long fingers to reach out and grab our bare legs.

My lip stung at the thought of Brett, his flying fist. Would I really try to take him for Pip? I tried to push the answer down, somewhere where I didn't have to face the truth.

I flicked on my torch and stood, my hand reaching down to take Pip's. Our fingers interlaced as I helped her to her feet, her palm warm in mine.

Of course, I'd take bloody Brett Wyatt for her.

'Come on,' I said. 'Let's go.'

# CHAPTER EIGHTEEN

The rain-slicked footpath of the main street needed repair. Sloping slabs of concrete and large pavers riddled with cracks set the whole path on an odd angle. Callum's leg gave a silent stab of pain with every second step, and he regretted not accepting Eddy's lift to the cop shop twenty minutes earlier.

'Just need to do a few quick things,' he'd told Eddy.

Once the motel room door had closed behind his friend, he'd flung the wardrobe open to reveal the folded blanket on the top shelf, undisturbed.

The vice around his chest loosened a notch.

Now, approaching the police station, thoughts of Amelia Wyatt rolled through his head. Brett and Pip's daughter. Not quite two years old when she'd vanished. How much had Pip gone through? First her sister, then her daughter.

And now her son.

He thought of what Steph had said—and Mrs Fenton from the school: Pip was lucky, after everything that had happened. He refused to agree.

A few doors down, an unmistakable hulking figure emerged from the cop shop, head bowed.

Brett.

Callum watched as he crossed the road without even a glance down the street, climbed into a white ute and slammed the door. A jolt of the vehicle and a spray of water as it pulled out. A moment later, it disappeared from view.

Callum closed the distance to the police station.

At the sound of the door—or the gust of wind that pressed inside—Steph looked up from behind the reception desk. A flicker of anger across her face as she opened her mouth to speak. A pause, then a quick reset.

'Three times in three days.' She smiled. 'Lucky me.'

He pressed forcefully against the door to close it. 'Well, at least one of us is lucky.'

Her face fell, dimple gone. 'Eddy told me about your car. It'll just have been a prank. There's a group of teens round here who think they rule the roost. Little shits.' Her smile returned. 'But weren't we all?'

He raised his eyebrows at her, thought back to Brett, the biggest of the shits.

'Hey, what was Brett doing in here?'

'Brett?'

'Yeah, I just saw him leave.' He paused. 'Seemed pissed.'

She snorted. 'Sounds about right. You know what he's like.' She waved her hand absently towards the door. 'He was just here fixing a leak.'

Callum turned. Aside from a patch of rain that had swept in with him—and a puddle now at his feet—the rest of the room was dry.

The phone rang and Steph snatched up the receiver. She waved him through to the back office then grabbed his arm as he passed. She wedged the phone between her ear and shoulder and fished around in the large handbag at her feet.

'Yes, Mrs Nolan, I understand your cat has gone walkabout again.' She rolled her eyes at Callum. 'But unfortunately that's not a police issue.'

The voice on the end of the line squawked, hysterical.

After a moment, Steph produced a large bunch of keys and, covering the mouthpiece of the phone, said, 'Take my car this arvo if you need to do anything. I won't knock off till three. It's the blue one parked out back.'

She pressed them into his hand, her fingers lingering, before ushering him through towards the back where he could hear Eddy's muffled voice.

He jammed the keys into his pocket. His fingers tingled where hers had just been.

'... great, thanks for that. Much appreciated,' Eddy was saying. 'Bye for now.' He hung up the phone and turned to Callum. 'How'd you go with the mechanic?'

'He's stuck at a call-out halfway down the range. A tree came down on a mini. Can't get back here till late arvo at the earliest. Thinks he should have the right tyres in stock though, so that's something.'

'Who the hell drives a mini in these conditions?' Eddy shook his head. 'Sure you don't want to fill out a statement in case we catch the buggers?'

'Nah, no point. I'm still gonna be slapped with the bill.' He waved his hand and took a seat at Eddy's desk. 'How are you progressing?'

While Callum had been tracking down Granite Creek's sole mechanic—*what the hell did the town do when the guy was on leave?*—Eddy had planned to chase up a few loose ends.

'Well, Josh Swindley did die on the eighteenth, so that all ties together with what Mike told us,' Eddy said. 'And I got hold of Tess and she's agreed to release the phone records for the landline at the house and Lachie's mobile, as well as his bank statements.'

'Sounds like it all happened easily.'

'She dug her heels in a little. Said that I should really be letting them grieve and move on, not stirring things up.' Eddy pulled his eyebrows together, the vertical line between them deepening. 'I just said that it wouldn't look good for her if I had to get a warrant instead.' He sighed and met Callum's eye. 'You'd better be bloody right about this not being an accident. I've already copped a few abusive phone calls that I'm poking my nose in where it's not welcome.'

'Jesus, really?'

Eddy hit a couple of buttons on the phone on his desk. A beep issued, followed by a croaky voice over the speaker.

'Just cos you grew up here doesn't mean you can come swannin' into town and messin' around with things. Leave Tess and Jack alone, ya abo prick. And tell ya journalist mate to fuck off back down south. There's no fuckin' story here.' Another beep.

*Ya abo prick.*

Callum sat, his ears ringing with the words. A smouldering anger within.

It wasn't Brett's voice.

'There's another two,' Eddy said. 'They both mention you as well.'

'Charming. Any way to trace them?'

Eddy shook his head. 'All blocked numbers and it's not worth my time.'

So, the people of Granite Creek might be arseholes, but they weren't complete idiots.

'Steph reckons that first one's Sammie Morgan, cranky old codger who's pissed I gave him a speeding ticket. Mates with Brett. She's not too sure about the other two.'

Callum thought back to his lunch at the pub with Steph, the two men with Brett. One young, the other older. The older one definitely fit the bill for a cranky old codger.

Callum leaned back in his chair; he hadn't realised he'd been perched on the edge.

'Well, that tells you something,' he said.

'And what's that?'

'Whenever someone tells you there's no story, it means there usually is. They just don't want you to sniff it out.'

'So, what are you suggesting?'

Callum clucked his tongue once. 'That we go sniffing.'

\*

Christ, another bloody hatchback. Steph's car's roof was barely up to Callum's navel.

He blew out a deep breath before resigning himself to an uncomfortable drive out to the walking track. He knew what Eddy would say and so hadn't mentioned his plan for the afternoon. His skin prickled at the thought of being so close to the rainforest, but he couldn't shake the image of Lachie sprawled on the granite boulders. He had to get closer.

A gust of wind blew his shirt collar up and an angry outburst from the clouds hastened him along.

He leveraged his left leg into the car, followed by the rest of his body, adjusting the seat back to its furthest position: not far enough. His knees still came level with the steering wheel, his left one fiercely protesting.

He took a few deep breaths through the pain of his knee's new angle. A stab turned to an ache, his breath steadied, and he registered something familiar: the scent of mango. Callum was thrust back over three decades, the feel of Steph's lips against his during a game of spin the bottle. A tug at the corner of his mouth.

He started the engine. The car lurched and his left shoe hit something that sent a jarring pain back up into his stump. The gearstick glared at him.

He gripped the steering wheel, closed his eyes. Frustration and pain coursed through him. He banged the steering wheel with one hand.

*A fucking manual.*

He wasn't going anywhere.

Gritting his teeth, he opened his eyes. A glint in the rear-view mirror and he whipped around to look through the back windscreen, heart pounding.

Nothing.

The wind picked up a notch and the car swayed slightly, his bulk doing little to anchor it. Another burst of wind, a whistle through the air, a whisper in his ear.

He squeezed his eyes shut again and took a deep breath, trying to ignore the slick sheen of sweat across his palms, the cramped car pressing back against him.

*Get it together.*

He opened his eyes and his gaze dropped to the back seat where a small cluster of silver sat. A moment's confusion and he reached back, his fingertips brushing the smooth objects. Cool to the touch. They were attached with a red twine to a charcoal folder, camouflaged against the fabric of the back seat. He scooped it up.

*Ting. Ting.*

The trill echoed around the small space of the car, loud enough to cut across the thrum of rain and the wind outside. He gripped one fist around the bells to silence them, his right elbow slamming into the car door. He swore and dropped the folder as a fresh zing of pain shot through his forearm.

*Ting. Ting.*

The pain passed and he looked around at the sprawl of papers. The memory of the inside of Lachie's car shoved its way into Callum's mind. Rubbish and old clothes scattered everywhere.

He began snatching up the papers, stuffing them back into the folder. A name caught his eye and he paused, clutching a printed set of documents. Columns of names and numbers lined the page, Steph's details in the top left corner, a familiar logo in the right.

A bank statement.

He scrolled his eyes along the entire length of deposits. One name stood out. Again and again.

He flipped the page. Again, the name.

And on the next page.

Every fortnight. The same name. The same amount deposited.

Callum's head spun as he stared at the statement so long he was sure his eyes were going to burn a hole right through the page.

His shirt collar tightened around his neck, the mango scent in Steph's car cloying.

He wedged the statement back into the folder and thrust the entire file onto the back seat.

One hand fumbled against the interior of the door, searching for the handle, while the other ripped the top two buttons off his shirt. A rush of warm, sticky air as he thrust the car door open.

He leaned over the small hatchback, palms flat on the roof, and sucked in great lungfuls of air. For the first time since arriving in Granite Creek, he welcomed the feel of the perpetual rain pounding down on him. Eyes closed, he tilted his head back. The rain swept over his face and the exposed skin of his chest. He willed it to wash away the last five minutes.

A smudge of a world welcomed him when he opened his eyes, everything hazy through his rain-streaked glasses. The grey of the police parking lot. The beige of the police station wall. The outline of his pale hands flush against the blue of Steph's car. He snatched his hands back.

*Steph, what the hell?*

# CHAPTER NINETEEN

The air clung to Callum's skin, sticky and heavy, as he walked down the main street. He didn't know where he was heading. All he knew was that he needed to put as much distance between himself and Steph's car as he could.

He'd stared at the bank statement so long that his eyes had begun to sting. He'd squeezed them shut and had felt a surge of disappointment when he'd opened them and the same name had stared back at him.

Brett Wyatt.

Brett's name. Again and again.

*What the hell was going on?*

Brett.

Steph.

Brett and Steph.

*Jesus.*

He felt sick.

He walked past deserted shopfronts, many with sandbags pressed against the foot of their door jambs. Steph's keys jingled with each step, pressing hard against his thigh.

The thought of confronting Steph—marching into the police station and demanding an answer—had sprung to his mind. But he'd dismissed it as quickly as it'd stomped its way to the front of his thoughts. Steph would rightly want to know what he'd been doing snooping around in her personal documents.

He remembered Brett stalking away from the cop shop earlier, head bowed and most definitely free of any maintenance gear.

*Fixing a leak, my arse, Steph.*

Callum knew that he was starting to recover from the shock when the ache below his left knee began to creep back, fighting Steph and Brett for domination of his thoughts. Each step brought an increasingly sharp jab, and he was considering heading to Cutters to recuperate with a seat and a bite to eat when he slammed right into something. Not something, someone, coming out of a shop.

'Shit, sorry.' He grabbed for the wall with one hand as the other reached for the arm of the woman he'd nearly bowled over. He registered her dirty blonde hair and swollen stomach a beat before he realised that he'd almost knocked Tess Wyatt clear off her feet. 'Are you all right?'

She clutched her stomach, doubled over.

'Mum?' Jack lingered in the shadow of the doorway behind Steph, red eyes puffy. A knot tightened deep in Callum's gut.

'I'm so sorry. I really didn't see you coming. Are you okay?' he asked again, worried she hadn't straightened. 'Tess?'

'I'm fine.' She gradually righted herself.

He tentatively removed his hand from the wall and they both looked to his other hand, still gripping her arm. He let go.

'I thought you were told to leave town.' She rubbed at her arm where his grip had reddened the exposed skin; a mottled bruise had formed beneath.

He shifted his weight off his left leg and Steph's keys dug into his thigh. A thought hit him. 'Sorry, I really didn't see you. Someone slashed my car's tyres.' He paused but she didn't react. 'So I was just borrowing Steph's car. Do you know her?'

Her hand paused over her blemished arm. The rain

pounding on the awning overhead did little to drown out the silence that stretched out between them.

'Steph Pemlington?' he said. 'She works at—'

'I know who she is.'

'Oh, well, do you have much to do with her? Maybe Br—'

'She has nothing to do with our family.' She made to step around him, gesturing at Jack behind her.

'Oh, I just wondered if—'

'I said we have nothing to do with her. End of story.' Her eyes looked past him, searching for escape.

'Look, I am sorry.'

He raised his hands non-threateningly, and she moved back, her heel kicking another sandbag. He went to grab her, but she regained her balance and pulled back further.

He took a step back, gave her space.

A pause. 'It's fine.' She gestured to Jack and made to walk past again.

'No, I mean, I'm sorry about everything. About coming by yesterday. That wasn't right. Getting Brett angry. And I'm sorry about Lachie too. I'm sorry you've lost your husband.' He turned to Jack. 'And you your dad.'

Tess's face flashed and Callum tried to read it, but her features had smoothed back over before he'd had a chance to interpret them. What was it? Anger? Fear?

'It's fine.' She grabbed Jack by the arm. 'Just leave us alone.'

'I can help you.'

What the hell was he saying? The words kept coming.

'If you need help. You don't need to be afraid. If Brett is—'

'I said we're fine.' Her voice rose and she stalked past him, Jack in tow. 'Just leave our family alone.'

At least she'd recovered enough to glower at him as she went.

\*

Callum watched Tess and Jack retreat down the street, picking up their pace as they dashed between shop awnings. A thought crossed his mind, and he pushed open the shop door and crossed the threshold.

The scent of rubber soles and dusty merchandise engulfed him as he made his way between the tightly packed aisles and stands displaying hiking poles and waterproof pants.

'Hi.' The curvy blonde he'd spotted through the window the morning before looked up from behind the counter. She wore a t-shirt that looked about two sizes too small. The words 'The Outdoor Store' were stretched enough to crack the faded paint of the logo. 'Can I help you at all?' Her voice had a guttural, not unpleasant, sound.

'How you going?' Callum asked.

'Great.' She closed the magazine she had open on the counter. 'Are you on the hunt for anything in particular?'

Callum scanned the cramped store. His eyes fell on the back wall. 'Yes, actually.'

Twenty minutes later, he walked up and down the short stretch of unoccupied carpet trialling his sixth pair of hiking boots. He'd learned that he preferred a lower cut upper with a non-slip sole. He'd also learned that the salesgirl, Hanna, was from a small town in western Germany, was twenty-three years old and had been in Granite Creek for almost six months.

She'd shrugged as she'd told him, 'It was either this or fruit picking south of Cairns. I thought there were worse places to see out the wet season and get enough work to extend my visa.'

Six months in Granite Creek during the wet season sounded as painful as shoe shopping with a prosthetic leg. Getting something that he could wedge his rigid left foot into while feeling comfortable on his right was harder than most would expect. Doubly as hard when the shoe at hand was a stiff, high-laced hiking boot.

Nonetheless, Hanna's easy banter and pleasant accent had made the chore somewhat more bearable. He hadn't even minded when she'd given him the customary pity face when she'd learned he was an amputee. Maybe it was because she'd followed it up with a cheeky smile and a stroke of his arm.

*Jesus, you're old enough to be her dad.*

As she stood at the counter, placing his new shoes into their box, he said, 'I noticed that Tess Wyatt was just in here.'

A shadow flickered across her face. 'Sorry, who?'

'Tess. Tess Wyatt. She was just in here.'

'Oh, is that her name?'

'Yeah. Was she after something in particular?'

'Oh.' Hanna fumbled with a pile of bright orange plastic bags. 'Just buying some new shoes for Jack.'

'Strange.'

'Why?' She looked at him, her face pulled tight.

'Well, her husband just died. Lachie Wyatt. Didn't you hear—'

'Of course, I heard. Everyone's heard.'

'Just seems an odd time to go shopping, that's all.'

'Well, that's what she did.' Hanna stuffed the shoe box into a plastic bag and thrust it across the counter. 'I guess she's an odd lady.' She didn't bother to wait for a response, instead walked around the counter, threaded her way between the towers of merchandise and opened the shop door. The rain, now coming sideways, swept in beneath the awning and began spraying water onto the shop floor.

'It was lovely to meet you,' she said, her face blank. 'I hope you enjoy your shoes. Although,' she added as he walked past her, 'I wouldn't go hiking in this weather if I were you.'

She pulled the door firmly shut behind him and flipped the sign to closed. Even over the pounding of the rain on the awning overhead, Callum heard the distinct click of the lock.

After a pause, he turned and began to trudge down the street, mindful of the puddles forming on the sunken and cracked pavement. The weight of his shopping bag was heavy in his hand as the memory of Tess and Jack disappearing down the same stretch of road only half an hour earlier pushed to the forefront of his mind.

Tess had clutched tightly to Jack's arm, not a shopping bag in sight.

# CHAPTER TWENTY

Secrets. The whole town seemed to have them.

Hanna. Tess. Steph.

And bloody Brett.

Callum tramped down the street towards the cop shop and pushed the door to the station open. Steph was on the phone.

Good. He'd just dump her keys, feign a smile and make his escape. He didn't know what he'd say to her anyway.

'Didn't have a bingle, did you?' she called as his hand reached for the station door. The receiver clicked into place.

He hitched a smile on his face and turned her way. 'Nah, couldn't even drive the thing.'

She frowned.

'Manual.' He pointed to his left leg.

It took a beat for her to understand. 'Oh, of course. Bugger. Sorry, I didn't even think about that.'

'No worries.'

'So where were you planning on going anyway?'

His eyes flickered to the door behind the reception desk that led to Eddy's office. Closed.

'To the hiking track, actually. See how far I could get along it.'

'In this weather?'

He shrugged. 'I probably won't be in town much longer and wanted to check it out.' He broadened his smile. 'For old times' sake.'

'The weather warnings say not to venture outside. You're a brave man.' She smiled. 'Or off your rocker.'

'The cyclone isn't due to hit until the day after tomorrow, and they're predicting it'll pass north of here anyway.'

Her brow furrowed, unconvinced, and he was reminded of her expression when Brett had left the station earlier. What the hell was going on with those two?

A hint of an idea crept into his mind.

He had to know more.

He took a step towards the counter. 'Come with me.'

\*

Twenty minutes later, Callum cracked Steph's car window as the pair drove towards Kingfisher Way. The rain filtered in, and she eyed him sideways as it landed steadily on his lap. A deep breath, and the sickly mango scent of the car, combined with the heady fug of the rainforest, almost gave him a headache.

Steph said she'd been due to finish up work anyway. It was Saturday and the station was usually closed, but with a cyclone en route, they were receiving an influx of panicked calls and Steph had offered to man the phone for a few hours, put people at ease.

Rain lashed the windshield and the wipers pelted across, only a screen of green and grey visible beyond. What the hell was he doing? Eddy was right. The weather was worsening, and he was in no condition to be traipsing through the slush of the rainforest. He was asking for an accident.

And what was he hoping to learn anyway? Did he think that Steph was going to open up to him, reveal her connection to Brett, if he cornered her in the rainforest? There was nothing to gain. He'd been to the camp site already, seen the photos of Lachie. Broken. Dead.

He took a deep breath but the mango scent lodged in his throat. He cracked the window further.

The wind picked up and the hatchback careened more than it should have as it took the turn onto Kingfisher Way.

The tyre hit a pothole and his leg gave a stab.

A moment later, Steph pulled the car in to park beside the main entrance to the hiking track. She kept the engine running.

'Here,' she said.

The deserted car park had the feel of something that had been discarded after everyone had lost interest. Deep puddles of water had pooled in the spots where police cars and ambulances had sat, and even from the car, he could tell the entrance to the track was a slopping mess thanks to all the feet that had tramped over it recently.

'Gosh, looks like a war zone.' Steph's eyes roamed over the muddy surface in front of them.

'Why don't we go back up the road a little? There's another entrance, less used,' he said.

A single nod and Steph pushed the car into first, angling it back down Kingfisher Way. Within a few minutes, Callum could see the distinctive kauri pine on the shoulder of the road that both marked and concealed the start of the track. He was about to open his mouth to point it out to Steph when she turned the wheel and edged the car off the road, coming to a halt on a firm patch of gravel, a mere five metres from the track.

'Here we are.' She turned to face him, her dimple winking.

He met her gaze and made an effort to mirror her smile, even as he caught the glint from the silver bells on the back seat.

\*

Callum swiped at a length of lawyer vine, the sharp barbs cutting across his palm. They'd been walking for only a few minutes, Steph ahead of him on the narrow track. He'd started with his shirtsleeves rolled up to help combat the heat. However, a few scratches and a dozen midge bites later, and he'd rolled them back down.

With his attention on the uneven rainforest floor, and his mind racing with Steph's ease in finding the track, he'd again found himself tangled in a low-hanging vine. He picked at the sharp vine that had entangled itself in his collar, his fingers smarting.

Dark shapes loomed, muted against the vibrant green background. Without the spotlights and crowd of searchers the rainforest felt like a different place. Bad different. He fumbled blindly at his collar.

'Here, let me.'

He hadn't heard Steph approach. The sodden floor of rotten leaves and mud deadened her footfall, and the downpour of rain on the canopy overhead all but drowned out the usual din of the rainforest.

She worked at his collar, her fingers brushing his jaw. He focused on a nearby branch. A small bird with a rusty breast and pinched black face stared at them.

*Symposiachrus trivirgatus*: spectacled monarch.

'You going okay?' she asked.

'Yeah, fine.'

'We've still got a way to go.'

'I know. It's just more overgrown than I remember.'

'Yeah, not many people use this track anymore. In fact, I think very few people even know about it. Most kids have been warned away from here anyway. Don't need them wandering off the path and getting lost.'

The word 'path' was generous. A faint track was etched out between mossy rocks, overgrown ferns and fallen trunks.

It dipped in and out of view, the rainforest swallowing it again every few metres.

It was hard to believe that only two days earlier the search team would've likely traipsed this very trail. The forest had already claimed it back.

He nodded. 'But you know the track.'

Her hands froze. A moment passed. 'I could say the same thing about you.'

'Fair call.'

'We grew up in a different time, you and me. Before the Amelias.' She began working at his collar again. 'I remember thinking about the whispering, but not really believing it. I mean, there were always good reasons why those other kids had wandered off and never turned up.' She suddenly laughed, her breath hot on his neck. 'Remember Brenda Sternspek got her knickers in a knot on grade nine camp cos she swore she heard the whispering? She went home a day early.' A small snort. 'It was just like a ghost story. But things have changed around here now. Parents are terrified their kids will drop off the face of the earth, and kids all wear those ridiculous bracelets. All afraid that if they don't keep the bloody things on, they'll end up flinging themselves off the boulders.'

His hand moved to his pocket, the bracelet with its bells beneath his fingers. He thought of the three silver bells attached with red twine to the folder on Steph's back seat. The same bells, loud enough to drown out the wind. Were they loud enough to drown out the whispering? Is that what kids thought?

He recalled the image from the front of last year's school yearbook. Kids holding the snake skin aloft, the silver bells on their woven bracelets winking.

'So, nobody really comes this way then?' he asked.

Her face was buried near his neck, and he felt, rather than saw, her shake her head. 'Lest they hear the whispering.' There was a smirk in her words.

'Not a believer then?' he asked.

'Of the whispering?' She gave a short laugh, her breath hot on his skin. 'Is anybody?'

He shrugged, his shoulder bumping her arm.

He felt a final tug on his collar and turned to look at her. Her auburn hair, secured in a ponytail, was slick with rain. A strand had come loose and ran down one cheek.

She sucked one of her fingers. 'Don't tell me you believe in it?'

He shrugged again.

She laughed and turned to continue along the track, mud splattered up the back of her calves and as high as the hem of her shorts. High.

The track angled upwards, and he started after her. His left leg gave a new stab of protest, his right heel already forming a blister from the new boots. His shoes squelched with each step and—according to his right foot—were already drenched through. *Waterproof, my arse.*

'And I suppose you believe in the boogie man and the Loch Ness monster too then?' she called over her shoulder.

'No, but you have to admit, there's something to it.'

'There's nothing to it. The whispering is folklore. A legend that kids say to frighten each other, or cruel parents tell to keep their children from falling to their deaths.'

'So, you've never told Noah about it?'

'He heard about it at school, and I told him it was a load of rubbish.'

'What about all the people who've died out there?'

'Coincidences. Tragedies.' She shrugged. 'And in Lachie's case, stupidity. Do you really think he heard it and came wandering out, unable to resist the call?' She took a few steady steps over a fallen trunk then stopped under a large strangler fig tree to wait for him.

A beat later and he pulled up next to her.

His mouth was suddenly dry. 'So.' He swallowed. 'You don't think any of the deaths out here had anything to do with it?'

'Aren't you an investigative journalist? Shouldn't you be basing your opinions more on fact than folklore?' She slapped a midge on her arm. 'Besides, if you're one for myths, then you'll believe that Brett chopped up poor baby Amelia and hid her in the walls of their house.' The corner of her mouth twitched.

He forced a smile. 'Well, that's morbid. I mean, Brett's a jerk, but I don't know if he'd knock off his own daughter.'

A flash of green eyes, rimmed with gold.

'Half of the town is convinced that's what happened.'

'And you?' he asked. 'Are you convinced?'

She paused. 'No. He's okay.'

'Okay? Did you go to school with the guy?'

'Yeah, all right.' She laughed. 'He was a jerk. But school was a long time ago. You might need to make sure that a thirty-year-old grudge doesn't cloud your judgement too much. The guy's had a rough time. First his daughter, then his wife.'

'And now his son,' he said.

Her expression was blank, unreadable. 'Sure. Now his son.'

He adjusted his weight, a sharp jerk below his left knee.

She grabbed his arm and steadied him. 'Besides, I'm surprised you don't think Brett flung baby Amelia off the boulders. From what I've heard from Eddy, you seem to think that he did just that to Lachie.'

Bloody Eddy.

'Well, I guess my judgement is a little clouded then.' He managed a half smile as he turned to face her. The rain overhead pressed through the thick branches of the strangler fig tree and fat droplets landed on her bare shoulders.

He placed his hand against the tree trunk, taking his weight off his now throbbing left leg, and took in his surroundings.

Green and more green. How long had they been walking for? Ten minutes? Twenty? The rainforest seemed to swallow the concept of time.

Still, he knew they weren't even halfway to the camp site. What had he been thinking coming out here? His leg ached at the idea of the trek ahead and his skin prickled as he thought of what lay beyond the camp site and the creek crossing.

Snatches of dark shapes and gaping caverns rushed through his mind. The mossy carpet of the rainforest suddenly falling away with nothing but the sheer drop to the boulders beneath him.

'You okay?'

'Yeah, fine.' He tried to mask a wince as he righted himself, letting go of the tree. His head spun.

'We should probably turn back.'

'I'm fine.'

'Well, the weather's getting worse, and ...' She hesitated. 'I've seen you in better states than this.'

'I said, I'm fine.' His voice sounded distant, even to him.

'Seriously, I can't carry you out if you collapse.' She looked along the track, towards the camp site. Towards the boulders. 'Let's turn back.'

'No, I need to see ...' His voice trailed off as he felt a slight prickle trace the length of his body.

He rubbed his slick palms on his trousers, his hands passing over three small firm lumps in his pocket: the bracelet. A flicker of relief.

He strained his ears as the sounds of the rainforest dropped away. The constant thrum of cicadas, the pulsating of the creek, the droplets of rain on the canopy above. Only in their absence did they become noticeable.

He closed his eyes; listening, straining.

Nothing. Silence.

Then, cutting through the air, a sound.

*Ting. Ting.*

Silence again. Then, a crunch and a rustle. Footsteps perhaps. Too far away to be Steph's.

A voice maybe. A whisper?

A laugh. It grew louder, a high-pitched whistle. Sharp, like a stab to the ears. It sailed through the air, carried on the wind, and burrowed into Callum's ears.

He thrust his hand in his pocket, fumbled for the bracelet.

A rush of wings. Birds. Everywhere.

The prickle over his body turned to a sweat, cold and consuming. He was coated in a thick layer of dampness, like a blanket draping over him.

A flash of the boulders, grey as smoke. The cover of the rainforest behind, the abyss of the drop-off in front. A large strangler fig tree to the side, its long roots reaching like fingers into the damp earth. A blue hat. Heavy clouds growing on the horizon.

Falling. The feel of nothing beneath you and the world above.

A voice.

*Please, no ... please don't ...*

A tight grip. Loosening. Slipping.

Then nothing.

He opened his eyes.

Pip. No. Steph. Tousled hair swept to cover her face as she bent to talk to Brett.

No. Not Brett. Jack.

The whistling in his ears still rang and he couldn't make out their words. A movement and he twisted, his whole body pivoting. He lost his grip on the fig tree and as he fell to the floor, he saw Brett again. No, Jack. This time further down the track. His face blurred. A smudge in the distance.

Callum hit the rainforest floor. Pain, sharp and blinding. Blackness taking over.

*Ting. Ting.*

A blurry figure, auburn hair. A boy moving behind, disappearing down the track. Callum tried to turn. Two figures, blurring into one. Then gone.

Nothing.

# CHAPTER TWENTY-ONE

Callum woke to a tickle on his face and the heady fug of the tropics lodged in his nostrils.

He opened his eyes. Steph's face was only inches away, worry lines etched across her forehead, around her eyes. He blinked a few times and her face came into focus, her features smoothed out and a slight smile hitched at her lips.

'Welcome back.' Her breath was a welcome warmth on his skin, the mild scent of mango cutting through.

She shifted her weight away from him and sat back on her heels. The world tilted: he was horizontal. A push through his arms to try to sit, and he was rewarded by an agonising pull in his leg. Steph's face dropped and he tried to smooth his own features out. He lay back down.

'I'm fine,' he said.

'I don't think you are.' Her brow furrowed. 'What was that?'

'Oh, um.' He heaved himself into a sitting position, pushed through the wave of nausea. 'I get these, ah, attacks.'

'Attacks?'

'It's nothing.'

'You just called them attacks.'

'It's nothing.'

'That wasn't nothing. You fell over and passed out.'

'Right. Well, I'm fine now.'

'That doesn't look fine.' She nodded towards his leg.

Callum's eyes moved downwards.

His leg was twisted, his prosthetic foot sitting at an almost ninety-degree angle from his knee.

\*

It took Callum and Steph three times as long to make their way out of the rainforest and back to the car. After righting his prosthesis as best he could, Callum had chosen a fallen branch to use for support and, with Steph's help, had managed to walk back.

Lurch. Falter. Limp.

Not walk.

Relief flooded him as the green of the rainforest gave way to the grey of the bitumen and the blue of Steph's car. They cleared the final trees and broke out into the torrential downpour of rain. At last, he took a proper lungful of air.

They drove in silence, and Steph's eyes flickered between the road ahead and Callum beside her. As they gradually left the rainforest behind, his shoulders relaxed and the vice-like grip on his chest lessened.

Memories flashed through his head.

The strangler fig tree. The rain on his face. The pain in his leg. And Brett. Or Jack. Or both. He couldn't be sure who he was remembering. Or what. It all blurred together so that he could no longer distinguish what had happened an hour ago from the snatches of memory from three decades earlier.

'Who were you speaking to?' he asked Steph.

'Huh?' She angled the car off the highway and onto the main street of town.

'In the forest, when I was out, you were talking to someone. A kid.'

'Oh, yeah. Just Jack.' A pause. 'Said he wanted to come out to feel closer to his dad or something. I don't know.'

'That's odd him being by himself out there.'

She shrugged. 'He's been through so much these last few days. Needed some space, I guess.'

Callum gave a slow nod. He'd traipsed through the rainforest plenty of times as a ten-year-old but never alone. 'Still, the weather's pretty bad and he's only a kid. Weren't you worried?'

She kept her eyes trained forward. 'I told him he should head home, back to his mum.'

The air in the car sat heavy.

'So, just Jack?'

She turned to him, shoulders stiff. 'Yeah. Just Jack.'

The silence stretched between them, riddled with sickly mango and unspoken words.

'We're here.' Steph's voice. 'Let me help you to your room.'

He blinked hard. They were parked in the motel car park, the large plastic green tree frog on the front lawn staring at them. 'No, I should be fine. You've done enough to help me out today. Sorry it wasn't the most enjoyable hike.'

'There's a cyclone coming. It was never going to be an enjoyable hike.'

Her face was deadpan for a beat, before breaking into a broad grin. Despite his pain, he smiled back. A long pause, then she leaned forward, crossing the chasm that had gaped between them only a moment earlier.

Her eyes—the same colour as the creek he hadn't seen in three decades—drew him nearer.

A splash of red and silver jumped at him from the back seat.

The folder. The bank statement. And Brett's name. Over and over.

He jerked back, away from her. His elbow banged against the door, a zing through to his pinky finger.

He cleared his throat and forced a smile on his face. 'I really should let you go. Don't you need to pick up Noah?'

A slight frown crossed her face. She recovered quickly, sat back, the gap between them widening. Her lips formed a tight smile. Forced. 'Yeah, you're right. I'd best head off.'

He paused a moment. Then fumbled for the door handle, an ache pulsing in his elbow. He shouldered the door open and heaved himself out of the too-small car. He bent down to say thanks and the words got lost on the way.

'Steph ... I'm sorry—'

'You're right.' Her eyes were focused forward. 'I need to go. Get Noah.'

He waited a moment, the rain licking at the back of his exposed neck. A nod, then, giving into the wind, he let the door slam shut.

Mud splattered on his trousers as she drove off.

He made his way gingerly towards his motel room.

She'd leaned in. So had he.

*Idiot. Don't get mixed up with someone who's already involved with bloody Brett Wyatt.*

Still, her body leaning in, lips inches away ...

He stopped. An open door. His door.

All thoughts of Steph vanished.

The door to his room sat wide open, banging against the wall in the near gale. The window that fronted the car park where he stood was raised, the glass broken, curtains billowing inward.

He took a step forward. Glass crunched underfoot. The doorway cast a long black shadow inward, and in the darkness beyond, he sensed a figure moving.

# CHAPTER TWENTY-TWO

Callum stood in the doorway of his motel room. The heady scent of wet earth pressed against him as if the outside had ebbed its way in. He squinted into blackness, trying to make out the dark blur of shapes and shadows. The outline of his bed. The angular set of the chair and desk, overturned. A shaft of dull light where the bathroom door sat ajar. A black rectangle against the far wall where the cupboard door had been thrust open.

*Shit.*

Outside, glimpses of the reception building and main street winked at him from between the parked cars, crammed together. Deserted.

A dim glow, flickering through the neighbouring room's window, told him they had the telly on.

He hesitated on the threshold. He should phone Eddy. Movement within. Footsteps. A drawer closing. A sharp breath.

'Hello?'

A rustle inside, hurried, urgent.

The hairs on the back of his neck stood up.

A bump.

'Fuck.' A voice from within. Familiar.

Callum reached around the doorway, fumbled for the light switch. His eyes burned against the glow. The outline of a man came into focus.

'Mike?'

Another bump.

'Ouch, shit. Yeah?' Mike righted himself, rubbing his head. 'Oh, it's you.'

'What the hell happened here?'

The room was chaos. A dull grey rock sat in a puddle of shattered glass under the window. What few belongings he'd brought with him had been strewn across the floor, along with the bedding and towels. Cupboards flung open, drawers upended. His eyes moved to the wardrobe, it gaped open like a chasm. His clothes, once hanging, now lay splashed across the floor; the innersoles of his shoes removed, thrown aside. His eyes landed on the blanket on the top shelf, folded neatly, undisturbed. The vice around his chest loosened its grip.

Mike looked around and shrugged. 'Dunno. But good thing you're here. I dunno what to tell ya.'

'But what the hell are you doing in here?'

'Heard a commotion, didn't I?' He was on the defence.

Mike's features were set. A moment passed before they softened. He bent, picked up the chair from in front of the cupboard. A few awkward steps and Callum crossed the room. Together they righted the desk.

The wind whipped outside, the rain on the car roofs in the parking lot deafening.

'You heard a commotion all the way from the front reception?'

'Nah.' A hesitation. 'I was in the room next door.' Mike rubbed his head again. 'Thought I heard ya come back. Then there was all this banging around. Sounded like you were ransacking the place. Thought I was gonna have to charge ya for damages.'

Callum raised his eyebrows.

'Obviously, I know it wasn't you now.'

Callum's eyes roamed over the squat room with its one exit. 'So, where'd they go?'

Another shrug. 'Out the bathroom window, I guess. That's what I was doing in there. Thought I heard someone.'

'And did you see anyone?'

'Nah. Not by the time I got in there. No way of knowin' who it was.' Mike's eyes shifted to the open door, the car park beyond. 'I'll get that window taped up for ya. Won't be able to get it fixed this time of the arvo. Can't offer ya another room either. With this cyclone coming, most people have decided to stay put and not risk the drive down the range.' He took a few steps to the door. 'Lucky the lock on ya door wasn't broken.'

Callum looked at the broken window. A locked door wasn't going to do much to keep anyone out.

Mike's figure receded into the gloom of the deserted car park. He flashed into view again as he ducked into the reception area, then was swallowed from sight.

Callum's eyes roamed the car park, vehicles crammed in. Anyone could be lurking between them. His own rental still sat towards the end of the row, low to the ground. Tyres still not bloody fixed.

A movement. Curtains snapped shut. A figure retreated from the window of the neighbouring room.

Someone was watching him.

His heart drummed and he turned to retreat back into his room. A flicker of red on the ceiling of the awning outside. His eyes followed and landed on a boxy black object.

The red light of the CCTV camera blinked back at him.

His eyes took in the broken window of his motel room, and he squinted back through the rain to the lit reception building. Mike's words echoed in his ears.

*No way of knowing who it was.*

\*

Wet clothes on a wet chair. Callum sat, his left leg extended, prosthesis screaming for removal. The metal box resting on his lap weighed more than he recalled. Its padlock—unlatched—winked at him in the overhead light, its lid thrown open.

The motel room door was locked—for what good it would do—and the curtains drawn over the broken window. They billowed inward, protesting against the onslaught of wind. Lashes of rain ploughed through, and a dark patch was forming on the soggy carpet, droplets of water gleaming on shards of glass yet to be vacuumed up.

He loosened his grip on the lockbox, his eyes focusing on the contents.

A grainy family photo smiled up at him. It was small, taken from a newspaper. A larger photo and article were folded on the page behind it.

Four faces. All familiar. Two he'd seen splashed all over the news.

The Wyatt family.

He traced his fingers over one of the faces, the paper worn.

No one in the picture smiled, not even the toddler who Pip held awkwardly on one hip. Cheeks so chubby that they made her eyes mere slits. The back of one starfish-shaped hand rested on her mother's chest, the other hung limply by her side in a bright pink cast: Amelia.

He tore his eyes from the toddler. He felt sick.

The photo had been taken only two weeks before she'd vanished.

The caption beneath the image read: 'Amelia Wyatt, with her parents, Pip and Brett Wyatt, and brother, Lachlan'.

The newspaper article was one of many from the time. Detailing the girl's sudden disappearance. Callum didn't need to read it to know what it said.

The Wyatt family had lived in a house on the cusp of the

rainforest. Father and son had gone on an extended camping trip for nearly two weeks.

Amelia had been napping, and Pip was sitting on the veranda with a book and the back sliding door open so she could hear her should she wake. The next thing Pip recalled was opening her eyes in the near dark, back door still open and no Amelia in the house.

Or anywhere.

Her doll had been found at the start of the rainforest track.

And so the search began. Hours turned into days. Weeks passed and rumours blossomed.

*Brett returned.*

*An accident gone wrong.*

*Swiped at Pip and got Amelia.*

*Dropped her body between two boulders.*

A weight settled in Callum's chest as he thought about the stories relayed through Eddy's parents to his own. His cheeks burned hot.

Of course, there were other stories too.

*She heard the call, the whispering. Wandered off into the rainforest herself.*

Snatches of the rhyme danced through his mind.

*The whispering wild will take your child if you dare to look away ...*

Pip had looked away. She'd fallen asleep.

*When she hears the call, she will meet her fall, never again to play ...*

Kids back then didn't wear the bracelets; there was nothing to drown out the sound.

*Winds from the boulders will snatch and hold her, where forever she will lay.*

Had there been winds? He couldn't recall if he'd read about the weather. It had been wet season though, so possibly.

But Brett had an alibi: Lachie. Lachie who'd never said otherwise. Lachie who'd only been a teenager and terrified of his dad. Terrified for his mum.

And then they'd found the body.

The weight in Callum's chest grew and he banished all thoughts of children and whispering winds. He dropped the newspaper clipping on the desk in front and rubbed his hands on his thighs.

Two other items lay in the open lockbox. The first was a letter in a sealed envelope of thick beige card. It was weighty, with more than just words. He'd never read it, never gone so far as to open it.

He placed it down, face up, a single name printed across its front in shaky writing.

The final item in the box was an A4 piece of paper folded in thirds. He picked it up and a wave of grief washed over him. He'd been holding it back for days. For years.

Unfolded, an official form from the registry of births, deaths and marriages lay open in his hands. The names shone from the page.

*Mother: Pippa Edith Wyatt (nee: Dyer)*
*Father: Callum Robert Haffenden*

His vision blurred and he snapped the paper closed before he could make out the letters of the third name. He squeezed his eyes shut. He knew exactly what it said. A heaviness had settled behind them. He blinked a few times, to clear his vision, and turned back to the worn newspaper image on the desk. One hand reached out and traced the outline of a face, as he'd done many times before. A familiar urge to pull back and not fade the photo further battled with an overwhelming desire to be closer. To touch, to connect to the child he'd never met.

His son, Lachie.

# CHAPTER TWENTY-THREE

*Thirty years earlier*

Pip's undies were plain black, her bra light blue with little white flowers on the front. She smiled at me before she turned and dashed for the creek, leaving her shorts and t-shirt on the bank.

I peeled my shirt off my sweaty chest and quickly pulled my shorts down. My old jocks sagged a bit and I hoped she didn't turn around. I ran after her.

The air around us already felt thicker, sticky almost. There'd been a shift in the seasons the last few days. It was hard to pinpoint exactly when it'd happened. But sure enough, somewhere over the last week or so, it'd gone from tourist weather to freakin' disgusting. Warm sun and blue skies had been replaced with low-hanging clouds and air so thick you could almost eat it with a spoon.

The creek was pretty still, the water not too high yet. Even in the middle, I could still touch the bottom with the tips of my toes. The mossy rocks were slippery though, so I treaded water instead.

I looked at Pip, floating on her back, her eyes closed. A long scratch shone on the top of her chest, red and angry, the skin around it a mottled brown. I wanted to ask her about it. Didn't really have to though.

Last night, after dinner, Dad had received a call. He was the only cop in town, so it was normal to get calls at all hours. Usually just brawls at Cutters that the barman couldn't handle. But sometimes it was different.

This time, Dad's voice had been soft down the line, reassuring. Kind.

He'd hung up, had a hasty chat to Mum and rushed out to the patrol car. His hushed words to Mum bounced around my head.

'… Dyer house … Amelia worried … Pip … Mum …'

Mum gave me a squeeze on the shoulder and told me to get back to the washing up. After the dishes, the ring of the phone made us jump. Five minutes later, Mum pecked me on the cheek, told me not to watch too much telly and that she'd be back in an hour.

The silent house had done nothing to quieten the thoughts in my head that Pip might not be okay. Neither Mum nor Dad had let anything slip when they'd arrived home two hours later. Just scowled at me for being up past ten thirty. I'd asked about Pip, of course. They hadn't answered.

I felt a wave of relief in the morning when Pip walked into class ten minutes late. She didn't meet my eye, shrugged me off when I tried to talk to her. When anyone tried to talk to her.

Another jolt of relief shot through me when I found a note telling me to meet her at the track after class. It'd been scrawled on a scrap of lined paper ripped from an exercise book and taped to the back of a firmer A4 piece of paper that she'd managed to slot through the side of my locker. I flipped the paper over and my breath caught.

It was a drawing.

A golden bowerbird.

Its beak was a bit too curved and its legs a little too long. But it was definitely a bowerbird.

Our bowerbird.

Pip floated on her back in the creek, the blue of her bra breaking the surface. 'Stop staring at me, bird boy.' Her lips hitched at the corners.

'Your eyes are closed, how do you know I'm staring?'

She smiled, sank down under the water and disappeared from view. A moment passed, a few bubbles surfacing, closing in on me. She came up, our bodies almost touching. Her bare legs bumped against mine.

'Were you staring?'

I shrugged. 'I might've been.'

A smile and she closed the distance between us, her arms wrapping around my neck. Her lips pressed against mine and her tongue dived into my mouth. Our bodies locked together and we sank below the surface, the sound of the rippling water and the birds gone in an instant.

I kissed her back for a moment before she pushed me away. We both resurfaced, gasping for air, and the gold in her eyes caught mine before she swam back to the shore.

A few minutes later we sat, dripping wet, on the bridge of boulders that spanned the creek. I used to think of the two banks as the safe side of the creek and the who-the-hell-knows side. Now there was the safe side and the Pip side.

We sat closer to the Pip side.

The who-the-hell-knows side felt like the right side.

I turned to her. Her freckles stood out against her skin and her face was expressionless. Flat.

'You all right?'

She blinked, the spell broken. 'Yeah.'

'No, you're not. What's up?'

She gnawed her bottom lip, kept her eyes forward. Green eyes, the same colour as the wings of the green-backed honeyeater. 'Amelia.'

I nodded. I knew Amelia from school. School was tiny. Two grades below us and not quite as pretty as Pip. Different. Weird. At least that's what everyone else said.

Trouble. That's also what everyone else said.

No dad. Drunk mum.

Pierced nose and dyed black hair. Wagged school. Smoked. Trouble.

Eddy had heard she'd hooked up with Stanley Rushton in our year, let him finger her in the sports shed and flashed him her tits. I told him that it was probably a load of shit. Stanley Rushton was full of shit and, given the state of his acne, Amelia Dyer could definitely do better.

I dunno, she seemed all right. Kept to herself mostly. Like Pip.

And Pip never spoke about her. Kicked Stanley in the nuts though when she heard what he'd said about her sister.

'Is she okay?'

'She heard me and Mum fighting.' Pip looked up, glared. 'I'm just so sick of it. Of her. Of the drinking.'

I nodded, my tongue too big in my mouth. This was new territory. I didn't know what to say. She never spoke about her family. Not Amelia. Not her mum's drinking.

'We were yelling. Mum threw a few things. I threw some things back.' Her hand reached absently to the scratch on her chest. 'One of us broke a window and I told Mum I wished she was dead.' She blinked a few times, swallowed. 'She told me that she would've been better off if she'd never had me. Should've had an abortion when she'd found out.'

'I'm sorry—'

'That's not why I'm upset.' A sniff. 'I told her that I wished I was dead too.' She turned to me. 'And Amelia heard. I didn't even realise she was there.' She blinked, a trail of tears ran down her cheeks.

'Oh shit.'

*What the hell? Did Pip actually wish she was dead?*

'You don't though, do you?'

'What? Wish I was dead?' She shook her head once. 'Nah. I'm almost eighteen so I can piss off outta this town soon and never look back.'

We sat in silence, eyes forward. I'd tried not to think too much about the end of the year. But it was creeping up and soon enough we'd be done with high school and most kids would move south. Me included. I'd wondered what Pip had planned. We hadn't really talked too much about the future.

'Now Amelia won't freakin' talk to me. She's angry. Thinks I'm going to fling myself off the boulders or slit my wrists or something.'

My body stiffened.

'I'm not,' she said. 'And I'll take her with me when I ditch this dump, I've told her that. My aunt said we can stay with her in Townsville. She didn't realise how bad things were with Mum till she came up to visit last holidays. Said we should stay till I finish grade twelve, then we can both move down. Amelia can do senior school there and I can, I dunno, work or something.'

I nodded along, happy. Townsville was one of my options for next year too. Either there or Brisbane. That's where the police academies were, where I was heading.

'Maybe I'll learn to dive and get a job on the reef.' Her voice perked up.

I laughed. 'Have you ever scuba-dived before?'

'No, but it can't be that hard and I'll just lure the tourists in with my winning charm.' She flashed me a smile. What'd felt like a fist around my chest loosened. I slung my arm around her.

'So Townsville?' I said. 'Maybe we'll both end up there then.'

'Constable Haffenden, eh?'

'Well, only for a little while. Then, you know, you'll be able to call me Detective or something like that.'

'Oh, Detective is it then?' She turned to me, looped her arms around my neck and stared me in the eyes. I tried not to look away under her gaze. 'So, Detective, can you detect what I'm thinking then?'

I snorted. 'Detective, not psychic.'

She laughed, pulled me close and pressed her lips against mine. It was the kind of full-on kiss where you barely stop for air and you almost feel like you're part of the other person, just for a moment. We were both out of breath by the end.

She wiped the corner of her mouth on the back of one hand, her eyes never leaving mine. 'But I have been thinking, you know. About us.'

*Shit. She's ditching me.*

*No, don't be stupid, she's not ditching you after that kiss.*

'Oh, yeah. About what?' I forced the words out.

'I was thinking, you know, with the end of school coming up and us both leaving this shithole at the end of the year, that maybe we should, you know, go out with a bang or something?'

'What do you mean?'

She shrugged. 'Do something to make all this extra special.' She waved her arm around. It landed on my thigh. 'So we never forget it.'

My heart, which had only just slowed, picked up pace again. *How the hell could I ever forget any of this?*

'What are you thinking?' My voice sounded higher than I'd wanted.

'You know. Maybe we should ... do it.'

*It? Like, sex? Was she serious?*

A somersault inside.

I shrugged. 'Oh, yeah. Okay. If you want.'

'Don't you want to?'

*Shit.* 'Of course I do.'

'Good. Well, I mean, we're both almost adults and it'd be nice to ... you know ... together ... before we leave Granite.' Her eyes roamed over my face, searching. 'But if you don't want to, that's okay too.'

'No. I mean, yes. Of course, I want to. I mean what seventeen-year-old guy doesn't, right?' I tried for a smile, but she didn't return it. 'I mean, with you. Yes, of course, I want to. With you.' Words tumbled out. 'I think it's a good idea.' I finished at last and squeezed my lips together to stop another onslaught of verbal diarrhoea that might damage my chances of doing it with Pip.

A moment passed. Then she laughed.

*Oh god.*

'Okay. At the end of the year then. After school finishes.'

My shoulders relaxed. With a quick peck on my lips, she lay down, her head in my lap, her legs stretched out on the boulders, ankles crossed. I twisted my fingers through her long hair and watched her chest rise and fall with each breath.

# CHAPTER TWENTY-FOUR

Tepid water poured over Callum's shoulders and ran down his back as he stood in the shower, his hands against the tiled wall. He wondered if he'd ever be able to wash away the weight of the lie he'd been carrying for what felt like a lifetime.

Lachie was his son. Not Brett's.

There wasn't enough rain in Granite Creek to wash that away. The guilt. The grief. The gaping boulder-sized piece of him that'd been missing since he'd learned he was a father. A father to a boy he'd never met, who became a man he'd never known.

And now never would.

His eyes stung, heavy, and he squeezed them shut against the water that poured down his face. His left stump ached and his right leg was tired, fed up with carrying the burden of his body. He rested his forehead on the shower wall.

Of course, he'd heard Pip was pregnant. He'd been surprised. And it'd been a kick in the guts when Eddy had told him that it was Brett's kid. But by that stage, Pip was already in his past.

No Pip. No police academy. No left leg.

His future had looked bleak, and his present had been filled with prosthesis fittings, intensive physio and sharp white unrelenting pain.

And long dark nights. Snatches of granite and the sensation of pounding rain. And always, he'd wake at 3.24 am, frantically wiping his palms on sweat-drenched sheets, feeling like he was going to drown under the weight of a boulder.

He bent his head as low as he could and wedged it beneath the shower head.

He'd learned the truth about Lachie years after he'd left Granite Creek. Lachie was seventeen by then—the same age Callum had been when he'd lost his leg. An age where you think you're invincible. An age where if some strange bloke came swanning into your life and told you he was your real father you'd tell him to piss off.

He'd justified it to himself countless times. Lachie was almost an adult. Didn't need a new dad. He was fine on his own.

And Pip's instructions had been clear: never contact Lachie.

*He's fine without you. He can't know the truth. No one can. Ever.*

She'd made him promise.

The photo from Tess's house slapped him in the face. Lachie standing with Pip and Brett. His eyes crinkled at the edges and his top lip turned upwards with a smile. His frame was smaller than Brett's. Slighter. Finer. He'd looked like Pip.

He should have done more for him. Lachie may have been seventeen, but he was still a kid. But at the time, he'd felt he'd had no choice. Contact Lachie and all would be lost. It would all be for nothing. Lachie only had one more year to endure with Brett. Then he'd be an adult, able to leave, start fresh.

The thought of Brett—knuckles smarting, face screwed up, spittle flying—in the same house as his—Callum's—son, made his chest ache.

What had Steph said?

*Who knows what happens behind closed doors?*

He thought about what that last year under Brett's roof must've been like for Lachie.

Why hadn't he done more to protect him? He should have at least tried.

Lachie's crumpled and bent body burst into view. Cold, unmoving. Broken.

Callum clenched his teeth, thought of his promise to Pip, and dug his fingers into the tiled wall. Well, Pip was gone, and he could do something now.

Thoughts of the last few days washed over him, and he tried to put them into some sort of order.

A heat up his cheeks as he recalled his hike with Steph that afternoon. The flicker of relief he'd felt when his fingers traced the outline of the bracelet in his pocket now made him cringe.

Jesus, he was as bad as the ten-year-olds.

He thought of Jack, that's who Steph had been talking to. His mind returned to the Wyatt house. To the looks of fear on Tess's and Jack's faces as Brett had arrived. To Steph's face after Brett had left the station.

He turned off the taps and stood for a moment, the last of the water running the length of his body. One hand on the shower door, the other on the wall, he hopped over the lip of the shower and banged his head on the door frame overhead.

'Shit.'

Head smarting, he lowered himself onto the closed toilet seat, his right leg thankful for the break.

No matter which way he looked at it, it was always bloody Brett. Brett and his threats.

*Leave my family alone. Or I'll come after yours.*

Milly. Who else could Brett have meant? But how the hell could he know about Milly? Callum had put as much distance between his past and his future as he could when his squirming, red-faced daughter had arrived.

But small towns talk and his parents were still, even now, in touch with Eddy's dad regularly. Brett would've heard regular updates on Callum's life down south. Callum had heard about Brett's, after all.

He thought back to the snippets he'd overheard his parents discussing over the years after they'd left Granite Creek.

Pip and Brett's son. Their marriage. The arrival of their daughter.

The loss of their daughter.

Then, the loss of Pip.

His eyes burned, heavy. He pressed his thumb and forefinger into them.

First her sister, then her daughter. Maybe everyone was right: it was lucky she wasn't around to see Lachie lost too.

But he refused to believe that Pip was better off.

The thought of losing Milly, of never seeing her again, created a deep ache inside him, a raw need to be with his daughter. The early days had been hard, but they were always going to be. A first-time parent, a single dad. The long nights, the constant crying, the inconsolable child.

But over time she'd changed. She'd grown into a little person, a little girl. His daughter. His world.

A warmth ran through him as he recalled the first time she'd smiled at him, held his hand, looked for him in a playground when she'd fallen over. And all the years since. The laughter, the tears, his irrevocable and unconditional love.

Everything he'd missed with Lachie.

The ache in his chest expanded.

He reached for his glasses and pushed them on. The bathroom window came into focus. Two vertical rectangles of frosted glass. Both small, and only one slid open, moving across the other, making the opening even smaller.

He stared at them for a moment, eyes glazed, until a cog clunked into place.

*Out the bathroom window, I guess.*

Isn't that what Mike had said about the intruder's exit?

He pulled on his jocks and, using his crutches, made his way out of the bathroom.

Images of Mike with his box of keys at reception danced through his head. Mike had access to all the rooms. He thought of Mike's face in the yearbook alongside Lachie's, and the story of Thacker pushed off the boulders.

And Josh. The third friend. Jumped off the boulders, didn't he? At least that's what Mike had said.

Callum's eyes shifted to his cupboard, doors firmly closed, lockbox hidden. Buried. He squinted at the motel room door, as if he could see through the timber and across the car park to the reception office where Mike most likely was.

With a grunt, Callum wedged the desk chair under the door handle and made his way to the bed. He tried his best to ignore the rattle of the garbage bag that was now taped over the broken window and the gaping entrance into his room that it offered.

## CHAPTER TWENTY-FIVE

The night was filled with granite boulders and whispering winds. Images of Lachie lying on his grey deathbed. His cold body against the warm stone. Lachie's face morphed into Milly's and Callum woke in a puddle of sweat and a familiar cool prickle all over his body.

A voice faded from his ears. He grasped at it, but it was swallowed by the howl of the wind outside.

He wiped his palms on the bedsheets.

His eyes were drawn to the patched-up window. The garbage bag had detached at the bottom and was now flapping in the gale that was blowing in.

A figure flashed past the window. Callum sat bolt upright, chest tight, and swung his legs over the edge of the bed. He snatched his glasses off the bedside table.

A few blinks and the dark room and the world visible through the sliver of uncovered window came into focus. Nothing.

His heart hammered and he shifted his weight on the damp sheets.

Just some late straggler from Cutters rushing to get out of the rain.

He blew out a slow breath.

The flapping of the garbage bag grew. He heaved himself off the sinking mattress, his crutches wrapped around his forearms. His stump pulsated with the rush of blood that pooled downwards and, with each laboured step towards the window, he could feel it swell.

With the garbage bag secured as best he could, he headed to the bathroom. His pants lay crumpled, discarded over the edge of the sink the night before. They'd never dry in the cramped musty room. He picked them up.

*Ting. Ting.*

He thrust one hand into the pocket, his fingers grasping blindly until at last he felt the small strip of woven red and blue fabric. It was damp, limp.

He rubbed the bracelet between two fingers.

*Ting. Ting.*

He gave it a squeeze. The fabric wet, as if it'd absorbed the dampness of the rainforest. Steph's voice rang in his ears.

*Kids all wear those ridiculous bracelets now.*

He opened his hand, released the bracelet.

*Ting. Ting.*

The red and blue stared back.

The pieces in his head, their shapes hazy, began to move themselves into place, edges sharpening. He looked out through the bathroom door to his room. It had been ransacked only hours earlier.

*For what?*

Nothing had been taken.

The child's bracelet lay flat in his open palm. Its three silver bells winked at him in the harsh overhead light of the bathroom.

\*

The skin was red and angry. The long scar at the end of Callum's stump was raised and a new shade of purple that he hadn't seen before. Despite a night of sleeping with his left leg elevated, his stump still remained swollen, the skin taut, and he knew—before he'd even bothered trying—that it wasn't going to fit into his prosthesis.

Apparently, his fall yesterday had done more damage than he'd anticipated. The stifling heat of the tropics hadn't done much to aid the swelling either and he felt an unexpected rush of gratitude towards his parents, who'd had the foresight to move the family south after his accident.

As if yesterday hadn't been a shit enough day. Slashed car tyres. Ransacked motel room. Panic attack. And Steph. His cheeks burned and he tried to forget the image of her set face as she'd pulled out of the car park after she'd dropped him off.

After she'd leaned in and he'd stupidly pulled away.

A soft knock at the motel room door made him look up.

'Come in.'

Mike cracked the door and stuck his head inside. The wind blew his limp hair across his face. 'Hello?'

'Come on in. Sorry, I can't get up too easily.' Callum nodded to his inflamed leg, which was elevated on his overnight bag.

Mike pushed the door closed against the wind. 'Just saw the mechanic leaving. Tyres fixed at last, eh?' Without waiting for a response, he plonked a large white ice-cream bucket on the desk, his eyes fixed on Callum's stump. 'Yikes, looks bad.'

'It is.' He propped himself further up the bed and was rewarded with a hot, white stab of pain.

'Room's looking a bit tidier. Sorry I couldn't move you last night. We're still booked up. I've called around to see if I can get someone to fix that up today. Our usual bloke's outta action. Well, you know that.'

Callum pulled his eyebrows together.

'Brett.' Mike finally pulled his eyes off Callum's leg. 'He usually does all the patchin' up round here. But, well, you know, with everything that's happening with that family at the moment, he mightn't get here today.'

'Brett's your maintenance guy?'

'Yeah. And his old man before him.'

Of course, why the hell hadn't he thought of that? Hadn't Steph said Brett had been fixing a so-called leak at the station?

'Look,' Mike continued. 'I know the guy's a prick, but it's slim pickings round here. Granite's not like it used to be. Not as many tradies as there were when my dad ran this joint. Brett's a bit of an all-rounder. Gets the job done well enough and doesn't charge me an arm and a leg.' His eyes shifted to Callum's leg and a redness crept up his neck. He looked away, nodded to the overhead light. 'Fixed your power the other night.'

'Brett fixed it?'

'Yeah, I know.' Mike shook his head. 'The sparky's been caught up all week. These winds are causing havoc with everyone's bloody power. Brett said he'd have a look, even though, you know, they'd just found out about Lachie. Said he wanted the distraction.' His eyes ferreted around the dimly lit room. 'Good job too, otherwise you'd still be in the dark.'

'So, Brett was in my room?'

'Yeah. Like I said, he's our maintenance guy. Been in all the rooms at some stage or another.'

'Were you with him?'

'In here? Nah, why would I be?'

A cool sweat washed over Callum.

Brett had been in his room. When? He racked his memory. Too much had happened since he'd arrived in Granite Creek and the timeline of events no longer felt linear. When had Brett been in here? Had Mike checked the room afterwards? Had Brett been the one to search his room? Maybe smash the window as a cover for a break-in?

His eyes flashed to the closed wardrobe.

'What time was Brett in here?'

Mike shrugged. 'Dunno. I think in the arvo sometime.'

'Can you be more specific?'

Mike gnawed his bottom lip, red and blistered. 'Maybe four-ish?'

'Four?'

'Or three. I dunno.' His eyes flickered to the door. 'Look, I brought you that ice and bag you wanted.' He pulled a plastic shopping bag out of his pocket, put it down beside the ice-cream bucket on the desk and made to reach for the door.

'Sorry, would you mind bringing it over here?'

Mike flushed. His eyes fell on Callum's red stump again, before quickly shifting away. He scooped up the container of ice and brought it to the bed along with the empty shopping bag, his eyes fixed on the end of Callum's leg.

Amputations were like eclipses to most people with four limbs: they knew they weren't meant to stare, but the temptation was too strong.

'Thanks,' Callum said as Mike handed him the container.

Callum's heart dropped. Melted brown slush wasn't going to fare too well as a makeshift icepack. A red bottle cap bobbed on the surface. His mind shifted gears.

'Hey, the camera outside …' He nodded his head towards the closed door. The force of the wind made it rattle in its frame. 'Can I get a copy of the footage? Might show who broke in.' He detected the note of hopefulness in his own voice.

'Ah …' Mike shifted, his body angled towards the door, one hand already extended. 'It's faulty. Doesn't work. Just for show.' His words rolled on top of each other, his eyes fixed on the handle.

Not waiting for a response, he opened the door. A gust of wind almost blew him back in. He pushed his wiry frame into the onslaught, pulling the door firmly shut behind him.

Eyes on the closed door, Callum's mind ticked over. Mike in his room last night; the bathroom window too small; the lock on the front door undisturbed. Mike had said he'd been in the next room. Had he had the key to Callum's room with him? He recalled flicking the light switch. Why hadn't Mike turned the lights on when he'd first entered?

He strained his ears. Over the flapping of the garbage bag, he heard the rain as it lashed against the wall of the building, against the door and the window's plastic covering. After three days, the rain had become a constant thrum. Background noise. But it was still there. Loud as hell. Had Mike really been able to hear a break-in from the next room?

He removed his glasses and pressed his thumb and index finger into his closed eyes, trying to put some order to the congestion in his head.

One thing was certain: broken CCTV cameras didn't have blinking red lights.

# CHAPTER TWENTY-SIX

'So, Brett was in your room yesterday?' Eddy sat at his desk, hands interlaced behind his head. 'It's hardly suspicious if he's the motel's maintenance guy.'

Callum raised an eyebrow. 'Not suspicious? Come on, it's Brett. Besides, what the hell's he doing working two days after his son's been found dead?' The words soured in his mouth.

Eddy shrugged. 'Paying his mortgage? Keeping his mind off it?'

Callum rolled his eyes.

'Tell me more of this Mike business.'

'It's what I've already told you. He just seems ... fishy.'

'I need something a little stronger than *fishy* to go off.'

'You know what I mean. The stuff about not knowing Lachie. Now this stuff about the CCTV not working. And him in my room, in the dark, window broken. You know.' He waggled his eyebrows. 'Fishy.'

'Well, we'll start with the CCTV stuff first. If it is working, it's probably not monitored by a security company. There's not too many services out this far north and they can be pretty pricey anyway. By the looks of the motel, I'd be surprised if that was in their budget.'

Callum snorted. 'I don't think new sheets are in their budget.'

'So, if that's the case, the footage might be recorded and kept at the motel. The more modern cameras send their videos straight up to the cloud.'

'It looked pretty archaic to me.'

Eddy nodded. 'So, we have to rely on Mike giving it up then.'

'He's not likely to do that, especially if it's going to show him breaking into my room.' Callum paused. He knew the answer to his next question before he even asked it. 'Could you get a warrant?'

'Probably not. With nothing taken and no damage, aside from the window, there's no grounds for it. The only person technically affected was Mike, and if he's not wanting to chase it up, there's not much that can be done.'

'What about my emotional trauma?'

'Sorry, mate. Not enough.'

Callum drummed his fingers on the desk.

'You can't decide if it was Brett or Mike, can you? Or maybe they're in cahoots with each other?' A small smile played across Eddy's lips. It vanished as soon as it came. 'I still can't believe you didn't phone me last night. What were you thinking?'

'It was nothing.'

'Your room was ransacked.'

'They didn't take anything.'

'Doesn't matter.' Eddy's features were firm. 'You slept all night with a broken window. They could've come back. After your tyres and with the threats that have been coming through here. Most of them include you, you know?' He sighed. 'You should've called me, that's all I'm saying. You could've spent the night at my place.'

The vertical line that ran between Eddy's eyebrows stood out, a dark crevice carving its way through his forehead. Had it actually become deeper these last three days?

Things couldn't have been easy for him this last week. New job. Dead body. Hostile town. Callum thought of Bill and the paramedic being called out to the Quade house; he added ageing father to the list. The last thing Eddy needed was a sleepless night investigating a break-in and a limping house guest on his couch.

The silence stretched.

A heat rose up Callum's neck. 'You're right. I should've called you.'

A pause, then a nod from Eddy. 'Any idea what they were after?'

Callum sank his teeth into his bottom lip. 'Maybe.'

'Maybe?'

Callum dug his hand into his damp pocket. 'Maybe this.' He slapped the woven bracelet down onto the desk between them.

*Ting. Ting.*

The soft tinkle cut over the groan of the air conditioner.

Eddy's eyebrows drew in and he leaned forward and scooped up the strip of fabric. 'What is it?'

'A friendship bracelet.'

Eddy cocked one eyebrow.

'Apparently the kids wear them. To ward off the whispering.' His mouth felt dry as he spoke, a chill down the back of his neck. 'The bells are meant to drown out the sound.'

'You think someone broke into your room for a soggy old piece of twine?'

'Nothing was taken, and I had this on me.'

Eddy placed the bracelet back down and clunked away at his keyboard; he'd insisted on completing a break-in report.

Callum thought a minute, almost didn't speak. 'Brett knows I have it. He saw me with it at the pub.'

'Enough with this Brett business. Where'd you find it?'

Callum ignored the question. 'I thought you said that kids didn't hang out around the boulders anymore.'

'Did you find it near the boulders?'

'Well, no. Just at the start of the old walking track.'

'So nowhere near the boulders then.'

'But I did see a kid out there yesterday.' Or two kids. The image was still fuzzy in his mind.

Eddy sat back in his chair, break-in report momentarily forgotten. He blew out a long breath. 'Look, mate, I need to talk to you about that.' He looked squarely at Callum. 'You can't go doing that again, okay?'

Callum swallowed, held Eddy's gaze.

'Steph told me about your adventure. It's not okay.'

'Because I'm a cripple?'

Eddy flinched at the word and Callum immediately regretted it. It was a low blow. Eddy had never treated him any differently than he did anybody else.

'Yes, actually. And no, also.' Eddy leaned forward, resting his arms on the desk. 'Like I told you last time, there's a bloody cyclone coming. There's going to be enough grief for me over the next few days if it hits. I've already had to hit the ground running with all this Lachie business. Last thing I need is to be traipsing after you because you've gone off into the rainforest on a whim.'

'It wasn't a whim.'

'Then what?'

Callum hesitated. 'I don't know. A feeling.'

'Same thing.'

There was no point in arguing. He sounded like a petulant child, even to himself. But why the hell didn't Eddy get it?

The two of them continued to look at each other. Though the laughter lines around the edges of his friend's eyes now seemed to be a permanent feature, Callum struggled to recall if he'd seen Eddy laugh, or even smile, these last few days.

After a while, Eddy sighed. 'Just promise me you're not gonna head out there again, okay?'

'Okay, okay.' Callum raised both hands up.

Eddy, satisfied, turned back to his computer. 'Still,' he said as he tapped away at the keyboard, 'last night was a break-in and you should've reported it. Or Mike should've.'

'See, fishy again,' Callum said. 'I'm here now though, aren't I?'

'You're here because I phoned and asked you to come in.'

Callum's eyes roamed the office, waiting for Eddy to finish the report. The box of his friend's stuff was still sitting in the corner, the leaves of the peace lily now drooping over the box's edge.

Steph gave a soft laugh outside. In on a Sunday, mostly redirecting the concerned citizens of Granite Creek to the SES or to the town hall to collect sandbags.

He hadn't told Eddy about the bank statements he'd seen in Steph's car. He wasn't sure why. He wanted to be certain of … he didn't know what … before he brought it up with Eddy.

Or Steph.

The thought of the statements triggered a memory.

'How'd you go with Lachie's bank statements and phone records?' he asked.

'Bank statements were easy enough to get. Still waiting on phone records.' Eddy reached down into his drawer and pulled out a manila folder. He opened it and Callum's breath caught as he braced himself for the photos of Lachie's mangled, crumpled body to appear. His shoulders eased as Eddy slid several sheets of stapled paper across the desk.

He scanned the document, trying to ignore the bright yellow logo in the top corner. It was the same institution that Steph used.

So what? Half the country used that bank.

He focused his eyes, and didn't have to look for long before he spotted what he was searching for.

He moved the papers back towards Eddy, pointing to several lines near the top of the statement. 'He spent twelve hundred dollars on fishing gear a week ago and he paid nearly nine hundred to a hotel company only two days before he died. I bet that's for the boys' weekend. It was on the calendar, remember? Hardly going to splash out on extravagant purchases if you're planning on knocking yourself off a few days later.'

Eddy looked at it. 'I knew you'd think that.'

'You don't think that?'

Eddy shrugged. 'Honestly, mate. I'm not sure what I think.' He leaned back in his chair again. 'But the hotel booking's easy enough to check out.'

'So, Tess gave these bank statements up willingly?'

'Willingly enough. She wanted to know why I wanted them.'

'Not exactly the friendliest of ladies.'

'Her husband did just die.'

'Pushed off the boulders by her father-in-law.'

'Cal.'

He raised his hands again, palms forward. 'Have you heard much about her?'

'Mate, I've been back in Granite only a few days longer than you.' Eddy pressed his fingers to his temples. 'What sort of stuff are you thinking I may have heard?'

Callum thought back to his encounter with Tess on the street the day before. Something skimmed the edge of his mind, like wings brushing by. 'Don't know.'

Eddy clicked his mouse a few times and a printer behind him whirred to life, Steph's voice trilling over the top from the front reception.

Her smile at Callum when he'd entered the station earlier had been unrestrained. She had the phone wedged between her ear and shoulder, her hands occupied as they flew across her keyboard. Callum had tried to ignore the flutter in his chest at the sight of her grin. He had a flash of her leaning over the gearstick, towards him. He pushed the image aside and instead tried to be thankful that she was on the phone, and he didn't have to find the words to say to her.

'Sign here, mate.' Eddy's voice brought Callum back as he slid the completed break-in report across the desk.

Callum signed, barely registering the document as his eyes flicked to the woven bracelet. He thought of the school, the yearbooks open with the faces of Lachie, Mike and Josh beaming up at him.

'What came of Thacker from the school? Any luck there?' he asked.

Eddy gave a nod. 'Tracked him down easily enough. Living in Adelaide. Wife and two kids. Sons.'

'Jesus.'

'That's not the worst of it. He's working at some boys' grammar school as head of PE.'

Callum's stomach rolled. 'How the hell did he manage that?'

'No charges were ever pressed. He doesn't have a record. It was his word against a bunch of twelve-year-olds.'

Callum shook his head. He couldn't speak.

'The best's still to come though. I phoned the school where he works. It's school holidays but they're open for admin. Apparently the teachers had an all staff meeting on Tuesday but Thacker wasn't able to make it. On holiday, got some last-minute flights with Qantas.'

'Where?' Callum's voice sounded distant, even to himself.

'Wanted a reef and rainforest experience.'

A jolt in his chest. 'You're kidding?'

'Nope. Whole family are on holiday in Cairns. I don't know when they flew in yet.'

'Shit.'

Callum could hear Steph moving about in the kitchen next door and his mind ticked back to his conversation with her at the pub. 'Didn't he get the shit beaten out of him for it?'

'Not sure. I can look it up, but if no charges were pressed, there mightn't be any record of it ... When was it again? Eighteen years ago? How long can someone hold a grudge for?'

'How long's a piece of string?'

Before Eddy could answer, Steph bustled into the room with two mugs of coffee. 'Sorry I took so long to bring them. That phone's been going non-stop.'

'Anything urgent?' Eddy's worry line was back.

'Mostly reporting damage from the winds. I'm redirecting the bulk of it to the SES. I think people get us confused.' She smiled. 'But I'm not trekking out in this weather to help heave a fallen tree off the road or deliver more sandbags.'

She paused as she placed the mugs on the table. Her smile vanished; eyes fixed on the friendship bracelet on the desk between Callum and Eddy.

'Where'd you get this?' She picked it up.

*Ting. Ting.*

'Cal found it out—'

'At the school. I was there yesterday. Found it in the yard on my way out.'

'Great.' She pocketed the bracelet. 'Noah's been looking for it all week. He's just like the others.' An exaggerated eye roll. 'All worried about the whispering.'

A smile played across her lips as Callum and Eddy watched her leave the office, the door snapping closed behind her.

# CHAPTER TWENTY-SEVEN

After leaving the police station, Callum's grumbling stomach sent him to the Cane Cutters' Tavern for lunch. The place was bustling. Many of the faces looked familiar. Search party members and fellow motel residents. A few nodded in recognition. One or two averted their eyes. An older man at the bar gave him an outright glare from under his cap. Brett's mate from two days ago, likely the culprit behind some of the threatening messages on the police station's phone. Callum gave him a nod and smiled.

*Screw you, you prick.*

Another figure, hunched in front of a half-filled pint further along the bar, stood out. A silver stud glinted through long greasy hair, a ferrety face: Mike. Callum waited at the bar as the barman poured his beer. He turned his head towards Mike, whose eyes were concentrated on the counter in front.

He couldn't be sure, but he felt the motel manager was intentionally avoiding his gaze.

Two light beers, an overcooked steak and seventeen phone calls later, and most of the crowd had died off, only a few afternoon drinkers remaining. Callum didn't plan to stay in Granite Creek too much longer, but his daily beer intake certainly needed to drop.

He sat with his phone pressed against his ear as he scrawled on the back of a damp cardboard coaster.

'Okay, thanks for your time.' He clicked the phone off and put a cross through the name of the hotel on his list.

Several decades as a journalist had given him a certain finesse when it came to uncovering the truth. Two kids and the crumbs of a teacher's salary had narrowed the hundreds of accommodation options in Cairns down to just thirty-four. He pushed aside the slight twinge of guilt he felt as he dialled the next hotel.

'Hello there, my name is Carl Lambert. I'm trying to track down my colleague, Simon Thacker. He works with me at Saint Paul's Grammar down in Adelaide. I have some rather distressing news about one of his students. He's not answering his phone and I was hoping to get in touch with him before he heard about the events on the news ... Yes, horrible accident. The entire staff are very shaken up ... I can't say anything about it though. You understand, the family needs their privacy ... I'm sure this is where he said he was staying ... What's that? No Simon Thacker checked in at your hotel? Oh no, I must've got the name wrong. Thanks all the same.'

His pen tip tore through the coaster. Another cross through the shortening list. Over halfway.

He stretched out his leg beneath the table. His prosthesis tapped the leg of the empty chair opposite him and sent a sharp stab into his stump.

He closed his eyes as he bit back the pain. His leg looked like a warning picture from the back of a packet of cigarettes.

*Don't smoke, or you too could have a festering stump.*

The few hours of elevation and icing he'd managed this morning had done little to alleviate the pulsating red mass. He'd swallowed back the bile as he'd all but jammed it into the socket of his prosthesis. A few sickening steps to the motel room door and he'd turned back to retrieve a single elbow crutch and down a handful of paracetamol tablets.

The skin pulled taut now as he bent and flexed his swollen knee and listened to the dial tone on his mobile. A monotone voice answered, welcoming him to the next mid-budget hotel: the Reef Inn.

The same sob story and, several moments later, the clerk on the other line had promised to get Simon Thacker to phone Carl Lambert back as soon as he arrived back from his croc encounter at the wildlife centre.

'Oh wonderful, thank you so much,' Callum said after he'd given a phone number off the top of his head with the South Australian area code. 'Oh, and also, just while I've got you on the line, I couldn't remember what day Simon went to Cairns. It's just that the family of the poor boy wanted to know if he was one of the teachers who went with their son on the cricket camp last week. They're wanting to do a memorial photo for the coach and teachers who were present. As it was Zane's last time ...' He swallowed audibly before continuing. 'They need to organise it with the printers today. Could you tell me when he checked in? That should clarify it for us.'

The tip of Callum's pen pressed through the soggy coaster as he jotted the date down. He hung up. A small flutter began in his chest and gradually transformed into the resounding beating of wings.

Hadn't Steph told him that Thacker had got the living daylight beaten out of him? And though Eddy hadn't been able to find a record of it, a local was as good as a recorded document when it came to a scandal in a small town.

He looked back down at the coaster. The Thacker family had flown into Cairns two days before Lachie was reported missing.

*How long can someone hold a grudge for?* Eddy had asked him.

Eighteen years perhaps?

\*

Callum paid his bill at the pub and stepped outside to a main street shrouded in a grey blanket. The clouds, heavy and full, appeared to have sunk and now hovered just above the rooftops. Pressing down, closing in.

The rain landing on the tin overhang of Cutters veranda was almost loud enough to drown out his thoughts.

The idea of Thacker dragging his wife and two kids from Adelaide to the far north to commit murder seemed a little far-fetched. Even to Callum.

And why only kill Lachie? What about Mike? If it was all just a messed-up story made up by a group of vindictive twelve-year-olds, then surely Mike would be as guilty as Lachie?

The questions tumbled over each other in his mind, and the scenario of Thacker tracking Lachie into the rainforest to knock him off seemed more and more unlikely the longer he thought about it.

Eighteen years was a long time.

He shifted his weight onto his left leg and a sharp jab of pain, familiar for three decades, cut through his thoughts. Maybe eighteen years wasn't that long after all.

The street was deserted, not even the odd person ducking in or out of shops to brave the torrent. His eyes landed two doors down from the pub, where the bottle shop had its door firmly shut. Sandbags lined its exterior, soldiers ready for battle.

A long-forgotten memory rushed into view. Callum in this very spot, maybe aged eight or nine, waiting for his dad to finish talking to the barman about a particularly messy brawl that had played out the night before. It must've been school holidays if he'd been shadowing his dad during the day.

The door to the bottle shop had swung open and Rita Dyer stumbled out, thongs scuffing, plastic bag swinging. The glass door went to slam shut behind her and a small hand had caught it, pressed it open. A short blonde-haired girl stepped out, turned to follow her mother.

Amelia.

Rita stopped a few metres from Callum, surveyed the pub. She pulled out a packet of cigarettes, lit one up and blew a puff of smoke directly at him. He looked away.

'Hurry up, girl,' she snapped.

Amelia pulled up alongside her mum. Maybe six years old, though she looked even younger. Feet bare, her pale skin matched the colour her dress would've once been.

'Stop draggin' ya feet.' Rita spun around, smacked Amelia across the shoulder with her plastic bag, the clank of glass bottles within. 'Take this and hurry the hell up.' Amelia took the bag and, eyes cast down, followed her mum along the footpath. The weight of the bag made her lopsided and the few people on the street, avoiding the first spittings of rain, gave the pair a wide berth, averting their eyes.

Callum had watched them until they'd disappeared from view.

The rain now came down in sheets and he blinked a few times before he tore his eyes from the sandbagged door of the bottle shop. Amelia Dyer. She'd looked miserable that day. Most days. He shook his head, let the image of the sad girl with the stained dress and bare feet fade.

He was unsure of his next move, and his eyes settled on the motel across the road as a large man with a wild ginger beard ducked out of reception and headed underneath the awning, presumably towards a motel room.

The thought of Callum's own room, damp, with its taped-up window did little to lure him. The car park was still full, and a white ute was double-parked out the front of the reception. Even through the rain Callum was able to make out the words 'Wyatt and Sons Handyman' plastered in bold letters on the side.

The air around him thickened and his throat tightened as he thought of Brett in his room, fixing the window. Metres from his lockbox; from the truth.

He took a gulp of heavy air and, without further thought, stepped out into the rain and onto the road. Water soaked his right shoe. He stopped as Brett's hulking figure emerged from the motel's main reception building and, shoulders rounded against the rain, headed with long strides to the ute.

Callum watched, the rain cascading down him as heavily as if he were in the shower. With his hand resting on the ute's door handle, Brett paused. After a moment, he turned straight on to face Callum. Brett shifted his weight as if to cross the road and Callum felt his body stiffen in response.

Fight or flight.

He planted himself firmly. Gripped his crutch in his right hand.

The wind picked up and whipped along the main street, sending palm fronds and debris skittering along the ground between the two men. Brett's earlier words rolled across him.

*Leave my family alone, or I'll come after yours.*

He swallowed, his mouth dry. Milly was safe, thousands of kilometres away.

Brett's mouth opened and closed, words lost, snatched by the wind. The shake of a buzz cut head and Brett threw open his ute door. Without a backwards glance, he climbed into the cab and slammed the door behind him.

Callum flinched and his leg gave a stab.

# CHAPTER TWENTY-EIGHT

Callum hadn't thought that the sound of rain lashing against a window could be considered pleasant. However, after a night of listening to the flap of a garbage bag, it was somewhat settling.

He wasn't sure which appealed to him less: having only a garbage bag to separate his room from the outside world, or that Brett had again been in his room to fix it.

He'd watched as Brett's ute drove all the way down the main street and took a left towards the outer edges of town and the rainforest. Ignoring his shaky legs, he forced himself back up the gutter to stand under the pub's awning. He gave himself a moment for his breath to slow and pushed thoughts of Brett's threats out of his mind.

How much did Brett know? Nothing. He couldn't know anything. Pip would never have told him.

A flicker of red caught Callum's eye.

On the underside of the veranda just in front of the pub door was a small CCTV camera, angled to capture the comings and goings. Two short steps and he stood directly beneath it, his back flush against the pub wall. He assessed the camera's angle and turned his body in the same direction. The motel and its cramped car park were directly in front, the illuminated 'No Vacancies' sign flickering in the growing gloom.

Thirty minutes later, with his laptop open and resting on his bare thighs, he was reclining on his bed in his jocks. His last pair of semi-clean trousers hung over the back of the chair, in what he was certain would be a failed attempt to dry them out.

The owner of the pub had been happy to hand over the footage after he'd heard what had happened to both Callum's car and room.

'Don't need more trouble round 'ere. Bad for business. Probably some riffraff from outta town. Place has been chockers since Lachie was stupid enough to get himself killed.' He'd shaken his head and not bothered to lower his voice, the few remaining patrons looking their way. 'Don't know if you'll get much of a shot of the motel though. But, still, you're welcome to it.' He'd given Callum a toothless smile as he'd slung a filthy tea towel over his shoulder and handed over a USB stick.

The shot wasn't the best. In fact, it was bloody crap. Callum felt a jab of disappointment when he flicked the video on and realised that the motel wasn't at all in view. A pixelated black-and-white image of the footpath and street directly in front of the pub was easily visible. The faces of the patrons coming and going, however, were not. The angle of the camera was too high to capture them, and instead it showed the tops of heads and shoulders. Akubras, caps and bald scalps.

He flicked through the footage, unsure what he was searching for. Even if he spotted Brett coming or going from the pub around the time his motel room was broken into, it proved nothing, except that Brett was around this part of town at the time and enjoyed a drink as much as the next bloke.

Still, he stared at his laptop screen as if in some sort of trance. The pub's security footage only dated back one week, he'd been told. After that, it began to record back over the top of the previous footage. It was a standard system and wasn't Callum's first time sifting through hours of footage on fast play. He'd learned early on in his career that if you wanted to find something out, you had to trudge through the shit yourself. Unfortunately that often involved long hours sitting on your arse staring at a screen.

The street outside the pub remained deserted for long stretches. Figures would flash across the screen, few and far between. He hit pause and rewound the footage, leaned into the laptop. Despite the poor angle, he recognised several people and had no doubt that the owner would be able to tell him who every single patron was that crossed his door based on this grainy video.

He yawned and ran his finger over the mousepad, slowing the footage, as a couple of uniformed firefighters entered the building. He recognised the bald head of one of them from the pub three days earlier: the man with the walrus moustache. Another, however, stood out; unfamiliar. Though the angle of the camera didn't capture their faces, a set of narrow shoulders and a high ponytail identified the unknown firefighter as a woman.

He paused the video, dumped his laptop on the damp sheets and threw his legs over the edge of the bed. He rubbed his jawline, the roughness beneath his hands unfamiliar. Had he already been back in Granite Creek three days? The days were blurring together. It felt like only hours ago that he'd seen the headline about Lachie missing in the rainforest, yet somehow, he felt as if he'd been drenched to the bone for a lifetime.

The throb below his left knee intensified as he made his way to the bathroom with the help of a crutch. Standing lopsided, and with one hand propped on the wall above the toilet, thoughts of the last few days rolled through his head.

Brett's threats. Tess's fear. Steph's lies.

And Lachie.

Smiling Lachie from the news footage. Family man Lachie from Tess's house. Teenage Lachie from the yearbook. Crumpled Lachie wedged between two boulders. Dead.

He shook his head, thrust the images away.

Back in bed he flicked the laptop back to life.

He hit the rewind button on the CCTV footage: people whizzed over his screen in reverse at a speed that rendered the figures no longer recognisable. His eyes were trained on the date and time ticking backwards in the top right-hand corner. Three days. Four days. Five days ago.

Bingo.

He hit play: 4 pm Tuesday. The day Lachie went missing. He pressed the fast forward button once and watched as the time began to move at double speed. He hit pause.

He didn't know Lachie; had never met him. But there was something familiar about the figure on the screen. This was Pip's son.

His son.

His build matched the photo of Lachie and his parents on Tess's wall. And there was something else. Something more definite. It took Callum a moment to realise what it was. His outfit. A dark t-shirt, a pair of suspenders over his shoulders. He was in his fireman's uniform, straight from work. The same outfit he'd seen in Eddy's office. The same outfit Lachie had worn when he'd plummeted to his death.

Callum reached one hand to the screen, pressed a finger over Lachie's figure as if to hold him in place; to stop the next few hours playing out. Lachie's last few hours.

He let his hand fall and stared at the screen long enough that the image began to blur at the edges and a heaviness took over his eyes. His head began to throb, heavy with the weight of a lifetime of longing, of knowing he should have done more. It pressed against his skull, itching for an escape.

He snatched off his glasses, rubbed his eyes and pushed down the guilt.

What more could he have done?

A deep breath and he replaced his glasses. He flicked through the footage further. The wiry frame and forward-poking head of the man in shot was familiar. As he went to enter the pub, the man turned to look up the road, tilting his head as he did so. The unmistakable glint of an earring reflected in the camera's lens.

Mike.

Another skim through the footage. At 4.52 pm, Lachie left the pub. Head bowed and shoulders rounded, it was hard to tell if he was crestfallen or just preparing for the onslaught of wind and rain.

Callum's hand paused. The mouse hovered over the fast forward button as Lachie's head turned to look up the street. A few seconds passed. Then Lachie moved his arm, rough, fast. An aggressive gesture. Callum sat up straighter and watched as Lachie's head jerked to the side, his arm waving again, almost thrashing. A moment passed before Callum realised what was playing out in front of him: Lachie was arguing with someone standing further up the footpath, out of shot.

Callum squinted at the laptop screen. A trousered leg appeared at the top of the video as the person neared. It was impossible to tell if it belonged to a man or a woman. Lachie stepped forward as if to approach the person off screen. Callum watched as Lachie's fist enclosed around an arm and yanked a figure into view.

Callum jerked in recognition. He leaned forward, squinting. He needed to be certain, hoped he was wrong.

The words from three days ago clawed their way from the depths of his memory. What had her response been when he'd asked if she'd known Lachie?

*No, not really. He was a fair bit younger than me.*

He focused on the screen. The tousled shoulder-length hair, the sculpted shoulders. He watched as Steph ripped her arm from Lachie's grip. She leaned into him and pressed her finger against his chest before she turned and stalked out of view.

# CHAPTER TWENTY-NINE

'How many calls to the police?' Callum had the phone pressed hard to his ear. The rain landing on the roof of his rental car and the groan of the air conditioner muffled Eddy's words at the other end of the line. He'd just been emailed through the phone records for Tess and Lachie's landline.

'Three in three weeks.'

'So, a lot.'

'Yeah. And the thing is, when I asked Tess about it this afternoon, she denied all knowledge. Said it must've been a mis-dial or that the phone company got the records wrong.'

Callum snorted. 'Who the hell accidentally dials triple zero three times in three weeks?'

'No one. And phone companies don't stuff up records. She's lying.'

'You think she made the calls?'

'Who else?' Eddy asked.

'Lachie?'

'Not possible. Well, not for the final call at least.' The sound of papers shuffling from Eddy's end. 'The third call was made the day we found his body.'

The rain on the car roof roared outside, the phone against Callum's ear silent.

'Jack then,' Callum said.

'Yeah, I've thought about that. I asked if I could chat to Jack about it.'

'I bet that went down a treat.'

'Like a bag of bricks.' A hesitation. 'Look, there's something else.'

'Something else—'

'I don't want you to go jumping to any conclusions,' Eddy said.

'You know me, no jumping.'

Another pause. 'The phone records, from Lachie and Tess's house. There were some outgoing calls the week before he died. Someone tried to make some interstate calls.' Eddy cleared his throat. 'To Adelaide.'

'To Thacker?'

'I tracked the number and it's for a hardware store, not Thacker's place or the school he works at.'

'We should call them.'

'I did. They've never heard of him. Or Lachie.' A pause. 'We're barking up the wrong tree with Thacker.'

The line was silent a few moments and Callum watched as a gecko clung to the driver's window of his parked car and made its way along the rain-slicked glass. 'Probably. But he's up here.'

'Cairns, not Granite.'

'Only a two-hour drive in a shitty rental. And he checked into a hotel in Cairns on Monday. What's the likelihood of him being up this way when one of the kids responsible for him getting the daylights beaten out of him and being driven out of town is murdered?'

Eddy hesitated. 'It's coincidental.'

'Still …'

Callum heard Steph's muffled voice through the line, faint. Eddy responded to her, and Callum tried to ignore the churn inside his gut as he waited for their conversation to finish.

He hadn't told Eddy what he'd seen on the pub's CCTV footage. The way Lachie had grabbed Steph's arm. The way she'd snatched it back, stepped towards him and pressed her finger against his chest. What was the meaning of it? Was he threatening her? Or she him?

Although their faces had been obscured, their body language had been clear: hostile.

Why would she have been angry at Lachie? Had she been angry enough to push him? Steph's dimple swam into view. Surely not.

Eddy came back on the line and Callum's thoughts of Steph scattered. 'I have to go. Duty calls.'

'Another feline fiasco?'

A tight laugh. 'Something like that.'

Callum was about to end the call when he remembered why he'd phoned in the first place. 'Hey, just quickly,' he said. 'Any idea how many female firefighters work out at the fire station here?'

'Odd question. But just the one.'

'Know her?'

'Yeah. Paige Sommerby. She was working with us on the search. Nice girl. Young. Pretty new to town.'

Steph was in the background again.

'Gotta go,' Eddy said. 'You'll have to fill me in another time.' He clicked off and the line went dead.

Callum had spent most of the afternoon sifting through the pub's CCTV footage. He'd rewatched the footage of Lachie and Steph until his eyes were heavy and his head had ached. Eventually, he'd decided to flick further along the footage, waiting for Mike to re-emerge.

On the video footage, minutes became hours. Two. Three. Then four hours and forty-seven minutes after Mike had entered the pub, he emerged. He paused, staggering a little in the wind, lit up a smoke and stepped out of shot.

Heavy drinking for a Tuesday.

In Callum's car, the windscreen wipers moved at double speed, the glass still streaked with rain and the view beyond hazy. He was parked outside a squat brick building, its wide roller door up, two large fire trucks inside like a pair of red smudges.

He recalled what Steph had said that first time he'd gone for lunch at Cutters and seen the group of men in their fluorescent yellow pants and navy shirts.

*The whole fire department's here to send him off.*

But not the whole department, he realised. The CCTV footage had shown a group of firefighters entering the pub, one of them with narrow shoulders and a long ponytail. A woman. Conspicuously missing from Lachie's send-off that day.

She might have just drawn the short straw and been left to mind the station, but his mind had reached for the darkest possibility.

He heaved himself out of the rental and gave his leg a moment to adjust to its new straightened position. Biting back a grunt, he closed the distance between the car and the fire station and pulled up alongside one truck, gleaming red with yellow stripes. The words 'Fire and Rescue' plastered along its side. Little except the rain outside was audible. More rescue than fire this time of year.

'Can I help you?' A man, older than Callum, poked his head around from the back of the truck. An impressive walrus moustache and two bristly eyebrows were the only signs of hair on his head. Callum recognised his bald scalp from the CCTV footage and his moustache from his first visit to the pub, guiding Josh Swindley's dad out.

'Oh, hi there.' Callum hitched a smile on his face. 'I was hoping to chat to Paige Sommerby. She around?'

A brief pause, then a nod. 'Just got back from a call-out. Busy as hell at the moment. Should be out in a minute.' He eyed Callum. 'New in town?'

'I grew up here. Came back when I heard about Lachie.'

'What's the name?'

Callum hesitated, considered lying. 'Haffenden.'

A blank stare, then a slight lift of the eyebrows and a scan down to Callum's leg, hidden beneath his drenched chinos.

*Great, another admirer.*

Callum forced himself not to roll his eyes.

'Yeah, this Lachie business is a bit of a shock.' The man shook his head and the corners of his mouth dropped slightly, pulling the ends of his moustache down even further. 'He'll be sorely missed round here. Good bloke, that one.'

A door to the side of the station opened and a woman with a long dark ponytail walked through, carrying two yellow jackets which she hung on hooks. She picked up a bucket and took a few steps forward before noticing the two men. Callum wasted no time. With a nod to Walrus he crossed the station, trying to omit any limp from his walk.

The woman was smaller than he'd assumed based on the video, her head just level with his chest. A twinge of recognition.

'Paige?'

'Yeah?'

'We met at the search site a few days ago.'

Her eyebrows pulled together; she was young, early twenties perhaps. 'Oh yeah, you're the whispering guy.'

'Callum Haffenden actually.'

'Right.' Her face was blank. 'And what can I do for you, Callum Haffenden?'

'I'm just looking into Lachie's death a bit. Wanting to gauge what he was like.'

'Why? He fell, didn't he?'

'Probably. But I'm just tying up a few loose ends. Just seeing what people who knew him best thought.'

'I'm pretty new around here. I didn't know him very well at all.' She frowned. 'You a cop?'

He glanced back over his shoulders. The man with the moustache was nowhere in sight. He made a snap decision. 'Just up helping out Quade. Poor sod only started this week. Think his hands are full as it is.'

She nodded, her eyes looking past him.

'So, can you tell me what he was like? Lachie?'

'You're probably best to ask one of the boys over there.' She jerked her head to the far end of the station as a group of firemen bundled in from the side door, their raucous laughter loud enough to challenge the sound of rain on the tin roof. A few shot the pair sideways looks.

'But you worked with Lachie, didn't you?'

Paige's face was firm, her eyes steady on the group of men. 'We got rostered on together a few times.'

'What did you make of him? You know, first impressions and all.'

She shrugged. 'Everyone liked him. One of the boys.'

'So I've heard.' He looked her square in the eyes, remembered her absence from the pub. 'But you're not one of the boys, are you?'

Her eyes snapped up to meet his.

He pushed. 'Did you like him?'

She bit her lip, her eyes moving back to the fireys. 'Look, I like it here. Everyone's been great.'

'Was Lachie great?'

He waited.

She shifted her weight, eyes moving from the group of men to the large roller door, then finally to Callum. She sighed. 'He was trouble.'

'What kind of trouble?' His mouth was dry.

'The usual kind.'

The silence stretched between them.

She bit her bottom lip. 'Look, I'm new here and let's just say that Lachie didn't waste any time having a crack.'

'In what way?'

Another shift of her weight. 'Started on my first day. He called me babe a few times, gave me a wink or two. Asked if I wanted to go for a drink after work more than once. Even offered to help me build my flat-pack furniture. He's nearly ten years older than me. Got a wife and kid. And another one on the way from what I've heard.' Her young face hardened with disgust.

'Then he walked in on me a few times while I was getting changed. He was a creep.' She raised her eyebrows then sighed. 'I just got on with the job. Then when he made a few less subtle passes at me and I didn't go for them, it got ugly.'

'He get physical?'

'Not quite. There are cameras all around this joint. He'd struggle to get away with laying a hand on me.' She hesitated. 'After I knocked him back a few times, he started saying things like I knew where to find him if I ever needed help christening my new bed. He'd laugh it off, like it was nothing. Like we were mates just messing around. I ignored him. But that just spurred him on. It was like he was looking for a reaction. He started detailing what he wanted to do to me. Said he knew I was gagging for it. That a bit of dick was just what a dyke like me needed.' Her eyes flew back to the group of men at the other end of the station. 'He'd only say it when it was just the two of us. No one seemed to have a clue. Everyone thought he was great. In the end, I asked not to be rostered on with him anymore. The chief didn't question me. That was the first time I thought that maybe they actually knew what he was like.' Her eyes narrowed towards the group of firefighters, laughing and carrying on. 'My roster was changed immediately. Wouldn't look good for the station if the only female on crew filed a sexual harassment complaint.'

'So you never officially reported him?'

She shrugged. 'Why would I?'

White hot anger pierced him, and his mind flicked to Milly, only a few years younger. He pushed the thought down. 'And yet you helped with the search?'

She snorted. 'Yeah, it's part of my job description. Probably would've got the sack if I didn't show up.'

A siren split the air and her muscles tensed, ready. She took a few hurried steps but stopped alongside him.

'Look, I don't know what the hell happened to him out at those boulders.' Her voice was barely audible over the screech of the siren and the drumming of the rain. Callum bent to catch her words. 'But I'm not sorry he's gone.'

# CHAPTER THIRTY

Callum felt as if he needed to scrub the last twenty minutes off his skin.

It sounded like Lachie had been a creep.

He'd been shocked by Paige's casual response when he'd asked why she hadn't reported the harassment. *Why would I?*

He felt stupid now for asking the question. Lachie was well liked in town. At best it'd be swept under the rug, at worst she'd be blamed for encouraging him and ostracised from the department, maybe even the town. And the next town.

He'd seen it before. Too many times.

He tried to stop Milly's face from replacing Paige's. What predators was she going to have to ward off in the future, if she hadn't already started? She was only fifteen, a kid. But if he were honest with himself, most men couldn't tell the difference between a fifteen- and an eighteen-year-old. And far too many just didn't give a shit. Not that age mattered. It was rubbish either way.

Milly. He pulled his phone out, jabbed at the screen. Half a dozen rings, then a lightening in his chest as Milly's sing-song voice hit his ear. A stab of disappointment: voicemail.

He left a message, hung up and tried to push her from his mind.

He thought of the last few days, since his arrival in Granite Creek. Fireys clinking glasses as they'd toasted Lachie. Jack's red puffy eyes. The sheer volume of searchers, volunteers. Everyone saying how much of a great guy Lachie had been. Firefighter, coach, volunteer. A top bloke, sorely missed.

None of it fitted with Paige's description.

And then Steph swam into his mind, her black-and-white outline pixelated on the pub's CCTV footage. Snatching her arm from Lachie's grasp, leaning in, a jab of her finger into his chest. He hadn't been able to see her face, but her body language had been easy enough to gauge. She'd been pissed off. Had she been threatening Lachie?

CCTV footage didn't lie. Nor the bank statement with Brett's name. He recalled her story about Brett fixing the leak at the station, the anger on her face, the hunch of Brett's shoulders. What the hell did she have to do with the Wyatt family?

And Tess's hostility when he'd asked her about Steph outside the Outdoor Store. Tess had been firm: *She has nothing to do with our family.*

His head pounded as he thought of Tess, with her snapping words and constant glare. Maybe Lachie had just had enough? Had Steph and Lachie had a thing? Maybe he was looking for an outlet, away from his wife's harsh tone and stern face?

But Steph was seventeen years older than Lachie. More likely she was having a thing with Brett.

And it was Brett's name on the bank statement, not Lachie's. Lachie may have found out, been fuming his dad had been giving her money.

*Jesus. Steph and Brett.*

His mouth soured at the thought.

He jammed the key into the ignition, pushed the gearstick into reverse and drove out of the fire station car park.

As he headed towards town the window wipers flew across the windscreen as fast as the ideas whipped through his head.

Each streaked across the forefront of his mind before quickly being swiped away, only to be replaced by another.

An affair. Had Lachie been having an affair? Had Tess found out? The image of Tess shoving Lachie off the cliff pushed its way forward. Swipe.

*Don't be crazy.*

Tess, thin, frail and nine months pregnant. Lachie, muscular, fit and more than physically capable. The notion was ridiculous.

His mind returned to Jack. Grieving. Terrified. He tried to recreate the scene at Tess's house. The front door closed. The washroom open, drop sheet on the floor, paint samples on the walls. The corridor with the family photos. Pip's face. He tried to focus. Tess. Jack again. Hiding behind his mother at the sound of Brett's return.

And Brett. It always circled back to Brett. Brett and his threats. Brett rummaging in Callum's motel room. Brett's name on Steph's bank statement. Brett arriving at Tess's house, slurring his words, and striking fear into his family.

And Lachie. Had Lachie been just as bad? Callum had no idea. He'd never met the man.

Never met his son.

An explosion of guilt ripped through his chest. He tried for a breath, but something was lodged in his airway. He fumbled for the window, pressed the automatic button. Nothing. Jammed. Another breath, again nothing.

He needed to get out, needed air.

He slammed his foot down on the brake and his front tyre hit the kerb. The sudden jerk bit into his leg and images of his son scattered.

*Find the door handle.*

He fumbled, palms sweaty, useless.

A gasp, still no air.

At last, the smooth plastic of the handle, a shoulder into the door as the wind pressed back against it, trying to contain him in the car; hold him captive.

He struggled to find his footing in the torrent of rain that ran along the gutter in search of a drain. His right foot told him he was ankle deep in water and he gripped the roof of the car for support.

His ears were muffled, as if stuffed with cotton wool. Pounding rain, whipping wind, flapping palm fronds—all muted.

He tried for deep breaths. The stifling humidity was heavy and wet with rain. He couldn't get any air. He was drowning.

Lachie.

His son.

Was Lachie as bad as Brett?

Pip's bruised skin swam across his vision. A field of blackish blues and purples tinted with tawny browns. Impossible. Lachie had only been a kid.

No, seventeen. He'd been seventeen then. Practically a man.

But violence was a learned trait: nurture, not nature. It ran in families, passed down generation to generation, like a twisted family heirloom. Lachie learned it from somewhere.

Callum's tongue flicked along the faint line on his lip, barely palpable, from where Brett had split it three decades earlier. The weight in his chest increased. What the hell had he been thinking, leaving Lachie with Brett?

He swallowed back the guilt, tried to let the rain wash it away, sweep it into the gutter and suck it down the drain.

It hadn't been his choice.

His head hung low, and the wind slapped a final wall of rain against his face.

Then nothing. Stillness. The clouds had seized up, as if at last empty. A squawk of birds overhead, a flurry of wings.

The air pressed against his skin, squeezing him. He tried to take another breath. Still nothing. A flush of panic. His ears unblocked, as if the wind had pushed within. He squeezed his eyes shut to block it, not daring to let go of the car to press his hands against his ears. The wind whistled and whispered.

A sickening chill ran over him as the old rhyme rang through his mind. There was nothing he could do to stop it.

# CHAPTER THIRTY-ONE

Fluorescent lights burned into Callum's eyes, and he blinked back the blinding brightness of his new surroundings. The familiar smell of disinfectant and latex stung his nostrils: he was in some sort of medical facility.

He lay on his back, the surface beneath padded yet firm. The mild chatter of voices in the next room hummed in his ears and the pillow beneath his head crinkled as he shifted. A wave of nausea rolled over him. He closed his eyes and tried to remember what had happened.

Rain had smacked against his face as he'd clambered out of the car, the air too dense to breathe. The whisper of the wind had pressed against him. Had there been a voice in his ear?

Now a voice in a nearby room picked up. Brisk, matter of fact. He propped himself up on his elbows and turned to face the door opposite him just as it nudged open. His head spun.

'Woah, woah, woah.' Heavy footsteps followed by a firm hand on his shoulder that guided him back down. 'Go easy, buddy. You've had quite the turn.'

He exhaled slowly through his mouth and heard himself speak. 'It happens.'

'Hopefully not too often.'

'More often than I'd like, I'm afraid.' His nausea began to settle. 'Especially here.'

He opened his eyes again. The fuzzy lines of his surroundings took a few moments to sharpen and become recognisable objects.

A boxy woman stood next to him. All angles, no softness. He heard the sound of velcro ripping, followed by an increasing pressure around his upper arm.

Her dark hair was streaked with grey and the spattering of wrinkles across her forehead put her at about Callum's age, he guessed. Not a bad age for a doctor: old enough to have seen enough; young enough to still give a shit.

'Blood pressure's a bit low.' She pulled the stethoscope out of her ears and cocked her head to the side. 'And pulse is a little high.'

'Sounds about right.'

'How long have you been having panic attacks?'

He paused, cringed at the accuracy of her diagnosis. 'Long enough.'

'And what do you do when you get them?'

He looked at her again. 'Panic.'

The edge of her mouth turned up. But she angled her body towards him and crossed her arms. 'I found you in your car. You could've hurt someone.'

'I believe you found me next to my car.'

'Much of a muchness, I'm afraid.' She moved towards the end of the bed. 'What's your name?'

'Callum.'

Her grey eyes bored into him, and the silence hung heavy between them.

'Haffenden,' he said.

'Alma Bacuzzi. Doctor.' She paused a moment before her brows drew together and the lines in her forehead deepened. Maybe she was older than him after all, wrong side of fifty perhaps. 'Haffenden?'

He waited for the name to sink in.

'As in Doctor Innis Haffenden?'

A jolt of surprise: not the usual response. 'Yeah. My mum was the GP here for nearly two decades.'

She nodded. No-nonsense. 'You look alike.'

His turn to frown.

She laughed. It was electric and sounded unnatural in a room probably used to mostly hearing bad news. 'Her photo's in the waiting room. Along with the other doctors that have worked here since her. None have lasted quite so long though.'

Callum nodded.

'She left when you lost your leg.' It wasn't a question.

'Better rehab down south.'

Without asking, she rolled up his left trouser leg to expose the titanium pylon shaft of his prosthesis. She couldn't get his trouser leg over his swollen knee. 'How are you finding the humidity on your stump?'

'It's delightful.'

That laugh again, impossibly loud for a room so small. 'I'll bet.' Her eyes ran the length of his prosthesis. 'You're going to have to take your trousers off so I can take a look.'

She didn't wait for a response, just whipped a blue plastic curtain across, masking her from view. 'Let me know if you need a hand undressing.'

Twenty minutes later, he sat on a hard plastic chair next to her desk as she typed up a script for antibiotics and some half decent painkillers. She slid two blister packs across the desk to tide him over until the pharmacy opened the next day. A touch of country charm, he guessed.

His stump had been worse than he'd feared. Red skin, on the cusp of breaking down. A raised purple scar wept at the edges. The makings of an imminent infection.

She'd dressed the wound and added an additional compression bandage. A grim warning and strict instructions to stay off his leg had followed, alongside a stern, and likely well-practised, you-should-know-better glare.

She tapped away at the keyboard, stubby fingers more dexterous than he expected, while Callum scanned her office. It was a sad excuse for an office really, as if the beige walls had absorbed the decades of poor diagnoses they'd no doubt been privy to. A lick of paint and a fresh privacy curtain was about all that had changed since his mum had worked there. Health budgets stretched about as far as police budgets, by the looks of things.

A framed photo of a buoyant border collie on her desk and a vacant ring finger suggested that Bacuzzi was likely single and child-free.

'How long have you been in Granite Creek?' he asked.

'Almost eight years now.'

'Long enough, then.'

The corner of her mouth lifted again. 'It's not for everyone. But I like the quiet life.'

'So how much longer till you're considered a local?'

She laughed. 'Another thirty years ought to do it, I imagine.'

Sounded about right. His mum had still been considered an outsider even after twenty years. Her Scottish accent probably hadn't helped.

There was a pause while Bacuzzi printed out his prescription, the hum of the printer filling the silence. She signed the form and slid it across the desk.

He pocketed it. 'But no doubt, being the GP, you'd be offered some kind of leniency.'

She reclined back in her chair and eyed him. 'Was your mum?'

'No.'

Another silence, and he wondered how hard to push. Harder, he decided. He leaned in towards her. 'But you'd know everyone's secrets.'

'If you mean I know who's got haemorrhoids and who's on anti-depressants, then, yes, I do.'

'It's more than that though, isn't it?'

She surveyed him. 'Surely you'll know how it is from your mum. I'm everyone's dumping ground, no one's friend.'

'Tough gig.'

'No job is without its downfalls.' Her broad shoulders rose up, dropped. 'It has its perks too.'

The plastic privacy curtain, the stained sheet on the examination bed. Surely the perks couldn't outweigh the knowledge that your neighbour had a terminal illness or that the guy at the petrol station had thoughts about flinging himself off the boulders.

He didn't know what to say, jerked his head. 'Lachie Wyatt—'

'Died in a tragic accident.'

'Maybe.'

A flicker of something across her face. She reset back to neutral before he had a chance to interpret it.

'What were his secrets?'

She raised an eyebrow. 'Not everyone has a story to uncover, Mr Haffenden.'

So, she knew more about his background than just his leg.

'Come on, you're the only GP in town. You must have known him.'

'Thirty-year-old men aren't known for their frequent visits to the GP.' Her eyes rested on his leg. 'A bit like teenage boys really when it comes to their health. Think they're invincible.'

A punch in his gut. A push to ignore it. 'Okay, what was he like then?'

'I'm under oath not to say.'

'No, you're under oath not to discuss his medical history with me. I'm just asking you what he was like.' He paused. 'As a person, not a patient.'

'What is it you're after, Mr Haffenden?'

'The truth.' Words he'd uttered often in his career and thought of too often since arriving back in Granite Creek. Always the truth. 'I've been back in this town for three days and I'm floundering.' The thumping in his head returned; the words streamed out. 'Everyone's hiding something.' He looked up, eyes bleary. It was a long shot, but the words came out before he'd even registered the thought. 'Brett?'

'Brett?' Surprised.

'Yeah, Brett. What do you think of him?'

She pulled her eyebrows back in together; they formed a dark bridge that spanned her forehead. 'I heard about you, you know. And your accident.' She didn't break eye contact. 'I know I came a long time after you left, but a small town never forgets. They talk.'

'And what do they say?'

'That Brett and you never got along.'

He snorted. 'That's an understatement.'

'And that he married the girl you loved.'

His heart jerked at the unexpected comment. A lump formed in his throat, threatening to rise up and fill his airway. He didn't dare try to speak.

'So, I know your thoughts about Brett, and I'm not going to entertain you with the notion that I agree. He's a hardworking man with a tragic family story. His daughter, his wife and now his son.'

Her eyes bored into him, and he fought to match her gaze.

'You'd do well to know, Mr Haffenden, that the talk around town is that no one is appreciating your poking about. Small towns will always band together, look out for their own. And while I may not be considered a local myself, after thirty years gone, neither are you.'

\*

His phone rang as he was leaving the doctor's surgery. He fumbled around in his pocket for it, ignored the drop in his gut when it wasn't Milly.

'You're not going to believe this.' Eddy didn't wait for a greeting.

'There's no more cats left for you to rescue?'

'That, and I talked Mike into giving me the CCTV footage from the motel.'

'You're kidding? Can you see who broke in?'

'Not quite. But let's just say I'm bringing Brett in for questioning.'

# CHAPTER THIRTY-TWO

'What the hell is he doing?' Callum sat on the chair opposite Eddy, the computer monitor between them angled towards him. The towel that Steph had given him, when he'd entered the station soaking wet, was draped around his shoulders.

'Don't know, but seems suspicious,' Eddy said from the other side of the desk.

'Rewind it.'

The grainy black-and-white image, slightly pixelated, showed the top portion of a door, the top half of a window and most of the door to the next room, a clear number seven plastered on its front. The rest of the shot was angled into the car park. The front of two cars were visible, parked noses to doors. Only the front fender, tip of the bonnet and one tyre of Callum's rental—furthest from the camera—was visible at the edge of the footage, his tyre popped up on the walkway. He inwardly cringed as he realised the only reason his rental was caught on camera was due to his shitty parking.

'So that's definitely your room there.' Eddy pointed to the closed door closest to the camera, only the very top of it visible. The half-visible window next to it belonged to Callum's room also.

'And my car.' Callum indicated the screen.

A ferrety figure, overbite prominent, came into view and gave a quick—silent—rap on the door of number seven,

Callum's neighbour. The camera caught a glint of an earring as Mike looked left and right along both lengths of the walkway that ran in front of the motel room doors. The door to number seven opened a fraction and he ducked inside before it snapped closed behind him.

'Fishy,' Callum said.

'Do you know who's in number seven?'

'Some SES bloke. Older guy. Ginger beard. I've seen him come and go a few times. Recognised him from the search. Must be staying on for a few days, maybe sticking round for the funeral.' He dredged up the memory of his trudge through the rainforest when he'd first arrived back in Granite Creek. So much had happened since then, his hike with Paige and the SES man was buried beneath a deep layer of mud, undergrowth and lies. Snippets of their conversation swam back to him. 'Seemed to know his local history.'

Eddy nodded. 'Well, Mike's in there with him. The man came back to his room over an hour ago and he hasn't left since.'

'The SES guy's an out-of-towner,' Callum said. 'So, how does Mike know him?'

Eddy shrugged. 'Mate, your guess is as good as mine. I've been back here for about four days longer than you have.'

'Could be a regular. At the motel, that is.'

'Yeah, I thought of that. But what's Mike doing sneaking about visiting guests? Could they have a thing going on?'

'Hooking up? Doubt it. I've seen Mike eyeing off some of the female journos staying in the motel. Not subtle, mind you.'

'Didn't think it was likely.'

The pair sat watching the monitor until a sudden change in the footage made Callum jolt upright. His leg gave a stab of pain.

'What the ...' He leaned further forward.

A flash across the screen and his window now gaped open. Glass shattered and frame raised, the curtains fluttered wildly inward. Next, the top portion of his motel door—the only part visible on camera—opened and closed.

Someone had entered his room.

He whipped around to look at Eddy. 'Who was it?'

'Don't know. The video doesn't pick them up. They're obviously ducking down so they're not caught on camera.'

'So, someone who knows the camera is there. That's a pretty narrow pool.'

Eddy's mouth was firm. 'The camera's in plain sight. Anyone with a set of eyes and any sense would scan for surveillance before breaking into a joint.'

'But how many people would know the angle of the cameras and what they can, or rather can't, pick up?'

'Mike. The security company.'

Callum's mouth went dry. 'The maintenance guy.'

'You're not letting go of this Brett thing, are you?'

'You've got to admit, he looks suss.'

'I'm not admitting to anything, mate. I'll chat to Mike all the same, get an idea of who knew about the cameras.'

The minutes ticked by, and Callum tried not to think of the person in his room rummaging through his stuff.

What the hell had they been looking for?

He thought back to the bracelet. A soggy strip of fabric with three silver bells. Noah's bracelet. Had that been it?

Another minute passed then the door to number seven flew open and Mike, eyes darting left and right, scurried along the walkway. He paused outside Callum's door, the side of his head only just visible. A hesitation. Then a raised fist high up on the door—a silent knock. A pause. Mike checked along the path and over his shoulder before he leaned forward and the visible section of the door opened— presumably by him. Another hesitation on the threshold, then he disappeared from view, the door left open behind him.

Callum blew out a long breath. His eyes began to ache from staring at the screen. He could feel his body sag into the chair, the weight of the last few days taking its toll at last. He barely registered his own figure flashing onto the monitor a minute later before disappearing inside the room.

'Rules out Mike at least,' Eddy said after a few moments of silence.

A slow nod, his mind elsewhere. Who the hell broke into the room? Brett? Had Brett had the foresight to duck from the camera's view? But how did he get out?

Another possibility washed over him. Perhaps Brett was still in his room when he'd arrived back from his hike with Steph. Had Brett been lurking somewhere all along?

The room had been chaos. Clothes everywhere, drawers opened, and the single chair upturned. Even his pillowslip had been removed and shoes searched, innersoles removed. He still hadn't found his shoehorn.

Had he checked the bathroom? He couldn't remember. He'd gone in there eventually. Surely no one would've been able to take refuge there. He visualised the rest of the squat room. A cupboard. Big enough to hide a grown man. But he knew that wasn't the answer. The doors had been opened, all contents laid bare.

His insides lightened as he recalled the folded blanket on the top shelf, untouched. Not all the contents.

His mind rolled over the room again, at last resting on his bed, its covers strewn across the floor. And underneath? He hadn't checked. His mind clawed at the image of his room, desperate to recreate it. What sort of bed was it? Was there space beneath? Space big enough for the hulking frame of Brett Wyatt? Had he made his escape when Callum had gone for a piss?

The cool sweat returned, spread up his neck and over his cheeks.

'You okay?' Eddy asked.

'Fine.' Callum's voice was distant, even to his own ears. 'Just my leg.' He straightened and flexed his knee, the bandage Bacuzzi had given him still restricting the movement.

'You should've told me you were at the doc's. I could've come and got you.'

Callum waved a hand. After receiving Eddy's phone call, he'd taken one look at his rental car—front tyre again popped up on the kerb—and decided that walking in the downpour was easier than cramming his swollen leg back into the tiny hatchback.

Eyes back on the screen, he swallowed. 'I thought you said you were bringing Brett in. What for?'

'Check this out.' Eddy hit rewind and, after a few minutes, play.

The time in the top corner of the footage told Callum that he was watching the events of yesterday morning, hours prior to the break-in. The top of Brett's buzz cut head came into view and, after a brief pause, entered Callum's room.

A chill crept its way along Callum's body. He knew it wasn't just the effect of the air conditioner and the rain on his skin. Brett had been in his room.

But he'd already known that. Brett had just been doing his job.

'He was there to fix the power fault in your room,' Eddy said.

Callum nodded. Only his room with a fault though. Only he got the blackout. Had Brett known that the electrician would be caught up? That he'd be summoned to the job? It was possible. Everyone knows everyone's business in a small town. How easy would it have been to cut the power to his room?

Eddy clicked his mouse and skipped through the video. An uneventful screen stared back at them. He hit play on the footage, the time showing twenty minutes or so had passed. Brett emerged, his entire head and top of his shoulders visible thanks to his height. His bulky frame paused for a moment in front of Callum's door, presumably locking it, before he turned to walk away. He halted. A flicker of emotion across his face. Surprise? Then his mouth was moving. It took Callum a moment to realise Brett was talking to someone out of shot and he felt a familiar jab of frustration as he recalled the CCTV footage from the pub. A minute passed. Brett intermittently silently talking. He took a step forward and lifted his arms towards the person he was speaking to, still off screen.

A jolt of recognition at the gesture. A distant memory, grappling to the surface. Brett's arms flopped back down by his side and the memory slipped away.

One last word mouthed, a half step forward, and then Brett's head dropped. Eyes down. The other person obviously gone.

A moment passed. Brett stayed put and, shoulders rounded, began to shake. A slight jerking to his hulking frame filled the screen.

Callum shifted uncomfortably in his seat. He leaned in closer to the monitor, unable to identify the stirring he felt inside. 'Is he ... crying?'

'Looks like it.'

A few more seconds, then Brett seemed to pull himself together. Standing taller, he wiped his nose on his wrist and briefly pressed his fists to his eyes. He stepped out of shot.

'Jesus.' Callum leaned back in his chair. 'Well, you can't bring him in for that.'

'Not that.' Eddy nodded to the computer. 'This.'

Callum looked at his friend, eyes trained intently at the screen, before returning his own attention back to the monitor.

A minute passed. Two.

A brief flash of a buzz cut head and broad shoulders came into shot. An arm. The shine of a blade.

Gone.

Eddy hit pause and Callum leaned into the screen again. Brett had disappeared from view.

He squinted through his glasses as the grainy image came into focus. The front tyre of his rental car sat low to the ground. Flat.

Brett.

\*

Brett crying. Brett slashing his tyres. Brett breaking into his room.

Brett. Brett. Brett.

Brett under his bed.

Callum shook his head. Stick to the facts.

The ideas skipped through his mind as he left Eddy's office.

'In a hurry?' Steph beamed at him from her chair behind the counter as he walked past.

'No,' he said before he'd had a chance to think. 'Yes, actually.'

The corner of her mouth fell, dimple gone.

'Sorry.'

She shrugged. 'Not to worry.'

A silence stretched between them. She stood and stepped towards him, eyes lifting to meet his. Her hands reached up and his breath caught.

'I'll take that.' She took the towel that still hung around his shoulders, lifting it over his head and spraying rain droplets on them both. 'Didn't seem to do you much good. You look as if you've been for a swim in the creek.'

She gave another smile and his breath returned. She hadn't stepped away.

He nodded, unable to speak. Her skin was smooth, her eyes warm. How the hell was she tangled up with the Wyatt family? With Brett?

'Thanks all the same.' He forced a lightness into his voice. 'I do have to be off though.'

'How much longer you sticking around?'

'Not sure. Another day or two, I guess. Gotta get home to Milly soon.'

'Well, it's been nice seeing your face around here again.'

'And yours.' The words flew out. 'It's been nice being back. You know, seeing Eddy and our old stomping ground again.' He fumbled over his words, unsure of what he was saying. He tried to ignore the slight drop in her shoulders.

'Right. Well, do come and say goodbye before you leave.'

Callum felt her eyes follow him as he left the station, the rain and wind doing little to wash away thoughts of her disappointment.

Rain immediately coated his glasses and he blinked a few times and tried to bring the road into focus.

Few cars were left on the main street—most no doubt parked safely beneath carports or in garages—and even fewer people were visible. The trees buckled in the wind, bent at impossible angles, the gale strong enough to make him feel unsteady.

He felt a stab in his leg. A pang at the thought of facing the next few minutes walking back to the motel, his leg no doubt throbbing the whole way.

He ducked his head and turned into the onslaught of wind. Half-a-dozen steps and he approached the corner of the building, and the driveway to the police car park behind.

A shadow between the cars. Hulking.

Brett.

His head was bent down, his back to Callum. He shifted his weight, dragging something in front of him, concealed from view.

Callum took a step forward.

Another shift from Brett, a turn of his body, so he was now side-on. His arm pulled—tugged—firmly at something. No, not something, someone.

Callum took two rapid steps towards them.

Brett's voice carried on the wind. '… keep your bloody mouth shut if you know what's good for you.'

Callum picked up the pace, his feet slipping on the wet concrete. 'Hey!'

Brett's head snapped around. His grip tightened around an arm. Jack's arm.

Callum lurched forward. 'What are you doing?'

'Fuck off, Haffenden.'

'Are you okay, Jack?' Callum took a step to the side to better see the boy. His face was red and puffy, streaked.

Brett tugged the kid behind his great hulk and stepped in front.

'Jack, are you all right?' Callum asked again.

'He's fine.' Brett stepped forward, letting go of Jack. 'More than you're gonna be if you don't piss off. What the hell are you doing here?'

'Could ask you the same question.'

'Being dragged into trouble because you're in town.'

'I'm not the one causing the trouble.'

'You've been nothing but trouble since the moment I met you.' Brett spat the words out.

'I'm not the one being called into the cop shop for questioning.'

Brett's eyes narrowed, his brow set in a scowl. 'This is your doing.' He pointed a finger into the centre of Callum's chest and Callum resisted the urge to step away. 'You need to get out of here. Go back to the city. Go back to—' he faltered '—Milly.'

'Don't you say her name.'

Brett stepped closer again. Callum had to tilt his face upwards to maintain eye contact.

'What did you say to me?' Brett asked.

'You have no right to speak about my daughter. Leave my family alone.' A pulse pounded in his temple and a wave of hot, white anger ripped through his body. A sudden memory of his daughter as a four-year-old. A ballet concert at home for him and her soft toys. Young. Beautiful. Innocent.

Brett could go to hell.

'Pop, please.' Jack's voice, soft.

Brett stepped back. He raised both his arms, as if in defeat, and a flash of the CCTV footage burst into Callum's mind. It was the same gesture.

A scurry from the depths of his memories as images, long supressed, sharpened at the edges. He grabbed for them, dragged them into focus. Callum, seventeen years old and hiding in the trees. Brett on the edge of the boulders, arms outstretched. Brett's face. Angry, surprised, shocked. He couldn't read it. The memories raced across Callum's mind, one after the other, a sick slide show he'd fought to keep down for three decades. Suppressed for almost a lifetime.

But a snippet was clear now, a fragment of footage sharp and crisp.

Brett's outstretched arms. Brett's face. Shocked. Then turning and running. No backwards glance.

A voice. A whimper.

Callum saw himself pushing forward to the boulder edge, the place where the rainforest dropped away to nothing but a sea of granite. Peering over the ledge, seeing white knuckles gripping tight to a granite shelf metres below. Wide eyes meeting his.

Amelia Dyer.

Her eyes were vivid in Callum's mind. He blinked, brought the police car park back into focus. His palms tingled, slippery with sweat, and he rubbed them firmly on his trousers as he watched Brett turn. Behind him, a glimpse of Jack, face white, eyes wide. Terrified.

Callum's mind cleared as the realisation of what Brett had done that day slotted into place. Brett had pushed Amelia Dyer. Pip's sister.

Brett had killed her.

All these years and the answer to what had happened to Amelia Dyer three decades earlier had been buried in Callum's head. He'd forgotten everything from the day of his accident. He'd been silent due to the fault in his memory.

Well, he'd stayed quiet long enough.

'You need to leave your family alone too.' Callum's voice held an edge.

A pause.

'What did you say?' Brett asked.

'You need to leave your family al—'

Brett spun. A flash of fury over his face and a fist almost too fast to see. Blinding pain across Callum's jaw and his leg gave way. A final terrified image of Amelia's eyes swam across his memory before his vision went black, and the ground rushed up to meet him.

# CHAPTER THIRTY-THREE

*Thirty years earlier*

It was the first day of no rain in almost a week. The torrential downpour, unseasonably early, had meant that Pip and I hadn't been alone together in what felt like years. I had blu-tacked her bowerbird drawing above my desk. Every time I looked at it my skin tingled, and the gold rim of her eyes would stare back at me instead of the bowerbird's.

Seven days can really drag.

The track through the rainforest was a sloppy mess. Pip led the way, mud splattered as high as the hem of her denim shorts. Her satchel was flung over one shoulder and bounced against her thigh with every step she took.

'We can't cross.' Pip's voice cut through my thoughts.

I pulled up behind her. We were at the creek crossing already. The water rushed along, white foam swirling over the top of the boulder bridge that sat fully submerged under about thirty centimetres of water.

She was right: we couldn't cross.

Seventeen years' worth of wet seasons meant that neither of us were stupid enough to cross flooded ground. Definitely not a flooded bridge.

I shrugged, it didn't matter. The boulders weren't why I came out here anyway.

I trudged a few metres along the bank to where another flat rock sat on high enough ground that the water didn't touch it. I threw off my backpack and sat down with my back against the trunk of a large tree.

A few minutes later, Pip sat angled towards me, with her back to the boulder bridge and her legs bent over the top of mine. Her sketchpad rested against her bare thighs, pencil in hand. Her hand moved effortlessly across the paper, the tendons in her wrist flicking with each movement. She was left-handed and her arm arced over her drawing in that way that lefties do so that they don't smudge their work. She had a freckle on her index finger.

I opened up my backpack, pulled out my binoculars. I tuned the focus, lifted them to my eyes. Pip's eyes flicked towards me. I tried to ignore them and scanned the canopy above.

A sleek grey body flittered from one branch to the next. It was too far away, but I knew that I'd be able to hold the bird in the palm of my hand.

Grey whistler.

Not much else.

Pip shifted, swapped some pencils, continued drawing.

I leaned forward to peer at the page. A jolt of surprise.

My own face stared back.

She snatched the pad to her chest. 'Don't look yet.'

'You're drawing me.'

She shrugged, pushed me back, kept sketching.

I stared at the back of her sketchpad. From the flash I'd seen, she'd done a good job. My cheeks were a little fuller and my eyes a little bigger, but she'd captured the way my hair flopped over my forehead and the cut of my jaw.

My bottom lip was smooth, unscathed. She'd left out the scar from Brett's fist.

'Is it for me?' I asked.

Her hand paused, and she didn't meet my eye. 'No.' Her finger traced close to the bottom of the page. Maybe where my lips were. 'This one's for me.'

Something in my chest pulled, an urge to hold her hand. She started sketching again.

I tore my eyes from her, rummaged in my bag and pulled out the book I'd brought along: *Tropical Birds of Far Northern Queensland*.

I flipped it open, read a sentence, the words blurring together, and let it drop onto my lap. I leaned my head back against the tree and closed my eyes instead.

My ears began to swarm, hum. The rush of the creek, a rummage in the foliage, the rustle of the overhead canopy.

The soft scratch of Pip's pencil against paper.

Minutes, an hour. Time slowed in here. My body became heavy, the rock beneath me pressing back.

A shift in the air. A rustle of wings, a flurry. A brush against my legs. A silence. Something had stopped.

No sound of Pip drawing.

My eyes flew open and took in our rock.

My face stared up from Pip's abandoned sketchpad. Her pencils lay on the rock and one rolled slowly to the edge. It dropped off, disappearing into the flowing creek below.

I whipped my head up, scanned the area.

Pip was standing at the boulder bridge. No, on the boulder bridge. She was about a metre across, water swelling up as high as her calves.

*What the hell was she doing?*

'Pip!'

She didn't turn, took a step further along the bridge. A branch flowing on the water's surface skimmed her shin and she wobbled. A drop in my chest. She steadied herself.

I dashed to the edge of the bridge. Water rushed over the toes of my sneakers.

'Pip!' A pause. 'Pip!' Louder.

She turned her head. Her freckles stood out against her skin, the gold of her eyes glowing. Her expression blank.

'Pip, what the hell are you doing?'

She blinked, looked down at the water swarming around her legs as if seeing it for the first time. She blinked again and her mouth opened, she looked back up at me. Terror.

I stepped my left foot out onto the bridge, my shoe fully submerged. 'Just walk back to me.'

She nodded, turned slowly, her arms wide for better balance.

I extended one arm out to her and she reached towards me. Our fingertips didn't quite touch.

I went to take another step towards her and she froze, her eyes upstream.

A trunk, large and fast, sped along the creek. She took a hurried step forward, slipped.

I stepped out onto the bridge, grabbed for her as she overcorrected. My fingers brushed her arm as she lost her balance and fell upstream. The force of the rushing water slammed her body into the boulder bridge, her face just above the surface.

'Cal! Hel—'

The tree trunk slammed into her head. The blonde of her hair sucked beneath the surface. I jumped off the bridge, onto the upstream side, onto firm ground. Two quick steps forward into the creek and the water rushed around my calves. Another two steps and it was above my knees.

Mid-thigh. Waist. Chest-level water.

It slammed me against the boulder bridge as well but I sucked in a breath and scanned the surface. A wisp of blonde just below.

*Pip.*

A gasp for air and I ducked below. A sudden silence.

I opened my eyes. Blurry, murky brown. I fumbled in front, my hands grasping nothing but water. A dig of my fingertips into the rock wall and I dragged my body forward. Another fumble, feeling, groping.

My chest was going to burst. I needed to go back up, get some air. But I couldn't.

*Find her. Don't leave her.*

But the pressure of the rushing creek pinned me in place.

I kicked my legs. My left foot skimmed something. Another kick and my toes hooked under it. A tree root maybe. I anchored my foot, wedging it in a small gap between the creek bed and the root. I bent my left knee and drew my body down further below the surface.

The sandy floor of the creek bed, mixed with dark patches of the granite grey boulders that dotted the bottom, came into focus. A dash of blonde.

*Pip.*

She was crumpled against the boulder bridge, her hair white against the granite. The pressure of the water wasn't allowing her to move back up to the surface.

I forced myself down further. My left foot, wedged under the tree root, cramped. The muscles in my leg ached, wanted to give up. My lungs were about to burst.

*Don't leave her.*

A lurch of my body forward and my left knee twisted. White hot pain.

I tried to scream and water rushed into my mouth.

*Don't take a breath. Get Pip.*

I snapped my mouth shut.

A grapple, and I clasped a handful of her t-shirt. I pulled her towards me, dragging her against the bridge.

My chest was going to explode. White dots filled my vision.

*Don't take a breath. Almost there.*

I wrapped my arms around her waist, fused her to me. One last twist of my left leg and my foot came free. I pushed off the tree root and a searing burn ran through my left knee as our bodies moved upwards.

We broke the surface.

*Air.*

My ribs expanded against the pressure of the water, still pressing us against the boulder.

Another breath and a scramble along the granite wall of the bridge. Arms pulling, right leg working hard. Kicking at first, then pushing into the creek bed as the ground angled upwards and we neared the bank.

I dragged Pip behind me, my arm a vice around her waist.

Firm ground at last.

I collapsed, pulling her down with me.

Deep breaths. The welcome scent of wet earth and the feel of the solid ground beneath.

A cough next to me.

*Pip.*

I rolled over and my left leg roared. I pushed down the pain, propped myself up on one elbow to hover above her, her face inches beneath mine. Her freckles shone against skin that was too white, and her eyes open, wide, reflected the canopy overhead.

We were so close I could practically taste her fear.

'What the hell were you doing?' My voice was raspy, waterlogged.

She searched my eyes and when she spoke I had to strain my ears to catch it, her voice barely a whisper, her lips as pale as her skin. 'Didn't you hear it?'

# CHAPTER THIRTY-FOUR

In the police station car park, the rain slapped the side of Callum's face and the metallic taste of blood pooled in his mouth. Images from thirty years ago raced through his head as he lay on the ground recovering from Brett's punch. Brett at the boulders. His outstretched arms. The look on his face. And Amelia Dyer. Hanging on to the cliff edge, her eyes flecked with gold.

*Amelia.*

Brett had pushed her. How had Callum not remembered that? Thirty years of not knowing.

Retrograde amnesia. That's how he hadn't remembered it. He didn't recall anything from the day of his accident. He just knew that the next day he had no leg. It was weeks later when he'd heard the news that Amelia had gone missing that day. His parents hadn't told him, had wanted him to focus on getting better, on his rehab. Eddy had eventually let it slip.

Callum had been found at the boulders. His parents had been worried he hadn't come home and eventually Pip had told them they'd been there together earlier that day. He must have gone back later by himself. *But why?*

*And Amelia? Brett?*

He urged his memories to come back, to sharpen. But everything before seeing Brett with his outstretched arms after pushing Amelia, and the fear in Amelia's eyes as she clung to the boulders, was still missing. Buried.

It was like he'd been given just a snippet, a scene, from that day. Nothing more. The reel of footage was blank either side.

He heard voices, their words muted by the pain in his leg and jaw. He opened his eyes. Blinked. The world was sideways, and it took a beat to associate the pressure against his cheek with the concrete of the footpath. He was horizontal.

Again.

Two figures, distorted around the edges, morphed into view. They stood a few paces away. One large and hulking, unmistakably Brett. The other finer with a smudge of auburn hair: Steph.

Callum squinted, willed them into focus. No luck. His glasses had shifted up, more over his forehead than his eyes. The frames dug into his temple, lodged between his head and the pavement.

Brett grabbed her, the gesture hazy yet unmistakable. Her body, pulled close to his, stiffened and angled away.

Callum lifted his head, tried to sit. He had to help her.

The pain across his jaw was like a hot iron and he bit back a groan as he tried to prop himself up. His head rolled and the two figures blurred together, then apart. At last they were swallowed by a blackness that snatched them away.

*

A wisp of something across his cheek; a wingtip. Soft and soothing. An image of a small bird, golden, spindly legs sticking skyward, eyes vacant. Dead.

'Cal?' The voice came from a distance.

His eyes flickered open, and the world shifted into focus. No birds. Steph's face shrouded in auburn hair, grey clouds pressing down from above. Her hair flittered across his cheek again and she removed her hand from his chest, sweeping his hair from his eyes and righting his glasses.

'Are you okay?' Her voice cut crisp through the rain.

'I'm okay.' Pain spread across his jaw, and he snapped his mouth closed, one hand flying up to cup it.

'Maybe try not to talk.' The corner of her mouth twitched upwards.

Relying on Steph more than he would've liked, Callum managed to make it back inside the police station a few minutes later. The kitchenette had a distinct smell of coffee and artificial lemons, the scent a little heavy for his pounding head.

'Here.' Steph perched next to him on the squat two-seater couch that was too big for the room, a first-aid kit resting on her lap. She pressed an ice pack wrapped in a tea towel against his jaw. He reached up to hold it in place and her hand lingered a beat longer.

'Thanks.' More pain.

'You know …' She smiled. 'Perhaps this would be a good time to consider keeping your nose out of other people's business.'

He snorted. A fresh wave of pain.

'I know you're used to digging around in things, trying to find a story everywhere. But sometimes there's no story to be found—'

Her words echoed Bacuzzi's.

'It's not a story I'm after.' He tried to ignore the pain that came with every word he spoke.

'Still, people are starting to talk.'

'What people?'

She shrugged, unzipped the first-aid kit.

'What are they saying?'

'That you're digging up the past unnecessarily.' A pause. 'That you're dragging the Wyatt name through the mud. That they've been through enough.'

Exhaustion washed over him. Was she right?

The memory of Amelia clinging to the cliff jarred him. And there was something else within that he couldn't pinpoint. A lightness maybe. It had been Brett.

No, Steph wasn't right.

She pulled his hand holding the ice pack away from his jaw and leaned in to survey the damage. He winced.

'Brett can be a bit of a jerk, I guess.' She rummaged through the first-aid kit.

He snorted, returned the ice pack to his jaw. 'You're not the first person I've heard say that.'

Her mouth flicked up again. 'I'm not surprised. But he's not all bad.'

Pip's words from thirty years ago rang in his ears.

*He's not so bad, I guess.*

He nodded to Steph. 'You're also not the first person I've heard say that.'

The thought of seventeen-year-old Pip was replaced by another memory of Pip. Older. Bruises on her skin. The photo of her daughter, Amelia; the toddler's arm in a cast. His chest swelled. He couldn't speak. He knew what Brett was capable of.

His eyes roamed around, avoiding Steph. A wall calendar from the previous year hung above the sink. A festive December picture of a cartoon dingo in a Santa hat grinned back.

The sound of voices muffled through the wall.

'I think he feels pretty bad about punching you.'

He snorted again. 'I think he felt pretty bloody good about it.'

'It's never been good between you two.'

'It's hard to have a good relationship with an arse.'

'I think he had his reasons for being an arse.' She eyed him sideways, continued searching through the first-aid kit. 'He didn't have it easy like you and me.'

A memory, sudden and crisp. Seventeen-year-old Brett, his back pressed against a ute, his father grasping him by the scruff of his shirt. Blue eyes filled with fear as his father had let go and stepped away. Callum's heart had sped up, his chest tight. A moment's hesitation, then, as he'd registered the trickle of crimson coming from Brett's nose and the clear glisten over his eyes, Callum had turned and walked away, an unsettling deep inside.

Steph's voice cut through the memory. 'Brett was trapped. The eldest of five. He was destined to take over his dad's business.'

Callum shifted on the squashy couch next to her. He'd never really given Brett's situation much thought. But now that he did, he wondered how he'd have felt as a teenager knowing he was never able to leave Granite Creek or amount to anything more than what his father had planned for him.

Steph gently pulled his hand supporting the ice pack away again.

The top of her head was level with his eyes. Her auburn hair caught the light overhead, flecks of gold reflecting beneath the rain drops that clung to the strands. He tried not to flinch as she dabbed some cream on his aching jaw.

'You know, I reckon he was pretty pissed off that Pip chose you, not him.'

A flicker of confusion as he processed her words. 'She didn't though.'

She looked up, face level with his. 'But she did.'

'No, she married Brett.'

'After you left.'

'She hooked up with him as soon as I'd gone.'

Steph's lips parted as if to say something. They hovered only centimetres from his. No words came out. He was uncertain if the fluttering in his chest was from the memory of Pip, or from Steph's breath warm on his lips.

'Straight after my accident.' His tongue was too big for his mouth, his voice struggling to come out. 'She chose him.'

'Of course she did. She had no one. Her mum died that day, don't you remember? Her sister went missing and her boyfriend was airlifted out of town with half his leg missing. She was totally alone. Brett was there for her. That's all it was.' Her eyes fixed on him. 'She was only seventeen. Still a kid. She would've been terrified, and he offered a shoulder to cry on. What else was she supposed to do?'

His head ached. He'd never thought about it from Pip's perspective. He'd been too caught up in his own issues. His leg. His future. Gone.

Then he'd learned about her and Brett from Eddy and a few months later he heard that she was pregnant. It'd been the final nail in the coffin.

Jesus, seventeen. Only two years older than Milly. Steph was right, she'd still been a kid. They all had been. It hadn't seemed that way at the time.

The air in the kitchenette pressed against him and he felt a fire creep up his neck and sear his cheeks.

'Hey.' Steph touched his cheek, her fingertips a cool relief against the heat that had formed beneath his skin. 'Don't be too tough on yourself. You were just a kid too.'

He met her gaze. Nodded.

'Besides, don't feel too sorry for yourself.' The smile across her lips returned. 'Any of the girls in our year would've chosen you over Brett, or any of the other boys for that matter.' Her voice lowered. 'I know I would have.'

His pulse raced. Images tore through his head. Her bank statement. Her argument with Lachie outside the pub. Her son's bracelet in the rainforest. The part of her lips, her dimple. He couldn't bring himself to pull away. Raindrops spattered her eyelashes. He swallowed. She was so close, breath warm. He leaned in.

'Mum?'

She froze.

'Mum?' Clearer.

Steph pulled back. The first-aid kit on her lap tumbled to the floor, its contents rolling everywhere.

'Shit.' She scooped down to pick it up, gathering the scattered items. 'In the kitchen, hon.'

The door to the kitchenette opened and a boy poked his head inside.

A wall smacked into Callum. He blinked several times, trying to clear his vision, figure out what he was seeing.

The boy's hair had a wild quality to it and was worn long, below his shoulders. His eyes were hazel like Steph's. His build was lean too.

But the sandy colour of his hair and the cut of his jaw were pure Wyatt.

Callum swallowed, his mouth dry.

Pure Brett.

## CHAPTER THIRTY-FIVE

The ache in Callum's stump turned to a throb as he sat on the closed toilet lid drying himself. He'd hoped the shower would wash away the image of Noah. The kid's likeness to Brett was undeniable and Callum's stomach rolled at the thought of Steph having ever been with such a prick.

His mind raced back to the hazy memory of what he'd seen when he was lying with his face pressed into the footpath and his glasses askew after Brett had punched him. Brett had been threatening Steph. He was sure of it. He'd grabbed her, pulled her close. Threatening.

Another explanation swam to mind, the thought bitter in his mouth. What if it wasn't a threat, but something else? Maybe his opinion of Brett was so skewed that he only saw what he wanted to: Brett the jerk. Brett the abuser.

Brett the killer.

There was a reason why Noah looked so much like Brett. Why Brett was transferring her money every single fortnight.

It was so bloody obvious, and Callum should have accepted it when he'd first laid eyes on the bank statement.

The fact that they had been involved once was undeniable. But were they still involved? Brett had pulled Steph to him. Had Steph resisted? Had he just imagined her body stiffening, leaning away? He couldn't be sure. His head had pounded, his glasses absent, and the hazy rain had made the whole image warp and bend until reality became something else entirely.

Now the bathroom swam in and out of focus, and he took a slow breath and an even slower blink.

The pieces of the last few days began to fall into place.

The bank statement. Brett stalking away from the cop shop, Steph angry inside. Even Steph's words about Noah's dad.

*He'd been more trouble than he was worth.*

Brett.

He closed his eyes, but the unanswered question gnawed at him: were Brett and Steph still involved? And why not just say so? Was Steph embarrassed by him? She didn't seem the type to care what others thought. But then she didn't seem the type to hook up with Brett either.

And she'd leaned in, tried to kiss him.

Another idea crept into view: Tess. Her hostility was palpable. Her body stiffened as if a physical barrier was erected every time he spoke to her. He recalled the conversation he'd had with her on the pavement outside the Outdoor Store. She'd said Steph had nothing to do with their family. Her body, however, had said something else entirely. She clearly didn't like Steph. But why? Something to do with Lachie?

He remembered the fuzzy image of Steph and Lachie from the pub's grainy CCTV footage. Lachie had been rattled, clearly angry to see her. But why? Because she was involved with his dad? Because Noah was Brett's kid? Lachie's half-brother?

He remembered Noah's striking similarity to Brett.

He took his glasses from the vanity. The toilet lid groaned beneath him. With his vision restored, he surveyed the damage to his leg. He'd been reluctant to remove the bandage Bacuzzi had given him, both afraid of what he'd find beneath and that, once removed, the stump would expand exponentially.

He'd been right on both counts.

Post shower, things weren't looking much better, and he didn't hold high hopes of his leg fitting back into his prosthesis come morning. He downed a handful of the painkillers Bacuzzi had given him in one swallow.

Back in his room, the dim light from the lit walkway outside shone around the edge of the curtains. It flickered.

*Jesus, not another bloody blackout.*

Dressed, he sat on his bed and pulled out the old yearbooks he'd borrowed from the school and flipped aimlessly through.

Coloured photos of smiling faces in green uniforms beamed at him. School camps. Concerts. Science fairs. He stopped flicking. The page lay open on the sports carnival. Bare-legged kids jumping, throwing, running. Ribbons shining from the chests of beaming winners. Kids bending over to catch their breath after the hundred metre dash.

He scanned the images across the double page, didn't recognise anyone. His eyes fell to a photo in the bottom corner. An image taken from the back of a crowd, the tail end of a sprint just in shot. He lifted the page closer, squinted through his glasses.

Two figures at the back of the crowd stood out.

*What the hell?*

He snatched his phone from the bedside table, snapped a photo and zoomed in on the image on his screen. The two figures were now enlarged enough for him to make out.

Two faces, both turned sideways to watch the race pass. The prominent overbite and wiry frame of a young Mike was unmistakable, though his short, cropped hair rid him of any scruffiness. Next to him, a taller man in a pair of running shorts, with dark sideburns that came down past his ears.

An unfamiliar face.

He flicked back through the yearbook, towards the front where he knew the teachers' portraits were. A quick scan and the man was easily recognisable among the staff of twelve: Simon Thacker.

He flicked back to the sports carnival page.

Thacker and Mike stood at the back of the gathered crowd. Callum examined the enlarged image on his phone again. His stomach tensed, the knot bound and pulled taut.

Thacker's mouth was open, one fist in the air, cheering on the race. Callum's eyes focused on Thacker's other hand, which was lodged firmly down the back of Mike's shorts, unmistakably on the young boy's arse.

Hot bile rose up Callum's throat. He took a sip of water from the glass on his bedside table, but the taste lingered, grew. He couldn't push it down. He heaved once, saliva pooling in his mouth. A second time, then he turned his head and threw up on the bedsheet.

He took a larger drink, then replaced the glass with a shaky hand.

*Jesus.*

His head spun. So, Mike had been telling the truth. And no one had done anything about it. Thacker had been able to continue on with his life: job, wife, kids. He thought of Milly, three years older than Mike, Lachie and their mate Josh had been when Thacker had taken advantage of them.

Callum felt a fresh wave of nausea sweep over him as he thought of his son. Thacker with his son.

He should've done more to protect Lachie. He was only a kid. He hadn't known about Thacker, but somewhere, buried deep for the last thirty years, he'd known exactly what kind of man Brett Wyatt was.

Why the hell hadn't he intervened?

A flash of terrified eyes and Amelia Dyer flittered across his memory.

A bang on his door ripped through his thoughts. He thrust the yearbook under his pillow and wiped his hands along the front of his shorts. He scooped up the loose sheet, struggled to take it to the bathroom, and closed the door behind him, containing the smell of vomit.

A gust of wind pushed against the motel door as he opened it, and he almost lost his footing as it flung back and banged against the wall. A wave of humidity rolled into the room.

'Eddy.'

'Hey.' His friend didn't wait for an invite, just strode inside, leaving the onslaught of rain behind. 'I'm calling it a night and wanted to stop by.'

Callum closed the door and turned in time to see his friend collapse into the desk chair, a puddle of water already pooled at his feet. Shadows had formed beneath his eyes that hadn't been there three days earlier, and his shoulders slumped forward.

'Are you all right?' Callum asked.

'I was about to ask you the same thing. You look like you've seen a ghost.'

'Worse.' Callum made his way to the edge of the bed and leaned the crutches against the bedside table.

He showed Eddy the photo from the yearbook and the zoomed-in version from his phone.

'Jesus.'

'Yeah, it's pretty damning evidence. Can't exactly sweep this kind of thing under the rug when it's staring you in the face.'

'I can't believe no one's ever noticed it. How the hell did that make it into the yearbook?'

'It was tiny, I blew it up, and if you think Granite Creek District School has some kind of committee that's scouring the photos …'

'All right, all right.' Eddy's head looked as if it were getting heavy. 'So, it's very likely that Josh Swindley did commit suicide because he was messed up after it all.'

'And it's also more than likely that Lachie and Mike were meeting to commemorate his anniversary.'

'Yep. I guess something like that bonds you for life.'

Neither spoke for a few moments. Rain and wind blended together to create a cacophony that barely allowed Callum's thoughts to fully form. He was the first to speak. 'So why's Mike acting all fishy next door?'

'I asked around. That SES guy is Bernard Burns from the Atherton Tablelands.'

'Bernard Burns?' Callum didn't bother to mask his smile.

Eddy shrugged. 'Apparently.'

'And what's Bernie Burns up to?'

'Word is, he comes for a visit every month or so.'

'What the hell for?' Granite Creek generally wasn't considered a tourist destination. One visit was usually enough for most.

'He's the local—well, not so local—pot dealer.' Eddy smirked. 'I'd wondered who it was. I'd almost thought it was Mike, there's such a strong stench of the stuff around this joint.'

Slot, slot. More pieces of the puzzle slotted into place as Callum recalled the heady earth scent embedded in his bedsheets, the carpet, the whole bloody motel. He'd grown used to it. Hadn't he even got a strong waft of it when he'd returned after his hike with Steph? When Mike had been in his room? In the aftermath of the break-in, he'd forgotten all about it. But of course, marijuana.

'It's some kind of fancy new rainforest blend: Green Ganja. Smells a bit different from the usual bush bud. Grows it at the back of his cane farm and promotes it as medicinal. Supposed to cure all sorts of ailments.'

Callum thought of his leg and the shitty painkillers Bacuzzi had given him. 'So, Mike likes a bit of weed. That's it?'

'And a bit of a drink. Well, more than a bit. Barman told me he's in there most nights after reception here closes.'

'Makes sense. Need something to drown out the memories of being felt up by a man you're meant to be able to trust while an entire town turned a blind eye.'

More pieces clicked together.

'And Thacker?' Callum asked. 'Rumour has it the kids left him for dead off the cliff. We know he got the daylights beaten out of him by Brett at the time. And he was up north when Lachie died. Coincidence?'

Eddy shook his head. 'We know he's not exactly a stand-up citizen.' He nodded to the open yearbook. 'I'll look into it.'

Callum took in his friend's crumpled uniform and the shadow forming around his jaw. Eddy looked as if he hadn't slept or showered for days. 'I'll do it. You've got your hands full with this cyclone coming.'

'No.' Eddy's voice was firm. 'That's not your job. You're not police.'

The comment jabbed at Callum, picked at something deep inside. A festering wound he'd thought long healed. Not being able to join the police force had been one of the biggest disappointments of losing his leg.

Watching his best mate go through the process had been even harder.

'It's not police work,' he said. 'I'm just making a few phone calls. Enquiries. I do it all the time for work.'

'Nah, mate, better not.' Eddy paused. 'Look, mate, while we're at it. I've heard a few things. Complaints really.'

Callum didn't speak. Eddy continued, didn't quite meet Callum's eye. 'Paige from the fire station thought you were a copper. In fact, she said you told her you were one. She found out who you really were from one of the other fireys. She's not happy, mate. Similar story with Tess. Impersonating a copper is a major offence. They could press charges and you could get in serious trouble.' Eddy met Callum's eye at last. 'Like jail trouble.'

The wind picked up, a bang in the distance.

'Seriously, mate. You've gotta stop. Give it up and let me do my job.'

The crusted scab began to open. 'It's been three days since Lachie turned up dead and we're no closer to finding out what the hell happened to him.'

'*We're* not doing anything, Cal.'

'Well then, *you're* no closer to figuring it out.' Callum felt the wound burst open. A fetid fire escaped, snaked up his neck and left a trail of desolate anger in its wake. 'Where the hell was Thacker on Tuesday? And have you even bothered to have a proper chat to Brett, or have you just been skirting around him like the rest of the people in this bloody town for the last thirty years?'

'I'm not skirting around anyone, mate. I've put the firm word on Brett about your tyres, and about socking you. And if you want to press charges, I'm all for it.' His words spilled out. 'But in case you haven't noticed, I've got my hands full and if you think it's easy being the new cop in town when a body rocks up and a cyclone's about to hit, then you're more deluded than you were three decades ago when you thought Pip was going to up and leave Granite and rush to your side.' Eddy snapped his mouth shut, as if he'd gone too far.

The fire swept up Callum's neck and set alight a blaze in his cheeks. 'Don't bring Pip into this. Don't go dragging up the past.'

'I'm not the one dragging it up, mate. You're living in it. You're obsessed with Brett, you always have been. And now Thacker—'

'Brett's a fucking jerk and you know it. And as for Thacker.' He threw the yearbook across the widening gap between them. It hit Eddy in the chest, fell to the ground. 'Do you need more proof, *Sarge*?'

'We've no proof Thacker was even in Granite on Tuesday. And, yeah, Brett can be a jerk, but he's also a respected citizen around here, and I'm not doing myself any favours as the new cop in town by pointing the finger at him when, as far as I can tell, aside from bruising your ego, he's done nothing wrong.'

'Nothing wrong?' He went to stand, forgot he didn't have his prosthesis on and plopped back onto the bed. 'Open your eyes! Pip! Lachie!' He had to bite his tongue to stop himself adding Amelia. He couldn't yet. He needed something solid, more than a thirty-year-old memory to throw at Eddy.

'My eyes are open, you're the one with blinkers on and only Brett in sight. You need to back off. Why have you even come back? It's been three decades, this isn't your problem. You have no connection to the Wyatt family anymore.'

The fire bore into Callum's cheeks and laced his tongue. He wanted to open his mouth, let it all out. Smoke, flames, the festering truth. Lachie was his son. This *was* his problem.

'Go home.' Eddy stood, reached the door. It banged open, hard, the force of the wind outside bursting to get in. He threw a final look at Callum—unreadable—and strode into the rain.

Callum went to the open door, crutches wrapped around his forearms. Eddy's figure darkened as he stalked across the car park, not bothering to follow the sheltered walkway. He was briefly illuminated as he passed the lit entrance to the motel reception before being swallowed entirely by the darkness. Beyond, the outline of the rainforest stood watch, trees bent over, inching closer.

# CHAPTER THIRTY-SIX

Bleary-eyed and mouth filled with the aftertaste of bitter espresso, Callum sat on a rickety metal chair inside the bakery. From his window seat, he watched as locals parked their cars and swept through the doorway's PVC flaps into the tiny shop. A carpet of towels had been laid on the floor in the hope of preventing a lawsuit. The bakery was doing a roaring trade. Apparently, an encroaching cyclone wasn't enough for most locals to forgo their morning meat pie.

Phone pressed up against his ear, he listened to the upbeat tune of the Reef Inn's waiting music and stifled a yawn.

Sleep had come in fits and starts. Granite boulders and whispers had interrupted his dreams. Snatches of Milly's face had come and gone all night until at last a grey granite floor had flooded his vision and he'd woken as abruptly as if he'd been slapped.

At 3.24 am.

Covered in sweat and his stump tangled in his bedsheets, he hadn't managed to drift off again. His argument with Eddy had played on his mind for the remaining hours of the early morning. His friend's words ran through his head, like news headlines at the bottom of the telly screen.

*You're not a cop. You need to back off. This isn't your problem.*

He'd carried a weight the size of a boulder in his chest all morning. It dragged him down and made him sluggish. Guilt.

He knew Eddy was right. He wasn't a cop. And he remembered from his dad how isolating it could be being the only cop in a small town. Everyone likes to keep a safe distance between themselves and the eyes of the law. Even those with nothing to hide. Life in a small town as a single bloke with no mates and an ageing father was going to be rough. He couldn't blame Eddy for wanting to make a good impression.

His morning had got even worse as he'd struggled to jam his still swollen stump back into its too small prosthesis. A phone call to Milly, unanswered, and another to his folks who told him she'd spent the night at a friend's and wasn't back yet, rounded off the start of his morning.

He took another sip of his shitty coffee.

'Thanks for holding,' the now familiar monotone voice said as the music cut off. 'I'll put you through to Mr Thacker's room now.'

Another pause, more music. A familiar curvy blonde entered the bakery. Hanna from the Outdoor Store made her way to the counter. She pointed to the takeaway coffee cups lined up behind the counter and her t-shirt rode up to reveal an intricate tattoo on the side of her waist. A splash of black, yellow and red on a mottled background of brown and faded purple. Callum's mind ticked over as her t-shirt slid back down to cover the mark.

Black, yellow and red. The same colours as Eddy's tattoo. The same colours on the flag proudly sported on his friend's desk at the station. The boulder of guilt nestled deeper, settled in.

'This is Simon Thacker.' The voice at the other end of the line snapped Callum's attention back. It was soft. It didn't fit with the image of a man with dark sideburns who liked to feel up young boys.

'Good morning, Mr Thacker, sorry to contact you so early in the morning. My name is Paul and I'm phoning you from Qantas Airlines. I understand that you missed your return flight last Tuesday and you're wanting to rearrange an alternate flight back to Adelaide for you and your family.'

'What?'

'I said, I under—'

'No, I heard you, but we didn't have a flight booked for Tuesday. We're going home next week.'

'Oh, are you certain? I've got it right here in front of me. Flights for four, Cairns to Adelaide.'

'Nope, not us. We only got to Cairns on Monday. We wouldn't have booked to return one day later. I can pull up my email.'

'Oh, that won't be necessary. Let me just check a few things at my end. It'll just take a few minutes.' Callum tapped away on his laptop and mentally cursed the sound of a barrel-chested man ordering a sausage roll at a near shout. Hanna had moved to the other side of the shop, awaiting her order. Her body angled slightly away, she avoided his eye and looked intently at the coffee machine.

He stifled a yawn and drained his espresso, managed to catch the eye of the girl working the machine and raised his hand and pointed to his empty cup, indicating another.

He needed the caffeine hit, shitty coffee or not.

'So, how's the trip going so far?' Callum spoke into the phone, his voice light, airy.

'Good.' Thacker's answer was clipped. Clearly pissed off about the flight debacle.

'Been up to the rainforest yet?'

'Nope.'

'Oh, you should go, it's beautiful. So much to see. They do lots of bus trips up north.' Tap, tap on the keyboard. 'We're actually partnered with some of the major tourism companies—'

'I'm not interested, mate. Look, how's this flight stuff going?'

'Just a few more moments. Yes, here it is.' A pause. 'Oh. Oh dear …'

'What?'

'You did check in on Tuesday.'

'No, I didn't.'

'Yes, sir. It's right here. The 0900 hours flight. The Thacker family. You paid for four tickets—'

'Look.' Voice raised. 'We didn't check in for a bloody flight on Tuesday. I was two hundred kay north of Cairns, nowhere near the bloody airport.'

A jerk in Callum's chest.

*Bingo.*

'And my wife and kids went out on a glass bottom boat. Left at 8 am, gone all day. Definitely not at the airport at nine. I've got the booking for the boat trip and for my car rental if you need some damn proof. We weren't at the bloody airport. We're still in Cairns.'

Callum tapped loudly on his keyboard. 'And you weren't tempted to join them?'

'What?'

'On the boat. You said your wife and kids went out on a boat.'

'I don't like boats.' Short, curt. Pissed.

'Of course, sir, this should only take another minute to sort out, so sorry for the inconvenience. Just bear with me a moment.'

A deep sigh down the other end of the line; a kid's voice quiet in the background. Callum's skin crept.

'You mentioned you were nowhere near the airport.' Callum's mouth was suddenly dry. He fought to keep his tone light. 'Off seeing the sites? I hear the Daintree is meant to be spectac—'

'I'm not interested in sightseeing. Had some business to deal with.'

Another sigh and Thacker switched his tone to that of a man who knew he should control his anger if he didn't want to be charged twice for his flights. 'Could you hurry this up a bit, it's just I've got stuff to do today, mate.'

'Yes, of course you do. This will only take a few more moments. We've been having these glitches all week.' Callum wondered how much harder to push. Harder. 'Have you spent much time up north before?'

A deep breath down the end of the line and Thacker gave up on his nice-guy tone. 'What the hell's that got to do with anything?'

'Oops,' Callum said, sensing he wasn't going to get anything else out of Thacker. 'Mr Shane Thacker, is it?'

'No, Simon. Simon Thacker.'

'Oh no. Mr Thacker, sorry, our mistake. I had the Mr Shane Thacker family checked in on Tuesday. Oh bother. Like I said, we've been having these faults all week with this new system upgrade. It's been blotting out first names and going off initials only. It's been such a bungle …'

Thacker's voice escalated in Callum's ear.

*Screw you, Thacker.*

He clicked the phone dead.

\*

Callum stared unfocused at the collection of pale blue espresso cups on his table, a dark circle of coffee granules around the rim of each. His conversation with Thacker replayed in his head on a loop.

*I was two hundred kay north of Cairns.*

Did he mean Granite Creek? Had he been here the day Lachie died? Had he had contact with Lachie? Could Thacker's grudge really have lasted eighteen years?

A fresh gust of wind and the bakery's PVC flaps blew

inward. Callum's thoughts of Thacker scattered as Bill Quade tottered inside and stood, sopping wet, gazing around the bakery.

Bill shuffled along the soggy towel-covered floor, his upper back rounded, his head poking out the top of his shirt like a turtle coming out of its shell to survey the world. He paused just in front of Callum's table, facing the counter.

At least he was wearing shoes.

'A tea, please.' His voice was lost over the racket of the rain outside and the chatter within the small space. 'A cup of tea, please.'

'Bill.' Callum reached out and touched Eddy's dad on the arm.

A brief pause, then Bill's eyes tracked down to Callum's hand.

'Bill, why don't you take a seat?'

Bill turned. Confusion, then recognition. He smiled his lopsided smile. 'Can't seem to get a bloody cuppa.'

'Take a seat. I'll get you a cuppa.'

A few minutes later, and Callum had texted Eddy to let him know the whereabouts of his dad, told him not to rush. A pang of annoyance that he'd had to bother Eddy. But he'd registered the worsening wind, the ongoing downpour and that he himself was in no state to escort Bill down the street to his car and drive him home. They'd both probably end up in a heap on the side of the footpath.

'A lot of people in town.' Bill's eyes roamed the cramped bakery, his hand wrapped around his half-empty teacup. The remnants of a sausage roll sat at the corner of his mouth.

'A lot of people came to help with the search,' Callum said. 'Most are stuck up here due to the cyclone coming.'

'Another cyclone, eh?'

'Hopefully it'll hit north of here.' Hope wasn't the right word. No one wished a category five cyclone to hit anywhere.

'Who were they searching for? Not another kid? It's always a kid.'

'Not a kid this time. It was Lachie Wyatt.'

'Wyatt, eh? He wasn't a bad kid.'

'So I've heard.'

A chuckle as Bill wiped his hands down the front of his shirt. He'd missed a button and a flake of pastry stuck to the tuft of grey hair that poked out from his chest. 'That's certainly not what you thought of him back in your day.'

A pause as Callum tried to put the pieces together.

'The Wyatt boy,' Bill said. 'The eldest one. You never liked him.'

Of course, he was talking about Brett, not Lachie. Eddy was right, there was more going on with Bill.

'Not a bad kid,' Bill repeated.

'No? I don't think Eddy got along with him too well either.'

Another chuckle. 'Oh, Eddy and you didn't know him very well.' He sipped his tea. 'But I did. Well, knew his dad at least, so knew what that boy had to put up with. A real brute that man was. The kid took the brunt of it.'

A weight in Callum's chest. He'd always suspected as much, had never said anything. Done anything. As bad as the rest of the town.

'But a good boy. Always worked hard. A good family man too when his kids came along. Loved that Pip of his.'

A stab within.

'Shame about the kids though.' His words begun to slur the longer his spoke. He took another sip and a trickle of tea ran down his chin. 'That little girl of his ...'

Something soured in Callum's mouth. He drained his espresso, washed the taste down. 'And what about his son? Lachie?'

A pause and Bill closed his eyes, leaned further back in his chair, mouth ajar. A minute passed, maybe two. Asleep?

An onslaught of wind, PVC flaps tangled with a cloud of auburn hair and Steph pressed her way into the bakery. She smoothed her hair, looked around. Her face lit up when she saw Callum's. His chest lightened.

'Bill,' she said, stepping towards them. She placed one hand on the old man's shoulder, crouched so that they were eye level. 'Bill.'

Bill opened his eyes, looked at her. A few blinks before he gave a smile.

'Good to see you got your cuppa. I've popped over to drive you back home before this weather gets any worse.'

'Oh.' His eyes scanned the bakery, surprise crossing his face. 'Home, eh? Well, that's good of you.'

Steph steadied him as he stood, dusted the front of his shirt and did up his missed button. 'There. All ready now.'

The two smiled at each other before Steph gave a quick wink to Callum and turned to guide Bill out.

As they reached the door, Bill turned back, eyed Callum. 'He took after his granddad, that one.'

The pair pressed through the doorway, and Callum watched as they passed by his window, Steph's arm looped through Bill's.

His mind whirred.

*He took after his granddad.*
*Who? Brett? Lachie?*

He sat for a moment, replaying the conversation with Bill in his head, ordered another coffee. A few minutes later, the waitress moved his way and placed an espresso cup in front of him. Its dark liquid brimmed so close to the surface that it looked more like a long black. Or dishwater. His eyes focused on the cup. The pale blue of the porcelain and the murky liquid within.

The wisp of an idea sharpened at the edges and began to take form. He snatched at it, brought it into focus. He opened the search engine on his phone and began tapping away. After a quick search, he drummed his fingers on the table, looked at his watch and, deciding they would be open at this hour, dialled another number.

After a few moments, a cheery voice answered the line and he injected a serious note to his voice, the lie fluid as it slid across his tongue.

'Good morning, sir, this is Senior Sergeant Ian Beaconsfield. I've just got a few questions I'd like answered for a case I'm looking into.'

# CHAPTER THIRTY-SEVEN

With the lingering taste of lighter fluid coffee, and a nagging thought in his head, Callum left the bakery. The smack of the rain and humidity were both so intense, he couldn't decide which was more oppressive.

He pushed the discomfort away and tried to free his thoughts. Something snagged his mind, like the wait-a-while vine capturing its fleeing prey.

Ignoring the ache from his prosthesis, he turned and walked head-on into the rain.

A hundred metres or so and he stepped into the air-conditioned relief of the Outdoor Store.

Hanna looked up at the jangle of the doorway bell and the gust of wind that swept in with him. Between the shelves of bushwalking guides and racks of waterproof jackets, he saw her face fall. He picked his way towards the counter, and by the time he stood in front of her, she'd managed to hitch a smile on her face. 'Didn't think I'd see you again. I thought you would have escaped the rain as soon as possible.'

'Just been catching up with some old mates. Besides, need to wait for this cyclone to blow over now. Didn't think you'd be open.'

She shrugged. 'Just for a few hours. Boss thinks that the waterproof ponchos and torches should sell themselves. So, what is it you're after?'

He scanned the cramped space. His eyes fell on the cheap birding binoculars that looked as if they wouldn't withstand a light shower or a gentle breeze.

'One of these.' He picked up a Nordic walking pole on the next stand.

'They come as a pair.'

'Well.' He smiled. 'Two of these then.'

A flash across her face. A beat later, the smile returned. 'Did you get to go for that hike?'

'Yes. Trickier than I'd expected in this weather. The boots were good though.' He tried to block the memory of his soaking right foot, and the blister that was still bothering him.

'I told you they were the best.'

'Yeah, I actually think they were the same one's Lachie had.'

A definite flash across her face. She started rearranging things on the counter.

'Were they?' Her smile gone. 'I can't recall.'

He knew the pair sitting on the shoe rack outside Tess's house had been higher cut and grey, not brown. But her reaction to Lachie's name had been what he was chasing. The idea in his head tugged a little firmer. He pushed on. 'But weren't Lachie and you, you know, close?'

Her eyes snapped up to his face. 'What makes you say that?'

'Oh, sorry, that was just the impression I got.' He hesitated, wondering how hard to push.

Probably couldn't piss her off too much more.

'I know Tess wasn't in here buying shoes.' He took a guess. 'She was confronting you.'

'I told you, I don't know the family.'

'Yeah, but you referred to their son by name.'

The scowl across her forehead deepened, her accent thickening. 'It's a small town. People know people's names.'

It wasn't working. Change tack.

She fiddled with a display of waterproof matches on the counter and he lowered his voice. 'You weren't the only one, you know.'

Her hands paused, gripping the matches.

'He did the same to one of his colleagues. A female firefighter at the station.'

Her shoulders stiffened. 'I don't know what you're talking about.'

'Hanna, it's okay to speak up.' He softened his voice. 'Lachie's gone and he's not coming back. The truth needs to come out.'

She took a deep breath. Her shoulders dropped slightly, but her knuckles remained white, squeezing the matchbox.

'He was so nice. Charming.' Her voice was low. 'This town is so small, nothing ever happens. But then Lachie came in. He was cute and funny and was the first person under the age of fifty to show any interest in me. I knew he was married. But Tess was always scowling and moping about. I felt a bit sorry for him. Anyway, we started seeing each other. Nothing serious. Mostly we'd meet in my flat or he'd take me for a drive. It was just a bit of fun at the start.' She faltered. 'Then he got a bit intense.'

'Intense?'

'Controlling. Like, I told him I was going to Cairns later in the month for a weekend and he got all funny about it. He tried to convince me not to go, then he asked if he could come with me.' Her frown returned. 'Actually, he told me he was coming. Said it could be my birthday present to him, to let him come along with me. He booked us a hotel before I could even say no.'

Callum's mind returned to the calendar on Tess's kitchen wall; the boys' trip to Cairns. 'Was that all he did?'

A deep inhale before she spoke, her voice thickening. 'He came into the shop once and I was serving the guy who owns the motel. Lachie just pretended to look around. When Mike left, Lachie just snapped.' Her face hardened. 'He grabbed me and pushed me up against the wall. He told me I was never to talk to other guys like that. To flirt. I wasn't even fucking flirting. Mike's a doped-up mess, I was just doing my job. But Lachie wouldn't hear it. He was hurting me. He had me pressed up against the shoe rack.' Her hand touched her waist, where Callum knew a mottled bruise lay beneath the clingy fabric of her t-shirt. 'It cut into me. I've never seen someone so mad before.'

'What happened?'

'Another customer came in. Thank god. I'm not sure what Lachie would've done otherwise.' Her skin had paled, and she seemed to have folded in on herself.

'When did this happen?'

'The same day he went missing.'

He nodded. 'And who was the customer? The one that came in?'

'Bernard. Big ginger guy with a beard. Stays at the motel every few weeks.'

Bernie Burns.

'Know him well?'

'He comes in to see me when he visits.' She smiled. 'For business.'

He nodded. Green Ganja.

'And why was Tess in here the other day?'

Her eyes glassed over, lost in thought. She took a moment to respond. 'She came to apologise.'

'Apologise?'

'Yes.' Her brows pulled in together. 'She said she was sorry that he'd got to me too.'

## CHAPTER THIRTY-EIGHT

The icy blast from the air conditioner was stifled by the smell of sour milk and disinfectant. Callum stood in the doorway of Granite Creek's nursing home and aged care facility, puddles of rainwater pooling at his feet, unsure why he'd come. The small reception area was adorned with vases of flowers and cheery pictures of green tree frogs and cassowary chicks. Neither overrode the clinical feel of the easy-clean lino and passcode-locked glass doors.

His encounter with Hanna was still tumbling around his head. Tess had apologised to the woman who'd been sleeping with her husband.

*Sorry he got to you too.*

A sudden image of Hanna's mid-drift as she'd stretched up in the bakery. The black, yellow and red of her German flag tattoo hadn't concealed the damage that had occurred beneath.

Lachie's aggression, his threats, his control. Callum thought back to Hanna's planned Cairns trip. Lachie had invited himself along, for his birthday. It was around the same time Tess would be due to give birth. Jesus, what sort of husband does that?

Callum scrunched his eyes as he recalled his run-in with Tess in the street two days earlier. He'd grabbed her arm to stop her falling, his fist tight. The skin had reddened. A bruise had shone beneath. But it couldn't have been from his grip. Her skin was already brown and mottled. At least a few days old. It had been right where he'd grabbed her. Right where anyone would grab her.

A sensation coursed over him, like an electric current, pulsating and alive.

Hanna and Tess.

And Paige. She had no one to turn to: the only female firefighter at the station and an out-of-towner.

Tess was from Brisbane, and Hanna from Germany. It seemed Lachie had had a pattern. He chose isolated women who had nowhere to go. No one to turn to.

No, Callum corrected himself: Lachie didn't choose them, he targeted them.

He recalled other blemishes, covered by long sleeves too hot for the Queensland heat. Unnatural blues and purples shining out on milky skin.

Pip.

He thought of the photo of the Wyatt family in the newspaper clipping, buried in his lockbox. Brett, Pip and Lachie. And baby Amelia, her tiny arm dangling limply in a cast.

He felt sick.

His son. Was it possible? What he'd thought he'd known about Lachie—what he liked to believe about the man he never knew—was slowly morphing. Moving from light, swallowed by shadows.

'Are you all right, mate?' A male nurse, with a grey beard that made him look as if he should be sitting on a Harley and not at a nursing home reception, ran his eyes over Callum.

'Yeah.' His tongue chafed the roof of his mouth.

'Here to visit someone?'

'Yeah.'

'Just need to sign the register here then.' The nurse indicated an open book on the desk, and stood as Callum approached, as if to catch him.

God, he must look like shit.

The last few days were catching up with him. His shirt was crumpled, and he'd worn the same pair of trousers for the last two days, his belt now loosened by one notch thanks to an almost week-long diet of pub meals and beer. He hadn't shaved since his arrival and his face itched from the unfamiliar growth around his jaw.

As he signed in, he looked at the names listed above his on the page. A few familiar names that he recognised but couldn't quite place. Then, at the top, one he'd thought he might see but that still caught him off guard.

Lachie Wyatt.

The date next to it was for six days ago. The day Lachie went missing. The day he probably died.

Callum's finger traced the name, the contours of where the pen had pressed into the paper. He flicked back a page.

Lachie Wyatt.

One week earlier. And another week earlier, Lachie's name again.

Callum flipped through the visitor book, page after page.

Lachie had visited every week.

'Everything all right?' The nurse asked, eyeing the visitor book.

'Yeah.' He stared at Lachie's name before looking up at the nurse. 'It's just that Lachie Wyatt visited every week, did he?'

The nurse paused a moment, scratched at his beard. 'Well, yeah. His mum's in here, you know?'

He nodded. He knew. 'And Brett?'

The nurse shook his head. 'Never comes.'

Never comes. Never bothers to visit his wife. Pip.

\*

Callum walked down the sterile corridor of the nursing home. The lino was sticky underfoot and he was pretty certain he was walking over some half mopped-up bodily fluid.

His head spun with the image of Lachie's name in the visitor book.

Open doors passed him by as he gripped the stainless-steel handrail. Glimpses of people inside tiny rooms. Frail, miserable, alone; separated from the next poor sod by two sheets of plasterboard and a lessening will to carry on. Names printed on small whiteboards adorned each door, easy to wipe clean when the time came. Make room for the next one no longer considered safe in their own home.

He thought of Bill Quade. A tug in his chest, a heat behind his eyes. *Jesus, life was cruel.*

His palms were slick and his chest tight. Should he even be here? He slowed his pace, came to a stop.

The next door gaped open, empty. The neatly made bed and strong lemon disinfectant scent suggestive of a life just passed, packed away neatly and cleaned up after. His eyes flicked to the whiteboard on the door. The name, yet to be erased, glared at him in red marker.

*What the hell?*

'Thought you were meant to stay off that leg.' Bacuzzi's voice jolted him back as she came to stand alongside him.

'I am. I mean, I have been.' He took in her no-nonsense expression and lanyard. 'You work here too then?'

'I look after the residence.'

Of course. Small town, one doctor. Jack of all trades.

He nodded towards the name on the door. 'Not here anymore?'

She looked at the door. A long pause, as if she was registering the name for the first time. 'No. Passed away last week.'

'Any visitors?'

She cocked her head to one side as if deciding if she'd be crossing some ethical line by answering. 'Never. His son came up from down south and picked his stuff up after he'd passed.'

'What day?'

She eyed him for a beat before answering. 'Tuesday.'

*Tuesday. Christ.*

She swiped a broad palm across the whiteboard, erasing the name in one sweep.

Gone.

The letters burned into Callum's mind.

\*

The door was open, and Callum stopped a few metres shy of it. The walls of the corridor were an off white, the silver metal handrail running either side broken every few metres by a doorway to another resident's room.

He knew he'd come.

If he were honest with himself, he'd known he would come from the moment he'd seen Lachie's name in the news. Over a decade had gone by in which Callum had wondered if he should visit. He'd always pushed the thought aside, telling himself he was too busy. Work. Single parent. Life. Everything. Anything.

He'd been in Granite Creek four days. Part of him was surprised it'd taken him this long to come.

For years, he'd played the scene out again and again in his head. How would she look? Would there be any signs of recognition?

He knew there wouldn't be.

His leg jerked as he took a step forward, the opening to the doorway closing in.

What the hell was he doing? *Turn back.* He couldn't face her.

Another step.

Seriously, what was he expecting to get out of this?

A shadow flitted across the opening and a soft hum caught his ear. The voice was familiar, deepened slightly by the years, but still the same.

A final breath and he crossed the threshold.

A willowy figure swayed around the room, just out of time to the tune she was humming. Her back to the door, long limbs protruded out of a blue cotton dress that hung too loose. The sash of a belt was undone, one end dragging on the floor next to her bare feet. Her ash blonde hair, nearly waist length, still held its colour. It wrapped around Callum's heart and dragged him back thirty years to the boulders. Pip's head in his lap, her blonde hair sprawled across the granite.

He watched her move, her hips shifting side to side as she rearranged belongings on a shelf with one hand, the other clutching something close to her chest. Thin milky fingers held each item for a beat before placing them in another spot. A mug. A hairbrush. A photo.

A flash of a chubby toddler with crinkled eyes and a slight upturn to her top lip. Her daughter, Amelia.

He held his breath, wondering if she recognised the face smiling back at her from the photo. She returned it back to the shelf. He exhaled, and she turned at the sound.

She looked different. The Pip he remembered was the Pip of thirty years ago. He'd seen her since then, of course. But that was different. Her green eyes had been mostly clear then, full of recognition, anguish, a mother's grief. Her tears had been for her daughter, but her smile had been for him. Now he was certain she was smiling because she had a visitor.

Any visitor.

His eyes dropped to her arm, and the bundle she was clutching close to her chest. A baby doll hung limply, its face pressed against her, its little white gown smeared brown and red.

'Hi, Pip.' His voice came out steadier than expected.

'Oh, it's you. It's about time.' She beamed at him.

His heart flittered, the wings of a bowerbird in his chest: she remembered. He stepped further into the room, his heart racing like he was seventeen again.

'You're late again, I've been waiting ages.'

A tug in his memory: their bikes at the kauri pine, Pip looking at her watch when he arrived.

'I've got something for you,' she said.

'Oh?'

'Yes, here.' She took something off the shelf and reached out towards him. A tight bracelet was around her wrist and her pale skin had a shine. He took in the length of her arm and noticed a few patches of purple dotted along it.

'Take it.' She thrust the item at him.

He looked to her hand. There was a freckle on her index finger. He took the item, looked at it blankly. 'Thanks.' His voice caught as his fingers brushed hers, her skin papery. Her hand lingered longer than necessary.

He didn't move, waiting, searching her eyes.

Nothing. No flicker of recognition. No spark at their touch.

She let her hand drop limply to her side.

*Ting. Ting.*

His eyes shifted to her bracelet. Three silver bells entwined within red and blue thread. He absently reached for his pocket, feeling for the bracelet he'd kept on him the last few days. Not there. Of course, Steph had taken it.

Pip began patting the baby doll again, shushing it softly.

'Did you bring my hat?' she asked.

He blinked. 'Sorry, your …?'

'My hat.' She turned, snatched up a yellow feather from the shelf behind her. 'I've been waiting for it. Did you bring my hat back?'

The feather caught the fluorescent light overhead. It shimmered dully. Surely it couldn't be the same one? It'd been thirty years.

But the angle of the barbs and the length of the vane told him it belonged to a golden bowerbird. Where else would she have found it?

His throat tightened, his voice struggling to come out. 'No, sorry. I forgot your hat.'

Her face fell, and a wisp of guilt filtered through him.

'Oh, that's too bad.' She returned the feather to the shelf and picked up a grey rock instead, the baby doll still held close with her other hand.

She resumed her humming and he watched her shift her weight methodically side to side, just shy of the beat once more.

A few notes in and the rush of the rainforest flooded his memory. His heart quickened.

She pressed the grey rock to her chest and, humming the tune for the whispering, placed it on the shelf in front of the framed photo, blocking the unmistakable eyes and upturned smile of her daughter.

Amelia Wyatt.
Their daughter.
Milly.

# CHAPTER THIRTY-NINE

*Thirty years earlier*

Grey clouds hung low overhead and a faint spatter of rain sprinkled across Pip's nose. The boulders dug into our backs, the flimsy picnic blanket I'd brought was useless. Legs entangled, we lay a few metres back from the edge, tucked among the roots of the huge fig tree that clung to the cliff face. I ignored the fact that the granite was getting more and more uncomfortable and tried to focus on what'd happened: I'd just had sex with Pip.

The words ran on repeat through my head.

Sex.

With.

Pip.

*Holy shit.*

I tried to remember it all. Her skin soft against the hard granite. Her long hair tangled in our mouths. Pressing inside her.

Sex. With. Pip.

I blew out a long breath.

Her hair sprawled out across my chest, and I picked up a strand and wound it between my fingers. I closed my eyes, blocking out everything except the rise and fall of her chest.

She'd been the one to suggest we do it at the boulders. I'd told her that we could go round to my place. Mum and Dad both worked long hours, and summer holidays meant whole days with an empty house. But she'd insisted.

She'd wanted to come here.

The wind swept across us, and her hair lifted and tickled my face. A soft whistle ran across the boulders.

Her body stiffened. 'We should go.' She sat up, her hair slipping between my fingers. 'It's getting late.'

I shrugged, tried to sit up. My knee twisted against the hard granite and gave a twinge. I lay back down. It still wasn't right from when I'd pulled her out of the creek. A sprained ligament or something. Mum said it'd come good in a few months, in time to try out for the academy's mid-year intake.

'Seriously, it'll be dark soon.' The sky was still light, grey clouds brewing in the distance.

Pip stood, pulled her shorts back on and rearranged her t-shirt. I propped myself up on my elbows and watched her. What was the hurry? There was nowhere better to be.

She bent and grabbed my wrist, twisting it to read my watch. 'Shit. It's late. Amelia will be waiting.'

She scanned the ground, eyes roaming over our stuff strewn across the boulders. She started frantically picking things up.

'Hey, it's okay, calm down.'

'Calm down?' She turned to me, wedging one sneaker on without undoing the laces. 'I need to get back. There's a stupid social worker coming round in half an hour. I've gotta make sure we're both there. They're expecting us to be there.' She snorted. 'Mum's got no bloody clue what's going on.'

I knew Pip worried she and Amelia would be split up if social services got whiff of what a deadbeat mum they had. Pip seemed to think that foster care was the worst thing that could happen to them, but I didn't think it could be much worse than how they were living now. But she seemed to think so.

'It's all right, you'll get there.' I heaved myself up and pulled my t-shirt back on. 'I'll pack this stuff up. You head off.'

She gave one last glance around before jamming her other foot into its sneaker. She smiled, and the gold in her eyes caught the rays of the sun.

'Thanks.' She stood for a moment, her weight shifting from foot to foot.

The first spattering of rain began.

*Kiss her.*

She waited.

'Well, see ya later then,' I said.

'Oh, yeah, okay. Bye.' A quick look at me, her face blank, the gold in her eyes gone. She turned and left. Within a few steps she'd disappeared into the rainforest, only the swaying trees visible.

*Dickhead.*

# CHAPTER FORTY

Callum gripped the metal handrail that lined the corridor outside Pip's room with one hand. His other hand held the object she'd given him. He looked down at it and turned it over in his hand. Milly's name stared back at him in pink glitter pen. The *y* distinctly angled the wrong way.

His shoehorn.

How the hell did Pip get it?

He sucked in air that tasted faintly of urine. A shuffle of feet and a sudden grab from behind. A wisp of a woman leered at him. What teeth she had were yellowed and her grey hair was thin enough that he could make out her patchy scalp beneath.

She made a grapple for him with crooked fingers and a sudden waft of rotten food and shit made him heave.

'Rhonda, there you are. Leave him be.' A familiar brisk voice. 'It's time for tea. Why don't you head down to the dining room? Bobby's there.'

Another waft of shit, a wink, and she was gone. The lingering disinfectant scent a relief.

'Thanks.'

'No worries.' Bacuzzi stood a few metres along the corridor, arms folded. Then, with an inclination of her head, she turned and walked back up the hall, her boxy figure disappearing through a doorway halfway along. He looked back to Pip's open door and caught a few notes of her humming. The old rhyme sent a shiver creeping over his skin. He followed Bacuzzi.

A few pained steps and he stood outside a door, white on white. Staff only.

He pushed it open. Bacuzzi was buried in the fridge of the small lunch room, her back to him. She straightened, gave him a glance before putting a plastic container in the microwave and punching the buttons.

'You really should get off that leg if you don't want to lose your knee.' She nodded to a chair at the dining table. 'If you think life is hard now, you should try it with an above-knee amputation.'

He sat. The smell of bolognese wafted through the room and he realised his stomach was running on empty. Three espressos were not quite a meal.

Bacuzzi plopped a packet of dry crackers and a mug of black tea in front of him. He nodded his thanks and took a sip. The liquid scalded his tongue, and he fumbled with the crackers instead.

She sat down. 'Have you seen Pip since her diagnosis?'

'No.' *Yes.*

'This must be hard for you then.'

He nodded.

'Dementia's never easy on the ones left behind.'

The cracker had turned to dust in his mouth, threatened to suffocate him. He placed the packet back down.

'She's happy here though. They forget their past, their sorrows.'

He thought of the doll Pip had been holding. The sound of the whispering tune she'd been humming. Had she really forgotten?

'At least she's safe now.' Bacuzzi's voice was distant, foggy.

His mind drifted back thirteen years. Pip had said it was rapidly progressive dementia. Rare. Especially for someone in their thirties. She had a few months at best until she was in the advanced stages. She'd joked that it must've been all the drinking her mum had done while she was pregnant. He hadn't thought it the time to joke.

'I'm sorry I didn't tell you sooner,' she had said.

He'd looked down at the bundle squirming around in her arms, fat rosy cheeks and legs that looked like hams tied in string. He knew she wasn't talking about the dementia.

'Pip, I can't—'

'Yes, you can.' Her eyes were clear. 'You have no choice.'

'Of course, I have a choice. She's not even mine. She's Brett's kid.'

'She's not safe in Granite. I need you.' Her voice dropped. 'You owe me. Seventeen years ago, you left me—'

'I lost my leg. I didn't choose to leave you. My folks moved me away. You know all this.' He pointed to what remained of his left leg and his voice rose. 'This was not my choice.' His chest ached. Too many emotions. Anger. Guilt. Confusion. What the hell was going on? Pip was in his apartment in Brisbane. She had this kid with her, wanted him to take it.

'No, Cal.' She reached out with one hand, touched his arm. Her shirtsleeve slid up, a purple bruise blossoming beneath. The kid squirmed onto the floor. 'Seventeen years ago, you left me pregnant.'

Her words took a moment to take shape in his head. 'What? No, you got pregnant to Brett. After I left.'

She shook her head. 'No. I was scared. Devastated. Amelia had disappeared. Mum was gone. You'd left. I had no one. But Brett was there. Then I realised I was pregnant, and I just freaked out. I hooked up with Brett and pretended it was his. He was so good about it.' She met his eyes, her hand still on his arm. The skin beneath her touch began to burn. 'I'm sorry. I should have told you sooner. But I was just some stupid grief-stricken kid. I know it's no excuse.'

Her words tumbled over one another. He had a child. A son. Seventeen.

'I should meet him. Explain—'

'No.' Her voice rose, and she took a moment before she spoke again. Softer. 'He has a dad. They don't need to know. Lachie's almost eighteen and doesn't need you.'

Lachie.

'But Brett—'

'Brett nothing.'

'Does he know?'

She sighed. 'I don't know. Brett's a lot of things, but he's not stupid.' She cast her eyes to the floor. 'No, I don't think he does.'

The air sat heavy between them.

'And he never said anything to you?'

'He loved me.' A pause. 'Loves me.'

His eyes moved to her arm, the bruises. The purple glowed stark against her pale skin and his leg gave an unexpected twitch of pain.

'I can help Lachie.' What the hell was he saying? Was he planning on taking two kids now?

'Lachie doesn't need your help. He can look after himself. He'll be an adult in a few months. But you have to take her, Cal.' Her fingers dug into his flesh, her other hand gripped the fabric of her skirt. 'She won't be safe in Granite once I'm not able to protect her. You have to take her far away, never bring her back. You must. You owe me.'

They both looked at the kid, rolling on the floor, chewing on the ear of a bedraggled stuffed teddy. A pink cast wrapped around one chubby little arm. Her gold-rimmed eyes were almost swallowed by her round cheeks.

Those eyes, Pip's eyes. A flash of a memory of being at the boulders, a voice in his ear and a weight inside. Guilt.

He wasn't sure what he was remembering, the image shrouded in nearly two decades of fog. He grappled for it, tried to bring it into focus, but it slid away and was swallowed by darkness. He wiped his hands on his trousers.

'It'll never work.' His voice had come out thick.

'Of course it will, I've planned it all.'

A lifetime flashed in front of his eyes. Lachie's lifetime. Seventeen years. All the things he'd missed as a father. Bedtime stories, footy games, camping trips.

He nodded.

He sat watching the girl on the floor for a moment before he found his voice. 'You called her Amelia.'

She tore her eyes away from her daughter. The gold that rimmed her green eyes had dulled. 'I thought, in some way, it might help bring her back to me.'

*

The wind slapped Callum's hair against his forehead. The smell of disinfectant lingered in his nostrils and he felt as if he needed to wash off the last forty-five minutes. Heck, the last thirteen years.

He stood in the almost vacant car park, welcoming the lashings of rain against his face.

Pip's bruises. Thirteen years later, still there.

Thirteen years ago, she'd been so desperate to get Amelia—Milly—out of their house, out of Granite Creek, before the dementia took hold and gnawed its way through her memory. At the time, he'd assumed—no, he'd *known*—it had been Brett that Milly had needed protecting from.

But what had the nurse told him? Brett never even visits Pip.

And Bacuzzi's words: *At least she's safe now.*

He hadn't even registered them at the time, too caught up in the memory of Pip. The doll. Milly.

Did Bacuzzi know? Did she know that Lachie was beating his mum within the nursing home? Why hadn't she done something?

*At least she's safe now.*

His stomach heaved and the visitor logbook swam into view.

Lachie Wyatt.

Lachie Wyatt.

Lachie Wyatt.

Every week he'd visited. Every week, without fail, he'd been left alone with his mum.

It didn't make sense. Lachie had only been a kid.

*He was messed up. We all were, after what happened.*

Mike had been talking about Josh, not Lachie. About the gambling and the suicide. But he said they'd all changed. Mike himself had turned to alcohol and marijuana to mask his past. Had the abuse from Thacker been enough to trigger something in Lachie? An evil?

Or had it been there all along and Thacker had just been the one to unleash it, set it free? To seep out from wherever it lurked, to run through his veins and poison him?

Callum thought about himself, his own actions. *Who the hell takes someone else's kid?*

Him. He'd taken Milly when Pip had asked. He'd wanted to protect her, keep her safe. He'd needed to make it up to Pip.

And he knew the other reason. The reason he'd always refused to admit to himself. He'd wanted Pip for himself, he always had. And Milly was Pip's.

Pip's image burst into view. Barefoot, long hair limp and down to her waist. Her sway just offbeat to the tune she hummed. Nursing the doll.

He hadn't lived in Granite Creek for three decades, but even he knew the whispers that ran through the town, whipped from mouth to ear.

Grief had sent Pip crazy. She'd been driven to the nursing home after her toddler had waddled off into the rainforest, lured by the whispering. The call too strong for the child to withstand.

Callum's mind jumped back thirteen years, to the news footage that had been splashed around the country during the search for Amelia Wyatt. The sight of the cold granite boulders had made his left leg tingle. The country had held its breath as the small body had been dragged up from a gap between the boulders.

Bernie Burns's words bounced around his head.

*The gaps between some of those bastards are big enough to stow a campervan.*

The body had been wrapped up, draped in a cloth by the time the news cameras had caught a glimpse of it. But he'd known that the body was too big to be the toddler that was playing on his lounge room floor.

Everyone knew.

It was the body of fifteen-year-old Amelia Dyer. Pip's sister. Dragged up seventeen years after she went missing. Seventeen years after Brett had pushed her.

That's what others say drove Pip mad. The discovery of her sister. Dead.

After that, a heavy blanket had settled over the town. Even thirty years later, Callum could still feel the weight of it. Guilt. Everyone recalled the words that had been said when Amelia Dyer had disappeared.

*Skipped town. Working the streets. Supporting her habit.*

The guilt of letting a fifteen-year-old down, of calling off a search less than forty-eight hours after it began. It seeped through the town, ran deep in the creek and blew along the streets with every gust of wind. Granite Creek had spent the last thirteen years trying to make up for it, to wash their conscience clean. Every missing person since had been searched for extensively. Feet on the ground immediately, help in the air, volunteers from down south recruited. Nothing was spared.

The search for Amelia Wyatt had continued for weeks after Amelia Dyer's body had been discovered. But they'd never found her.

Pip's plan had worked.

'I can give you two weeks' head start,' she'd told him.

'Two weeks?'

'Brett's taking Lachie camping for the school holidays, week after next.' Her eyes bored into him. 'They'll be gone for two weeks. It'll give Amelia and me a break.'

A break? From Brett, he'd thought. But what about Lachie—his son—alone with Brett for two weeks?

Callum's stomach rolled. He couldn't think about that now.

'We'll book a unit, somewhere down here. We can spend the week together, the three of us. She's really easy, she'll take to you just fine. Then you'll have a week to get further away. Move south, or west.' She gripped his arm. 'Just get her as far from Granite as possible.'

And he'd agreed.

A week with Pip to help Amelia warm to him. A week driving to Hobart, settling in.

He'd questioned what he was doing, but he'd resigned from his Brisbane job, rented a house in Hobart, told his friends he needed a sea change. It had been off the back of his big breakthrough story. There'd been a lot of backlash; he'd received threats. Both at his work and his home. People understood the move. The need to disassociate himself from his old life.

In the week with Pip and Amelia, he'd gone from being unsure to knowing he was doing the right thing.

'What's her favourite song?' Callum had asked as he'd rocked the wailing toddler.

'I've made one up.' Pip walked over and stood next to them. 'And she likes when you do this.' She stroked Amelia's forehead with her index finger and started singing.

Amelia calmed within a few seconds, her wails replaced with small hiccups that jerked her warm body in Callum's arms. Maybe he could do this.

'I think I'll call her Milly.'

Pip's eyes had glazed over and she stood for a long moment before she walked to the window, looked out. 'It's getting dark. I'll have to head home soon.'

Callum frowned. 'Pip?'

'Amelia will need me.' Her voice dropped. 'It's getting dark.'

Callum had looked beyond her, through the open curtains, where the midday sun reflected against Pip's golden hair.

He'd known at that moment he was doing the right thing.

Pip had headed back up north after their week, and Callum down south. With Milly.

On the last night of Brett and Lachie's camping trip, Pip reported her daughter missing. Said she'd dozed off on the veranda with the front door open, Amelia asleep inside. Their house was on the cusp of the rainforest. The girl's doll was found at the start of the track.

They'd scoured the rainforest for her. The boulders too. Nothing.

Well, not nothing. The body of Amelia Dyer, hidden for seventeen years, was not nothing.

In the months that followed, Eddy's parents told Callum's that Pip was slipping further away. Her mind failing her. Within six months, she had been admitted to the Granite Creek nursing home. Her dementia had taken hold, entwined its fingers deep enough.

Everyone said it was a blessing. That she was better off.

Callum had looked at his daughter, nearly two and a half years old. Chubby, smiling and full of cheek. He knew that they were all wrong.

# CHAPTER FORTY-ONE

Over the years, Callum had often wondered what his life would've been like if he'd never lost his leg, never lost Pip. He would've moved south, joined the police academy—he was sure of that. Would've worked his way up the ranks and found his niche. Would he and Pip have stayed together? He'd liked to think so. They would've settled down, probably married young. Maybe she would've taught art part-time while their kids were little.

The image yanked at his heart and something sat awkwardly in his chest. Kids. But not Milly. Their kids wouldn't have been his Milly. The feel of his daughter's weight in his arms, her head lulled on his shoulder, from a time when she was still small enough that he could carry her.

It was better this way. What he'd once thought of as no leg and no future had turned out to be the best kind of life he could've imagined.

And he would've lost Pip eventually anyway. The black fingers of her dementia would still have taken hold, woven their way around her memories and ripped their years of happiness away.

*

Callum wiped his hands on his trousers, the nursing home still looming in the background, the car park still deserted.

Yes, he'd needed to make things up to Pip. To protect Milly.

The memory, newly recalled, of Brett's outstretched arms and Amelia Dyer hanging on to the cliff flooded over him. The heavy weight of guilt.

Her death wasn't his fault and he recalled the sudden wash of lightness that had spread through him when the memory of Brett's act had first returned. Relief. But he still didn't know why he'd even been there. He never went to the boulders without Pip.

It couldn't have been his fault.

But the idea that something in himself wasn't right pushed its way to the surface. He'd taken someone else's kid. He'd lied to everyone. Everyone he'd ever known or loved for the last thirteen years. To Eddy. His parents. His daughter.

But Milly wasn't his daughter.

*Yes, she is.*

He'd raised her. Loved her. Done everything for her.

Just not told her the truth.

He'd told no one the truth. Made up a story about an old fling, a child he hadn't known he'd had. The questions had come. He'd managed to find answers for them all. In the end, his folks were thrilled to have Milly in their lives and he'd left his Brisbane life—and his mates—behind. The questions soon died down.

But wasn't this about Lachie, not Milly? Had something in Callum—something not right—been passed down to his son? Had the abuse from Thacker been enough to flip a switch? Was Callum's own switch buried deep within, just waiting for the right kind of trauma to set it off?

No, violence wasn't pre-wired into a person. It was learned, copied from someone else. A father.

Or a teacher.

His head snapped up. Thacker. He'd forgotten about the letters on the door of the vacant room in the nursing home, swiped away in one quick swoop by Bacuzzi's broad hand.

Thomas Thacker.

Simon Thacker's father. Presumably.

*His son came up from down south and picked his stuff up on Tuesday.*

So, Thacker had been up here on the day Lachie disappeared.

Thacker's soft voice rang in his ears. *Had some business to deal with.*

Was knocking Lachie off his business?

Was Thacker the reason Lachie turned out like he did? Had it been Lachie all along? Not Brett?

His mind raced back thirty years. He knew what Brett was capable of.

He pushed the past away, tried to focus on the present.

Who else was involved?

Tess and Jack. Their fear at the sound of Brett's return, faces pale, eyes wide. Tess's protective hand over her son and her unborn child. He thought back. The ute's engine as it pulled up. The slam of the door. His memory hashed out the image of the white car parked in the pouring rain outside Tess's house. Plain white. No Wyatt and Sons logo plastered on its door. Lachie's ute, not Brett's.

It wasn't Brett they were frightened of. He'd been driving Lachie's ute, bringing it back from the camp site car park. The ute's engine was a sound they associated with Lachie's return. With terror.

The ideas were flooding in faster than he could put them into place.

And Steph.

The CCTV footage of her with Lachie. Her glass, remaining on the pub table while everyone else raised theirs in a toast to the newly lost firefighter.

And Noah.

Not like Brett. No, not Brett's kid.

Lachie's.

# CHAPTER FORTY-TWO

'I was worried about you after yesterday.' Steph beamed at him from behind the station's reception counter. 'You looked like you'd seen a ghost.'

Callum finished wiping his shoes on the entry mat and strode towards her. He was sick of not knowing any answers, sick of guessing. 'Who's Noah's dad?'

Her dimple vanished. 'Excuse me?'

'Is it Lachie?'

'What on earth are you on about?'

He hesitated only a moment before pushing on. 'He looks like Lachie. Like Jack. He's a Wyatt.'

'He's my son, and that's all that matters.' She stood, the desk between them not enough to shield him from the heat radiating off her.

'I'm not saying he's not. Of course he is. But he should know.' He thought of Jack, Noah's half-brother. 'You need to tell Tess.'

She pointed a finger at him, leaning across the desk. Her voice hushed. 'Don't you stand there, Callum Haffenden, and accuse me of having an affair, of being a home-wrecker.'

A jolt of surprise. She'd misunderstood. 'I'm not accusing you of anything.' He lowered his voice to match hers. 'I'm accusing Lachie.'

She leaned back and her hand dropped to her side. Her shoulders sagged and Callum watched as the weight of a decade slid off her.

\*

'He made me feel as if it were my fault that it'd happened.' Steph's eyes were fixed on the floor.

They sat side by side on the squashy couch in the station's cramped kitchenette. Callum tried not to think back to the last time they'd sat there together. Steph so close, lips parted, raindrops on her eyelashes. Had it really only been yesterday?

The background hum of the air conditioner battled over the roar of the rain outside, which felt as if it'd embedded itself permanently in his eardrums. Despite the noise, the police station seemed quiet, still.

Steph's breaths were deep, and he could feel the rise and fall of her shoulders next to him.

'I came back around Christmas. Mum wasn't well and Dad needed all the help he could get. I hadn't enjoyed city life and thought the move back might do me good. I'd hardly been back a week when I met Lachie at the pub one night. Boxing Day. I knew straight away he was Brett's kid. We'd been having a chat, nothing serious. He was funny, charming even. Maybe I'd been flirty. I don't remember. Anyway, I decided to walk home. I'd had a few drinks and it felt safe enough. It's Granite after all. I'd walked the streets at night hundreds of times as a teenager without thinking twice. Half the time pissed.

'He offered to drive me because the weather was terrible, but I said no. He must've followed me. I was staying in the granny flat at the back of my folks' place and was unlocking the front door when I heard him behind me. He startled me and I remember wondering why he was there. He said he was thirsty and asked to come in. Mum and Dad were in the main house and I knew he was married. What could happen, right?' She shook her head.

Callum sat frozen next to her. The room was too small and the walls pushed Steph's words against him. A beat began to pulse in his temple.

'I poured him a beer for Christ's sake.' She faltered. 'He forced me on the bed, pinned me down. I cried out. Of course, no one heard.'

The rain banged against the kitchenette window and roof, as if coming from all directions. It echoed and bounced around the room. Of course no one heard her.

'After he'd finished, he dressed and told me that Tess had been so unwell with morning sickness that she wasn't putting out and that a man had to get it somewhere. I remember not being able to speak. I wanted to scream, but nothing came out. Just before he left, he said that I should be grateful that a guy like him had been interested in an old bird like me. He bet I hadn't had it that good for years. He even kissed me goodbye, like he'd thought it was consensual.'

Callum's head pounded. 'He raped you.'

A nod.

'And you never told anyone.'

She shook her head.

'Why?'

Another shake. 'I don't know. Maybe I believed everything he said.' She lifted her head at last and turned to him. 'You know, the next time I saw him, only a few days later, he smiled and asked how I was going. Gave me a little wink. It was like he thought we shared a cheeky little secret. Like he thought I was in on it from the start.' Her gaze dropped again. 'I guess I was afraid of what people would think. What they'd say.'

'What people would say?' He fought to keep his voice level.

'This is a small town and people talk. I'm nearly twenty years older than Lachie. He was only nineteen at the time, newly married to a gorgeous woman, baby on the way and he had just started at the fire station. I was mid-thirties, single, living with my parents. It would've been his word against mine. And I'd been stupid enough to invite him in, he would've said I wanted it.' She paused. 'After all, why would someone like him want to be with someone like me?'

Callum took in her hazel eyes, glossy from the sheen of tears.

What the hell wasn't to like?

'People looked down their noses at me when I first returned to Granite. Like I couldn't cut it in the big city and had to come crawling back. No one was going to see my side of the story.' She took a deep breath, sat taller. 'The cop at the time was a young bloke, hung out with Lachie. It seemed easier to move on than report it. So, I just carried on. I avoided him of course. I was terrified of ever being alone with him again. I didn't go out at night and didn't go back to the pub for months, and never alone. And I always drove and never drank.'

The injustice of it twisted into him like a knife. Had all women experienced something like this? Had Milly? Had she ever kept a secret this big? Was there something she felt she couldn't share? Couldn't tell him?

He brought his attention back to Steph. 'And then you found out you were pregnant ...'

Her eyebrows pulled in, but he was relieved to see she didn't crumple under the comment.

'I was distraught at first. Didn't know what to tell Mum and Dad. In the end I just said I'd had a one-night stand in the city the week before I'd returned and didn't know who the bloke was. They didn't ask any more questions. My sister has never wanted kids and I think they were just thrilled they were becoming grandparents. I'd almost given up hope myself.' She gave a dry laugh. 'So, nine months later, Noah arrived. I never thought about not having him. He's changed my world.' The corner of her mouth lifted, and he caught a glimpse of a dimple.

Milly swam into view again. He understood.

'But when he was born, something in me changed. I decided to confront Lachie. Let him know that what he did was wrong. I told him that Noah was his. He didn't believe me. Said I was a gold-digging slut. I didn't bother to follow it up. It was better if he wasn't involved in Noah's life anyway.

'But as Noah got older, it became pretty obvious. Jack was only a few months older, and they were the spitting image of each other. A new teacher at the kindy thought they were twins, for god's sake. And then people started talking. There was a rumour going round that Brett was the father. I guess because he and I were the same age it just seemed logical to everyone. Brett never said anything. Never denied the gossip. I guess he was trying to protect Lachie. I always thought Tess knew the truth though. Well, to some extent. I think she thought we'd had an affair. Over the years, I've caught her watching Noah, probably wondering if he's her husband's other son. Plus, she's never liked me.' Steph snorted. 'I've never really liked her either. She seems cold. Distant. Though, being married to someone like Lachie has probably done that to her.'

'I suspect Tess knew the truth. I think she knew what Lachie was,' Callum said.

'You think?'

He nodded. 'Unfortunately, I think she'd experienced both sides of him.'

'And Jack?'

Callum shrugged. 'If I had to have a guess, I'd say he knew what his dad was.'

Callum recalled the school admin clerk's—Mrs Fenton's—comments about Jack. Quiet. Subdued. And the way he'd tucked in behind Tess's legs.

He'd stuck up for Noah though, when he was being bullied. Jack couldn't change the abuse happening at home but could face the bullies in the school yard. A small consolation for a kid stuck in an abusive family.

They sat in silence. Steph's skin had lost its usual glow and was coated in a sticky sheen, as if she were going to be sick.

Callum was the first to speak. 'But Brett knew, didn't he?'

They looked at each other, her face drawn of colour.

'He was giving you money, to help out with Noah.' He searched her face. For a moment, he thought she was going to deny it.

Then she nodded. 'He's not stupid.' Her word's echoed Pip's from thirteen years earlier. 'When the boys started school, it was pretty obvious. It was easier to deny before then because they were rarely in the same room as each other. I remember seeing Brett at a school play. Lachie and Tess were there too. I kept my distance from them, obviously. But I saw Brett watching me. Watching Noah. A few days later, he came to speak to me. I tried to deny it at first. I thought he was going to accuse me of having an affair. Get up me for ruining his son's life. But he just broke down. Said he's known for years about Lachie. That he should have done more to stop him. To protect her. I didn't know who he was talking about. Tess, I guess.'

'Pip.'

'Pip?'

He nodded.

Steph blew out a breath. 'But he was only a kid then.'

'Yep. And he was still doing it right up until his death.'

'But she's—'

'He visited her every week. She's got bruises.'

'Jesus.'

Pip. Tess. Steph. Hanna. Paige.

How many others had there been? The list was too long already.

And there was one name he knew he'd forgotten to include. Purposely pushed it down, not wanting to believe Lachie had ever hurt her.

A wave of bile swarmed up. The acidic taste burned his mouth and filled his nostrils. A heave in his stomach as his eyes searched the room.

A chubby toddler waddled across his mind, the pink cast on her arm catching his eye. Tumbled down the back veranda stairs, that's what Pip had told him.

His empty stomach retched. He stood, fumbled for the kitchenette sink and the splash of his morning's coffee pooled in the bottom.

Milly.

\*

The tepid water in his cup did little to settle Callum's stomach.

Steph had immediately been at his side, rubbing his back and passing him a tissue as he hung over the sink. She settled him back down on the couch, brought him a glass of water and offered him a small smile, her dimple just forming.

'It was a long time ago. I've moved on.'

He nodded. He should be consoling her.

The station phone rang and, with a squeeze of his shoulder, she headed back to the reception, excusing him from coming up with some insufficient response. A moment later, her voice carried through the closed kitchenette door, and he could hear her directing someone to the town hall to collect sandbags.

Lachie had raped Steph.

He'd assaulted Hanna and Paige.

He'd beaten Pip. Beaten Tess. And probably Jack.

Another roll of his stomach.

And Milly. Her broken arm. What else had she endured before he'd taken her? Pip had tried to protect her in the end, but why hadn't she acted sooner? She'd known what Lachie was. Jesus, Brett had known. They'd all bloody known and chosen to ignore it.

This whole town seemed to turn a blind eye. The entire nursing staff to Pip's bruises. The entire fire department to Paige. The entire school to the three boys. The entire town to Amelia Dyer.

Thacker had managed to get away with it. Pip's bruises had continued. Amelia Dyer was still dead.

There was no justice.

And Brett. What the hell was he playing at? Paying Steph to help support Noah. What else had Brett done? Pushed Lachie off the boulders to protect the rest of his family? His wife. His daughter-in-law. His grandson.

And why did Callum even care anymore? By the sounds of it, Lachie had got what was coming to him. He'd grown into a predator, whether helped along by Thacker or not.

Thacker had been in town that day. Had they bumped into each other? Had Thacker sought Lachie out? Had they had an altercation? Surely Lachie would've recognised Thacker despite the years passed. The face of your childhood abuser would be etched into your memory, wounds gouging deep.

And Steph. Her warm touch, her unrestrained smile. Raped by his son.

Her story washed over him. Raped on Boxing Day. Nine months later, Noah was born.

He looked up. The wall calendar above the sink swam into view. The cartoon dingo with its Santa hat grinned back.

Nine months later was September.

Another calendar came to him: Tess's. Lachie's birthday written in neat black pen, only a couple of weeks away. Hanna's comments about his upcoming birthday. January. Lachie was born in January.

Nine months earlier was …

The truth locked into place. Weighed down by thirteen years of guilt, it sank into the sodden earth, too heavy to shift.

Pip had lied.

He took a rapid breath and reached for memories. She'd said Lachie was his. That she'd realised she was pregnant after he'd left. He'd left in December. Lachie was born in January, thirteen months later.

He recalled Steph's words when she'd described first meeting Lachie.

*I knew he was Brett's son.*

He thought about Noah. His carefree face and wild hair did nothing to change his resemblance to Jack.

And Jack. So much like Brett. The wisp of an idea that had bugged him every time he'd seen the kid over the last few days finally began to take shape. Jack looked like Brett. Callum had known it the first time he'd met the kid back in Tess's lounge room. Yet he hadn't managed to put it together.

Or maybe he had and had decided to push it down because the reality was too hard. The reality that Pip had lied. That Lachie wasn't his son. And that he never should have agreed to take Milly.

Thirteen years of lies bit into him and he was overcome with a deep weariness. How long had he been in Granite Creek? Four days? A lifetime.

He thought of his daughter. It was time to go home.

Using the worn armrest of the couch, he heaved himself up, ignoring the jab in his left leg. The thought of seeing Milly soon made his chest swell.

He rinsed his glass and rested it in the draining rack. A glint of red and blue caught his eye, poking out from Steph's handbag on the kitchen bench. He took a step towards the bag and peered inside. The blaze of an idea swept across him.

Steph was hanging up the phone as he entered the reception area and raised both her eyebrows at his hand brandishing the red and blue woven bracelet that he'd found in the rainforest.

*Ting. Ting.*

'Trying to make a fashion statement?' she asked.

'You didn't give it back to Noah.' It wasn't a question.

Eddy banged through his office door, cutting Steph off before she had a chance to respond. The door smacked against the wall and threatened to knock Eddy backwards. He shoved it aside, passed the desk and came to a halt when he noticed Callum.

Eddy's eyes flickered. Relief? His features then set in a grim expression, the memory of their argument clearly still fresh in his memory. 'You're here.'

Callum nodded and his hand dropped to his side.

*Ting. Ting.*

A beat passed and Eddy's features softened. 'Good. I think I'm going to need an extra set of hands.' He turned back to the door. 'You're coming with me.'

With a fleeting smile at Steph, Callum followed Eddy out into the deluge of rain. It took longer than it should have for the two men to make their way to the rear of the station and to Eddy's patrol car. Callum forced his door open against the onslaught of wind before he was able to fold his legs into the police SUV.

He waited until both doors were closed before he spoke. 'Where're we heading?'

'Tess Wyatt's place.'

'What?' Callum turned to Eddy. His friend's skin was sallow, the corners of his mouth turned down. 'Why?'

'It's Jack.'

A chill ran along Callum's body and his fist tightened around the woven bracelet that he still clutched.

Eddy's eyes stared through the windscreen, the wipers unable to shift the rain long enough to gain a clear view. He manoeuvred the SUV onto the street, flicked on the siren. Callum strapped on his seatbelt as the speed kicked up a notch, the car buffeted by the wind.

Callum managed to catch Eddy's words as they drove towards the wall of green ahead.

'He's missing.'

# CHAPTER FORTY-THREE

The drive out to the Wyatt house was slow. Flooded roads didn't respond to sirens or flashing lights.

Neither Eddy nor Callum spoke the entire drive as Eddy tried to navigate the rising waters and poor visibility. Callum distracted himself by squeezing each of the three bells on the bracelet in turn, over and over again.

*One, two, three.*

Lachie wasn't his son.

*One, two, three.*

Pip had lied.

*One, two, three.*

He should never have taken Milly.

He squeezed one of the bells so hard that he felt it compress beneath his fingertips. No, Milly had still needed protecting, and no one else was doing it. Her arm in its pink cast, hanging limply by her side, shot into view. He pushed away the thought that his daughter should never have been his. He squeezed the bells again.

*One, two, three. One, two, three.*

Eddy pulled up in the Wyatt driveway, alongside Lachie's ute. Before they even had time to slam their car doors, a faint figure hurried down the wooden stairs of the house. Callum made his way down the driveway after Eddy, the crunch of gravel underfoot inaudible through the thunderous downpour.

Tess's figure came into focus, barefoot and hunched over. Her grey dress, drenched through, clung to her thin frame, accentuating her swollen stomach. By the time he got to her, Tess's face was bone white and she was bent over, one hand braced on her knee, the other clutching Eddy.

Her mouth opened and closed forming the outline of words, whipped away by the wind before they could be heard.

*He's gone.*

Her face contorted and her back arched. She buckled, her knees failing, and Callum lunged forward to help Eddy support her weight. Her skeletal fingers dug into his arm with such force it almost overrode the roar in his leg.

*Jesus Christ, is she about to have the kid?*

A high-pitched noise pierced the air. He scanned the sky. Nothing. His eyes flew to the rainforest that loomed behind the house.

The noise again.

It was coming from Tess. He let out a breath, and a faint voice drew him back. He looked up to see Eddy shouting across the metre of space that separated them. He may as well have been shouting across a footy field. Nonetheless, his meaning was clear: get Tess inside.

Together, they hoisted her along the path, supporting her weight as she stumbled. More than once, she looked back over her shoulder, along the road, her feet digging into the path, her body instinctively drawn away from the house.

No, not away from the house. Towards the rainforest.

He sucked in the warm air. It caught in his throat as it coated his mouth and clogged his airways.

He fought to push the growing sensation down.

They half dragged Tess the last few metres along the driveway and up the steps to the veranda. Black spots filled his vision and he leaned against the outer wall of the house as Eddy tried to settle her into a timber chair. She tried to stand but collapsed back down.

Callum sucked in a lungful of air. Thick, sticky.

His vision cleared. A slow breath, and his shoulders eased as he registered the familiar rise and fall of his chest.

He turned to Tess. One of her hands gripped the armrest of the chair. The other gestured frantically towards the rainforest, her words silenced by the pounding rain overhead.

He stumbled forward to catch her words.

'... he ran away.'

Eddy was crouched in front of her. 'We'll find him.'

'No, he's gone.' Her eyes darted outwards again. 'He said he heard it.'

Callum swallowed. He knew the answer but forced himself to ask anyway. 'Where'd he go?'

Her face was stricken as she met his eye. 'The boulders.'

A cool prickle again, this time running up the back of his neck. His stump throbbed.

'I'm sending out some searchers.' Eddy pulled out his radio and stepped inside the open front door.

Tess opened her mouth to speak but let out a wail instead and bent over. A step closer and Callum was at her side. A moment passed and her grip on the armrest eased, and he helped to lean her back in the chair. A dark pool of blood swam in her lap, her grey dress stained.

Jesus.

He stepped away and peered through the doorway. Eddy had his radio pressed against one ear, a finger firmly lodged in the other, mouth silently forming words. Callum moved back to Tess, her breath shortened, laboured.

'He's gone,' she said again, sucking in another breath. 'I can't lose him.'

'We'll find him, Eddy's calling for help now.'

'There's not enough time.' She looked to the wall of green visible through the steamy rain that was lashing sideways past the house. Trees bent, their tops flapping wildly. The cyclone was coming. 'Brett's gone after him.'

*

Sweaty palms slipped on the steering wheel as Callum fumbled to angle Lachie's ute through the rising waters covering the road from the Wyatt house.

With a nod from Tess, he'd snatched the keys from her and left her bleeding in the chair. An oblivious Eddy had still been on the radio.

Callum almost missed the turn-off to Kingfisher Way. His chest gave a jolt as he pulled the wheel of the car sharply, and the back tyre spun out, skidding in the mud. The front driver's side tyre hit a pothole. His leg gave a stab.

He scanned the side of the road. A barrier of foliage, then a white blur began to take shape ahead. A car, parked on the shoulder. He eased his foot off the accelerator and the grey of the Wyatt and Sons logo loomed through the rain. He fought the urge to push his foot down and continue past.

A flash of Jack's fear-stricken face and an image of fingers digging into granite, slipping.

He gave the steering wheel a yank. The car spun onto the shoulder and the bonnet dipped down sharply as the front wheels sank into the sodden mud. The front fender crunched into the tail-light of Brett's ute.

He pressed his weight against the door, threw a leg out and paused. A quick scan of the back seat. His eyes focused for a moment before he reached back with one arm and snatched up Lachie's head torch and jammed it into his pocket.

A red bike lay discarded at the foot of one of the trees, a low shrub almost engulfing its frame.

A deep breath and eyes forward, he took a steady step beneath the canopy. The rainforest's dark silence swallowed him whole.

# CHAPTER FORTY-FOUR

Darkness. Silence. Sunlight had been unable to penetrate the grey clouds all day, but when Callum crossed the threshold into the rainforest the dense canopy above blocked out any signs of it being daytime altogether.

He paused a beat, allowed himself to adjust. Dark forms began to take shape. A tall trunk. A fallen log. An angular fern. He was able to make out the ground, sodden and littered with fallen foliage. No sign that he and Steph had tramped over it only two days earlier.

Or that Jack had done so within the last hour. Or Brett with his hulking frame.

His leg tingled. He pressed on.

Beneath his feet, the ground slid, and he worked to find purchase with each footfall, frustrated by his slow progress.

He shifted his attention to why he was here.

Jack.

A terrified boy. Frightened by the sound of his dad's truck. Bruises on his mother.

How much had the kid seen of the abuse? How much of it had been directed at him? Had Brett pushed Lachie off the cliff? Had Jack found out the truth?

*... keep your bloody mouth shut if you know what's good for you.*

Brett's grip on Jack's arm, his threatening glare. Jack's red eyes and blotchy skin. Would Brett hurt his grandson to cover his secret? But it didn't make sense. Hadn't Brett pushed Lachie to protect Jack? Why was he so angry with the kid?

Or was there something Callum was missing? Had Brett pushed Lachie for another reason entirely? Had Thacker been involved somehow?

He bit back against the pain in his left leg and picked his way through a narrow stretch of path, the trees pressing in against him.

A whistle overhead, shrill and high-pitched.

*Accipiter novaehollandiae*: grey goshawk.

His eyes flew around the dark trees, searching. Nothing. He was too deep in the forest for it to be a goshawk.

He fumbled one hand into his pocket, and his fingers met the woven bracelet within: Jack's bracelet. He was sure it was Jack's. It was a replica of the one he'd spotted around Pip's wrist. Jack must've given it to her. He gripped the bracelet and a firm lumpy object brushed his knuckles. Confused, he grasped it, pulled it out. Lachie's head torch rested in his open palm.

*Idiot.*

He strapped it to his head and flicked it to life. A beam of light cut through the darkness, illuminating a world of greens and browns. He swiped at strips of vines and ferns and picked up the pace, pushing on.

The track angled upwards, and his thighs burned with the effort to lug himself up the incline. As the terrain evened out, he caught a glimpse of the long intertwining roots of a large strangler fig tree towering on the edge of the track. The spot he and Steph had stopped and turned around. He continued past.

He thought of Jack, also here two days earlier. At this very spot. The image of the boy came back, hazy. He hadn't been alone. There'd been two boys. One with Steph—Jack—and another further down the track. Wild hair that hung free made the shape of him blur, a smudge in Callum's memory. Jack wasn't alone in the rainforest that day. He had been with Noah.

Another sharp jut upwards, a rock protruding out from the earth, and the catch of his prosthetic foot on its lip. His body careened forward.

A slide show of images: Jack. Tess. Pip. Milly.

Just before the edge of the rock connected with his head, one final face came into view: Amelia Dyer.

\*

A sharp pain at the end of his left knee and blackness all around. Callum blinked a few times and the black faded enough that he could make out the shapes of the rainforest, the image darker than he recalled. He reached for his forehead, for the head torch. Nothing.

*Shit.*

The damp smell of earth pressed around him. He was flat on his stomach. He shifted his weight and blinding pain rolled over him. Tears pricked behind his eyes and a drumbeat started in his temple.

He fumbled one hand around the sodden rainforest floor, his fingers at last hitting the firm, lumpy shape of the head torch. He pressed his thumb down on its button.

*Nothing.*

He pressed it again, harder. Nothing.

*Fuck.*

He sucked in a deep breath, the earthy scent of mud and rotten leaves making his head spin. He bent his elbows and pushed himself up into a sitting position.

Another deep breath, and he hauled himself onto two legs, both hands on a slick mossy trunk. He scanned the rainforest; shapes jutted and waved in and out of focus. A tentative touch to his glasses told him that the right lens was cracked, the sharp split of the glass catching the skin of his fingertip.

He shifted his weight and a blinding pain made his breath catch. He picked up a sturdy branch nearby, the bark rough beneath his palm.

The minutes dragged as he picked his way through the dense foliage.

*Too slow.*

He swallowed the protest from his leg and increased his speed.

*Jack. Pip's grandson. Milly's nephew.*

He ripped through the snag of a lawyer vine, the flesh of his forearm smarting as he pulled free.

Brett was after Jack.

The dark pool of blood in Tess's lap and the mottled bruise on her forearm forced him onwards.

Tess's words echoed in his head.

*He said he heard it.*

Had Jack heard the whispering?

Did the kid believe it was real? Is that why he wasn't wearing his bracelet? Was he giving up?

Callum dug his stick firmly into the soft ground. A step later and a soft whisper caught his ear. A prickle crept over his skin and travelled into his missing left calf, all the way down to toes he no longer had.

He stopped, turned his head one way, then forward again. Had the trees in front moved closer? The sound grew; sharper, louder. It sang out, whistling through the trees and snaking its way around his body, tightening.

The thick air felt like wet soil in his chest. He sucked in another breath. Nothing.

One hand gripped his stick while the other fumbled for

his pocket. He dug in. Empty. The bracelet was gone, it had probably fallen out as he'd removed the head torch.

The whisper again, as loud as a scream. A wave of panic rolled through him. He dropped his stick, pressed his hands against his ears.

He had to get away, move. His feet loosened in the soil, and he spun. Trees everywhere. Tendrils of ferns and vines reached for him, their long fingers tethering him.

*Move.*

A rush of wings through the air.

*Don't stop.*

Forward again. He pushed through the trees. More green. And then a dash of black and a streak of blue across his vision, gone almost before he had time to register it.

He halted. His heart hammered in his ears. He scrambled to think, trying to put some logical explanation to the last few minutes.

The whispering was in his head, it wasn't real.

A low primitive rumble rose from between the trees, vibrated his teeth and stopped his breath. He swung his head around and peered into the darkness, searching.

*Hide.*

A dark twist of shadow to his left, and he was at the foot of another large fig tree. He sidled up to it, a branch snapped underfoot, cracked like a gunshot.

*Shit.*

He found a nook among the roots that was large enough for him to slip into. He strained his ears. It was impossible to tell which way the sound had come from. A moment passed, then another.

The same low rumble, heavy footfalls, and the outline of a cassowary ambled across his view. The silhouette of its prehistoric helmet sent a cool sweat rushing over him as Bernie Burns's words rang in his ears.

*Gut ya like a barramundi.*

He pressed back into the tree.

The sound of clawed feet, deadened by the dank underbrush, diminished.

A deep breath. A long pause.

*Jack. Keep moving.*

He stepped out from his shelter. Green. Everywhere he looked. More green. It all looked the same. He could feel his breath shorten again as the panic began to set in.

His dad's words: *Never step off the trail.*

A glance down. The earth beneath his feet was a tangle of tree roots, dead leaves and vines. Not a trail in sight.

*Fuck.*

He was lost.

\*

Five minutes? Fifteen? How much time had passed?

Leaves whipped across his face and hanging vines snagged his clothes, tore his skin. More than once, he stumbled over fallen trees and ropy undergrowth.

He pushed on.

There'd been no point staying where he was. That would've been a death sentence for both himself and Jack.

*Keep moving.*

He scanned the dim outline of large trees and angular ferns for any sign of a clearing. Every few moments he stopped, held his breath, listened.

A high-pitched wail.

*Ailuroedus maculosus*: spotted catbird.

A punctuated shrill whistle.

*Oreoscopus gutturalis*: fernwren.

A rapid staccato machine-gun call.

*Meliphaga lewinii*: Lewin's honeyeater.

Never what he was straining to hear.

An ache in his chest caught him and he bent over double, both hands on his right knee. He listened. The constant thrum of the rainforest continued, even over the roar of his breath. He went to straighten, and a distant sound caught his ear. He froze. Head angled, eyes shut, breath held. A rush, distant and faint. The distinct churn of water filled his ears.

His eyes flew open and he pulled his feet free from the sodden earth and began to push his way through the scrub, towards the rushing creek.

\*

Water broke the banks, and Callum made his way down the steep embankment. He needed a clearer vantage point. The body of water swarmed over fallen branches and protruding boulders. A large trunk swept past and was sucked beneath the surface. The constant rain had given the creek its fill from which it had spawned a life of its own.

The rising waters made it impossible to get low enough to clear the thicket of trees that lined the upper part of the embankment. He waded in, using the bendy trunks of saplings to steady his progress.

Water snaked around his knees as his prosthetic foot slipped out beneath him. A lunge and a jerk of pain as he fumbled for a nearby tree.

*Shit.*

His torso was half in the murky waters, his feet slipping on the mushy earth beneath. Then he spotted a break in the creek ahead. The water rushed down suddenly, dropping into a lower section. A wide short waterfall. It spanned the width of the creek, like a belt.

Not a belt, a bridge: the boulder bridge.

With a last heave, he righted himself, his feet at last finding solid ground, and began to pick his way further along the bank, his feet sloshing through the water, quickening with each step.

He reached the waterfall and his chest tightened: the boulder bridge was fully submerged, a frothing foam churning over the top. The rushing water moved with such force and the image of the tree trunk hurtling down the creek made him pause. He'd be swept clean off the bridge.

He thought back. Dug into the recess of his memory and pressed down into the flowing waters. He tried to push down a growing sense of foreboding.

He'd done this before.

He stepped into the rushing creek, upstream of the bridge. He held his breath as the water swept beneath his feet and pushed his body along. A brief moment where he was weightless. Then, a bone-crunching slam as his body hit the boulders hidden beneath the murky surface.

The churning water sloshed at his chin and dived into his mouth. He reached his arms over the boulders, his chest pressing against the rock. His arms grappled along the mossy rocks, dragging himself along. A slip. Then another. He sucked in a mouthful of water, his lungs burning, his chest unable to expand against the vice made by the rushing water and solid boulders. He made himself press forward, one hand after another, dragging himself along the submerged rocks.

The image of Pip, motionless on the sandy creek bed, sent a rush of terror running over him.

At last, his feet hit solid ground, and he scrambled to heave himself out. Using a tangle of tree roots and vines, he dragged himself clear of the water's edge and, flat on his stomach, heaved in great big lungfuls of air, the damp earth a welcome scent.

*Get up. Move.*

He wasn't far now. He pressed through the thick undergrowth of the rainforest and hauled himself over uneven terrain, the rush of the creek diminishing with each scramble forward. His breathing settled, his heart slowed.

There was no clear path to the boulders. He worked on memory and the faint trail of smaller rocks that were scattered along the way. Breadcrumbs. There was no sign that two others had just trampled ahead of him. Had he got it wrong? Were they not at the boulders?

The sharp sting of a wait-a-while vine caught his exposed forearm. He picked at the barbs, and a murmur of voices caught his ears.

He tore himself free. A clearing through the trees ahead allowed the weak light of the grey sky to penetrate the darkness. The wind whooshed through the opening and pressed against his body, like a warning holding him back.

A familiar voice. He paused. A child's wail pierced the air.

He lurched forward and his prosthetic foot hit the hard ground of the boulders. A vibration ran up its shaft, into his stump, along his bones. He stopped.

The small figure of Jack, heels bordering the cliff edge and rain slamming against his frail body, came into view. The boy's face was riddled with terror as he looked towards the rainforest. Towards a second figure standing in the shadows of the trees.

A gruff voice.

A seething fire ran over Callum.

When he had read the headlines about Lachie's disappearance, he'd known who he'd find at the end of it. And when Lachie's body was found at the boulders, he'd known who had pushed him.

He'd come back to this hellhole of a town to protect a son that wasn't even his to protect. Pip's son.

To protect a daughter he'd hoped he'd moved far enough away that the tendrils of Granite Creek would never be able to touch her. Pip's daughter.

His daughter.

At last, the rainforest let him go and he moved forward with ease, as if he was always meant to return.

He planted his right foot firmly into the soil, drew his shoulders back and took in the hulking figure nestled on the cusp of the rainforest.

Brett.

# CHAPTER FORTY-FIVE

*Thirty years earlier*

The trees overhead gave good cover from the rain, but I knew it was coming down more heavily now. The pattering sound on the leaves muffled the swishing of the creek behind me.

I'd made it most of the way home before I remembered I hadn't packed Pip's hat. It had been sitting in a nook between the fig tree roots at the cliff edge. I'd put it there after we'd started snogging and its rim kept bumping my forehead. As I'd taken it off her head, her hair had tangled in the bowerbird feather sewn to its side. The feather pulled loose and she'd eased it out of her hair, placed it between the pages of her sketch pad that poked out of her open satchel beside us.

I pulled my bike over on the side of the road and rummaged through my backpack.

'Shit.'

I looked at the greying sky and, with one last glance down the road towards home, I spun my bike around and headed back.

It was Pip's favourite hat. Her sister had given it to her.

The visibility beneath the trees was fading fast and I knew it would be pitch black by the time I returned. The weight of my torch was comforting in my hand as I hurried along. The boulders were just ahead.

The trees thinned and a faint light pierced through. A voice caught my attention. I stopped behind a wide tree.

Muffled talking. A gruff voice.

I edged closer.

A scream. No, just the wind.

I peered around the trunk.

A hulking figure, arms outstretched, a fraction away from the cliff edge.

My body stiffened.

Brett.

# CHAPTER FORTY-SIX

Jack stood too close to the edge, one back heel moving closer to the sheer drop. Rain came down hard and made the sloping ground soft. Slippery.

His eyes, filled with terror, glanced back over one shoulder. Over the edge. A sea of granite boulders lay below, stretching to the horizon. Giant crevasses gaped open between the rocks, grinning their toothless smiles. Dark. Still. Waiting.

'Jack, step away from the edge, buddy.' Callum raised his voice to battle the wind.

A hard blink and a sob, whipped away almost as soon as it'd reached Callum's ears. The upper branches of the large fig tree next to Jack swayed in the wind.

Callum took a step towards the edge, towards Jack. His body pleaded to stay back, to shelter in the trees. He pushed the protests down and took another step. He reached both arms out, as if to lure Jack to him, or catch him should he slip. A slick sweat covered his palms.

Jack's eyes flittered between Callum and Brett. The movement made his foot slide a fraction in the wet earth. His small body jerked.

Callum's chest lurched.

Jack regained his balance.

Callum stopped, hands up. 'Step away from the edge.' He fought to keep his voice level, to mask the panic threatening to spill over. 'I can help you, you don't have to be scared any—'

'Jack, please don't jump.' Brett's voice was firm. 'He's gone now.' His feet were anchored to the ground, his arms outstretched.

Reaching …

'It's my fault,' Jack said, his voice matching his grandfather's.

'No.' Brett took a step, his voice softened, unlike anything Callum had heard before. 'It's my fault.'

'I pushed him!'

Jack's words reverberated around the boulders, around Callum's head.

Even the wind paused to listen.

'I know,' Brett said. 'But it wasn't your fault.'

'Yes, it was.'

'No.' Brett squared his shoulders, his eyes trained on Jack. 'He wasn't a good man. You were just protecting your mum. And the baby.'

'He had Mum. Same as the other times.'

'I know,' Brett said.

'Here.' Jack peered over the edge. 'He made her stand here.' A sob. 'Why did he do that to her?'

'Because he was a bad man. He liked to hurt people.' A catch in Brett's voice. 'He had since he was a kid.'

'I don't want to be a killer.'

'You're not.'

'She was going to fall. She was so tired. He wasn't looking and …'

'You did nothing wrong.'

'I pushed him.'

'You did the right thing.'

'Mum won't forgive me.'

'There's nothing to forgive.'

A sudden beat of bird wings and the wind rolled over the sea of boulders behind Jack. A soft whistle pitched up and off the boulders from the cracks and crevices where solid rock didn't quite meet. Jack pressed his hands against his ears, blocking the sound, and Callum's hands flew up to cover his own ears too. The old rhyme danced through the air, whispered by the wind, and wedged its way between fingers held tightly together.

*The whispering wild will take your child,*
*If you dare to look away.*
*When she hears the call, she will meet her fall,*
*Never again to play.*
*Winds from the boulders will snatch and hold her,*
*Where forever she will lay.*

Tears and rain blended together and, with one last glance at the impenetrable wall of green in front, Jack dropped backwards over the edge to the sea of granite below.

## CHAPTER FORTY-SEVEN

*Thirty years earlier*

Brett stood frozen.
*I couldn't piece together what I was seeing.*

He snatched his outstretched arms back in and took a step away from the edge. Then a second step. His foot caught on a root of the strangler fig tree, and he stumbled. A few hurried steps and he found his footing, now only metres from me.

*Shit, move.*

I took a few steps to my left, ducked in behind a large trunk and held my breath.

A few more hurried steps on the granite. Another stumble. The muffled sound as Brett ran down the dirt path in the direction of the creek.

I watched until he'd disappeared from view. He didn't turn back.

I let my breath out and stepped into the open. I edged towards the fig tree roots, scanning for Pip's hat.

A whip of the wind. Then a whimper.

I snapped my head around, scouring the area. Nothing. Just the wind.

*Get the hat and get the hell out of here.*

The sun had almost set, and I squinted into the orange glow that pierced the grey clouds. I moved quickly towards the tree. Nothing. No hat.

That sound again. I froze. The wind picked up and swept my hair across my eyes.

A sob. Loud, clear. One step forward, and I peered over the edge. The floor of granite stared back, almost sucking me down towards it. A splash of blue on grey. Pip's hat had blown down.

Another cry.

My heart raced. What the hell? Was someone down there? 'Hello?'

One hand on the fig tree, I angled my body further, so I could see closer to the cliff face. Fingers. White and thin.

A strangled cry. 'Help.'

I leaned a fraction further and the top of a dyed black head came into view. The girl angled her face upwards and the last of the dying light caught the gold flecks in her eyes.

Amelia.

Pip's sister.

# CHAPTER FORTY-EIGHT

Gone.
Jack had fallen. Over the edge.
*The whispering wild will take your child ...*
Nothing. Silence.
Then, a scream, carried on the wind, closer than expected.
Memories from thirty years ago, suppressed all these decades, slammed into Callum. A flash of Brett out of the corner of his eye and Callum lurched forward. The carpet of granite boulders opened up in front of him as he approached the edge.
One step, then another.
*If you dare to look away.*
Eyes focused. Time slowed, the wind silenced.
One last step on solid ground and he bent his right knee, dropping his whole body to the ground. A skid along his right-hand side and both his legs thrust off the edge of the cliff. His hands grappled for a fig tree root that dropped vertically off the cliff face. Another second and his whole body left the solid support of the cliff.
As the memories from three decades earlier ripped through him, it all fell into place. And so did his body.
He fell—weightless—as the granite rushed up to meet him.

# CHAPTER FORTY-NINE

*Thirty years earlier*

Oh shit. Fuck.
'Hold on!' I called.
A sob, carried on the wind, almost didn't make it to my ears.
I looked around. There was no one. Nothing.
*Oh god.*
I dumped my backpack and looked down. A ledge of rock jutted out from the wall of the cliff face, not even a metre deep. Amelia's fingertips dug in to its edge, her body dangling into the abyss.
'Climb up!' I knew it was useless before the words had even left my mouth, and I was already on my stomach, edging closer.
A fig tree root dived down off the boulder, ran past the rock ledge, into oblivion. I gripped it, my sweaty palms slick on its surface. Swallowing down the fear, I guided my legs over the edge.
'Hold on. I'm coming.'
My feet scrambled for something to grip on to. The smooth rock face, now slick with rain, was all they found. A whip of wind swept across us and this time I didn't miss her scream.

My stomach rolled as my torso left the edge and my arms burned as they clung to the tree root.
Another wail.
Deep breath.
*Don't think. Just do it.*
I let go.

# CHAPTER FIFTY

A crunch as Callum's body slammed into solid rock. About two metres wide and less than a metre deep, the ledge's surface sat at a slight angle towards its edge. His left leg flew out over the open chasm below, and his hands scrambled at the slick surface, searching for grip. An ache in his jaw from where it had smashed into the rock.

As the spots across his eyes faded, pale fingers, gripping on to solid rock, came into focus, centimetres from his face.

*When she hears the call, she will meet her fall ...*

Another scream.

Jack.

Callum reached his left hand over the edge to grasp the boy's thin wrist just as his fingers lost their grip on the wet granite. Jack's weight slid Callum's body further along the small ledge.

The boy cried out again, and the sound echoed in Callum's head as the past rushed back at him.

Amelia.

*... never again to play.*

# CHAPTER FIFTY-ONE

*Thirty years earlier*

My body smacked into the rock, hard, and my left leg lodged itself down a gap between the ledge and the rock face. A sickening crack rang out across the boulders.

I screamed. The sound gripped my throat and ripped out of me.

Blinding white hot pain rushed up my leg, took over my body. My vision faded and my mouth swam with spew.

I grappled for my leg, wedged almost up to its knee.

Another scream. It took me a moment to realise it hadn't come from me this time.

My vision was blurred with spots but small fingertips gripping the rock ledge in front of my face came into focus.

Amelia.

My hands flew out. I snatched at one thin wrist as her other hand lost its grip.

The weight of Amelia, as her body fell, jerked on my leg, and shot a new pain through my body. I fought to stay conscious, tightened my grip.

'Hold on.' The words barely left my lips.

Her wrist slipped. I dug my fingers into her skin, but she

slid further again. A push of wind swept at her small body and a whisper filled my ears.

'Cal, please, no … please, don't let me fall!' Her voice tight, eyes wide.

*Don't let her go.*

A final gust as a high-pitched whistle pierced the air.

The pain took control of me, threatened to burst from my seams. My vision faded at the edges, slowly went black.

One last fight and I tightened my grip around a wrist that was no longer there.

## CHAPTER FIFTY-TWO

Callum tightened his fist around Jack's wrist. Rain and sweat combined, and he felt the boy slip further.

His ears rang with wind so strong it dragged Jack's body along the cliff.

*Winds from the boulders ...*

Dirt and mud from the rainforest had washed off the edge above and littered the small ledge, making the rock face slippery. He slid another fraction along the ledge.

The weight of his left leg and prosthesis dragged them further off the edge and he tried to lift it back up onto the rock. As he swung his leg up, the wind pushed back against it and the tip of his shoe hit the corner of the rocky edge. With no sensation to guide him, and unable to see behind him, he twisted his left leg to leverage it up onto the solid surface.

His shoe slipped, and his whole leg dropped back over the edge, the weight sliding them both further down. He caught a glimpse of the bed of rock below, and a gaping abyss between two boulders. His breath caught.

'Don't let me fall!' Jack's eyes wide, light green with flecks of gold. Like Pip. Like Amelia.

*God, not another one. Not another Amelia.*

A fresh gust of wind drew Jack down, pulled him towards the boulders.

*... will snatch and hold her ...*

Find a foothold, a crack, anything.

The idea smacked him hard in the face and his right foot immediately fumbled blindly for the point where the small ledge met the rock face. He found it: the crack in the granite that had cost him his left leg thirty years ago.

He jammed his toes into it as his torso slipped over the edge. He anchored his foot, wedging it as far down as it would go. Using the crack for leverage, he swung his prosthetic leg up onto the ledge. Trusting his right leg, he let go of the rock with his right arm and flung it out over the edge and reached for Jack. Jack's free arm flailed upwards, towards him. Nothing. Their fingers separated by centimetres.

'Please!' Jack's voice cracked.

Callum tried for a breath. The rock edge dug in and crushed his ribs, the wind swooped, a ferocious blow that rattled around them.

His left hand was losing its grip on Jack's wrist. Panic washed over him.

*... where forever she will lay.*

He swung his arm supporting Jack, and the boy reached up again for Callum's spare hand. They brushed fingers. As Jack's body swung back down, Callum's grip slid further along the boy's forearm.

*Don't let go.*

Callum dug his right foot further down into the crack and, with his left shoulder screaming, he swung again.

Contact. A grapple, and he had Jack's second wrist. A scramble from Jack's feet against the rock face, one last heave, and Callum pulled the boy up, grabbing the back of his shorts as he heaved Jack onto the small ledge with him. With his right foot still lodged down the crack, Callum didn't loosen his grip on Jack.

He sucked in great lungfuls of heavy air.

'Jack, here!' A gruff voice above. Urgent.

Brett.

A frantic scramble and Jack's wrist was pulled from his grip. Callum's hand froze, reluctant to let go. His palm burned where he'd just held on to the boy.

'Jack, up here!' Brett again.

His head lurched into gear.

*Get Jack off this ledge.*

From the awkward position on his stomach, Callum tried to push Jack upwards with his right hand. A final burst of effort and Jack was pulled off the ledge, back to solid ground. The boy disappeared from view.

A breath of relief.

He eyed the ledge above. Waiting.

Nothing.

No one.

A hard blink and he took in the angled rock beneath him and the sea of granite below. He was alone on the ledge again. The terror of thirty years ago ripped through him.

## CHAPTER FIFTY-THREE

*Thirty years earlier*

Darkness. Pain.

My eyes flickered open. My watch glowed at me: 3.24 am.

Rain drummed down on me and I tried to move. A wave of pain swept over my left leg and coursed through my body. I screamed, but the sound was stopped by the spew that rose up and filled my mouth. Everything went black again.

My body pressed into rock, and I tried to shift. Something tethered me to the ground. I opened my eyes and confusion washed over me. Light on the horizon and grey boulders everywhere. Rain spattered on my face. A distant *thump, thump* overhead.

I couldn't feel my left leg.

No more pain at least. No more anything.

I closed my eyes.

# CHAPTER FIFTY-FOUR

Callum lay facedown on the ledge with his head pressed against the rock face, too terrified to move. The rain drummed down. Water filled the crack that his right foot was wedged in and its grip loosened. He slipped another inch and flailed his arms to find something, anything.

Nothing.

A large abyss in the floor below yawned open. Amelia's resting place for seventeen years. A sickening wave over his whole body.

Another slip.

'Haffenden, grab it!' A gruff voice called above and there was a flash of green.

Another small slide down the rock face.

'Haffenden!'

He snapped alert.

A branch. Long and covered with leaves. No, a sapling. It dangled down, swept at his cheek. He swung for it and wrapped his arm around its wet trunk, entwined his fingers around the leaves and gripped.

A heave. He slid back up the ledge. He dug his toe back into the crack and used his right foot for leverage. Another heave and his torso lifted from the solid ground of the ledge.

'Take my hand!'

Callum looked up. Brett was on his stomach, his head and shoulders over the edge of the cliff. One arm still holding the other end of the branch, the other now reaching down to Callum. Reluctantly, Callum let go of the tree and, pressing his torso up with his left arm, he reached his right hand up to take Brett's.

Brett gripped his wrist and Callum wrapped his fingers around Brett's thick forearm. A grunt and a pull. Callum's left leg fumbled on the slick rock ledge, barely finding purchase, no sensation to guide it. He pushed through the roar of his stump.

The sapling flew past him as Brett let it drop and extended his free hand downwards. Callum reached up with his left arm and Brett snatched it firmly in his grasp. Another heave from Brett and a push through Callum's legs. A scramble of dirt and rain flicking off the edge. Jack's face, anxious. The boy lay on his stomach, gripped the back of Callum's shirt and then trousers, pulled.

A grunt and a jab of pain and at last he felt the ledge disappear beneath him as the damp smell of earth and the rainforest returned.

## CHAPTER FIFTY-FIVE

The photo of his mum smiled back at Callum from the waiting room wall of Bacuzzi's surgery. His leg throbbed, his jaw ached and the toes on his right foot felt as if they'd been crushed.

The adrenaline had faded, and he lingered somewhere between an overwhelming desire to curl up in a dark room with a pack of strong painkillers and an utterly raw urge to go home to his daughter. His chest ached at the thought of her, at the thought that she'd very nearly lost her second parent.

The journey back from the boulders had been arduous. Brett had supported most of Callum's weight from the boulders to the creek. The water was churning, and crossing it seemed like a death sentence. But to stay in the rainforest with a cyclone en route was even more dangerous.

Brett had helped Jack across the creek, upstream of the boulder bridge, then as he'd been stepping back into the water to help Callum, a group of people in high-vis clothes broke through the green behind him. Fluoro yellow pants, navy t-shirts: fireys.

The help Eddy had radioed for had arrived at last.

Callum made the rest of the trek out with the support of two men. Paige guided the way and a fourth firey brought up the rear.

Jack was silent the entire walk, his face pinched, pale. Clearly in shock.

He had pushed Lachie. Jack. Not Brett. Brett had been trying to stop Jack from jumping. What else had Brett done to protect the boy?

Callum thought of Brett and Jack outside the police station the day before. Brett had been threatening Jack.

*... keep your bloody mouth shut if you know what's good for you.*

But why had Jack even been at the cop shop? To confess?

Had Brett been trying to prevent him?

At last, they cleared the rainforest. The rain came down in sheets and the wind tried to push Callum back into the trees. He gripped the shoulders of the two fireys supporting him. It was impossible to speak—or at least to be heard—and Callum allowed himself to be guided into the fire engine. Brett bundled Jack into the passenger seat of his ute and, with the driver's door open, caught Callum's eye, gave him a nod.

The fire engine led the way, Brett just behind.

Callum had watched Lachie's ute shrink behind them in the wing mirror, the fireys making a beeline for Bacuzzi's.

The clinical smell of disinfectant and latex in the surgery waiting room was a welcome relief from the rainforest's heady scent of wet earth and rotting leaves.

The murmur of voices floated through the closed door, interrupted occasionally by the small wail of a newborn baby. Tess and Lachie's baby. Jack's sister.

Milly's niece.

Callum's eyes flicked back to the photo of his mum. Young and worry-free. Taken before the events of thirty years ago. Before his accident, before his leg.

Thoughts of Amelia Dyer raced through his head. The memory of what had happened that day, suppressed for decades, had at last resurfaced in full colour. Her eyes flecked with gold, terrified; the grey boulders below; her wrists slick with rain.

He'd let her fall.

His breath caught and his palms began to sweat. He wiped them on his filthy trousers.

And Brett. What had Callum really seen that day? Brett with his outstretched arms. The same as with Jack today. Reaching. Not pushing.

Saving. Not killing.

Or trying to save.

A few breaths and he refocused his eyes on his mum's. Her rich brown eyes stared back. The same eyes that stared back whenever he looked in the mirror. Not like Milly's, not like Lachie's. Had he really been that stupid to believe that Lachie was his son? Why had he never bothered to find out more? Maybe he hadn't wanted to know. The chubby toddler with the squinty eyes had found a way under his skin. She was Pip's. And he'd wanted her.

His gut tightened as he realised what would have happened if, thirteen years ago, he'd known Lachie wasn't his. How different the outcome would've been: he would never have taken Milly. She would've been left in Granite Creek. His chest tightened and his eyes grew heavy.

His beautiful daughter.

Her fresh face. Her hand in his. Her goodnight kisses on his cheek. None of it would ever have been his. A void in his chest. He'd have missed it all.

Pip had made the right call.

The surgery door opened and Brett stepped out. Callum blinked back the weight behind his eyes and caught a glimpse of Tess lying on the examination bed, a bundle on her chest and Jack curled up at her side. Brett drew the door shut behind him and his eyes flicked to Callum.

Brett with his hulking frame and set scowl. Brett with his blue stare and buzz cut, now grey, but once blond. Just like Jack.

Brett shifted awkwardly under Callum's stare. After a pause, he closed the gap and sank down in the chair closest to him.

Minutes passed. Decades.

'Thank you.' Brett's voice was hoarse. 'For Jack.'

Callum nodded, his eyes still on his mum's photo.

'You need to know, I never hurt her.' Brett's eyes were trained forward. 'Pip. Or any of them. It wasn't me. It was never me.'

Callum's lips fused. Thirty years of unjust anger at the man beside him was hard to push down. They sat in silence.

'Lachie ...' Brett said after a few moments. 'He was cruel. Used to drag Tess out to the boulders. Make her stand at the edge, her toes hanging over. Used to do it to scare her. I think he'd hoped she'd just jump, but she'd never leave Jack. He didn't have the guts to push her.' He laughed, the sound short and dry. 'I knew Jack had followed them out there more than once. I overheard him asking Tess about it. She said it was just a grown-up game they played.' He shook his head. 'I just ignored it. Pretended I didn't know what was going on, like I'd never heard it.' His shoulders shook once. 'I should've done something. Protected them. Tess and Jack. Pip.'

Callum searched for words but found none.

'The day he died, I'd gone out to their house. I must've arrived not long after Tess and Jack got back from the boulders. I overhead her telling him just to say that Lachie had fallen. That it wasn't his fault. That Lachie had just slipped and not been pushed. I spoke to Tess. I told her I would protect them. It was about time I did something. I drove his ute back out there and dragged his gear out to the camp site, set it up. Tess came and picked me up.

'But Jack blamed himself. Couldn't see that by pushing Lachie he was saving his mum. He was always trying to protect her. He felt so damn guilty about Lachie though. He bottled up, wouldn't talk about it. But I think he tried to fess up a few times. I couldn't let him do that. Ruin his whole life. And Tess's. Jack's got a future ahead of him.'

Callum's mind drifted to the phone calls to triple zero from Tess's house: Jack trying to confess. Even the ones before Lachie's death: Jack, trying to protect his mum.

Brett sighed. 'He was acting irrationally though. Doing all sorts of wild things. We all were. I'd seen you with Jack's bracelet at the pub. Thought maybe you'd clued on to him. That you were poking around. He must've heard me tell Tess about it.'

Callum thought of Tess's hostility towards him. At her house and on the street. She'd thought he was sniffing out Jack.

The thought made his stomach knot. He'd never considered the boy, would never hunt down a kid like that.

But now the events from the last few days began to sharpen and slot together. Brett pleading with someone out of shot on the motel's CCTV: Jack. The break-in: Jack. The door opening and closing: Jack. Too short to be captured on camera yet small enough to escape through the bathroom window. And too short to reach the top of the wardrobe and the lockbox concealed within the folded blanket. He recalled the chair on its side in front of the open wardrobe. Had Jack been interrupted by Mike's arrival just in time?

Callum's breath caught at the thought of what would've happened had Jack got hold of his lockbox. All his secrets in one sleek box: the newspaper clipping of Milly's disappearance, Pip's letter to Milly, Milly's birth certificate. The final name on the document: *Amelia Innis Haffenden.*

Haffenden. Not Wyatt. And Innis: Callum's mother's name. Pip had planned it all. From the moment she was diagnosed with early onset dementia. Before she'd even given birth to Brett's daughter.

Milly. Beautiful, glorious Milly. Her name danced around, and he thought of it written in shaky handwriting in pink glitter pen, the *y* distinctly backwards. His shoehorn. Had Jack taken it from his room? Given it to Pip? Why? Had she mentioned her daughter to Jack? Recalled that Callum was going to call her Milly? The questions tumbled over each other, no answers within reach.

Jack and Pip's matching bracelets came to mind. They obviously had a relationship. Callum shifted uncomfortably at the thought that Jack might be aware of Milly's connection to Pip. To Brett.

'It was my fault that it ever happened though.' Brett's voice dragged Callum back.

Callum turned to face him. Brett's cheeks were reddened, dark shadows had blossomed beneath his eyes, like the inky sky outside.

'He was never right after he got hurt,' Brett said. 'After that teacher up at the school got hold of him. Got hold of a few of the kids actually. He never got done for it. No one wanted to say anything. I beat the shit out of him, for what it was worth.' He shook his head. 'But I couldn't even bring myself to talk to Lachie about it. I just pretended it never happened.

'Should've got him some counselling or something. I dunno. The school didn't help either. Just swept it all under the rug. Hush, hush, nothing happened here sorta thing. Pip tried a bit. But he wouldn't talk to her either. In the end we just moved on with our lives.

'But it changed him. Brought out an anger. He became aggressive. It was only small things at first. A bit of picking on kids at school, that sorta stuff. But then it grew. He started hitting Pip. Most of the time she didn't even bother to fight back. Thought she deserved it for not protecting him better. For not knowing what was going on. She'd struggled with him from the beginning. We were so young when she fell pregnant. Still kids really. I was flat out trying to help Dad with the business, bring in enough to support them. I wasn't involved enough. She was still grieving her sister and ... and you, I think. She struggled to ... I dunno, connect to him right from the beginning. She thought she deserved his beatings later on.' He snorted. A pause. His eyes looked heavy. 'I always loved her. More than she loved me, I think.'

Callum couldn't speak. He blinked as he acknowledged the obvious common thread that had always linked him to Brett: he'd loved Pip too. As a teenager, but more so the last thirteen years. Every time he looked at his daughter, he saw Pip. Thanked Pip.

'That day when you had your accident,' Brett continued, 'I'd been with Dad at Pip's house. We'd gone to fix some stuff. When we arrived, her mum had had an overdose or something, I dunno. Amelia was all panicked and had called the ambulance. Said Pip was hanging out with some guy from school and she left to find her. I knew it was you. All the kids at school knew about you and Pip. Knew you hung out at the boulders too. Amelia knew too, I guess.'

Callum looked up in surprise. He'd thought it had been their secret. He shook his head. *Stupid.*

'Anyway, I thought I'd better go and get Pip myself. Her mum didn't look too good at that stage. So, I took Dad's truck and drove out to the rainforest. I saw Pip coming out of the trees just as I pulled up the car. I told her what had happened with her mum. She got in the car and I threw her bike in the tray, saw yours stashed in the scrub. I knew you'd been together.' His hands made fists.

Thirty years on, was he still pissed?

Callum nodded, found his voice at last. 'It was getting late, Pip was worried about Amelia. She said they needed to be home for something to do with her mum. That's why she went ahead of me. She raced off while I was packing up our things. I went back later because I realised I'd forgotten her hat.'

Brett's face was blank. 'By the time we'd returned to her house, your mum had arrived. Pip's aunt must've called her or something. The ambulance had been stuck. A tree had fallen and blocked the range. Your mum was doing CPR. It didn't look good. Pip was panicked because Amelia wasn't back, and your mum said she hadn't seen her on the drive over from her house. It was pissing down rain by then and Pip was worried that Amelia had followed you both out to the boulders. She wanted to go and look for her, but she was in no state to do anything, so I said I'd go.'

Brett's head drooped further, and he sucked in a great breath. The air must've caught halfway because he cleared his throat loudly before continuing. 'Amelia's bike wasn't at the start of the track where I'd picked up Pip, so I drove up to the main track's car park and found it there. It had a flat tyre.'

Callum nodded. Pip and he always used the smaller, unmarked track, closer to town. But not everyone knew about it. Maybe Amelia hadn't. The two tracks didn't join until the camp site. Had she been walking into the rainforest on one track as Callum had been walking out along the other? He felt sick at the thought. If only they'd crossed paths. He could've stopped her. Saved her even. Instead, he'd cycled back home, grinning from ear to ear. Turned around to get Pip's hat, still grinning. Oblivious.

Brett took a deep breath. 'The weather was pretty bad, and I hurried out to the boulders. When I got there, she was just standing at the edge. She was looking down at something below. I don't know what it was.'

*Pip's hat.*

Callum remembered peering over the edge of the boulders and seeing it, right before he saw Amelia.

'She pressed her hands against her ears,' Brett said. 'Then she turned and saw me. She was terrified, it was like she'd seen a ghost or something. There was no colour left in her face.'

Like Jack. Had they both heard it? The whispering? Pip had said she had. Callum's palms tingled and his stump throbbed as if it were about ready to explode out of his prothesis.

Brett sucked in a breath. 'Her feet were so close to the edge. I was afraid she was going to fall. She said something. I didn't quite catch it. Something about Pip maybe. "Pip's fine," I tried to tell her. She didn't hear me. The wind was so loud, it was doing that whistling thing it does sometimes. The whispering.' He snorted. 'And her hands were still pressed against her ears. She looked so scared. Her heel slipped back, and I went for her. I didn't want her to fall.'

Brett shook his head. 'I've spent the last thirty years going over that moment again and again in my head. She slipped. I'm sure she slipped. She didn't jump.' His voice caught and his shoulders gave a heave. 'I tried to grab her. I was just back from the edge, and I missed. Pip's sister. I was so scared I just left. I didn't know what else to do.'

His whole body began to shake, to tremble with thirty years of grief. Of guilt.

'I panicked. I didn't think anyone would believe me. I knew I wasn't popular. Thought I'd be done for killing her or something. I was eighteen, would've been tried as an adult. When I got back to Pip, I didn't know what to tell her. Her mum had literally just died.'

Brett's hulking frame shook. Silent sobs filled the small waiting room.

'It wasn't your fault.' Callum's throat was tight, he struggled to press the words out. 'Pip had thought she'd heard the whispering before. She would've told Amelia it was true.' He squeezed his eyes shut. The darkness of the gaping crevasse below the boulder cliff shone back at him. He pushed the image away, opened his eyes. 'Pip's hat had been blown over the edge of the cliff. Amelia must have seen it, thought Pip had fallen, that the whispering had got to her.'

'Pip pushed so hard for the search to continue,' Brett said. 'Amelia's bike at the rainforest meant that she must've been lost. But Pip was just a kid, and a Dyer. Her opinion didn't matter. They called the search off. Said Amelia had done a runner. She was a troubled kid and had just fled town, that was all. But Pip said she knew otherwise. Amelia knew they had a plan to leave Granite in only a few weeks. Pip was right. And I never told her.' Brett hung his head in his hands. 'I didn't know you'd gone back out to the boulders.' Brett's voice was barely a whisper, but Callum caught every word. 'If I did, I never would have left you there.'

## CHAPTER FIFTY-SIX

Callum was slow to pack up his room and stow the last of his belongings in the boot of his rental car. His stump was so swollen that he'd taken one look at the stretched purple skin and scooped up his crutches. His prosthesis was one of the first things he'd packed.

The warmth of the sun shone down through the clouds, which were at last an iridescent white rather than the angry grey they'd been this past week. The threat of the cyclone had passed, the worst of the storm hitting further north.

The previous night, he'd lain awake for hours, unable to switch off the events of the day.

Jack falling, nearly dying.

The realisation of what had really happened to Amelia Dyer thirty years ago, and how he'd come to lose his leg.

The isolation of the ledge. The terror.

And then Brett.

Brett, the biological father of his daughter. Perhaps not a good man, but not a bad man either. The thought was difficult to process, to accept.

Had Callum done the right thing thirteen years ago, taking Milly? Hadn't Brett suffered enough? Didn't he deserve to know the truth?

The thoughts tumbled over in Callum's mind. Nothing seemed clear. Then something took shape, sharp and beautiful, its edges defined. Milly's image blazed through the fog.

She was his daughter. That's what he knew. That's what Pip intended.

He pushed down the doubt, the questions. There was no use opening up wounds long healed and letting the fetid truth out.

He thought of the letter in his lockbox, its thick envelope with the scratchy handwritten name: Amelia. Pip's parting words to her daughter. Callum had never read it. What did it say? He thought of giving it to Milly when he returned home. He rolled the idea around in his head until he found himself toeing the line between right and wrong, unprepared to tip either way.

A decision for another day.

His body had eventually given in, and he woke to the light shining in beneath the curtains. An uninterrupted sleep. Blank, deep. He'd slept through for the first time since arriving in Granite Creek.

He showered, dressed and put on his cracked glasses. The scenes of the day before ran on repeat through his head, and as he sat on the closed toilet lid drying his stump, he thought about his conversation with Brett in the doctor's surgery. Brett's words about Pip hadn't made him feel the warmth he'd expected.

'She never loved me like she loved you,' he'd said. 'I was always second best.'

Callum had remained silent.

'I think she was just lost. You'd moved to the city after your accident. Most of the other kids from school had left for holidays and then uni. Her mum was dead, her sister too. Though she didn't know that.' He'd swallowed. 'I think that's why she stayed in Granite. She always held out hope that Amelia would turn up. I think I was just familiar to her. And I cared. I really did care about her. We never really started dating. Things just sorta progressed on their own. At first, I think she just wanted to feel something. Anything. That's why she started up with me. And I was just a horny teenager who was finally getting with the girl I'd always fancied.' He'd shaken his head. 'Then all of a sudden she was pregnant and, before we knew it, we were parents.' The silence stretched out between them. 'I like to think she grew to love me over the years.'

Several minutes passed, the air heavy with the burden of the last thirty years. Brett gave a nod to Callum, then rose and walked back into the room where Tess, Jack and the new baby were. He didn't look back, the door pulled closed behind him.

After Bacuzzi had finished with Tess, she'd checked Callum over, dressed the blister on his heel and driven him the few hundred metres back to the motel. He'd nodded as she gave him a stern warning about resting if he didn't want to lose his right leg too.

Now, as Callum stepped out into the balmy sunlight, he wasn't sorry to be locking the motel room door behind him for what he hoped would be the last time.

'Will we see ya again?' Mike asked as he handed in his keys.

'Not too soon, I hope.'

Mike gave him a knowing look and the heavy, earthy scent of marijuana followed Callum out of the cool reception room and into the heat.

He drove the two blocks to the station, the car roomier without his prosthesis on.

'What a bloody night. I can't believe everything that happened,' Eddy said once the pair were settled in his office.

Callum smiled for what felt like the first time since returning to Granite Creek. 'Look at you, first rescuing cats, now delivering babies.'

'It was dumb luck, really.' Eddy laughed before his face fell flat. 'Don't know what I would've done if things had got complicated. We were lucky the roads hadn't totally flooded, so we were able to get to the doctor's surgery afterwards, at least.'

'It sounds like you did a good job, mate.'

'Yeah. Left behind a bit of a mess in the lounge room though.' Eddy leaned back in his chair, his shoulders relaxing. 'Brett actually came by this morning to tell me that Tess and the baby are doing fine. And to say thanks. Didn't think I'd ever see the day Brett Wyatt thanked me for anything.'

'You deserve it.'

'You don't seem too surprised.'

Callum took a moment before answering. 'Maybe he's not as big of a jerk as we suspected.'

Eddy blew out a long whistle and smiled. 'Callum Haffenden, I never thought I'd hear you sing Brett's praise.'

'I was hardly singing his praise.'

'Still, that was practically a compliment.'

'Well, it was off the record, so you can scratch it from your memory bank, thanks.'

Eddy snorted, then after a moment said, 'You'll never guess what she named her.'

Callum's brow furrowed.

'Tess. The baby,' Eddy added. 'She called her Amelia.'

Something in Callum's chest twitched before nestling down and creating a heaviness that made his breath catch.

'Hope the name's not bloody cursed.' Eddy raised his eyebrows, shook his head.

Callum tried to find something to say but nothing came.

After a few moments, Eddy spoke. 'I can't believe Jack blames himself for his dad's death.'

Callum had filled Eddy in on a modified version of the events at the boulders the night before. 'Kid stuff, I guess.

I think he feels that if he had been with his dad he could've helped in some way, that Lachie wouldn't have slipped.' Callum managed to look Eddy in the eye as he spoke, the lie sliding out easily. 'Survivor's guilt.'

Callum had failed to save Pip's sister, but maybe in some way he could help save her grandson.

Just then, Steph cracked the office door and poked her head in.

'Phone call,' she said apologetically. 'Some hotel in Cairns.'

Eddy picked up the phone. 'Sergeant Eddy Quade speaking.'

Steph gave Callum a quick wink before pulling the door closed with a soft click.

'Okay,' Eddy said into the receiver. 'And they're certain? Did they look at the photo I sent through?' A pause. 'All right. Thanks for that then.'

Callum raised his eyebrows in question as Eddy hung up.

'The Reef Inn,' explained Eddy. 'Staff have identified Thacker as returning to the hotel about four o'clock last Tuesday afternoon. One of them remembers him requesting new towels as he went up to his room, so he would've left Granite well before Lachie even finished his shift at the fire station.'

The phone call to Adelaide from the Wyatt house had been a dead end also, as Eddy had concluded. Callum had called the hardware store from the bakery the day before, asking questions that they were only too happy to help an investigating senior sergeant with. Tess had ordered some vintage ornate bathroom taps from them. A special order. Not available anywhere else in the country. They remembered her clearly as she'd apparently been quite abrupt on the phone, and they'd never heard of the delivery destination before: Granite Creek.

'So, Thacker had an accidental slip then?'

It was a charged question and it hung in the air between the two friends. Eddy looked at Callum, and after a pause nodded. 'We'll be looking into it further. I've already forwarded the image from the yearbook to the guys down south. There'll be a full investigation. They'll nab him,' Eddy said. 'I just hope Mike's ready for the onslaught of questioning that he's going to have to withstand. And a likely trial.'

A few minutes later, Eddy walked Callum out of his office. They hugged. Callum felt his body slacken as he registered that the tension in Eddy's shoulders seemed less than it had five days ago.

'Don't suppose we'll get you back here again anytime soon?' Eddy asked as they held each other at arm's length.

Over his shoulder, Callum saw Steph's lips toy with a smile. 'Well, never say never,' he said.

Callum and Eddy finished their goodbyes and Steph stood up from behind the station's counter. 'I'll walk you out.'

Out in the car park, Callum leaned against his tiny rental car. With only a spattering of clouds in the sky, the air felt lighter.

'So, never say never, hey?' Steph said.

Before he could think of a response, she'd closed the distance between them and pressed her lips gently against his. He squeezed his crutches to steady himself.

She pulled back before he had a chance to completely register what had happened.

'Well, let's hope never comes sooner rather than later.' Her lips turned upwards, and her dimple firmly planted itself in her left cheek. The sun reflected off her auburn hair. It looked like a fire against the backdrop of the green rainforest.

She stood waving as he pulled out of the car park and turned onto the main street. The pressure of her lips against his lingered as she disappeared from view.

The windscreen was finally free of rain. He kept his eyes trained on the road ahead and the open blue sky. He might just be beginning to dry out at last.

He glimpsed the green wall of the rainforest that filled the rear-view mirror. His left leg gave a tingle. He fixed his eyes ahead and pressed his right foot down on the accelerator.

# EPILOGUE

## *Six months later*

I sat on the low wall outside the nursing home, my Doc Martens making my feet sweat as I banged the heels against the brick wall. Should've worn thongs.

Dad sat next to me, his hand rubbing his knee. His leg must have been sore. He hadn't said anything since I'd come back out from meeting Pip. Mum. Shit that word seemed weird.

Mum.

He'd wanted to come in with me, but I'd said no. I'd needed to meet her on my own.

She'd looked younger than I'd imagined. Her hair was longer than mine and the same colour, before I'd dyed it pink at least. Maybe I'd wash the colour out after all. That'd make Dad happy.

He looked at me.

'Milly—'

'I'm fine,' I cut him off. He worried too much.

I saw him open his mouth to say something. But then he closed it again.

'Honestly, Dad. You don't need to worry. It was fine.'

He nodded.

Neither of us spoke. I twisted my nose ring around and it caught the skin and stung. I fiddled with the bracelet Mum had just given me instead.

It was a handwoven friendship bracelet. Like those dumb things we all used to wear in primary school. It was red and blue, and it had three silver bells threaded onto it that tinkled when I moved my arm. They winked at me in the sunlight. I guess this one wasn't so bad.

We sat for a few more minutes. The sun was warm, though not as hot as Dad said it got over summer. If this was winter here, I could definitely get used to it.

'Come on,' I jumped down off the wall. 'You promised me a snorkelling trip, old man.'

Dad snorted. 'We've got a bit of a drive before we hit snorkelling territory.'

He limped a little as we headed back to our rental car. I opened up the passenger door and turned to look back at the sad brick of the nursing home one last time. Behind the building, the rainforest shivered in the still air. My eyes trained on the shifting trees in front, the wall of solid green.

I blinked. The trees moved closer.

There was something about them. It was like they were alive, watching me. The sound of the engine rumbling and Dad's murmurs slipped away. One hand let go of the door and my feet took a half step away from the car.

A soft whispering swam across the heavy air and buried into my ears, calling to me. My head fogged and the air pressed in, warm, comforting. A flurry of wings as birds, hundreds of them, danced from the treetops.

Beautiful.

Something tugged deep inside. An urge, raw and urgent. I needed to go. I had to. Nothing else mattered.

I took another step and my other hand fell from the car door.

*Ting. Ting.*

The soft tinkle of bells cut through the air. Sliced through the whisper. I blinked hard and tore my eyes away from the green. Everything was fogged but slowly cleared.

'Come on, slow coach.' Dad's voice seemed further away than it should. 'Close the door and let the AC do its job.'

With a final look at the rainforest, I got into the car and slammed the door shut behind me.

Dad hit the accelerator.

# ACKNOWLEDGEMENTS

I feel that all debut authors must dream about the day that they get the privilege of writing an acknowledgements page for a novel. I'd thought about this long before I even knew that this book would ever see the light of day, and yet I'm still stumped. Thank you are two simple words that just don't seem to convey enough. But let's give this a go (and see if I can manage it without crying on my keyboard).

A mammoth—and yet what feels like an inadequately insufficient—thank you to HarperCollins. Thank you for running The Banjo Prize and for offering emerging Aussie authors the opportunity of a lifetime. Thank you to your team for selecting *The Whispering*, for seeing the potential in my story, and for giving this newbie author a chance at the big game.

To my incredible publisher, Anna Valdinger, thank you. You were the first person who expressed such deep enthusiasm for the story and that first conversation with you will be forever etched in my memory. As we've moved through the publishing process, your zeal for my novel has never wavered (nor has your tolerance for the bombardment of emails you receive from me), and for that I am truly grateful.

A very big thank you to my agent, Benjamin Paz, and the entire Curtis Brown Australia team. Thank you for holding the torch out in front for me so that I don't feel as if I'm wandering aimlessly in the dark as I navigate this completely foreign industry. Thank you, Ben, for championing my writing and for always being in my corner.

To my editors, Madeleine James and Deonie Fiford, thank you. I had no idea how often my characters snorted and shrugged, nor that there was any other way for something to go from A to B other than to *dart*. Thank you for unjumbling my story, smoothing it out and sharpening its edges. You are true wordsmiths and I wish I could bottle your talent. Thank you also to my proofreader, Bronwyn Sweeney, for your keen eye and final polish.

Thank you to Lucy Inglis, my publicity campaign manager, for getting the book into the hands of others, and for helping it to spread its wings and soar.

Thank you to Christine Armstrong for the stellar cover. Unique, eye catching and completely ominous. You hit the nail on the head.

To my writing buddies Anna Johnson, Terence Phillips, Elyse Harrison and Kate Burns, thank you. You were the first readers of snippets of *The Whispering* and your ongoing enthusiasm, support and brainstorming helped to evolve and grow the story.

To Brian Short, thank you for the hours of bookish conversation in the Pilates studio, and for broadening my reading horizons beyond our shores.

Thank you to my dear friend Shauna Brown. Before The Banjo, and before publishing was even on the horizon, every time we met you asked me, without fail, how my writing was going. Thank you for recognising its significance in my life and being the person who told me that my face lights up when I talk about it.

To my wonderful friend and star-crossed-mother Beth Colvin, thank you. For the early days of hours pounding the pavement and the 3 am text messages when sleepless nights stretched to the horizon. And more recently, thank you for shouting about my book from the rooftops. I hope you continue to do so after you've read it.

Thank you to both the Matlock and the Lando families for welcoming me into the fold. The Matlocks for grounding me earlier on, and the Landos for later when I was looking for a place to call home. Your generosity and open arms are things I will always hold dear.

Thank you to my sister Emma. For being my first reading buddy and for the lifetime of support, love and laughter. Thank you for the endless cups of tea and the quick phone catch-ups that go for nearly two hours. Thank you for understanding me, for never judging, and for your undying enthusiasm for my writing. No one knows me quite like you do.

To my daughters, Lucia, Sofia and Isabella. Thank you for the sticky hand holds, the warm hugs and the irrevocable love. Thank you for letting me experience the magic of the world through your eyes and for keeping my imagination sparkling.

And of course, to Tito, thank you. Thank you for the little world that we've built together that feels bigger than what just two people should be able to create. And thank you because when I told you that I wanted to write a book, you simply said 'do it'.